THE
LAST
GOOD
MAN

A. J. Kazinski is the pseudonym of filmmaker and author Anders Rønnow Klarlund and author Jacob Weinreich. An instant bestseller in Denmark, *The Last Good Man* is their first collaboration.

THE
LAST
GOOD
MAN

WITHDRAWN

A.J. KAZINSKI

Translated from the Danish by Tiina Nunnally

SIMON &
SCHUSTER

London · New York · Sydney · Toronto · New Delhi

A CBS COMPANY

First published in Denmark by Politikens Forlag under the title
Den sidste gode mand, 2010
First published in Great Britain by Simon & Schuster UK Ltd, 2012
A CBS COMPANY

Copyright © A. J. Kazinski, 2010
English language translation © Tiina Nunnally, 2012

1 3 5 7 9 10 8 6 4 2

Simon & Schuster UK Ltd
1st Floor
222 Gray's Inn Road
London WC1X 8HB

www.simonandschuster.co.uk

Simon & Schuster Australia, Sydney
Simon & Schuster India, New Delhi

A CIP catalogue record for this book is available from the British Library

Trade Paperback ISBN 978-0-85720-579-7
Ebook ISBN 978-0-85720-581-0

Printed and bound in by CPI Group (UK) Ltd, Croydon, CR0 4YY

Two notes to the reader

The myth mentioned in this novel about "God's righteous men" stems from the Jewish Talmud—a collection of religious texts set down in Israel and Babylonia—which, according to the Jewish faith, is a direct transcription of what God said to Moses. One of the things God said was that there will always be thirty-six righteous people on earth. These thirty-six protect all of us. Without them, humanity would perish.

The thirty-six do not know that they are the chosen ones.

On September 11, 2008, at the United Nations headquarters in New York and under the leadership of Dr. Sam Parnia, the world's largest scientific conference on near-death experiences was held. The objective was to discuss the growing number of near-death experiences that are reported each year from around the world. These are reports of people who have been revived and afterward have described the most unbelievable phenomena—things that science cannot explain.

Part I

BOOK OF THE DEAD

O earth, cover not thou my blood, and let my cry have no place.

—Job 16:18

P eople die all the time. Often in hospitals. For that reason it was a brilliant plan. Simple, almost banal.

All the near-death experiences that the doctors heard about would be verified. But how? In the emergency rooms, of course. Because there was a pattern to what people described—those people who had been declared clinically dead, people who had stopped breathing and whose hearts were no longer beating. They floated upward. They hovered near the ceiling and looked down on themselves. They were often able to describe details that their brain couldn't possibly have invented in the last throes of death: how a doctor had knocked over a vase, what he or she had shouted to the nurses, who had come into or left the room and when. Some people could also recount what was happening in the room next door. Even so, it was not considered scientific evidence. But this situation was now going to be rectified.

Emergency rooms, intensive care wards, and trauma centers—the places where people were most likely to be revived—would be recruited. As part of a worldwide investigation, small shelves were installed. Small shelves set high up on the wall, close to the ceiling. On these shelves were placed pictures, illustrations turned faceup—impossible to see from below. Only someone who was hovering near the ceiling would be able to see the pictures.

Agnes Davidsen was a member of the Danish team. The doctors had laughed at the plan but hadn't objected, as long as the team paid to put up the shelves. Agnes was present the day the shelf was installed at the National Hospital in Copenhagen. She even helped hold the ladder as the janitor climbed up with the sealed envelope in his hand, and she was the one who switched off the light when the seal was broken and the image was placed on the shelf. Only headquarters knew what sort of image it was. No one else had the slightest clue. A television could be heard in the background, broadcasting news about preparations for the climate summit in Copenhagen. The French president, Nicolas Sarkozy, announced that Europe refused to allow the temperature of the earth to rise more than two degrees Celsius. Agnes shook her head as she helped the janitor fold up the ladder. How crazy it sounds when expressed like that, she thought. *Refused to allow.* As if we humans could turn the earth's temperature up or down like a thermostat.

She thanked the janitor and looked up at the shelf near the ceiling. Now all she had to do was wait for the hospital to call her with the message that someone had died in this room.

And then had come back to life.

1

Yonghegong Temple—Beijing, China

I t was not the shaking of the earth that woke him. He was used to that. The subway ran right under the Yonghegong Temple, constantly threatening to topple the 350-year-old temple complex in the center of the Chinese capital. He woke because someone or something had been leaning over him as he slept. Studying him. He was sure of it.

The monk named Ling sat up in bed and looked around. The sun was just setting; pain had sent him early to bed.

"Is someone there?" The pain kept moving. He couldn't tell whether it was his back, his stomach, or his chest that hurt. He could hear the young monks talking in the temple courtyard. The last Western tourists were leaving.

Ling defied the pain and stood up. He still had a sense that somebody was in the room, but there was no one in sight. He couldn't find his sandals, so he tottered barefoot across the stone floor. It was cold. Maybe I'm having a stroke, he thought. He was having trouble breathing. His tongue was swollen, and he staggered as he walked. For a moment he almost lost his footing, but he knew that he needed to stay upright. If he fell now, he would never get up again. He took a deep breath that sent a burning sensation down his windpipe and into his lungs.

"Help me," he tried to shout. But his voice was too weak, and no one heard him. "Help me."

Ling stepped out into a narrow, damp corridor and went into another room. Rays of orange sun were filtering through the skylight. He looked down at his body. There was nothing to see on his arms, stomach, or chest.

A powerful stab of pain made him feel faint. Briefly, he closed his eyes, gave up resisting, and disappeared into a darkness that was boundlessly unpleasant. Then he had a moment of peace. The pain came in small jolts, and each time it was stronger than before.

His hands were shaking as he opened the drawer and began fumbling through it. Finally, he found what he was looking for: a little, scratched pocket mirror. He looked at himself in the mirror. A face filled with fear. Ling tugged his loincloth down a bit and held up the mirror so he could get a view of the lower part of his back. What he saw took his breath away.

"Dear God," he whispered, dropping the mirror. "What's that?"

The only answer he received was the sound of the mirror shattering on the floor.

The old-fashioned pay phone on the wall didn't look at all like a means of salvation, but it was his only chance. He dragged himself over to it. A new wave of pain made him stop. It seemed to last an eternity. He opened his eyes and looked at the pay phone, which he had objected to so strongly when it was first installed. The authorities had required it because of the visiting tourists—in case something happened to any of them, there had to be some way to summon help. For the same reason, the emergency number was printed on the wall in large type, and next to it stood a pot filled with coins. Ling stretched out his hand and tried to reach the pot. He managed to get hold of the rim but lost his balance and was forced to drop it in order to lean on the wall for support. Pottery shards and coins scattered over the floor. Ling hesitated. The very thought of bending down seemed inconceivable. Was one of his last deeds on earth really going to be leaning down to pick up the shiny little coins that he'd spent most of his life renouncing? But he didn't want to die yet, and with trembling fingers he picked up a coin, dropped it into the slot, and punched in the three numbers printed on the wall. Then he waited.

"Come on, come on," he whispered with difficulty.

At last he heard a woman's voice say: "Emergency Center."

"You must help me!"

"What is the emergency? Where are you calling from?" The voice on the line was calm and composed. Almost robotic.

"I'm burning up. I'm . . ."

Ling fell silent and turned around. There was someone there; he was sure of it. Someone was watching him. He rubbed his eyes, but that didn't help. He couldn't see anyone. Who could be doing this to him?

"I need to know where you are, sir," said the woman.

"Help me—" With every word he spoke, a stab of pain raced from his back up through his throat to his mouth and swollen tongue.

The woman interrupted him, sounding kind but firm. "What's your name?"

"Ling. Ling Zedong. I . . . Help me! My skin . . . it's burning!"

"Mr. Ling . . ." Now she sounded impatient. "Where are you right now?"

"Help me!"

He stopped abruptly. He felt that something inside him had collapsed. As if the world around him had taken a step back and left him in a state of unreality. The sounds vanished. The bursts of laughter from the courtyard were gone. The voice on the phone was, too. Time stood still. He found himself in a new world. Or on the threshold of another world. Blood was running out of his nose.

"What's happening?" he whispered. "It's so quiet."

At that instant he dropped the phone.

"Hello?" said the robotic voice in the receiver dangling from the wall. "Hello?"

But Ling didn't hear it. He staggered a few steps toward the window. He looked at the three glasses standing on the windowsill. There was water in one of them. Maybe that would help. He reached for the glass but couldn't get a good grip on it. It fell out the window and shattered on the stones in the courtyard.

The monks outside looked up. Ling tried to signal to them. He saw their lips moving, but he heard nothing.

Ling could taste and feel the blood running out of his nose. "Dear God." He groaned. "What's happening to me?"

He felt as if he were about to be obliterated. As if he'd been reduced to a chess piece in somebody else's dream, somebody who was about to wake up. And he could do nothing to fight it. The sounds around him were gone. He fell, landing on his back, and looked up. He was enveloped in silence. Then he smiled and raised his hand in the air. Where the ceiling had been a moment ago, he now had an unobstructed view of the first faint stars in the night sky.

"It's so quiet," he murmured. "Venus. And the Milky Way."

The other monks came rushing into the room and leaned over him. But Ling didn't see them. His hand slowly dropped. He had a smile on his lips.

"He tried to use the phone." One of the monks was standing with the receiver in his hand. "To call the Emergency Center."

"Ling!" One of the other monks—the youngest, no more than a boy— tried to make contact with him. "Ling. Can you hear me?" No answer. The young monk looked up at the others. "He's dead."

No one said a word. They all bowed their heads. Several had tears in their eyes. The eldest monk broke the silence. "Get Lopön. We don't have much time."

One of the others was going to send the boy, but the eldest monk stopped him. "No, go and get him yourself. The boy has never witnessed this before. Let him stay here and watch."

The monk ran off, and the boy looked at the eldest monk. "What's going to happen?" he asked anxiously.

"*Phowa*. We are going to send his soul onward. Lopön will be here in a minute."

"*Phowa?*"

"*Phowa* helps the soul onward. Through the body and out through the head. We have only a few minutes to do it."

"What will happen if we don't do it in time?"

"We'll make it. Lopön is quick. Come and help me. He can't stay here on the floor."

No one moved.

"Pick him up."

The boy took hold of Ling's legs. Two other monks came to help.

They lifted him up and placed him on the bed. He was lying on his side. When the eldest monk tried to roll him onto his back properly, he caught sight of something. "What's that?" he asked.

The others came closer to see what he meant.

"Look. There, on his back."

Everyone stood leaning over the dead monk.

"What is it?" asked the boy.

No one answered. They simply stood there in silence, staring at the strange mark that had appeared on Ling's back. It had spread from one shoulder to the other and halfway down his spine. Like a tattoo or a burn.

Or as if a fire had been burning inside his back.

2

Suvarna Hospital—Mumbai, India

G iuseppe Locatelli had received the e-mail three days ago, asking whether he could help locate an Indian economist who had recently died. Giuseppe wasn't much interested in complying, but he was eager to get out of India, and he hoped that if he made a good effort at discharging his duties, it might serve as a springboard to a better job at another Italian embassy. Maybe in the United States. That was his dream. Washington, D.C. Or the consulate in New York, which handled everything related to the United Nations. Anything but these stinking streets. So he didn't hesitate to say yes.

It was a long and tedious drive even though it was early in the morning. The taxi could make only very slow progress through the teeming slum. During his very first week in India, Giuseppe had learned not to look at the poor. Not to look them in the eye—that was how first-time visitors ended up with a swarm of beggars in tow. But if you kept your eyes fixed straight ahead and remained ice-cold, they left you alone. In India it was a matter of ignoring the poverty when you were out on the streets and waiting to weep until you were alone. Otherwise it would tear you apart.

The cab stopped. "Suvarna Hospital, sir."

Giuseppe paid the driver and climbed out. There was a line of people in front of the hospital. Damned if there weren't lines everywhere in this country. Lines at the beach, lines at the police station, lines in front of every little clinic that might have a Band-Aid and a piece of gauze. Giuseppe pushed his way through without looking a single person in the eye. Without taking in anything about his surroundings.

He spoke English to the receptionist. "Giuseppe Locatelli. From the Italian embassy. I have an appointment with Dr. Kahey."

Dr. Kahey didn't seem bothered by the workload. He appeared calm and composed as he spoke about Sardinia, where Giuseppe had never been, as they went downstairs to the morgue. Giuseppe couldn't help expressing his admiration for the busy doctor. "All those people waiting outside. How do you ever take care of them all?"

"They're not here for treatment," Dr. Kahey said with an indulgent smile. "Don't worry."

"Then why are they here?"

"They've come to show him their respects."

"Who?"

Dr. Kahey gave Giuseppe a surprised look. "The man you've come to see. Raj Bairoliya. Didn't you notice that all those people were carrying flowers?"

Giuseppe blushed. He hadn't seen anything. He'd stared straight ahead, fearing any eye contact that might make him a target for beggars. Kahey went on in his characteristic singsong Indian accent: "Bairoliya was one of the closest advisers to Mr. Muhammad Yunus, the inventor of microloans. Do you know Mr. Yunus?"

Giuseppe shook his head. But of course he'd heard of microloans—the loans had made it possible for thousands and thousands of people to start small, innovative businesses.

"Yunus was awarded the Nobel Peace Prize in 2006," said Dr. Kahey as he pulled out the drawer holding the body of the deceased economist. "But they could just as well have given it to Bairoliya."

Giuseppe nodded. The doctor moved the sheet aside. The dead economist looked peaceful. His face was ashen. Giuseppe recognized the color from his grandmother's wake. He cleared his throat and explained that he would call the Italian police authority who had sent him here.

"Sure, sure."

He punched in the number on his cell phone. It was answered immediately. "Tommaso di Barbara?" he asked.

"*Sì.*"

"Giuseppe Locatelli. *Chiamero dall'ambasciata a* Mumbai."

"*Sì. Sì!*"

"As you requested, I am now standing next to the body of Mr. Raj Bairoliya."

The man on the phone sounded agitated and as if he had a cold. "His back. Can you see his back?"

Giuseppe turned to the doctor, who had stepped aside to have a smoke. "The Italian authorities are asking about his back."

"Ah. You want to see the mark." Kahey shrugged and set his cigarette on the windowsill. "Perhaps you can tell me what it is." He gave Giuseppe an encouraging look. "You're going to have to help me."

Giuseppe held his cell in his hand, not sure what to do.

"We have to turn him over."

"Call me back," the man on the phone commanded before disconnecting.

"Come on. Don't be afraid. He won't hurt anyone. On three. Ready?" Dr. Kahey laughed as Giuseppe grabbed hold. "One, two, three!"

The body fell onto its side, with one arm hanging stiffly off the edge. Giuseppe Locatelli stared in amazement at the dead man's back. A mark stretched from one shoulder to the other.

"What's that?" he asked.

3

Tommaso di Barbara had been waiting for the call all day. He'd done practically nothing but sit and stare at the phone as he nursed the first symptoms of the flu. And now the call had come through—at a hell of an inconvenient moment. Tommaso glanced at his phone as his boss studied him with an accusatory expression.

"And you don't know anything about it?" demanded Commissario Morante. "A package requested from this station, sent by diplomatic pouch from China?"

Tommaso didn't reply. He wondered why Morante was at the police station today. Usually, he put in an appearance only when there were important visitors. Tommaso had an unpleasant feeling that his days at the station were numbered.

The commissario persisted: "Are you sure? Someone used official channels to get the Chinese authorities to send the package with the cassette. Via Interpol. Without my knowledge." The commissario's breath smelled of Chianti and garlic.

"My shift starts now," replied Tommaso, evading the question.

He got up and fled outside into the rain.

The wharf that led from the police station to the police boats was the first part of Venice that prominent guests to the city encountered. After being transported over from the mainland, they were received by Commissario Morante, then escorted through the old police headquarters, which had once housed monks, and out to the Grand Canal along the police wharf. Tonight there were no guests. Only rain. Tommaso jumped down into the boat and tapped on his phone to retrieve the last missed call.

"Hello?"

"It's Tommaso again. Are you still there?"

"Yes. Yes!" Giuseppe Locatelli sounded distressed.

Tommaso swore. This damn rain. It was impossible to hear anything. He pressed his hand over his other ear and strained to listen.

"I'm still in the morgue."

"Did you turn him over?"

"Yes. It's—"

"Talk louder," shouted Tommaso. "I can't hear you."

"He has a mark. It looks completely crazy. Like a . . ."

Tommaso broke into the silence. "Like a tattoo?"

"Yes."

Flavio and the new man from Puglia came running through the rain. They were on the night shift with Tommaso.

"Can you take some pictures with your cell phone?" asked Tommaso.

"Yes. But I've also brought along a camera. As you requested in your e-mail."

Tommaso thought fast. If he had interpreted the boss's mood correctly, he might not have much time left at the station. Not enough time to wait for photographs to travel by snail mail from India.

"Take pictures of his back with your cell. Do you hear me? This is an urgent matter. Take pictures showing his whole back and also some close-ups—as close as you can get without losing focus."

Flavio and the new colleague opened the door and stepped into the cabin of the boat. They said hello to Tommaso, who nodded.

"Did you understand what I said?" asked Tommaso.

"Yes," said Giuseppe.

"And send them to me as an MMS."

Tommaso ended the call. He dug a bottle of pills out of his pocket and took two without any liquid other than his own spit as he tried to figure out how he could have gotten the flu. Maybe he'd caught it from somebody at the hospice. The nurses and nuns who took care of his mother were in constant contact with illness. The thought of his dying mother sent a pang of guilt through him.

Santa Lucia train station—Venice

The man's passport said that he came from Guatemala. It was the thinnest passport Tommaso had ever seen: nothing more than a small piece of paper folded in half. No space for seals or visas, just a dingy photograph of the owner, who looked like a Mayan Indian, and a few dubious official stamps from an equally dubious authority on the other side of the Atlantic.

"*Poco, poco*," replied the owner of the passport when Tommaso asked if he spoke Italian.

"French?"

He didn't speak that language, either. The man knew only a little English, which was far from Tommaso's strong suit. But Tommaso was not the only one in Italy who didn't speak English. Not even his English teacher in school could speak the language properly. On the other hand, French had been pounded into the heads of the students. Tommaso would have preferred to learn English, but by now it was too late, he thought. If you're over twenty-five, it's too late to learn anything new. That was what his father had taught him. And when you're over thirty, you need to become your own doctor. Tommaso's father, who had never left Cannaregio in Venice, died because he refused to seek medical help when he began having problems with his lungs. Now Tommaso knew: Fathers shouldn't talk so much. He also knew that in many ways, he was a tired copy of his father.

Tommaso straightened up and caught sight of his own reflection in the window of the train compartment. Normally, he would have seen a sharp, clean-shaven face with penetrating eyes, hair sprinkled with gray, and a firm jaw. Tonight he looked like he should be home in bed. Tommaso was the first to admit that his good looks had been a hindrance to establishing any sort of stable relationship with a woman. There were simply too many temptations. But not in the past couple of years, since he'd reached his mid-forties. Not that his appearance had changed appreciably, but people around him had changed. They'd gotten married and were enjoying the pleasures of settling down. Tommaso told himself almost every day that he ought to find himself a wife. But that's probably not going to happen tonight, he thought as he again caught sight of his reflection.

"*Grazie.*" Tommaso nodded to the Mayan from Guatemala and stepped out onto the platform.

He immediately checked his cell phone. No new messages. No photo files. Tommaso looked at the train station clock. Tuesday, December 15, 2009. 1:18 A.M. He knew it could take several minutes, sometimes even several hours, for a message to reach his phone from Asia. Their intelligence services delayed the signal so they could check what was being sent in and out. They diligently monitored everyone's conversations.

"Flavio," Tommaso called to his colleague. "Flavio!"

The three of them were the only ones on the night shift, which had started in the rain seventeen minutes ago. Police headquarters was located down the street from the train station. They knew that the train from Trieste arrived at one-thirty and often carried illegal immigrants from Eastern Europe, seeking their fortune in the West by working for lousy wages in some miserable kitchen.

Flavio stepped out of the rain and under the platform's steel roof. He had to shout at Tommaso to make himself heard over the noise. "We're letting them go."

"Why?"

"Suicide on Murano."

"Suicide?"

"Or murder. Out on those islands, it could be either." Flavio blew his nose hard three times and then stuffed the tissue back in his pocket.

Tommaso took another look at his cell phone. Still nothing from India. Am I afraid of what I'll find out? he asked himself on his way down to the boat. Almost every other time, he'd been right. A couple of months ago a body was found in Hanoi. Dead in the same way. With the same mark. Also a humanitarian.

Before Flavio turned the boat around in the canal, Tommaso noticed that the lights were on in the commissario's office. Tommaso knew only too well what that meant. Commissario Morante was moving heaven and earth to find out who had convinced the Chinese authorities to send the package with the cassette. Soon he would know—the commissario was a thorough man—and he would also know that Tommaso had used Interpol to send warnings to a number of European police departments. Including the one in Copenhagen.

4

cy-cold hours in the Nordvest district of the city.

The rain was drumming on the roof of the police car in a relaxed, monotonous pattern. The drops were getting heavier. Soon the rain pouring down on Copenhagen is going to crystallize and land on the ground as soft snow, thought Niels Bentzon. His fingers shook as he tried to pry the next-to-last cigarette out of the pack.

Through the foggy panes, the world around him was like an impenetrable veil of water, dark with shifting lights from the cars driving past. He leaned back and stared into space. He had a headache and thanked the higher powers that the team leader had asked him to wait in the car. Niels didn't care for Dortheavej. Maybe it was because of the area's particular ability to attract trouble. It wouldn't surprise him at all if it wasn't raining in the rest of Copenhagen tonight.

Niels tried to recall who had taken up residence here first. Was it the Islamic religious community or the occupants of the Youth House? The two groups both served as an open invitation to troublemakers. Everyone on the police force knew it. A call on the police radio from Dortheavej in Nordvest meant a bomb threat, demonstrations, arson, or general mayhem.

Niels had participated in raiding the old Youth House; almost every police officer in the country had been called in. It was a bad business, and he hadn't liked the way things played out. Niels had ended up in a side street where he tried to pacify two very young men wielding very big clubs. Niels was struck on the left arm and in the lower rib cage. Hatred had streamed out of the two youths, a supernova of frustrations directed at Niels. When he finally managed to knock one of them to the ground and get him cuffed, the young man began screaming the ugliest epithets right in his face. His accent was unmistakable. The kid was from northern Sjælland, probably Rungsted. A child of wealth.

Tonight it wasn't angry youths or Islamists who had brought him to this street. It was a returning soldier using surplus ammunition on his own family.

"Niels!"

Niels ignored the pounding on the car window. He still had three fourths of his cigarette left.

"Niels. It's time."

He took two deep drags before he stepped out into the rain.

The officer, a young guy, looked at him. "Great weather, huh?"

"What do we know so far?" Niels tossed his cigarette butt on the ground and made his way past the police barricade.

"He's fired three or four shots, and he has a hostage."

"What do we know about the hostage?"

"Nothing."

"Are there children?"

"We don't know anything, Niels. Leon is in the stairwell." The officer pointed.

Tuesday, December 15, 2009

Fuck you!! That was what some honest soul had scratched into the wall above the names of the residents. The stairwell was both a wreck and a testament to the political decisions of the past few years: *Save Christiania, Fuck Israel,* and *Kill the cops.* That was as much as Niels had time to read before the rusty front door slammed shut behind him. It had taken only seconds for him to get soaked through.

"Is it raining?"

Niels couldn't tell which of the three officers on the stairs was trying to be funny. "The third floor, right?"

"Yes, sir."

They may have been laughing behind his back as he continued up the stairs. On the way he passed another pair of very young officers wearing bulletproof vests and holding automatic weapons. The world had not become a better place since Niels was admitted to the police academy more than twenty summers ago. On the contrary. He could see it in the eyes of the young officers. Hard, cold, withdrawn.

"Take it easy, boys. We'll get home alive, no problem," Niels whispered as he passed them.

"Leon?" called one of the officers. "The negotiator is on his way up."

Niels knew exactly what Leon stood for. If Leon were forced to choose a motto, it would be: *The operation was successful, but the patient died.*

"Is that my friend Damsbo?" Leon called from the landing before Niels came around the corner.

"I didn't know you had any friends, Leon."

Leon leaped down two steps and looked at Niels in surprise, both hands gripping the small Heckler & Koch automatic. "Bentzon? Where the hell did they dig you up?"

Niels looked into Leon's eyes. Dead, gray—a reflection of the typical November weather.

It had been a long time since Niels last saw Leon. Niels had been on sick leave for the past six months. The stubble on Leon's face had turned white, and his hairline had receded, leaving behind a whole parking lot full of wrinkles.

"I thought they were going to send Damsbo."

"Damsbo called in sick. Munkholm is on vacation," replied Niels, pushing the muzzle of the Heckler & Koch away so it was no longer pointed at him.

"Can you handle this, Bentzon? It's been a long time, right? Are you still on medication?" A condescending smile appeared on Leon's lips before he went on. "Isn't it mostly speeding tickets that you've been handing out lately?"

Niels shook his head, trying to hide the fact that he was out of breath. He pretended that the deep breaths he was taking meant he was thinking about the situation. "How bad is it?" he asked.

"Peter Jansson, twenty-seven years old. He's armed. A veteran of the Iraq war. Apparently, he even won a medal. Now he's threatening to kill his whole family. A colleague from the military is on his way here. Maybe he can get Jansson to let the kids go before he pops himself."

"Maybe we can even talk him out of popping himself," replied Niels, giving Leon a hard stare. "What do you say?"

"When the hell are you going to face facts, Bentzon? Some guys just aren't worth the money. A prison sentence, disability pension, you name it."

Niels ignored Leon's diatribe. "Anything else, Leon? What do we know about the apartment?"

"There are two rooms in front. The door opens directly onto the first room. No entry hall. We think he's in the room on the left. Or in the bedroom in back. Shots were fired. We know there are two children and a wife. Or ex-wife. Or maybe only one kid and a foster child."

Niels gave Leon an inquiring look.

"Yeah, well, the story varies depending on which neighbor you talk to. Are you going in?"

Niels nodded.

"Unfortunately, he's not completely stupid."

"What do you mean?"

"He knows there's only one way he can be sure that the negotiator isn't hiding a weapon or a transmitter."

"You're saying that he wants me to strip?" A deep sigh.

Leon gave Niels a look of sympathy and nodded. "I understand if you don't want to do it. We can storm the place instead."

"No. That's okay. I've done it before." Niels unfastened his belt.

———————

Next summer Niels Bentzon would mark fifteen years with the homicide department—the past ten years as a negotiator, the kind sent in during hostage situations or when someone threatened to kill himself. They were always men. Whenever the stock market took a nosedive and the economists warned of financial crisis, the guns all came out on the table. Niels was constantly surprised to discover how many guns were out there in people's homes. Handguns from World War II. Hunting rifles and target rifles, none of them with permits.

"My name is Niels Bentzon. I'm a police officer. I have no clothes on, just as you requested. I'm not carrying a weapon or a transmitter." Cautiously, Niels pushed open the door. "Can you hear me? My name is Niels. I'm a police officer, and I'm unarmed. I know you're a soldier, Peter. I know it's a difficult thing to take somebody else's life. I'm just here to talk to you."

Niels stood motionless in the doorway and listened. Not a word in reply, just the stench of a life that had disintegrated. Slowly, his eyes got used to the dark.

Off in the distance a Nordvest mongrel was barking. For several seconds Niels had to rely on his sense of smell: cordite. He inadvertently stepped on some cartridge cases. He picked up one of them. It was still warm. Niels was able to make out what had been etched into the bottom of the metal: 9mm. Niels was very familiar with that caliber. Three years ago he'd had the honor of taking a German-made bullet of precisely that caliber in his thigh. Somewhere in the top drawer of Kathrine's bureau at home, he'd hidden away the slug that the surgeon had dug out of him. A 9mm parabellum. The most popular caliber in the world. The name parabellum came from Latin. Niels had found it in Wikipedia: *Si vis pacem, para bellum. If you want peace, prepare for war.* That was the motto of the German manufacturer. The Deutsche Waffen und Munitionsfabriken—the company that had supplied ammunition to the German army in the two world wars. And what a splendid peace had resulted.

Niels put the cartridge case back on the floor, where he'd found it. He stood still, collecting himself. He needed to get rid of the unpleasant memory before he could continue. Otherwise fear would take over. The slightest quaver in his voice could make the hostage-taker nervous. Kathrine. He thought about Kathrine. He had to stop doing that or he wouldn't be able to continue.

"Are you okay, Bentzon?" whispered Leon from somewhere behind him.

"Close the door, Leon," replied Niels in a harsh voice.

Leon obeyed. The headlights of cars passing on the street below sent flashes through the windows, and Niels caught sight of his own reflection in the pane. Pale, frightened, naked, and defenseless. He was freezing cold.

"I'm standing here in your living room, Peter. My name is Niels. I'm waiting for you to talk to me."

Niels was calm. Utterly calm. He knew that it might take most of the night to negotiate, but he didn't usually require that much time. The most important thing in a hostage situation was to find out as much as possible about the hostage-taker in the shortest possible time. To find out something about the *human being* behind the threats. Only when you saw the real person was there any hope. Leon was an idiot. He saw only the threat. That was why he invariably ended up shooting.

Niels was looking for traces of *the man named Peter* in the apartment. The essential details. He looked at the photographs on the refrigerator:

Peter with his wife and two children. Underneath the pictures, it said *Clara* and *Sofie,* spelled out with magnets. Next to those names it said *Peter* and *Alexandra*. Clara—the older daughter—was nearly grown up. Maybe a teenager. Braces and pimples. There was a big age gap between the two girls. Sofie couldn't be more than six. Blond and delicate. She looked like her father. Clara didn't look like her mother or her father. Maybe she was the product of a previous marriage. Niels took a deep breath and went back to the living room.

"Peter? Are Clara and Sofie with you? And Alexandra?"

"Piss off," said a firm voice from the back of the apartment. In the same instant Niels's body gave in to the cold, and he started shaking. Peter wasn't desperate. He was determined. It was possible to negotiate with desperation; determination was worse. Another deep breath. The battle was not yet lost. *Find out what the hostage-taker wants.* That was the most important task of a negotiator. And if there's nothing he wants, help him find something— *it doesn't matter what it is.* The point was to make his brain start looking forward. Right now Peter's brain found itself in its last minutes; Niels could hear that in the confident tone of his voice.

"Did you say something?" asked Niels, trying to play for time.

No answer.

Niels looked around. He still didn't have the one detail that might resolve the situation. Sunflowers covered the wallpaper, big sunflowers from floor to ceiling. There was another smell mixed in with the smell of fear and dog pee. Fresh blood. Niels's eyes located the source of the smell in the corner, curled up in a position that should have been impossible.

Alexandra had taken two bullets right in the heart. It was only in movies that anyone would bother to feel for a pulse; in reality, he saw a gaping hole in the heart and a life that had gone to waste. She was staring at Niels with wide-open eyes. Niels could hear the muted sobbing of one of the children.

"Peter? I'm still here. My name is Niels—"

A voice interrupted him. "Your name is Niels, and you're a police officer. I heard you! And I told you to piss off."

A deep, decisive voice. Where was it coming from? The bathroom? Why in hell hadn't Leon found a floor plan?

"You want me to leave?"

"Yes, goddammit."

"Unfortunately, I can't do that. My job is to stay here until it's over. No

matter what happens. I know you can understand that. You and I, Peter—
we both have work that demands we stay, even if it's impossible."

Niels listened. He was still standing next to the body of Alexandra. In
her hand she was clutching several pieces of paper. Rigor mortis hadn't set
in yet, and it wasn't hard to tear the papers out of her hand. Niels stood up;
over by the window he made use of the streetlights on Dortheavej. The letter
was from the defense department. A discharge. Too many words, covering
three pages. Niels quickly scanned what it said. *Personal problems . . . unstable
. . . unfortunate incidents . . . offer of assistance and retraining.* For a few
seconds Niels felt that he was caught in a time warp. That he'd crept into the
last photograph of the family. He could just imagine the situation: Alexandra
found the letter. Peter had been discharged. He provided the family's only
income. Discharged while, at the same time, he was trying to digest all the
shit he had seen and done in the service of his country. Niels knew that they
never talked about it—the soldiers in Iraq and Afghanistan. They refused
to answer the most obvious questions: Did you shoot anyone? Did you kill
anyone? They always gave evasive answers. Wasn't the answer simple? The
shots the soldiers fired that ripped apart the veins and arteries and organs of
their enemies did almost as much damage to the soul of the shooter.

Peter had been discharged. He had gone away a real man and come
home a wreck. And Alexandra couldn't handle it. Her first concern was
for the children; that was always true of a mother. A soldier shoots, and a
mother thinks of her children. Maybe she shouted at him or screamed. Told
him he was incompetent, that he'd let them down. And then Peter did what
he'd been taught to do: If conflicts cannot be resolved in a peaceful manner,
you shoot the enemy. Alexandra had become the enemy.

Finally.

Finally, Niels had the detail he could use. He would talk to Peter as a
soldier. He would appeal to his sense of honor, his masculinity.

5

Murano—Venice

Early winter—the high season for suicides on the European continent. But this was no suicide. It was revenge. Otherwise the man wouldn't have used steel wire to hang himself. It wasn't exactly difficult to find rope on this island, with all of its boat builders.

Flavio was outside, throwing up into the canal. The widow of the deceased glassblower had long since disappeared. She'd gone up the road to seek comfort from the neighbors. Tommaso could hear her wailing every so often. Outside the house, a microcosm of the island's inhabitants had gathered. The shop steward from the glassblowing workshop, a monk from the San Lazzaro cloister, a neighbor, and a storekeeper. Tommaso wondered what the storekeeper wanted. Was he hoping to collect payment for the last bill before it was too late? It was unbelievable what the financial crisis had done to men and their self-esteem. And islanders were even more susceptible because of the isolation, the closed society, the rigid roles. No wonder Venice had crept to the top of Italy's suicide statistics.

The house was damp and poorly lit, with a low ceiling. Tommaso looked out the window and caught sight of a woman's face. She was in the process of wolfing down a sandwich. She gave him a guilty look, smiled, and shrugged. She couldn't help it if she was hungry, even though the glassblower was dead. Tommaso could hear the people talking outside. Especially the shop steward. About all the cheap glass imitations from Asia that were being imported and sold to tourists. It took work away from the locals, everyone who had produced and developed glassblowing into an art down through the ages. It was scandalous!

Tommaso glanced again at his cell phone. Where the hell were those pictures? The glassblower's body swayed slightly. Tommaso was afraid the steel wire might not hold him much longer. If the vertebrae in his neck were broken, the wire would soon work through the flesh and slice off the body.

"Flavio!" shouted Tommaso.

Flavio appeared in the doorway.

"I want you to write up the report."

"I can't."

"Like hell you can't. All you have to do is write down what I tell you. You can sit over there with your back turned."

Flavio picked up a chair, turned it to face the damp wall, and sat down. The place smelled of soot, as if someone had doused the fire in the hearth with a bucket of water.

"Ready?"

Flavio said nothing as he sat there holding his notebook and staring resolutely at the wall.

Tommaso began with the official part. "We arrived just before two A.M. The call came in from the glassblower's widow, Antonella Bucati. Are you writing this down?"

"Yes."

There was the siren. At last he heard it. Tommaso listened. The ambulance switched off the siren as it made its way from the lagoon and down along the dilapidated canal. The rattling engine and the monotonous attempts of the waves to break down the half-rotten bulwark announced the arrival of the ambulance several seconds before the medics jumped ashore. The blue lights lit up the room in flashes, reminding Tommaso how dark it was in Venice in the wintertime. The damp seemed to steal the scattered remnants of light from the few buildings still occupied. The rest of Venice was submerged in darkness. Most of the city was owned by Americans and Saudis who came to visit two weeks a year, at most.

Tommaso caught sight of it the same instant that his cell phone beeped. The black shoes of the hanged man had white heels. Tommaso scratched one of the heels; the white stuff came off easily.

"Can we take him down?" asked Lorenzo, the ambulance driver. Tommaso had gone to school with him. They'd gotten into a fight once. Lorenzo won.

"Not yet."

"Come on, you're not going to tell me it was murder, are you?" Lorenzo got ready to cut down the glassblower.

"Flavio!" yelled Tommaso. "If he touches the body, put the cuffs on him."

Lorenzo stomped his foot on the floor in fury.

"Flashlight?" Tommaso held out his hand.

Flavio covered his mouth and kept his eyes lowered as he gave Tommaso the flashlight. There was no evidence visible on the floor. And yet. The kitchen floor had been swept clean under the spot where the glassblower hung from the ceiling joist. Unlike the living room, where the floor was filthy. Tommaso's cell beeped again. He opened the back door. The garden was overgrown. A grapevine reached up several yards in the air. Once, long ago, somebody had tried to make the vine grow around the eaves of the terrace, but had then given up and let it follow the sun instead. Now the vine was creeping along the roof. The light was on in the workshop. Tommaso walked the short distance through the garden and opened the door. In contrast to the rest of the house, the workshop was very neat. Meticulous.

Yet another message appeared on the display of his cell. They were appearing in frantic succession. He didn't dare look at any of them right now.

The floor of the workshop was white cement. Tommaso bent down to scratch at the surface. It was porous, as if made of chalk. The same substance was on the glassblower's heels. He sat down on a chair. Flavio was calling him, but Tommaso pretended not to hear. His first instinct was correct. It wasn't suicide. It was revenge. The wife's revenge. The glassblower had been killed out here and then dragged through the workshop, which had left traces of white on the heels of his shoes.

"What are you doing out here?" asked Flavio.

Tommaso looked at his colleague standing in the doorway.

"Are you okay? You're looking a little under the weather."

Tommaso ignored the diagnosis. "We're going to need the medical examiner. And the tech guys from Veneto."

"Why?"

Tommaso ran his finger along the floor and held it up in the air so Flavio could see how white it was. "If you look close, you'll see the same stuff on the dead man's heels."

It took a few seconds for Flavio to process this information. "Should we arrest the widow?"

"That would probably be a good start."

Flavio shook his head, looking sad. Tommaso knew exactly what Flavio was experiencing in those seconds. Dismay. The story they were going to hear from the widow over the next few hours would be all about poverty, drunkenness, and lost jobs, domestic violence and island disputes. That was the story of Venice in recent years. A life insurance policy was undoubtedly tucked away somewhere. Or maybe the glassblower's wife had simply had enough? Flavio called the station and pulled himself together so he could make the necessary arrest. Tommaso took a deep breath. Tonight the world is going to end, he thought. He hardly dared look at the messages on his cell. Four photographs from Giuseppe Locatelli in India. Tommaso got out his reading glasses and studied the first image: the mark on the back of the deceased man. Exactly the same as the others. Then he looked at the close-ups.

"Thirty-four," he murmured to himself. "Two to go."

6

Manic-depressive. Niels heard Leon whispering with the other officers outside the door. He was well aware of the term used to describe him. He also knew how the term was defined in their dictionaries: off his rocker. But Niels was not manic-depressive. Occasionally, he could get wound up a bit. And sometimes he found himself way down in the dumps. The last time it had lasted a couple of months.

Niels looked at his naked legs as he moved into the middle of the room. They were still shaking; the cold was making it difficult to achieve the desired self-control. For a split second he considered leaving. Fleeing. Letting Leon handle the situation the hard way. He himself had never fired his service weapon—and he never would. He knew that. He just couldn't. Maybe that was the simple explanation for why he'd ended up as a negotiator. It was the only position on the police force for which the officer never carried a gun.

Niels cleared his throat and shouted: "Peter! Do you think I'm stupid?" He took two steps closer to the bedroom. "Don't you think I know how it feels? To do the kind of work that you and I do?"

He knew that Peter was listening. He could hear him breathing. Now it was a matter of winning his trust so he would let the children go.

"People don't know what it's like to take somebody's life. They don't know that it feels like you're killing yourself, too."

Niels let his words hover in the air for a few seconds. "Talk to me, Peter!" he shouted in a commanding voice. Even he was surprised by the harsh tone he used. But Peter was a soldier. He required orders. "I said talk to me, Private!"

"What do you want?" Peter yelled from the bedroom. "What the hell do you want?"

"No, what do *you* want, Peter? What is it you want? Do you want to get the fuck out of here? I can damn well understand that. It's an ugly world out there."

No reply.

"I'm coming in now. I'm unarmed, and I'm not wearing any clothes. Just like you requested. I'm going to push open the door very slowly so you can see me."

Niels took three steps over to the door. "I'm opening the door now."

He waited a couple of seconds. It was essential that he get his breathing under control. He couldn't show any sign of nervousness. He closed his eyes. Opened them and pushed open the door. He stood in the doorway. A girl was lying on the bed. Fourteen or fifteen years old. Clara. The firstborn. Lifeless. Blood on the bedcovers. Peter was sitting in a corner of the bedroom, looking with surprise at the naked man in the doorway. The soldier had put on his uniform. His eyes shifted back and forth. He was a wounded animal. He was holding a hunting rifle, which he pointed at Niels. An empty bottle stood on the floor between his legs.

"You can't tell me what to do," whispered Peter. He no longer sounded very sure of himself.

"Where is Sofie?"

Peter didn't answer, but faint sounds were coming from under the bed. He lowered the rifle and aimed it at little Sofie, who had curled up under the bed.

"We've got to get out of here," said the soldier, looking Niels in the eye for the first time.

Niels held his gaze, refusing to look away. "Yes. We need to get out of here. But not Sofie."

"Yes, the whole family."

"I'm going to sit down now."

Niels sat down. Blood from the dead girl was dripping from the bed frame onto the floor. Some drops landed on Niels's naked foot. An oppressive stench of alcohol and unwashed bed linen hung in the air. Niels allowed a few minutes to pass. He could tell that Peter wasn't ready to shoot his younger daughter. There were many different ways of negotiating with a hostage-taker, many techniques. So many that Niels was no longer up on the latest methods. His two colleagues had gone to the United States to take a course from the FBI. Niels was supposed to go with them, but his fear of travel had kept him home. The mere thought of getting into a huge metal cylinder to fly over the Atlantic at an altitude of thirty-five thousand feet was beyond his comprehension. The result was inevitable: His superiors seldom used Niels anymore. Only if the others were sick or on vacation, like tonight.

According to the manual, his next step should be to initiate negotiations with Peter. Get him to make some requests or demands, anything at all. Something that would win them time and get his mind to relax. It could be something very banal. A little more whiskey or a cigarette. But Niels had abandoned the manual long ago.

"Sofie!" Niels shouted again: "Sofie!"

"Yes?" he heard from under the bed.

"Your father and I are going to have a little talk. It's grown-up talk. We want to be alone!"

Niels spoke in a harsh voice, very harsh, and he didn't take his eyes off Peter even for a second. Sofie didn't answer. Niels was now Peter's commanding officer, his superior, his ally.

"I want you to do as your father and I say. Get out of there now! Go out to the stairwell!"

Finally, Niels heard the girl moving under the bed. "Don't look at us! Get out now!" he bellowed.

He heard the girl's light footsteps as she ran through the living room and then the sound of the front door opening and closing. Left behind were Niels and Peter with the body of a teenage girl.

Niels studied the soldier. Peter Jansson, twenty-seven years old. Discharged soldier. A genuine Danish hero. Peter had turned the gun around and placed the muzzle under his own chin.

The soldier closed his eyes. Niels could hear Leon whispering in the stairwell. "Let him do it, Niels. Let the maniac blow his brains out."

"Where do you want to be buried?" Niels was completely calm. He spoke to the soldier as if they were close friends.

Peter opened his eyes but didn't look at Niels. He fixed his eyes on the ceiling. Was he a religious man? Niels knew that many of the soldiers sent off to war made more use of the military chaplain than they were willing to admit.

"Do you want to be cremated?"

The soldier tightened his grip on the gun.

"Is there a message that you want me to give to somebody? I'll be the last one to see you alive, you know."

No reaction from Peter. He was breathing heavily. This last act—the taking of his own life—apparently required more courage than killing his wife and daughter.

"Peter, is there anyone you want me to contact? Somebody you want to leave a message for?"

Niels spoke to Peter as if he had one foot in heaven. On the threshold to the next world. "What you went through in Iraq—no human being should have to go through something like that."

"No."

"And now you want out."

"Yes."

"I can understand that. Is there anything you'd like to be remembered for? Something good?"

Peter was thinking. Niels could see he'd hit home. For the first time Peter was thinking about something other than blowing up himself and his family and the whole fucking world. So Niels kept at it.

"Peter! Answer me! You've done something good! What is it?"

"There was a family . . . a village outside of Basra that was under heavy fire," Peter began, but Niels could see he didn't have the strength to go on.

"An Iraqi family? And you rescued them?"

"Yes."

"You saved lives. You didn't just take lives. That will be remembered."

Peter lowered the gun. For a moment he let the blows pummel him like a boxer who'd been stunned but was still on his feet.

Niels reacted with lightning speed. In a flash he was next to the soldier, grabbing hold of the rifle barrel. Peter looked up at Niels in surprise. He had no intention of letting it go. Niels promptly slapped the man on the head with the back of his hand.

"Let go!" he yelled at Peter, who finally released his grip.

At first Niels thought it was Peter making that rattling and moaning sound. But the soldier was just sitting there, looking like someone who had given up. Holding the rifle, Niels turned around. The girl on the bed was moving.

"Leon!" shouted Niels.

The officers stormed in. Leon was in front, like always. They threw themselves over the soldier, even though he offered no resistance. The medics came thundering up the stairs.

"She's alive!" Niels hurried out of the room. Someone stood ready with a blanket that was thrown over his shoulders. He paused in the doorway and looked back. Peter was crying. He was in the process of falling apart. Tears were good; Niels knew that. If there were tears, there was hope. The medics had put the girl on a gurney and were on their way out.

Niels retreated to the kitchen, wrapped in the thick blanket that smelled of police dogs, and let the others do their jobs. The family had eaten meatballs for dinner. With béarnaise sauce from a package mix.

Outside it was still raining. Or was that the first snow of the year? The windowpane had misted over.

"Bentzon." Leon came into the kitchen. He stood very close. "There's one thing I've been meaning to ask you."

Niels waited. Leon had bad breath.

"What the hell do you think about?"

"Do you really want to know?"

"Yes."

Niels took a deep breath. Leon used the pause to eat the family's last meatball. He smeared it around in the béarnaise sauce and stuffed it into his mouth.

Niels said, "I think about something I once heard on the radio. About Abraham and Isaac."

"I was afraid you'd say something like that."

"You asked."

Leon was still chewing. "So what about them? I don't really know much about that kind of stuff."

"There was a pastor on the radio who said nobody should ever preach that story. Do you remember how it goes? God tells Abraham that he has to sacrifice his son to prove his faith."

"I agree with the pastor. It sounds like a sick story. Ban that shit."

"But isn't that exactly what we do? Send young men off to a war in the desert and ask them to sacrifice themselves for a belief?"

Leon looked at Niels for a few seconds. A little smile, an exaggerated shake of his head, and then he was gone.

7

My revenge will be my redemption.

That thought was crystal-clear in the mind of Abdul Hadi as he stared with contempt at the security guard. If I really wanted to hijack a plane, your ridiculous security check wouldn't stop me.

But it wasn't that simple. He didn't want to hijack a plane and fly it into EU headquarters. There weren't going to be any pictures on TV of the passengers' relatives screaming and crying when the airline posted the names of the victims. This revenge was going to be different; it was going to be a righteous vengeance.

The security guard gave him an annoyed look. Abdul Hadi had of course understood his question the first time, but making the guard repeat his unreasonable request gave him a feeling of power.

"Could you take off your shoes, sir?" The security guard raised his voice.

Abdul Hadi looked at the Westerners who had slipped right through the airport security check without taking off their shoes. He shook his head and went back through the strange free-standing doorway that beeped if you had coins in your pocket. He took off his shoes, calmly and self-confidently, and placed them in a plastic bin. Maybe they think I'm hiding a knife in my shoe, like Mohamed Atta, he thought before he stepped through once again. A second security guard called him over. This time it was his carry-on bag that was submitted to different treatment. And with great suspicion. Abdul Hadi looked around the airport while they rummaged through his toiletries kit. Chocolate and the comic strip *Tintin*. He didn't know much about Belgium, but he now knew that it was famous for these two things. He also recalled that two middle-aged Belgian women had been killed a year ago in Wadi Dawan. Some of Allah's warriors had attacked a convoy of Westerners, and the two women had died. Abdul Hadi shook his head. He would never drive through the Wadi Dawan desert without protection.

A map of the world hung above the tax-free shop. He studied it as they opened the side pockets of his bag and took the batteries out of his shaver. Terror has created a new map, he thought. New York was the capital. Mumbai had also acquired new significance, along with Madrid and the London tube. Sharm el-Sheik, Tel Aviv, and Jerusalem. His people had taken out a broad brush and were beginning to paint the world red. They were in the process of creating a new map of the world in which people no longer thought of castanets when Madrid was mentioned, or the Statue of Liberty when the conversation turned to New York. Instead, they thought about the horrors.

A different security guard came over to join the others bending over his bag. Was this man their boss? Without lifting his eyes from the contents of the bag, the man asked in English: "Did you pack this bag yourself, sir?"

"Yes, of course. It's my bag."

"Where are you traveling?"

"To Stockholm."

"Do you work there?"

"No. I'm going to visit family. I have a visa. Is there a problem?"

"Where are you from, sir?"

"Yemen. Is there a problem?"

The guard gave his bag back without even a hint of an apology.

Abdul Hadi stopped in the middle of the departure hall. Shops, advertisements for movies, and advertisements for specific lifestyles. He was filled with contempt. Toward the West and the bizarre relationship of Westerners to security. It's pure fiction, he thought. Just like the dream of what all their products will do for them. Now travelers believe that everything is fine, that they're safe. But none of them are safe! Abdul Hadi wouldn't dream of trying to bring a gun to an airport. Why make things more difficult for himself? Everything had been prepared for him at his destination. He knew where he was supposed to go. He knew who was going to die and how he was going to do it.

Stockholm—delayed

He looked up at the monitor showing departure times. The delay didn't matter; he had plenty of time. He would land in Stockholm with time to spare. Someone would meet him at the airport, drive him to the train station, and help him find the right train to Copenhagen.

He looked at the passengers around him and thought: No. You're not safe at all. The thought pleased him. You can rummage through my bags, you can ask me to take off my shoes, you can demand that I strip off all my clothes, like you did at the first airport where I changed planes. But that won't save you.

He thought about the humiliation he'd suffered at the airport in Mumbai. He was the only one in line who was taken aside. He had obediently followed his escort down to the basement. Two airport security guards led the way, and two Indian police officers brought up the rear. The room had no windows. No chairs, no table. He had to put his clothes on the floor. He'd asked for a chair, since the floor was so dirty. Their answer was to ask him whether he wanted to catch his plane or make trouble. He considered making trouble. Westerners weren't treated like that, not even when they were under suspicion. But he focused his thoughts on his goal. On revenge.

And then he thought: We will never be accepted in your world. Tolerated, maybe. But not accepted. Not on an equal footing. He'd talked about this with his younger brother just before he left. If he didn't return, his little brother would become head of the family. That was why his brother had come home from Saudi Arabia, where he'd been a guest worker. The Saudis were almost worse than the Westerners. Decadent. Pathetic. Liars. Everybody knew that their women covered up their bodies merely for show. On Friday evening they boarded chartered planes and headed for Beirut. The women changed clothes on the plane. They threw off the burka, while the men changed into Hugo Boss suits. Abdul Hadi had studied at the American University of Beirut during the years before the civil war. He saw the Saudis arriving every weekend, completely transformed in appearance.

The women lay on the beach in bikinis, while the men got drunk and played blackjack in the big casino. He didn't know whom he hated most: the Saudis who played weekend-Westerners in the only city in the world that would play along with them, or the Westerners who had enticed them there. Enticed with promises of freedom. The freedom to try to get the same things the Westerners had. But they couldn't. That was something Abdul Hadi knew from bitter experience. Even though he was a handsome man, especially before his hair turned gray, he'd had no chance with the American girls at the university.

Well, one of them did say yes to his invitation. *Caroline.* She was from Chicago. Wanted to be a movie director when she went back home. They went to see a film together. *Jaws.* But she lost interest in him when she found out he wasn't from Lebanon. Caroline was just looking for a little local color. Someone who could take her inside the tent of the Bedouins; someone who could show her the real Lebanon before she went back home.

Stockholm—delayed

After the day when Caroline pretended not to recognize him on campus, he'd sworn never to make any more attempts with the American girls. He was living with his brother in a rented room in the building behind the Hotel Commodore. The high-rise had a swimming pool on the roof, but there was never any water in it. They shared the courtyard with a private clinic, and every afternoon human offal from the plastic surgeries was carried out in big sacks. The Saudi women had their fat sucked out and their beaked noses straightened so they would look like Caroline and her friends. But they would never be like the Western girls. And until the rest of the Arab people realized this, they would never be truly free. To be locked inside a dream in which you can never participate is a prison. So it was good that someone had started to remake the map of the world.

"Boarding card, please."

Abdul handed his boarding card to the Swedish stewardess. She smiled at him. It had been a long time since anyone had smiled at him.

"The airport in Stockholm is still closed because of snow, sir," she added, and it sounded as if she meant "sir" with respect. Not like the security guards, who used "sir" as a free pass to subject a person to degrading treatment. *Open your bag, sir. Take off your clothes, sir.*

"We'll be boarding as soon as the airport reopens."

The stewardess was still smiling at him, and he felt a slight spark inside. No, it doesn't matter, thought Abdul Hadi. It's too little, too late.

8

Carlsberg silo—Copenhagen

The elevator door closed with a gentle sigh and waited for what Niels would do next. He did the same thing he always did: put in the key, turned it, and pressed "21." He felt a faint hum in his diaphragm as the elevator began its dialogue with gravity. The feeling made him think of sex. It had been a long time.

A few seconds later, the door opened, and he stepped directly into the apartment. Either he had some uninvited guests, or he'd forgotten to turn off the light. Probably the latter, he decided as he went into the large living room. It was as empty as he'd left it. And yet. Someone had been there. A faint scent of . . . He'd have to ask Natasha in the apartment below tomorrow. She had a key to his place so she could let workmen in and out. Considering the fact that the building had been completely remodeled a few years ago, there was a surprising amount of trouble with the ventilation system, wiring, and gas lines.

Carlsberg had originally built the 280-foot-tall silo for storing malt. But after the royal brewing company had merged with the other big breweries, the malt warehouse became superfluous. Niels actually didn't care much for beer anymore. Like so many people his age and in his salary bracket, he'd switched to cabernet sauvignon. And why not have half a bottle tonight? Or a whole one? Should he be celebrating or in mourning? Celebrate that someone had survived or mourn the fact that someone had died? Oh, fuck it. Niels opened the bottle, his mood still undetermined.

It was almost two in the morning, but Niels didn't feel tired. The rain was pelting the big picture windows. He put on the Beatles and turned up the volume so he could hear "Blackbird" from the bath. He washed the girl's blood off his feet before, true to ritual, he sat down in front of his computer. He always did that when he got home. And when he got up in the morning. He hesitated before turning it on. He missed Kathrine, he missed having somebody in the apartment. He felt out of sorts when she wasn't there.

———— ——

Kathrine was a partner in the architectural firm that had handled the remodeling of the silo into luxury apartments. She was the one who wanted to buy the most beautiful of the lot. She was completely in love with it, she said. Niels was also drawn to the apartment. The high elevation at Carlsberg appealed to him. It had the best view of the city in all of Copenhagen. Back then the smell still permeated the whole area whenever the brewery fired up the boilers. Since then the beer production had been moved far away. Niels had no idea where. Maybe to Asia, like so much else. He was glad that the stink of yeast no longer poured in over him every morning. It had felt like having an old drunk breathing on him.

Niels looked around the room. The two designer sofas facing each other. The solid, rectangular coffee table. A hollow in the reddish granite of the table, which allowed them to light a small fire in it. Bioethanol. Scent-free, and it evaporated completely, as Kathrine had explained to a skeptical Niels. It did look beautiful when they sat there with a fire glowing on the table. He hadn't yet invited anyone from the station up here, although there'd been no lack of urging from Kathrine. "Invite your colleagues over," she often said. But Niels couldn't do it; nor could he tell Kathrine why: He was ashamed. Not because it was Kathrine's money that had paid for the view from the beer tower—he'd gotten used to that idea—but because his colleagues would never be able to afford a place like this. A 360-degree panoramic view. If you lay in the bathtub in the evening and the only light was from glowing candles, the tiny white flames would glitter on the Italian marble and compete with the lights of the city and the stars in the sky.

He switched on the computer, wondering if Kathrine was awake yet. What time was it in Cape Town? An hour later . . . three in the morning. On the list of online friends, it said that Kathrine was logged on, but she almost never turned off her MacBook. So that didn't mean she was awake.

"Where shall we go tonight?" Niels asked himself as he ran through the list of online friends. Amanda from Buenos Aires was logged on. So was Ronaldo from Mexico. It was too early in the morning for most Europeans to be online. Only Louis from Málaga. Damned if he wasn't always online. Did he even have a life away from his computer screen? Niels didn't feel as sickly or abnormal since he'd discovered this network. A global network for people who couldn't travel. People who, for the most part, had never left their own country. The phobia took many different forms. Niels had chatted with people who couldn't even leave the city where they lived. So he'd begun to feel quite normal. After all, he'd been to Hamburg and Malmö. And to Lübeck on his honeymoon. The physical discomfort hadn't set in until he got to Berlin. Kathrine had once forced him to go to that city, but he'd spent the whole weekend shaking and feeling sick.

"It will pass, it will pass," she'd chanted over and over as they walked along Unter den Linden. But it hadn't passed. Nobody understood. Nobody except a couple of hundred people who were part of this network. Or at least it *sounded* as if they understood. Because it was not an uncommon phobia. "Air and Travel Phobias." Niels had done a lot of reading on the subject. Several studies said that more than one in ten people on the planet suffered from it to a greater or lesser degree. He'd also tried to explain this to Kathrine. If he got more than a couple of hundred kilometers away from home, his whole system simply stopped functioning. First his digestion. He couldn't take a shit. That was why he could never be gone more than a weekend. After his intestines stopped working, he would start having trouble breathing. In Berlin, his muscles had begun to protest. Those were the sort of details he exchanged with others on the network. Niels knew that this phobia was the reason why he had a tendency to get depressed. To freeze up. Because he couldn't travel, on some days he felt like he had a heavy cement block tied to his waist. During other periods, he felt a surge of energy. He could see the positive in life—and that was when people thought he was manic.

Hi, Niels!!! How are things in Copenhagen?

That was Amanda from Argentina. She was twenty-two. She was studying at the art academy and hadn't left Buenos Aires in fifteen years. Her mother had died in a plane crash when Amanda was seven, so for her there was probably a psychological explanation for her travel phobia. For many others, there was no obvious explanation. At least none that Niels knew about. Not for himself, either. He'd tried everything. Psychologists. Hypnosis. But no explanation had ever surfaced. He just couldn't travel.

Hello, Beautiful. It's colder here than where you are.

He regretted writing "Beautiful." It made him sound like an old man. But Amanda really was beautiful. He looked at the photo in her online profile. Almond-shaped eyes, thick black hair, full lips. She hadn't stinted on the red lipstick when the picture was taken.

Amanda's answer appeared at the bottom of his screen:

Wish I could be there to warm you up.

Niels smiled. Everybody did a lot of flirting with each other in this forum. Good Lord. A couple hundred people who would never meet. And who all possessed the deepest longing to go abroad. They sent each other pictures of their hometowns, personal reports, recipes. Niels had posted a recipe for some good old-fashioned Danish liver pâté for anyone to use. It turned out to be a big hit. He had made Louis's mother's recipe for paella while he listened to Spanish music played on a twelve-string guitar—also supplied by Louis. It was almost like being there himself. That was the good thing about their forum. It wasn't devoted to everything they couldn't do: travel, drive, fly. It wasn't devoted to talk about illness. It was about what they *could* do: tell each other about themselves, their countries, their cultures. Through each other they experienced the world.

Niels exchanged a few trivial comments with Amanda, and then she had to leave for school. She promised to take a picture of the school and the sculpture she was working on.

Bye, Niels. Handsome man, she wrote, and then she was gone before he could reply.

He was just about to log off when Kathrine's face appeared on the screen. "Niels?"

The screen flickered a bit. As if it needed a moment to get in sync with its African counterpart.

"You're not in bed?" Her voice sounded slightly groggy.

"I just got home."

She lit a cigarette and smiled at him. Smoking was something they had in common. Since they couldn't have children. Niels could see that she was slightly high.

"Can you tell that I've been drinking?" she asked.

"No. I don't think so. Did you go out?"

"Could you turn off the Beatles? I can hardly hear what you're saying."

He turned off the music, adjusted the screen, and studied her.

"Is something wrong?" she asked.

"No. Not at all."

She smiled.

Niels didn't want to tell her about his evening. There was no reason to share the misery; that was how he'd always felt. He hated it when people told horrible stories about sick or dead children. Drowning accidents, car crashes, disasters . . . Why did other people need to hear about it?

Kathrine adjusted her webcam. She was sitting in the usual hotel room. In the background he could see something glittering faintly. Was that the city behind her? Moonlight skimming over Table Mountain? Or maybe the Cape of Good Hope? Were those tiny bright spots from ships putting the Indian Ocean behind them?

"Did I tell you about Chris and Marylou? The American architect couple who've just arrived here? They're fucking brilliant. One of them even worked with Daniel Libeskind. Well, they had a little housewarming . . . You'll meet them yourself in a couple of days. They've invited us over on Saturday."

She gave him an encouraging look.

"I'm looking forward to it."

"Did you get the pills?"

"Yes. Of course I did."

"Can I see them?"

Niels got up and went out to the bathroom. By the time he came back, Kathrine had taken off her white shirt and was sitting there in her bra. Niels knew perfectly well what she had in mind.

"Is it hot down there?" he asked, teasing her.

"It's great, Niels. The best climate in the world. And you're going to love their red wine. Show me the pills."

He held the package up to the camera.

"A little closer."

He did as she asked. Kathrine read aloud: "'Diazepam. 5 mg. A sedative for fear of flying.'"

"Allan has a friend who used them with great success," said Niels.

"Allan?"

"From the police SWAT team."

"I thought you were the only police officer who couldn't fly."

"I don't mind flying. I just have a hard time traveling anywhere."

"What's the difference? Just take the pills. Take two while I'm watching you."

Niels laughed and shook his head. He put two little pills on his tongue. "Cheers."

"Swallow them, sweetheart."

After he'd downed the pills with half a glass of red wine, Kathrine's mood changed, just as he'd expected.

"Shall we play?"

"Is that what you want?"

"You know I do. Stop teasing. Take off your clothes."

———

Kathrine had been in Cape Town for six months. At first she hadn't wanted to go. Or rather: She pretended she didn't want to go. Niels knew this game well. Right from the start he sensed that her reluctance mostly had to do with him and his reaction: What would he say if she left?

When the decision was finally made, Niels experienced a great sense of relief. Not because he was happy about the idea of being away from Kathrine for an entire year, but because the uncertainty was over. Every once in a while before she left—this was something he never told her—he'd even caught himself looking forward to being alone. He couldn't explain why, because he knew that the loneliness would hit him hard. The last evening they'd had a terrible fight before they made love on the sofa. Afterward Kathrine had wept, saying that she couldn't leave him. She was going to call her boss and cancel the whole thing. But of course that hadn't happened.

They said goodbye early in the morning as he sat in the car. The air was thick with invisible rain. Niels felt completely drained. His eyes swam. When Kathrine leaned down to kiss him, her lips were warm and soft, and she whispered something in his ear that he didn't quite catch. All day long, after she'd left, he wondered what exactly she had said. *If we don't see each other again . . .* At the same time, he had an inexplicable feeling that it was good he hadn't heard the rest of her sentence.

———

"Move over so I can see you," said Kathrine.

When Niels again looked at the screen, Kathrine had beaten him to it.

She was sitting naked on the chair, having pushed herself back a little so that Niels could see everything he was missing.

"Do it slow, sweetheart. You look so good. I want to enjoy it," she said.

When it came to sex, Kathrine was from another planet. A planet where sex was not associated with shame or embarrassment or being a little shy. He loved that, even though it did challenge his own boundaries. Kathrine had taught him to like his body; not that there was anything wrong with it. On the contrary. Niels was born with all the right attributes: tall without being lanky, compact without looking like a bulldog. The hair on his chest had turned gray; that was something Kathrine loved, and she'd eagerly observed the transformation. But before he met her, his body was something attached to his head, and it did only what his brain commanded. Kathrine had taught him that his body had its own will, its own desires. And when it came to sex, the commands moved in the opposite direction. Now his body sent messages to his head about what it wanted. And he had to obey.

"Turn around. I want to see your ass when you take off your pants," she ordered.

Niels stood with his back to the camera and slowly let his jeans fall, the way he knew she liked. He looked down at himself. Hmm—it was surprising, actually—he hadn't expected to see any life down there after what he'd been through tonight. But why not? Sex and death. *Desire and fear.*

"Let me look at you, sweetheart," whispered Kathrine in Cape Town.

9

The airspace over Europe

Her again. That stewardess. Now she was walking up the narrow aisle, serving coffee and tea, juice, and peanuts. Abdul Hadi smiled at the thought. Nuts, coffee, and tea. They were the most important goods sold in the Middle Eastern bazaars. The reason why European merchants had flocked to Arabia for centuries—to bring these items back to the barren north. Now the glories of Arabia were handed out to airline passengers in fancy plastic packaging showing pictures of blond young people. The motive behind the West's frantic marketing of their products was something that no American or European would notice: The West was selling primarily the idea of itself. Advertising had been invented to sell the West to Westerners.

"Coffee or tea?"

Abdul Hadi looked up. It was her. Again that smile, the insistent eye contact. In spite of the many hours spent waiting in the airport, she looked as fresh as if she'd just gotten up.

"Orange juice."

"Peanuts?"

"Please."

Her hand brushed against his as she set the juice on the tray table. A warm current rushed through him. It had been a long time since he'd felt anything like that. The stewardess placed a single package of peanuts on the little tray table. Just before she moved on, she added another package. Not hastily, but calmly and pleasantly as she said, "Enjoy the flight, sir."

Abdul Hadi glanced around the cabin. Of all the passengers seated nearby, he was the only one who'd been given two packages of peanuts. Was there some message behind her advances? He leaned into the aisle to look at her. He shouldn't have done that because at the same instant she turned around and looked back. He could feel the heat. The blood draining from his head to fill a whole different part of his body. He imagined himself with the stewardess in a hotel room. How she would sit on the edge of the bed. He would touch her hair. He'd never touched blond hair; the closest he'd ever come was Caroline's. He wondered what it felt like. Was it softer? Angel hair. He would run the palm of his hand gently over her hair as she unfastened his belt. In his fantasy, he remained standing while she sat on the bed and slowly wrapped her hand around his genitals. She was wearing nail polish. A discreet red. Was that something he imagined, or was she really wearing nail polish? He turned around and tried to catch her eye. But she was far away, at the other end of the narrow aisle, and a baby had started crying behind him. He tried to push the stewardess out of his thoughts. Tried to think about something else. About the West and its sham self-image. Gunpowder was no longer invented by the Chinese but by the Americans so they could celebrate the Fourth of July. The number system no longer originated in Arabia but in Europe. How many people in the West realized that the cradle of the world's culture was the Arabian Peninsula? Storytelling, mathematics, science . . . everything on which the West was built and had claimed as its own. It all comes from us, Abdul Hadi reminded himself. *From us.*

He ate the two packages of peanuts, and then his stomach began to rumble. He hadn't had a proper meal in a long time. He promised himself that when they landed, he would get something to eat. That was another reason why his brain was having a hard time focusing. But things were going better now, and he was thinking clearly again, without the fantasies about the stewardess. First you stole everything and made it yours, then you denied the rest of the world access. That was how it was. The West was built on theft and the oppression of others. At some point people would strike back. That was only right.

The baby behind him was still crying. The eternal problem of the innocent. If I went up to the cockpit right now and forced the plane down into the sea or into a building, everyone would be talking about the killing of the innocent, Abdul Hadi thought. But the argument doesn't hold. It's your taxes, your money, financing the oppression of my brothers. Is a person innocent simply because he does nothing but give money to the oppressors? You hide behind your children. As long as you use them as a shield, you're the ones who have put them in the line of fire.

He drank the little glass of juice in one gulp and thought about his sister. She would be about the same age as that beautiful blond stewardess, if she had lived. For many years he hadn't thought about how she was killed, but lately, the memory had returned. As if it were trying to come to his defense. Help him to understand the innermost mechanism and ultimate justice of revenge. Abdul Hadi closed his eyes and played through his most crucial memory: He was sitting in the backseat along with his two brothers, with his parents and sister in front, when the car struck the boy. He hadn't seen or heard a thing. The road in the desert was so rough that there was a constant bumping sound as the underside of the vehicle struck rocks or the exhaust pipe scraped against the ground. But his father had jumped out, and his mother had screamed. They were far away from the city, out in the Wadi Dawan desert where, many years later, the Belgian women would also die.

"What's happening? What's happening?" Abdul Hadi's brother had shouted when their father jumped out of the car.

Abdul's father had run over a boy by accident, and he died on the spot. His awful scream had drawn the rest of the village, and soon the car was surrounded. Abdul's father tried to explain. "I didn't see him, he ran out in front of the car. It was so dry and dusty, almost like driving in a fog."

The wailing started up, and the other mothers joined in. It was a horrible sound. A chorus of grief that rose up to the sky. Abdul Hadi couldn't remember whether the village elders and the father of the dead boy had been there the whole time. He remembered only how the adult men flung open the car door and hauled him out. He was sitting closest; that was why he ended up being the one they grabbed. His father tried to fight back but was restrained. Someone had to die. Revenge. Justice. He looked at his siblings still sitting inside the car.

"I didn't see him." His father wept.

Some men pulled his father's papers out of his pockets. They read his name aloud to each other. "Hadi. Hadi," they said over and over, as if his father's surname held the key to why everything had gone so wrong. His father shouted at them, "Let my son go. He has nothing to do with this." The women screamed their distress. The dead boy was lifted up while Abdul's father tried to make his pleas heard. When that didn't work, he tried threatening them. He shouted the names of police officers he knew in the capital. But people in the city meant nothing out there in the desert. They forced him to his knees. He was still shouting, but someone squatted down and stuffed sand into his mouth. Vomit and screams and death. They lay the dead boy down on the ground again, in the center of one the circles formed by the villagers.

"Your son for my son," cried the man with his hands around Abdul Hadi's neck, and he began squeezing tighter. With sand and blood pouring out of his mouth, his father watched in resignation as the horror unfolded in front of him.

Abdul Hadi remembered how the dead boy's father had let go of his neck. Instead, the man grabbed him by the arm; with the other hand, he grabbed Abdul's sister.

"You will be allowed to choose," shouted the dead boy's father to Abdul's father. "The boy or the girl?"

Only now did Abdul recall how his mother started to scream. Had she also wept and shouted when he was the only one standing at death's door? Maybe. I just couldn't hear it, Abdul told himself again and again. There were so many people screaming.

"The boy or the girl?"

"It was an accident . . . I beg you."

"Your son or your daughter?"

A knife appeared. There was dried blood on the blade. To provoke a decision, the tip was placed right under his father's larynx.

"Which do you choose?"

Abdul's father looked only at his son when he replied. "The girl. Take the girl."

10

Carlsberg silo—Copenhagen
Wednesday, December 16

Niels Bentzon woke up late, feeling anything but rested. He should actually call in sick. He was entitled to a day off anyway, after such a night. Yet fifteen minutes later, he was sitting in his car with wet hair, a cup of coffee in one hand, and a tie around his neck that a teenager could have done a better job knotting.

Police headquarters—Copenhagen

Niels could hardly see headquarters behind the wall of green buses being used for members of the police force. Officers from all over Denmark had been called in for the climate conference. In a few days *Air Force One* would land on Danish soil. Niels's uncle had already called to ask whether Niels would get to meet *him*. Protect *him*. But Niels had to disappoint his old uncle. "Obama is bringing his own army of bodyguards," he explained. "And his own limousine and his own food, a hairdresser, and a little briefcase that contains the codes to America's nuclear arsenal." Afterward Niels wasn't sure whether he believed the part about the nuclear weapons. He had a feeling that he would have disappointed him even more if he'd told him the honest truth: that the only people he was going to meet were the angry demonstrators in front of the Bella Center.

Niels elbowed his way through the crowd of provincial officers who had come to the big city. They looked as if they were on a school outing. Laughing. Clearly looking forward to this change in their daily routine.

Today they wouldn't be issuing speeding tickets on small country roads in northern Jutland or stopping fishermen from getting into a brawl in the village hall in Thyborøn. Soon they would be standing face-to-face with the Attack Movement, various environmental and climate organizations, and an ugly conglomeration of highly talented left-wing activists and neglected children who called themselves anarchists and were filled with anger.

"Good morning, Bentzon!"

Before Niels could turn around, he received a resounding masculine slap on the back.

"Leon. Sleep well?"

"Like a rock." He scrutinized Bentzon. "You, on the other hand, look slightly frazzled."

"It takes a few hours to come down."

"Not for me." Leon smiled.

A thought settled in Niels's mind and refused to leave: I don't like you. That was simply how it was. Niels didn't like Leon. It was fucking disgusting that the man could go home and sleep like a baby after spending a night in the company of a dead body and a pair of emotionally shattered children.

Luckily, Anni interrupted them. "Sommersted is asking for you."

"Sommersted?" Niels repeated, looking at Anni.

His secretary nodded. Maybe there was a hint of sympathy in her eyes.

A private meeting with Chief of Police W. H. Sommersted was something that very few officers experienced. According to popular legend at police headquarters, no one had ever had more than three private meetings in Sommersted's office over the course of a career: when you received the first warning, when you received the second warning, and when you had twenty minutes to pack up your things and get out. Niels had been there twice. Two warnings.

"As soon as possible," added Anni, giving Leon a pleasant smile.

Niels pulled her over toward the coffee machine. "Am I the only one he wants to see?"

"It was his secretary who called. She asked me to send you up when you came in. Why? Is something wrong?"

It said w. h. sommersted in black letters on the glass pane of the door leading to the outer office. No one knew what the "H" stood for. Maybe it was just for appearances.

Sommersted was on the phone. His wide jaw didn't move when he talked. Niels thought he would make the perfect ventriloquist.

"Fax it immediately." Sommersted got up and went over to the window to look out as he continued to talk. On the way he gave Niels a glance that revealed not even a hint of recognition. Niels tried to relax, but it was difficult. Fuck him if he fires me, thought Niels. He tried to imagine what he would do with his time. His mind drew a blank. He could only picture himself stretched out on the sofa in his bathrobe. He would let the depression wash over him. Wallow in it. Dive all the way down to the bottom.

"Bentzon!" Sommersted had finished his phone call and jovially stuck out his hand. "Sit down. How's it going?"

"Fine, thanks."

"It's pure hell here."

"I can imagine."

"*Air Force One* will be landing soon. Copenhagen is bursting with international VIPs. And the intelligence team sees terrorists everywhere. Personally, I think we've got the hostess jitters. Everything will go fine." Sommersted snorted. He took a deep breath and suddenly seemed to remember why Niels was sitting in front of him. "I'm glad you're back, Bentzon." He took off his glasses and put them on the desk. "I hear you had to strip. They're getting smarter and smarter."

"Is she going to make it?"

"The girl? Yes, she'll live." Sommersted nodded solemnly. His bushy eyebrows moved a tad closer together as he put on a concerned expression. Quite credible, but Niels wasn't buying it. Sommersted was a skilled communicator. Five years ago he'd taken the media course that Niels had declined to attend. Today a police chief had to be a combination of talk-show host, politician, and personnel manager.

"You're good at talking to people, Niels."

"Really?" replied Niels uncertainly, knowing that Sommersted had just set a trap for him.

"I mean it."

"Well, thanks, then."

The trap fell shut. "Maybe a little too good at it?" Sommersted's gaze became more piercing.

"Is that a question?"

"Miroslav Stanic, our Serbian friend. Remember him?"

Niels shifted position uneasily. He promptly regretted doing so, because he knew that Sommersted had noticed.

"I hear you visited him in prison. Was that a one-time deal?"

"Is that why you wanted to see me?"

"The man is a psychopath."

Niels took a deep breath and looked out the window. He didn't mind awkward silences. While Sommersted was clearly waiting for an answer, Niels ran over in his mind what he knew about Miroslav Stanic.

It was seven or eight years ago. Suspected of being a war criminal in Bosnia, the Serb was supposed to be turned over to The Hague. Inexplicably, he'd ended up in Denmark and was granted asylum for humanitarian reasons. The error soon became all too apparent to the Danish authorities. Stanic was not some poor, persecuted Serb but a former guard at the infamous Omarska prison camp. He was now enjoying three healthy, balanced meals a day, free of charge, at Restaurant Denmark. But just as he was about to be handed over, he went berserk. He took two other refugees hostage at the Sandholm camp. When Niels arrived, Stanic demanded safe passage out of the country; otherwise, he was going to cut the throat of one of his hostages. He was obviously serious, because he had almost managed to kill one of them—a young Albanian woman. It was due only to the miraculous efforts of the doctors at the National Hospital that her life was saved. Afterward the air was thick with reproaches aimed at Niels. Leon in particular came down hard on him. Why the hell hadn't Niels blown that psychopath's head off? he asked. The incident had ended with Niels negotiating with the Serb for half the day. Miroslav Stanic showed absolutely no remorse for his war crimes. Sommersted was right. He was a genuine psychopath. And charming. Once he even got Niels to laugh. But Stanic was afraid of prison. The loneliness. He was fully aware of the fact that the jig was up and that he was looking at twenty years behind bars. Niels's job was to get him to move from acknowledgment of the situation to surrender.

Sommersted was still waiting.

"It was a promise I made him, Sommersted. And since he ended up serving his sentence in Denmark, I had the chance to keep that promise."

"A promise? You promised to visit him in prison like some Red Cross representative?"

"That was the price for letting the hostages go."

"Forget your promise, Bentzon. The hostages were released. Stanic was convicted. Do you realize what the others on the force are saying about you?"

Niels hoped this was a rhetorical question.

"Do you?" For a second W. H. Sommersted looked like a doctor who had to deliver the sad but irrevocable truth to a dying patient.

"That I'm manic-depressive?" suggested Niels. "That I've got a screw loose?"

"Especially the last part. They can't figure you out, Niels. One moment you're out on sick leave, and the next you're running around visiting all the psychopaths."

Niels was about to protest, but Sommersted was too quick for him. "But you've got talent. No doubt about that."

"You mean I'm good at talking to people?"

"You're a good mediator. You almost always talk them out of a crisis. I just wish you weren't so . . ."

"So what?"

"So strange. With your travel phobia and manic behavior. And making friends with psychopaths."

"Only one psychopath. You make it sound like—"

Sommersted interrupted him. "Can't you just toe the line once in a while?"

Niels stared at the floor. Toe the line? Before he could reply, the police chief went on. "I hear you're about to take off on vacation."

"Just for a week."

"Okay. Now listen here. I'm pleased with your efforts yesterday. What do you say we try again? We'll start off with something small."

"Sure."

"I've got an assignment for you. Nothing major. I want you to contact a few citizens. Have a talk with them."

"You say I'm good at that." Niels couldn't hide his sarcasm.

Sommersted gave him an annoyed look.

"So who am I supposed to talk to?"

"Good people."

Sommersted began searching for something among the modest collection of papers on his desk as he shook his head and commented on the daily flood of red notices from Interpol.

"Can you remember the sound of the telex machine in the old days?"

Of course. Niels remembered all too well the telex machine that received updates and warnings from Interpol's headquarters in Lyon. It had been replaced by a computer. Or rather, thousands of computers. In the past the telex machine ran nonstop. The monotonous sound of the mechanical printer reminded them that the world was steadily becoming a more and more fucked-up place. If anyone wanted a brief, concentrated look into the world's misery, all he had to do was spend twenty minutes in front of the humming machine: serial killers, drug smuggling, women kidnapped for prostitution, cross-border traffic with stolen children, illegal immigrants, enriched uranium. In the less urgent department, traffic in endangered species: lions, leopards, rare parrots, dolphins. The list was endless. Art objects and rare historical artifacts. Stradivarius violins and jewels that once belonged to the Russian czar. Not even one thousandth of everything that Nazi Germany had stolen from the occupied countries had been recovered. Hidden in the nooks and cellars of small German homes, there were still diamonds and amber and gold jewelry from the Byzantine Empire; there were paintings by Degas and gold bars that had belonged to Jewish families. The search for these items was still going on. You could get a headache simply from standing in front of the fax machine. It made you want to scream and run away; to jump into the sea and wish that life had never crawled up out of the water, that the dinosaurs still dominated the earth.

Now everything was on Interpol's database, and all member countries were linked. It was called, in all simplicity, I-24/7. Just like a 7-Eleven, it never closed. But along with the development of new technology, the threats had increased. Suicide bombers, bioterrorism, computer hacking, distribution of child pornography, credit card fraud, illegal trade in CO_2 credits, tax fraud, money laundering. Not to mention the fight against corruption in the EU. Interpol may have acquired a new weapon to fight crime, but the criminals had gained just as much expertise with the new technology. Maybe the world really hasn't made any headway. That was a thought that often occurred to Niels. Maybe it was better in the past when there was only a telex machine that was on round the clock, when the agitated sound of the print wheel cut through the air as a constant reminder of the world's misery.

"A red notice," said Sommersted when he finally found what he was looking for among the papers. He handed it to Niels. "Apparently, the good people are being murdered."

"The good people are being murdered?"

"That's what it looks like. In different places around the world: China, India, Russia, the United States. Many of the victims worked for humanitarian causes. You know what I mean—aid workers, doctors, advisers."

Niels read the words: "Red notice." The text was in English, composed in the laconic, staccato style that was so typical of Interpol: *Possible sectarian killings. First reporting officer: Tommaso di Barbara.* Niels wondered if that was the way they talked down there in Lyon. Robot language.

"In the old days we wouldn't have wasted time on something like this. But now, after the Muhammad cartoon controversy . . . Globalization, whatever that means."

"What's the connection between the murders?" asked Niels.

"Symbols on the backs of the victims, as I understand it. Some sort of mark. Maybe the murders have a sectarian motive. Pretty soon there's going to be a lunatic with a saber and half a ton of dynamite strapped to his chest on every other street corner."

"You think the motive is religious?"

"Possibly, but we're not involved in the investigation. Fortunately. 'Holy' killings. That would mean a hell of a lot of paperwork. And going through a pile of dusty old reference books. Whatever happened to greed and jealousy? Those were motives we could understand."

Sommersted broke off and stared out the window for several seconds. Niels had a feeling it was the word "jealousy" that had sent his thoughts elsewhere. He'd seen Sommersted's wife on several occasions. A pampered little rich girl, blond, a slightly faded beauty who had probably never seen much of the sleazy side of life. But maybe it wasn't that easy to be a stay-at-home upper-class girl. Where would you find your triumphs and minor setbacks? The personal confirmations that provide nourishment for the soul? Sommersted's wife found hers in the looks she attracted from other men; Niels had noticed that the very first time he saw her at a reception. She stood close to her husband, even held his hand several times, but always aware of the looks directed at her from others in the room.

"I think you should spend today making contact with the . . . let's say the eight to ten good people here in Copenhagen. Find out if they've noticed anything unusual. The head of the Red Cross, people who have something to do with human rights, and the local environmentalists. Those kinds of organizations. Ask them to be on the lookout. That should cover our back."

"What about all the delegates coming here for the conference?"

"No." Sommersted gave a forced laugh. "I think we've already got them sufficiently covered. Besides, in four days they'll all be leaving. I think this is more of a long-term threat."

Niels skimmed through what it said on the two pieces of paper, even though Sommersted was clearly eager to hustle him out the door. "Are there any suspects?" Niels asked.

"Bentzon. Timely precaution, nothing more."

"But why have they come to us about the case?"

"Listen up: This is nothing. You can almost think of it as a day off to thank you for your help last night. If we were going to take these sorts of unspecified threats seriously, we'd have no time for anything else. There's plenty to keep us busy here. If we make the slightest mistake, tomorrow there are going to be three morning newspapers and 179 members of Parliament demanding an explanation and an investigation, telling us we need to prioritize our work. Even though I'd like to tell them all to shut up, I'm forced to stand there and smile and nod like a schoolboy at a prom." Sommersted gave an exaggerated sigh and leaned back in his chair. He'd given this speech before. "This is my reality, Bentzon: to consult with the justice minister and the attorney general. To send e-mails about why we didn't reach the crime scene two minutes earlier. To take calls from journalists about why we're doing such a lousy job. Because that's how they see us."

Sommersted pointed out the window, toward the general public. "Think of me as your defender. I'll handle the bloodhounds at Christiansborg and various newsrooms. All you officers have to do is what you've always done: Catch the criminals, toss them in prison, and throw away the key."

Niels merely smiled. Sommersted did have a sense of humor.

"Timely precaution, Bentzon. Consider this a confidential assignment. Just between you and me. And have a good vacation when you get there."

11

Police headquarters archives—Copenhagen

"**G**ood people?" There wasn't a trace of sarcasm in Casper's voice. Only genuine curiosity. "You're looking for 'good people'?"

"Exactly." Niels sat down on the edge of the desk and looked around the computer room with its clinical atmosphere. "We need to locate the good people. Can you help me?"

Casper had already sat down in front of the computer. Niels wasn't offered a chair; that was standard procedure in the archives. Even though the office looked like all the other offices, just a little bigger, Niels felt like he'd forced his way into a stranger's home. No offer of coffee or a chair. No polite introductory remarks. Niels couldn't figure out whether the archivists didn't like him or whether they simply lacked social skills. Maybe spending so many years in the dusty archives, surrounded by index cards, file folders, and computer systems, had gradually desocialized them and filled them with the fear that foreign bodies like Niels might destroy their meticulous order. The fear that anyone entering through the heavy black-painted wooden doors would bring chaos along with him.

"The art of being a good person," said Casper as he Googled "good person." He went on: "First hit: Jesus."

"I'm glad we got that established, Casper."

Casper looked up from the screen, genuinely pleased with Niels's compliment. Irony doesn't work in here, Niels reminded himself. Of course not. Irony can create misunderstandings, and misunderstandings can cause index errors, and then an important book, a file, or maybe a crucial letter might be lost forever. The archives storage rooms supposedly contained more than three hundred thousand registered items. Niels had never been there—access was strictly forbidden to unauthorized personnel—but the few people who had seen it described the place as a treasure trove of police history. There were things from as far back as the thirteenth century. And way too many unsolved murder cases. More than a hundred since the end of World War II. Of course, a lot of the perpetrators had long since gone to their graves and received their judgment in the next world. But from a statistical point of view, there were still at least forty murderers running around loose. Not to mention all the Danes who had disappeared. Some of them had run off, while others had gone to ground so successfully that they weren't included in the statistics about unsolved murders.

Many of Niels's colleagues had asked for permission to hunt through the archives after they retired. So even though irony was of no use down here, the place wasn't lacking in its own overriding irony. Only when officers retired did they have enough time to do the work they'd been hired to do. Way too much time was spent on unnecessary paperwork. Reports that nobody read, documentation that was of no interest to anyone. Soon they wouldn't be able to use the toilet without first consulting an Excel chart. Over the past eight or ten years it had gotten worse. The government had talked about cracking down on all the excess paperwork and unnecessary bureaucracy, but the reality was the exact opposite. In the meantime there was enough to deal with out in the streets and alleyways: biker clubhouses; gang wars; bestial violence in every imaginable abomination; the evictions of the squatters from the Youth House and the conflicts that followed in its wake; clueless young immigrants who couldn't tell the difference between a disposable grill and their neighbor's car; morally callous businesspeople who were constantly on the lookout for opportunities to strip a company of its assets; so-called gangsters from Eastern Europe and the Middle East; African prostitutes; poor wretches who were mentally ill but had nowhere to go because the number of hospital beds had been drastically cut back; and so on and so on. It wasn't surprising that some police officers found it necessary to work beyond the retirement age. Among the police chiefs, it was whispered—only half in jest—that the government ought to create a republican guard like in the Middle Eastern countries. A small army of willing agents to do the government's bidding. Such a guard could take care of clearing out the aging hippies from the Christiania settlement of Copenhagen and go to battle against the demonstrators here, there, and everywhere. It would create a breathing space so the police could do what they did best: *to protect and to serve.* To protect the people, to prevent and solve crimes.

Casper gave Niels a hesitant look. "Can you use Jesus?"

"We need to locate Danes, Casper. Who are alive today."

"Good Danes?"

"Yes. Good, righteous people. I'd like to have a list."

"Supreme Court justices and people like that?"

"Don't be stupid."

"Why don't you give me an example?"

"The Red Cross," said Niels.

"Okay, good. So you're talking about charity."

"Not just charity. But including that."

Casper turned back to his computer screen. How old was he? Probably not a day over twenty-two. So many young people today have learned so much by an early age, thought Niels. They've been around the world three times and finished their formal education; they can speak multiple languages and know how to develop their own computer programs. When Niels was twenty-two, he could patch a bicycle tire and count to ten in German.

"How many do you want? The Red Cross, Amnesty International, Lutheran Emergency Aid, UNICEF Denmark, the Peace Academy . . ."

"What's the Peace Academy?" asked Susanne, the oldest archivist, looking up from her work.

Casper shrugged and pulled up their website. Susanne gave Casper and Niels a dissatisfied look.

"What about Save the Children? I send them donations," she said.

"I don't want organizations. I want people. Good people."

"So what about the woman who's in charge of Save the Children?" asked Susanne.

Niels took a deep breath and decided to start over from the beginning. "Here's the thing: All around the world, good people are being murdered. People who have fought for the lives and limbs of other human beings. Their rights and their living conditions—"

"Okay, we'll try something else," Casper interrupted him. "We'll do a search on those words."

"What words?"

"Cross-referencing. The people that we label as 'especially good' will always be mentioned the most in the media, right? If there's an international terrorist traveling around murdering them, he has to be getting his information somewhere. And that somewhere is the Internet."

"Granted."

"So all we—and the terrorists—have to do is enter the words we think would generate a goodness hit list. You know, words like *environment, third world.* Things like that."

While Susanne thought about whether this was a good idea, Niels added more words to the list: "*Aid workers, AIDS, medicine.*"

Casper nodded and went on, "*Climate. Vaccine. Cancer. Ecology. CO_2.*"

"But what does it mean to be a good person?" Susanne asked.

"It doesn't really matter," said Casper. "The important thing is what other people perceive as good."

Niels had thought of other words: "*Research. Clean water*—no, *clean drinking water.*"

"That's good. More?" Casper began typing in the words.

Susanne finally threw her skepticism to the wind. "What about *infant mortality? Malaria. Health.*"

"Good!"

"*Illiteracy. Prostitution.*"

"*Abuse,*" Niels interjected.

"*Microloans. Working in developing countries, volunteers,*" said Casper.

"*The rain forest,*" Susanne said, completing the list and looking indignant, as if Casper and Niels were personally in the process of chopping the rain forest into kindling. Casper's fingers lifted off the keyboard as if it were a Steinway and he'd just played the last chords of Rachmaninoff's Piano Concerto no. 3.

"Give me ten minutes," he said.

——— ——

Niels spent the waiting time at the coffee machine. The mocha was insipid. It didn't measure up to the coffee from the espresso machine that Kathrine had dragged home from Paris last year. Niels was in an irascible mood. Maybe it was because of the place where he found himself at the moment. All those unsolved murders. Niels hated injustice more than he loved justice. An unsolved crime—murder, rape, assault—could keep him awake at night. Resentment and anger: That was the energy that drove him to fight injustice. But once he saw the criminal convicted, when he stood in front of the courthouse and saw him being driven off to prison, Niels was often struck by an inexplicable feeling of emptiness.

"Okay. How many names do you want?" asked Casper from his place at the keyboard.

Niels looked at his watch. A few minutes past ten. He wanted to get home by six o'clock at the latest so he could pack. He also needed to take more pills. Eight hours. One hour for each conversation. He would have to meet with all of them in person. He reasoned that a warning about a potential murder, no matter how unlikely, couldn't be delivered over the phone. "Give me the top eight," he said.

"Do you want a printout?"

"Yes, please."

The machine hummed. Niels looked at the list. The cream of the crop of the humanitarian causes. *The best of the best.* He could stop anybody on the street, and they would most likely come up with the same names.

"Should we check them against our own database?" Casper glanced at Niels with almost a smile. It was tempting. These were the people who had gotten the most hits from the words "pertaining to goodness"—the ones who were most often in the media when it came to defending the weak and the helpless. Should they take a look at what the police database had to say about them?

"What do you think? It would take two minutes, tops," Casper went on.

"No. We don't need to do that. What matters is how the rest of the world perceives them."

Susanne scrutinized the list, looking over Niels's shoulder. "There, you see? The woman from Save the Children is on the list," she said with relief. "But why is Mærsk the shipping magnate included?"

Casper studied the search results and shook his head. "Mærsk is associated with so many different projects around the world and in Denmark that he almost always shows up, no matter what we search for. He probably pays for a hundred elementary schools a year with his taxes alone. If we ran a search for the most hated Dane, he would probably show up on that list, too. Shall I cross him out?"

"Yes, do that. I don't think he'd be first in the line of fire."

"Who's the person at the top?" asked Susanne.

"Thorvaldsen?" Niels was surprised she didn't know him. "That's the secretary-general of the Red Cross in Denmark."

A new list came out of the printer. Instead of Mærsk occupying sixth place, it was now held by a pastor who was frequently in the news.

"All old friends," Niels concluded. "Except for number eight. I don't know him."

"Gustav Lund. He got 11,237 hits on the words 'save' and 'world.' Let's take a look," said Casper as he Googled him. An intense-looking, aging professor in his fifties.

"Handsome guy," said Susanne drily.

"Gustav Lund. Professor of mathematics. Oh, okay: recipient of the Fields Medal in mathematics in 2003, along with two Canadian and three American colleagues. Hmm . . . his son committed suicide . . . at only twelve years old."

"That doesn't make him a bad person," Susanne said.

Niels and Casper looked as if they disagreed.

"Why is he considered good?" asked Susanne.

"Excellent question." Casper studied the screen. "Here it is: In connection with the award, he stated that 'it will be a mathematician who saves the world.' That remark was apparently quoted far and wide. Should I cross him off the list and take number nine instead? A climate spokesperson from—"

"No, that's okay." Niels looked at the list. "Let's leave room for a few surprises."

12

s Abdul Hadi disembarked, he kept his eyes on the floor instead of the stewardess. He couldn't do it. She belonged to the West; she was their possession. There was no reason to think anything else. She also reminded him too much of his sister, even though they looked nothing alike. The only similarity was their age, the age his sister would have been today: thirty-eight. She was only eight when she died.

At passport control, he got in the line for "all other nationalities." Citizens of the European Union whisked right through their privileged gateway. They were the ones who could be trusted. Abdul Hadi's line wasn't moving. He was used to that. An Arabic man had once called the line for other nationalities the "Orient Express." A Somali mother with three children was carrying on a hopeless discussion with the Swedish police officer behind the glass pane. Abdul Hadi could see at once that she would never be admitted. He witnessed the same scene every time he traveled: non-Westerners who were sent back home because of problems with their visas, a child's name that was not spelled the same on the passport and the plane ticket, no return ticket, or a passport photo that was too old. The slightest discrepancy could deny a person entry. Europe was a fortress—the passport control was the drawbridge over the moat, and if you didn't know the correct password, you would be turned away.

The Somali woman was crying. Her children were hungry; their skin was stretched tight over the bones of their faces, something that was usually seen only on people who were very old. It pained him to look at them. The woman had to step aside to make way for others. Abdul Hadi's face was subjected to intense scrutiny, both his passport photo and his features. While he waited, he counted the Europeans who were allowed to pass through in the other line. Five. The officer slid his passport through some sort of machine. Twelve.

"Business?"

"Visiting family."

"Do you have a return ticket?"

"Yes."

"Show me, please."

Abdul Hadi looked at the other line. Five more—seventeen. The officer inspected his return ticket. Admittance was denied unless you had a valid return ticket. They wanted to be sure that you would be leaving as soon as possible. Twenty-five. Abdul Hadi counted to thirty-two before the officer handed back his passport and ticket without comment.

"Next!"

There was only one Arabic man waiting alone in the arrivals area. He and Abdul Hadi exchanged glances and then approached each other.

"Abdul?"

"Yes."

"Welcome. I'm Mohammed. Your cousin."

Only then did Abdul Hadi notice the resemblance. The oval face, the hair that wouldn't last long on his head. The thick eyebrows. Abdul smiled. It had been years since he'd seen his mother's brother. His uncle had been granted asylum in Sweden almost twenty years ago, and since then he'd had several children. One of them was standing in front of him. Looking well nourished, relaxed.

"They feed you well."

"I'm fat. I know that. My father complains about it, too."

"Please give him my greetings and convey my respects."

"I'll do that. Let me carry your suitcase."

They headed for the exit.

"Why isn't your father here to meet me?"

Mohammed seemed to be searching for the right words.

"Is he ill?"

"No."

"Is he afraid?"

"Yes."

Abdul shook his head.

"It doesn't matter that he's not here. We are so many. An entire army. A sleeping army," said Mohammed.

"Yes. A sleeping army. But it's not always easy to awaken its soldiers," Abdul told his young cousin, who had eaten so well from the riches of the West.

A package was lying in the backseat. Abdul chastised Mohammed for leaving it there in plain sight. Not only was the sleeping army overweight, it was also careless.

"It's just photographs," Mohammed defended himself. "The explosives are in the trunk."

Abdul studied the pictures of the church. He didn't recognize it. "Are you sure this is the right one?"

"Positive. It's one of the most famous churches in Copenhagen."

Then Abdul saw some of the same pictures he'd found on the Internet. Including Jesus on the wooden cross. It bothered him that the figure would be destroyed in the blast. But it wasn't really Jesus—it was just an image, nothing more than an image. The execrable and unceasing attempts of the West to create images, figures, and drawings of everything that was sacred. Nativity plays, carvings meticulously shaped out of wood to depict scenes from the Bible. Statues and paintings. It never ended. The people of the West tried to use images to convince themselves; it was what they had always done and still did. These days the images were nothing more than advertisements for their lifestyle. Not like Hadi and his people, who could sense the divine inside of themselves. They didn't need to hold it out in front of them. He looked at the figure of Jesus again. A childish conceit, he thought.

"We've loosened the screws." Mohammed pointed at the basement window visible in the photograph of the church. "It took us three nights to do it, but nobody saw us. We're sure about that. All four screws are loose. All you have to do is push up the window."

Abdul Hadi's stomach growled. It had been hours since he'd had anything to eat other than the peanuts the stewardess had given him. His thoughts returned to her briefly: her blond hair, her hand touching his. But he couldn't think about her without seeing his dead sister. And the boy his father had run over. Two lives. It had cost two lives for him to be sitting here now. It was only right that he should repay the debt. It was pointless to think about the stewardess. How he wished that she hadn't smiled at him. At least not in that way.

13

The package lay on the table. Very likely the only recording of what had happened when one of the murders was committed. It had been almost impossible to obtain, but he'd managed it.

Tommaso di Barbara rubbed his eyes and then looked at the small, neatly wrapped package on the conference room table. He had tracked down plenty of victims, but he hadn't come up with any leads for finding the killer.

Commissario Morante had apparently decided not to come alone. Tommaso could hear their footsteps out in the hall. Official footsteps marching in time. A unified tempo is fine in music but appalling when applied to the human gait, thought Tommaso. When people march in step, it's because they're going about something too brutal to do alone. The door opened. The commissario sat down, and before even looking at Tommaso, he poured glasses of water for himself, the personnel manager, and the man from the mainland, who was a stranger to Tommaso. Di Barbara made an effort to look as healthy as he could, given that he had both a fever and a headache.

"That was some night. With the glassblower's widow," said the commissario.

"Has she confessed?" asked Tommaso.

"Yes. Early this morning. She waited to do it until a priest was present along with Flavio."

"Was it because of a life insurance policy?"

"No, there was no life insurance." The commissario cleared his throat and then changed the subject. "Tommaso, I'm now going to ask you for the last time."

"Yes," Tommaso hastened to reply.

"Yes?"

"I was the one who contacted the Chinese authorities. And got them to send the tape. It may contain information of great importance."

The commissario raised his voice: "Without authorization, you used official channels to send warnings to Kiev, Copenhagen, and a long list of other cities."

Tommaso stopped listening. He wondered how the commissario had found out about that. Somebody must have squealed. Or else they'd been keeping an eye on him for longer than he'd realized.

Tommaso again attempted to explain. "As I've been trying to tell you, these murders have been following a specific pattern, and we haven't seen the last of them."

Silence. Someone cleared his throat.

"But Tommaso," said the commissario, "you contacted our embassy in Delhi and had them send a man to Mumbai to look for evidence."

"Not evidence. An Indian economist had been murdered."

The commissario went on as if Tommaso hadn't spoken. "You asked the Chinese authorities to hand over material to us. And you've been in contact with Interpol."

"Because they're handling a case just like the one in Mumbai! Take a look at the reports. That's all I'm asking. Listen to what I'm telling you. I was also dumbfounded in the beginning. It was months ago when I first saw the picture that Interpol sent out. In the beginning it was just a body with a big tattoo. Then I started studying the documents. I got Interpol to send me the photos in the original high resolution."

"You asked them to send you more material?" The commissario shook his head.

Tommaso gave up on him and turned to look at the man on the right, the one who was a stranger. Probably some top brass from the mainland.

"First there was one murder victim. Then there were two. There was another common denominator besides the mark on their backs. They were both involved in helping other people."

The stranger nodded, looking interested.

"I contacted Interpol, but they said they didn't want to handle the case. They said it was too minor. So I started on it myself."

"You started on it yourself?" the commissario repeated, again shaking his head.

"Yes, I did. In my free time. I haven't shirked any of my duties. I haven't missed a single shift. I've used my own time for the investigation."

"Your own time! Do you really think this is only about *your* time? You've also used other people's time. An embassy employee in Delhi, for instance."

"We have a certain responsibility."

The commissario chose to ignore Tommaso's remark and continued, "Tomorrow we're welcoming a delegation of prominent visitors. The justice minister and a number of judges and politicians. How do you think this will look to them?"

Tommaso swore silently. That was the only thing the commissario was ever concerned about: receiving the plethora of prominent visitors who seemed to pour into the city every other week. Everyone wanted to hold conferences in Venice.

Maybe the commissario sensed that Tommaso had seen through his obsessive vanity. At any rate, he changed tactics. "What about the people on the other end, Tommaso? When you send out a red notice, somebody has to deal with it. You've alerted people in numerous cities. Ankara, Sligo."

"And Copenhagen. There's a pattern."

The commissario cast a plaintive look at the man from the mainland. The commissario glanced at him every time Tommaso mentioned a pattern. Now the man cleared his throat and ran both hands through his hair.

"A pattern that I haven't quite figured out yet," Tommaso went on. "But it's approximately three thousand kilometers between some of the murder sites. I thought it was only right to warn the police authorities who seemed to be within the danger zone."

Silence settled over the room. The commissario again looked at the stranger, who sat up straight and spoke for the first time. "Signor di Barbara," he began, then allowed a brief pause to hover in the air. "We understand that your mother is seriously ill."

Tommaso frowned. What did that have to do with anything? "Yes?"

"She's in a hospice. Is that right?"

"Yes. The Franciscan sisters are taking care of her."

"It can be very difficult to cope when one of your parents is dying. I lost my own mother just last year."

Tommaso gave him an inquiring look. And then turned to stare at the commissario, who was studying the tabletop.

"Sometimes when we're feeling stressed about situations that are beyond our control, we throw ourselves into senseless tasks. As a form of mental compensation. A kind of sublimation. Do you understand what I'm saying?"

"I'm sorry, but who exactly are you?"

"Dr. Macetti."

"Doctor? A doctor of what?"

"Psychiatry," said the man, looking Tommaso in the eye before he went on. "It's perfectly natural and completely acceptable for the brain to produce an excess of activity. That's actually a healthier reaction than remaining passive. Or becoming depressed. Or turning to drink." The psychiatrist's last comments were directed at the commissario, who nodded eagerly.

"So you think I'm going crazy?"

They smiled in embarrassment. "Of course not," said the psychiatrist. "Your reaction is totally normal."

Tommaso again focused his attention on the package lying on the table. It still hadn't been opened.

"Perhaps it would be best if you concentrated on your mother right now," said the psychiatrist. "And then you could come to see me once a week in Veneto."

"We don't even need to use the word 'suspension,'" said the commissario. "That sounds so dramatic. But I'm going to have to ask you to clean out your office and hand in your gun and ID."

14

Offices of the Red Cross—Copenhagen

The young secretary in the offices of the Red Cross had a nervous air. The nervousness was well hidden behind a mask of friendliness and candid self-confidence, but it was there nonetheless.

"From the police department?"

"Yes. Niels Bentzon."

A flush appeared at the base of her throat. The change in color was barely visible, but Niels saw it at once. It was the sort of thing he'd been trained to notice.

Police negotiators were ordinary police officers who'd been trained by psychologists and psychiatrists to resolve conflicts without the use of physical force. The very first course that Niels had attended about the secret language of the face had opened a whole new world to him. He and his colleagues were taught to register the tiniest of movements, the ones no one can ever control. The pupils of the eyes, the blood vessels that run up and down the throat. They watched films with no sound. Learned to study faces without listening to the words.

"Mr. Thorvaldsen will see you in five minutes."

"Thanks. That's fine." Niels picked up a brochure about a Red Cross project in Mozambique and sat down to wait in the small reception area.

Thorvaldsen was looking extremely solemn on the front of the brochure. Younger than he looked on TV the other day. *Malaria, civil war, and the lack of clean drinking water are some of the greatest threats to public health in Mozambique,* he stated in the brochure. Niels put it aside. Mozambique was far away. He could see Thorvaldsen sitting in his office on the other side of the glass partition. He was laughing about something. Niels opened the case file from Interpol and took out a dossier, so he wouldn't be sitting there staring into space. He looked at the phone number of the Italian police officer who had written up the case: *Venice*. Strange, but it didn't look as though any "good people" had been killed in Italy. There was one in Russia, though. Moscow. Vladimir Zhirkov, a journalist and social critic. According to the file, he had died in prison. Niels shook his head. In Russia things were apparently done in reverse order—the good were put in prison while the criminals went free. The Russian authorities stated that the cause of death was a blood clot. So why had Zhirkov ended up on the list of the good people who were murdered? Niels found the answer farther down on the page. The bodies all had the same tattoo. A tattoo in a specific pattern. Had Sommersted mentioned that? Niels couldn't recall. There was no other information. Well, it didn't matter, because the case didn't particularly interest him. Sommersted's lack of enthusiasm seemed to have infected Niels. Good Lord, a few murders committed in distant parts of the world. So what? Three or four hundred people died in traffic accidents every year in Denmark. Many of them children. And who worried about that? Was there some police officer on the other side of the globe thinking about those traffic deaths right this minute? Hardly. The only thing that interested Niels was the fact that he would soon be on his way to see Kathrine. He was going to toss back those tranquilizers like candy. Enjoy the sun. And not give a shit that the hotel—according to Kathrine—looked like some ugly citadel surrounded by barbed wire and armed guards. He was going to gorge himself on the fabulous food that the hotel's Filipino kitchen staff cooked for lousy wages. Make love to Kathrine. Enjoy her lovely body. Enjoy the fact that he could reach out to touch her whenever he liked. Forget all about Sommersted and—

"Hello?"

Niels was holding his cell phone in his hand. He hadn't even noticed that he'd made a call. It was as if his fingers had a will of their own. A circle was drawn around a name on one of the documents in the file. *Tommaso di Barbara,* then a phone number. Had he put that circle there?

"Hello?" said the voice again.

"Tommaso di Barbara?" said Niels aloud. He probably wasn't pronouncing it correctly.

"*Sì.*" The voice sounded tired, dejected.

"This is Niels Bentzon," he said in English. "I'm calling you from the

Copenhagen Homicide Division. I have a report here that says you were the first officer to—"

"*Scusa. Parla italiano?*"

"No."

"*Français?*"

Niels hesitated. He made eye contact with the secretary. "Do you happen to speak Italian? Or French?" he asked her.

"No." She beamed at him. Seldom had Niels seen anyone look so happy not to speak a foreign language. Or was it because he'd given her some unexpected attention? Thorvaldsen was now on his way out of his office.

"*Monsieur?* Hello?" said the voice on the phone.

"I'll call you back later, Mr. di Barbara. Okay?" Niels ended the conversation and stood up.

Thorvaldsen was standing in the doorway, taking leave of his two visitors. "Keep your cards close to your chest. We don't want to start a media frenzy at the moment," he said to one of the men, putting a hand on his shoulder. "Are we agreed?"

"There's a man here from the police asking for a brief meeting with you," murmured the secretary nervously.

"The police?" Thorvaldsen turned and caught sight of Niels. "Has something happened?"

"No, no." Niels took a step closer and held out his hand. "Niels Bentzon, from the Copenhagen Police."

Thorvaldsen had a powerful handshake and a resolute look in his eyes. He was a man who was used to having other people take him seriously. "The police?" he repeated.

Niels nodded. "This will only take a minute."

15

Tommaso wrote down the phone number of the Danish police officer. He felt almost elated in spite of his new status: officially on paid leave. It was the first time in all the months he'd spent on the case that anyone had ever responded. He closed the door to his office. The commissario had given him the rest of the day to write up his report on the glassblower's widow. Not that there were any problems with the case. It was a simple matter of a confession of guilt. The woman just hadn't been able to stand the jerk any longer.

His office had a view of the canal and the train station. The furnishings consisted of a desk, a chair, and a small sofa upholstered in imitation green leather. There was also a wardrobe, but Tommaso didn't use it for clothes. He opened the door to the wardrobe. The commissario hadn't found it. He was almost certain about that. Otherwise his boss would have mentioned it in the same breath as the suspension. The entire inside of the wardrobe was covered with clippings from the case. Photographs of the victims. Maps of the locations. Bible quotes. Tommaso's thoughts and theories. He heard footsteps and quickly closed the wardrobe door. He knew they were keeping an eye on him.

His secretary, Marina, had just come into the reception area, looking guilty. Of course—they'd gotten their mitts on her, too. She knocked on the glass door.

"Come in," said Tommaso.

Marina poked her head inside his office but made an effort to keep the rest of her body in the reception area. "They called from the hospital. Your mother has been asking for you all night."

"Come on in, Marina."

She complied, closing the door behind her.

"You told them about what I've been working on, didn't you?"

"What was I supposed to do? The commissario called me last night and asked me to come down to the station. It was past ten o'clock." She had tears in her eyes.

"Take it easy. I'm not blaming you for anything."

"You lied to me."

"I did?"

"I thought I was working in an official capacity when I translated all those documents that you asked me to read." She gestured toward the wardrobe. "Do you have any idea how many hours I spent doing translations for you? Both to and from Italian and English?"

"You've done a great job. But you didn't mention anything about . . ." He pointed to the wardrobe.

"They didn't ask."

"Good, Marina."

"Is it true what they're saying? That you've gone off the deep end?"

"What do you think?"

Marina straightened up and made an obvious attempt to evaluate Tommaso's mental state. He smiled. He needed her to get hold of the package from China for him. "Stop looking at me like that," he said.

"They say it's because of your mother."

"Ask yourself who you should believe. Me or the commissario?"

She considered the question. Marina was a sensible woman. He'd personally chosen her as his secretary. The mother of three, shaped like a barrel, with a heart of gold, and even more important: She spoke English. The language was like linguistic saffron in official Venice—very few were fluent in English, and those who were could command high wages. Marina's mascara was smearing. He handed her a tissue and gave up waiting for her to answer his question. "Could you find me a cardboard box? I'm going to take the case documents home with me. And then if you wouldn't mind doing one last favor for me."

She nodded. "All right."

"This is important, Marina. More important than you or me. When the commissario gives you the package from China and asks you to send it back, don't do it."

She was once again giving him an obedient look. That was what he wanted.

"Instead, you need to send it to the person who has this cell phone number." He handed her the napkin on which he written down the number.

"Who is this person?"

"A police officer in Copenhagen. A man who is also working on the case. Maybe the only one now that I've been fired."

"How am I going to find out who he is?"

"Call the number and ask him. Or send him a text message and ask for his name and address. Then send him the package. In a diplomatic pouch. That will be faster."

16

G ood people, you said?"

Niels couldn't tell whether Thorvaldsen was flattered or upset.

"All the murder victims were good people?"

"Yes. You know—pediatricians, human rights activists, aid workers. People in your line of work."

"The humanitarian business. You're welcome to use that term here."

Niels looked around at the impressive office. Danish Design furniture. Wegener. Børge Mogensen. Genuine Persian carpets. Huge picture windows. A large framed photograph of Thorvaldsen flanked by Nelson Mandela and Bono, possibly taken on Robben Island.

"Who else is on the list?" Thorvaldsen asked.

"Excuse me?"

"Your list. Who else are you going to warn?"

"I'm afraid that's confidential," Niels told him.

Thorvaldsen leaned back with an almost imperceptible shake of his head. "The police department's list of all the good men in the realm. I suppose I should consider it an honor to be included?"

Niels didn't know what to say.

Thorvaldsen went on, "Why do you think there's a connection between these murders? Couldn't it just be a coincidence?"

"Sure, that's possible. But we're not involved in the actual investigation."

"Then what *are* you involved in?" He gave a wry smile, so as not to seem skeptical. But it was too late for that.

"Just think of it as a warning light. A very small one. In case anything out of the ordinary occurs. A break-in. Vandalism. Anything like that. And then give me a call. I assume you haven't received any threats over the past couple of years, have you?"

"Constantly." Thorvaldsen nodded. "My ex-wife's lawyers have been threatening me day and night."

There was a knock on the door, and the secretary came in, carrying a coffeepot and cups.

"I don't think coffee is going to be necessary," Thorvaldsen said, giving her a sharp look. "We'll be done in a minute."

Niels saw it at once. She'd made another mistake. Her boss wasn't happy with her. He felt a need to come to her rescue. "Just one cup would be great. Thanks. In return for all the coins I toss into the Red Cross collection cans whenever you're doing a fund-raiser."

The secretary poured him a cup, her hands shaking slightly.

"Thank you," said Niels, looking up at her.

Thorvaldsen asked, "Are you going to offer me police protection?" He seemed to have moved from no longer feeling flattered to getting a bit scared.

"We haven't reached that point by any means," said Niels. "The threat level is minimal at the moment." He gave Thorvaldsen a reassuring smile. He knew full well that such a remark would cause the opposite of the intended reaction. It wasn't the word "minimal" that the man's subconscious would fasten on to. It was the phrase "threat level." If somebody was worried about various diseases, it didn't help to read about them, no matter how rare the illnesses might be; on the contrary, that would merely feed the person's anxiety. Niels suddenly felt an inexplicable urge to punish Thorvaldsen. To give his subconscious a few extra morsels to chew on in the nights ahead.

"Even though the murders were carried out with extraordinary cunning, at the present time there's no reason to believe that Denmark will be the next target." Niels smiled at the secretary again before she left the room.

"Then why are you sitting here talking to me?"

"Timely precaution."

"If you consider that my life is in danger, you need to ensure my safety."

"Not as the threat level now stands. If it should change, we will of course take the necessary measures. Until that time, you should just—"

"Take it easy?"

"Precisely." Niels looked out the window. The view was of Fælled Park. A fine layer of frost had settled over the grass and trees, making them look like part of an old painting whose colors had faded.

An uncomfortable silence ensued. Thorvaldsen's dissatisfaction was like a physical presence in the room. So Niels was not surprised when the man sighed and prepared to launch into a lengthy diatribe.

"Now, look here. I spend every waking hour of my life rescuing people in need. According to estimates, our drinking water project in East Africa alone has saved tens of thousands of lives, not to mention the attention that the Red Cross has focused on the disaster in—" He stopped short, apparently realizing that Niels wasn't listening. "The least we can expect in a situation like this is a little help from the authorities."

"I can give you my phone number. As I said, you're always welcome to contact me."

"Thanks, but I know the phone number for the police!"

Silence again descended. Niels stood up. "So, feel free to call me. Just keep an eye peeled for anything unusual."

"Sure. Great. Say hello to Amundsen at Amnesty International for me. I assume he's next on the list. Ask him whether we should hide out together—in his summer house or mine."

Niels nodded and left the office.

Don't worry, Thorvaldsen, thought Niels as he rode down in the elevator. You're in no danger. He took out the list. The list of all the good men in the realm, as Thorvaldsen had dubbed it.

He purposely crossed out Thorvaldsen's name.

17

The Copenhagen suburb of Lyngby

God knows what they need all this square footage for, thought Niels as he turned down one of the residential streets. Not a soul in sight. Parked in front of all the huge houses were the small cars belonging to the wives. This evening the big cars would return home and park next to them.

The brass plate on the front door, which was painted a dark Bornholm red, had only one name: Amundsen. Number two on the list. There were sounds from inside the house. Footsteps going up and down stairs. Unsteady footsteps. Niels rang the bell again and then followed up with a resounding knock on the aging wooden door. There was a huge dent in the middle of the panel, as if someone had tried to kick it in. Niels was getting impatient. "Come on, open up."

He glanced back at the street. No witnesses. With his finger, he flipped open the mail slot and caught a glimpse of a naked young woman running upstairs. Somebody was whispering, and Niels stood up at the very moment the door opened. The man had youthfully blond hair that reached almost to his shoulders. And clear blue eyes. "Can I help you?"

"Christian Amundsen?"

"Yes?"

"Niels Bentzon. From the Copenhagen Police. I went to see you at the Amnesty offices, but they told me you had called in sick today."

Amundsen stared at Niels in confusion before replying. "Well, I wouldn't exactly say that I'm sick. Everybody needs a day off once in a while. Does this have something to do with my car?"

"I also tried to phone. May I come in for ten minutes or so?"

"What's this about?"

Niels looked at the framed photographs on the wall: Amundsen in Africa, embracing two released prisoners. Amundsen in Asia, standing in front of a prison with two happy-looking Asians.

"That was taken in Myanmar." Amundsen came into the room.

"You mean Burma?"

"Political prisoners. I spent three years trying to get them released from Insein Prison. It's one of the most horrific prisons in the world."

"That must have been a big day."

"And do you think I was able to get them asylum in Denmark?"

"Not when you put it like that."

"Finally, the Australian government agreed to take them. After massive pressure from a lot of people, including us."

The girl whose legs Niels had already admired came in carrying a tea service on a tray. She was now wearing jeans. Tight jeans and lovely red lipstick that suited her smooth black Asian hair. She couldn't be a day over twenty. The chemistry between her and Amundsen was electric. Niels felt like he was standing in the middle of their bedroom.

"This is Pinoy. She works for us as an au pair."

"Hi," she said. "Tea?" A sweet voice, accommodating yet independent.

"Yes, thanks."

"Pinoy was also persecuted by the authorities. She was sent to prison twice. Even so, we had to give up trying to bring her here as a refugee. Instead, we were able to get her into the country as an au pair. That rule will never be touched. Not as long as the upper classes need their cheap labor force."

"Getting back to the matter at hand—" Niels began, but Amundsen interrupted him.

"That's just about the only way we can get anybody into Denmark anymore. We try to help as many as we can."

Niels let a few seconds pass to allow Amundsen's excuse to fade. "As I was saying—you don't need to worry. Just call me if anything unusual happens. A break-in, vandalism, locks that are picked, mysterious phone calls, et cetera."

"Nothing like that has ever happened to me. It all sounds a bit far-fetched—I mean, the idea that somebody's going around murdering good people."

Amundsen jumped at the sound of a car pulling up outside. "That's the kids. Could you wait a minute?"

Before Niels had time to answer, Amundsen was gone. From the window, Niels could see Amundsen's very pregnant wife trying to lift two little kids out of the car. Niels cast a glance at the front hall and caught Amundsen's eye. The Asian girl was standing next to him. She seemed angry. He whispered something to her right before the front door opened. Happy children, smiles, and heartfelt hugs. Niels used the waiting time to examine once again the photographs of Amundsen's victories. A framed article on the wall announced: *Amnesty International saves Yemenis from deportation.*

"I'm sorry." Amundsen stood in the doorway holding a child in his arms. He was a confused man trying to balance his personal urges with all the good that his superego wanted to achieve. Niels smiled at the little boy.

"That's all right. As I was saying: Call me if you see anything out of the ordinary. And there's no reason for concern."

Amundsen took Niels's card. "I'm not worried. Do you want to know my opinion?"

"Sure."

"You're looking in the wrong place."

"What do you mean?"

"It's not in my field that you'll find the good people. There's far too much ego and media attention involved."

"It's not my job to find the good people. I just have to warn those whom some lunatic might perceive to be good."

Amundsen hesitated. Then he calmly looked Niels in the eye and said, "Are you sure about that?"

Amundsen was sitting in his home office, alone. The officer had gone. It had not been a pleasant visit. The policeman seemed able to see right through his life. All the lies. Why hadn't he mentioned the anonymous phone calls? The caller who slammed down the phone in the night? Or the time when somebody threw a bottle at the front door? Amundsen could still hear the crash in his mind. The bottle had shattered into a thousand pieces and left a permanent dent in the door. Among the shards of glass, he'd found the label from the neck of the bottle. Amarula Cream. Amundsen was quite familiar with the brand—a creamy African liqueur, overly sweet and with the picture of an elephant on the label. He'd once gotten drunk on Amarula in Sierra Leone. Or maybe it was Liberia. Could the bottle flung at his front door have anything to do with one of those cases? Sierra Leone—the gateway to hell. Gruesome crimes, poverty, starvation, disease, corruption, mad dictators, and a nonexistent justice system that hampered the work Amnesty was trying to do. It was impossible to avoid missteps when operating in places like that. And missteps bred enemies.

One incident in particular had made an impression on him. Along with the other Amnesty directors, Amundsen had gone to Sierra Leone a couple of years ago. They were going to set up a crisis center for child soldiers. Amundsen had met two boys who were in prison, on death row, convicted of a grisly massacre in their village. One boy had shot his own younger brother, who was ten. The boy himself was twelve. The boy had demanded that the rest of his family be executed. Amundsen had never met anyone who was so alone. The country, the army that had kidnapped him, the social welfare authorities, if they could even be called that, his family—they had all abandoned the boy to his fate. Amnesty had collected over a hundred thousand signatures on his behalf. Amundsen had personally delivered them to the president of the nation's supreme court. It was a farce. Their courtroom was a hall once used for banquets in an abandoned hotel. The gods only knew where the pitch-black judge had found the ridiculous white wig that he wore. The gods had long since deserted West Africa, leaving behind organizations like Amnesty, the Red Cross, and Doctors Without Borders to clean up this shithole on earth. Their efforts to help were nothing more than snowballs in hell.

The other boy in prison still had the support of his family. He had been kidnapped when he was eight, and he was ten by the time Amundsen met him. He had been trained in two months to be a killing machine. They had practiced on children. They had practiced by shooting other children who had been kidnapped. The boys were either shot by an adult sergeant or learned to pull the trigger themselves. Mike, as this boy was called, had quickly learned the value of drugs and how important it was to dull the senses. Without the drugs, he would have gone crazy and shot himself. Amundsen would never forget his first meeting with the boy. He had expected to encounter a horrible situation, but the reality was far worse than he could have imagined. What he saw was a boy who had become an addict in order to survive in hell. A little boy, sweating and shaking in his cell, all his thoughts and words focused on getting another fix. Amundsen was in close contact with the boy's family. Maybe he tried to instill too much hope in them. Both boys ended up being shot in a filthy prison yard. Of course. All stories from Sierra Leone ended in death.

The boy's mother had reproached Amundsen, saying that he hadn't done enough and he might as well go home. He could still remember what she shouted after him: "My son's death pays your salary."

Amundsen often thought about those words. They had made a strong impression on him. An unfair conclusion, he told himself. He was fighting for *them*, after all. His job was to instill hope. But the boy's mother hadn't understood that, and her words continued to haunt him.

My son's death pays your salary.

18

Niels took out the list again. *Severin Rosenberg,* he read. The next-to-last name. After him, the only one left was Gustav Lund, the wild card, the mathematician who had won a Fields Medal. It appealed to Niels that the man was a dark horse and not just one of the well-meaning media darlings. It strengthened his sense that the list was trying to locate people who were *good,* people who had found other ways to help than by participating in climate demonstrations or torchlight processions in Town Hall Square.

Niels hadn't had time to do much research. What he knew was pretty much the same as what anyone would know from reading newspapers on a regular basis over the past few years. Meaning that on several occasions Severin Rosenberg had offered refuge to individuals who were denied asylum. He was the *refugee pastor,* as the media liked to call him. Various sectors on the political far right had chosen to direct their hatred at him. Joining them were large segments of the Danish population. But Severin Rosenberg had refused to be cowed; he had stood firm in his belief that brotherly love meant brotherly love. That it couldn't be interpreted to apply only to people with blond hair and blue eyes. Everyone had an obligation to help people in need. Niels had often seen the pastor discuss his views on TV. Rosenberg gave the impression of being an intelligent but slightly starry-eyed idealist who was willing to go through hell and high water to defend his beliefs. Two thousand years ago he would have been tossed to the lions in the Colosseum, persecuted like the other Christians who believed in sharing both love and earthly goods. There was something a bit naive about Rosenberg. Niels found that appealing.

On the other hand, Niels found churches boring. As far as he was concerned, if you'd seen one, you'd seen them all. He had always felt that way, but Kathrine had a soft spot in her heart for the vast sacred spaces. She had once dragged him along to Helligåndskirke, the Church of the Holy Spirit, during an evening cultural celebration in Copenhagen. A choir had sung hymns in Latin, and a writer with a long beard had talked about the history of the church. The only thing Niels remembered was that at one time it had functioned as a hospital cloister. During the Middle Ages, when Copenhagen was becoming known as a European metropolis, countless travelers began arriving in the city: knights, wealthy burghers, and merchants. This increase in traffic meant more prostitutes and more illegitimate children. The babies were often killed right after birth. Helligåndskirke was then expanded and given the status of hospital cloister for the express purpose of taking in the babies given up by women who had become mothers against their will.

Niels parked his car at the curb and studied the church. Copenhagen residents were still bringing their children here six hundred years later. The cloister was now a day-care center.

He sat in the car for a moment, glancing up at the sky, where the sun was struggling to shine through a thin layer of pale gray clouds. He looked at the people walking past on the sidewalk. A young mother with a stroller. An elderly couple holding hands as if they were newly in love. It was a beautiful winter day in Copenhagen. *Hopenhagen,* as the city had been dubbed in honor of the climate conference.

Niels crossed the square, noticing immediately the patrol car parked at the curb. From quite a distance away he could hear a man yelling at the police officers. The slurred, unmistakable sound of a voice box damaged from long years of heavy drug use. The officers had grabbed hold of the addict's arms.

"It wasn't me, you fuckheads!"

Niels knew the man well. He had even arrested him once a long time ago. Just one of Copenhagen's numerous deadbeats. An obnoxious figure who made everyone look the other way in a futile merging of empathy and disgust. The junkie tore himself out of the officers' grip and set off in what looked like a comical flight. He lurched forward on frail legs. But it wasn't his day, because he ran right into Niels.

"Hey, take it easy."

"Let go of me, man. Dammit!"

Niels took a firm grip on the junkie's arms until the officers caught up with him. The man was nothing but skin and bones. His arms felt as if they might snap in half. He clearly wasn't long for this world; his breath stank of death. Niels had to turn his head away as the poor guy used his last strength to curse at the world.

"Go easy on the man," Niels said as he handed him over to the custody of the young officers, seizing the opportunity to show them his police ID. One of the policemen wanted to make the addict lie down on the cold cobblestones so he could cuff him.

"I don't think that's really necessary, do you?" said Niels. The junkie was staring at him, but with no sign of recognition. "What did he do?"

"He was trying to break into the basement of the church."

"It wasn't me!" shouted the addict. "Listen to me, man. I just needed a place to give myself a fix."

Niels glanced at his watch. He was late. He didn't have time to find out exactly what had happened. Not if he was going to finish going down the list by six o'clock. The poor guy was still babbling. "Where are we supposed to go? Tell me that. Where the hell should we go when we need a fix?"

The cuffs closed around the addict's thin wrists with an innocuous-sounding click. Niels noticed the man's tattoo: a red snake and a little dragon wrapped around several symbols that he couldn't make out. The tattoo was relatively new; no dull colors or smeared lines like on tattoos from the old days. Nor was it some sort of unauthorized tattoo from prison. It was a professional job. Quite the little work of art.

It turned out that the screws on the small basement window had been loosened, and a used syringe lay on the ground. Niels tossed the syringe in a garbage can. He wasn't exactly fond of other people's blood. He also found a single screw lying in the crack between two cobblestones. He fished it out and tried to push it into the window's hinge. It fit perfectly. One of the young officers was standing behind him.

"Did you search the guy?" asked Niels.

"Yes."

"Did you find a screwdriver?"

"No."

Niels showed him the screw. "So he's not the one who unscrewed the window. Besides, he doesn't have the strength to manage anything like that."

The policeman shrugged. He didn't give a shit. Then he said, "If there's nothing else, we'll drive him over to the station."

Niels wasn't listening. He was thinking about the junkie's tattoo. Why would an addict who had a hard enough time coming up with the thousand kroner he needed every day for his drug habit spend as much as ten thousand on a new tattoo?

Basement of Helligåndskirke—Copenhagen

Rosenberg looked very much like the version of himself that Niels had seen on TV. A tall, corpulent, balding man with a slightly stooped posture. His face was as round as a smiling sun in a child's drawing. But behind the thick lenses of his glasses, a great solemnity lurked in his deep-set eyes.

"It happens a couple of times a year," Rosenberg said.

They were standing in the basement under the church office. The space was practically empty. A couple of chairs, a few dusty cardboard boxes, a bookshelf holding a stack of pamphlets. Nothing else.

"Typically, some drug addict or homeless person imagines that our collection box is bulging with cash. But I must say they're getting bolder. It usually happens at night. It's never happened in broad daylight."

"You didn't see anything suspicious? Anyone sneaking around?"

"No. I was upstairs in my office. Answering all the hate mail, you know, and going through the minutes from the last meeting of our parish council. I'll spare you the details."

Niels caught the pastor's eye. He smiled. People always told the police more than they were asked. "Is anything missing?"

Rosenberg surveyed the church's earthly goods with a resigned expression. Folding chairs, cardboard boxes. Things that pile up and are then forgotten.

Niels looked around the room. "What's behind that door over there?" He didn't wait for an answer but walked over and opened it. He found himself looking into a small, dark room. The fluorescent lights took their time switching on. More tables and folding chairs. And over in the corner, a pile of old mattresses.

"Is this where they were living?" Niels asked, turning around.

Rosenberg came closer. "Are you going to arrest me for that now?"

Something that might have been a criticism of the police smoldered in

Rosenberg's eyes. He had turned the damp cellar wall into a gallery: black-and-white photographs from the days the refugees had spent in the church. A testimonial. Niels looked at their faces. Fear. And hope. The hope that Rosenberg had given them.

"How many were there?"

"Twelve, in the biggest group. This isn't exactly the Hotel d'Angleterre, but they never complained."

"Palestinians?"

"And Somalis, Yemenis, Sudanese. Even a lone Albanian. If they were telling me the truth, that is. Some of them weren't especially talkative when it came right down to it. I'm sure they had their reasons."

Niels studied the pastor. They were standing only inches away from each other, but the distance felt much greater. An invisible shield enveloped Rosenberg. His personal space seemed stronger than most people's. He would allow someone to come this close and no closer. Niels wasn't surprised. He had often encountered something similar from other people who made their living offering closeness and attention. Psychologists, psychiatrists, doctors. It was probably an unconscious survival mechanism.

Rosenberg switched off the light. Niels found himself standing in total darkness.

"This is how I tell my confirmation students about the night when the police came. And how the refugees held on to each other. Some of them were crying, but they were brave, even though they knew what awaited them. I tell my students about how your colleagues broke down the door of the church and how their heavy boots could be heard moving across the church floor and down the stairs."

Niels stood there listening to his own breathing. "But they didn't come in here?"

"No. Your colleagues didn't come in here. You gave up."

Niels knew quite well that the police were not the ones who had given up. It was the politicians who had yielded to the pressure of popular opinion. Rosenberg turned the lights back on, and Niels again looked at the photos, trying to imagine what it must have been like.

"Aren't there more than twelve in this picture?" Niels counted to himself. There were clearly more refugees in this one than in the other photographs. Rosenberg was standing in the doorway. He wanted Niels out of there.

"Yes, you're right. A couple of them disappeared."

"Disappeared?"

Niels noticed at once that Rosenberg was hesitating.

"Yes. Two men from Yemen. They just took off."

"Why?"

"I don't know. I guess they thought they wanted to try and make it on their own."

Niels knew instantly that Rosenberg was lying.

———————————

The church was completely empty. Almost. An organist was practicing the same piece over and over. Rosenberg didn't seem worried by the information that Niels had given him.

"Good people, you say? What sort of good people?" he asked.

"Human rights activists, aid workers, that sort of thing," Niels said.

"What kind of world are we living in? Now that good people are being murdered?"

"Just be careful who you allow inside. Be vigilant."

The pastor handed Niels a stack of hymnals to hold. "I'm not afraid. I'm not in any danger." The mere idea made Rosenberg laugh, and he repeated, "I'm certainly in no danger of being considered a good person. I can promise you that. I'm a sinner."

"I don't think you're in any danger, either, but you should still be careful."

"There was once a man who went to see Luther."

"The man who made all of us Protestants?"

"Yes, that's the one." Rosenberg laughed again, looking at Niels as if he were a child. "The man said to Luther: 'I have a problem. I've thought long and hard about it, and do you know what? I have never sinned. I've never done anything that I shouldn't.' Luther looked at the man. Can you guess what he said?"

Niels felt himself carried back to the confirmation classes of his youth. It wasn't a pleasant memory. "That the man was lucky?"

Rosenberg shook his head in triumph. "No, he told the man that he needed to commit a sin. That God existed in order to save sinners. Not for the sake of those who were already saved."

The organist stopped playing. A couple of tourists came into the church and studied the interior with obligatory curiosity. Rosenberg clearly had more that he wanted to say to Niels, but he waited until the echo of the organ had dissipated up toward the ceiling.

"The Jews have a myth about the good people. Are you familiar with it?"

"I've never taken much interest in religion." Niels could hear how that sounded, so he added apologetically, "Though I probably shouldn't be saying that to a pastor."

Rosenberg went on as if Niels hadn't spoken, looking almost as if he were standing in the pulpit on a Sunday morning.

"It has to do with the thirty-six good people who keep the rest of humanity alive."

"Thirty-six? Why thirty-six?"

"Each letter in the Hebrew alphabet has a certain numerical value. The letters that spell out the word 'life' add up to eighteen. And so eighteen is a sacred number."

"And eighteen plus eighteen is thirty-six. That means it's twice as sacred?"

"Pretty good for somebody who doesn't take much of an interest in religion."

Niels smiled, feeling a childish sense of pride. "How did they find that out?"

"What do you mean?"

"How did they know that God had put those thirty-six people here on earth?" Niels held back a disbelieving smile.

"He told Moses about it."

Niels looked up at the huge paintings. Angels and demons. Dead people crawling out of their graves. The Son nailed to a wooden cross. Niels had seen a lot in his twenty years on the police force. Too much. He'd turned Copenhagen upside down in his hunt for evidence and motives to crimes; he'd searched every dark, grim corner of the human soul and discovered things that made him sick to his stomach just thinking about them. But he'd never seen a shadow of evidence that there was any sort of life after death.

"Sinai. Moses went up on the mountain and received the commandments. We still live our lives in accordance with what he was told. To such an extent, in fact, that we've made them into law. Thou shalt not kill."

"That hasn't ever stopped anyone."

Rosenberg shrugged and went on. "Love thy neighbor. Thou shalt not steal. I'm sure you know the Ten Commandments."

"Sure. Of course."

"Actually, it's your job to see that God's Ten Commandments are kept. So maybe you're more involved in the big picture than you know," Rosenberg teased Niels, smiling. Niels couldn't help smiling back. The pastor was clever. And experienced. He'd had years of training in how to tackle nonbelievers.

"Maybe," replied Niels. "So what did God say to Moses?"

"He said that in every generation He would put thirty-six good, righteous people on earth to take care of humanity."

"They're supposed to go around and proselytize or what?"

"No. Because they don't know that they've been chosen."

"You mean the good people don't know that they're good?"

"That's right. They don't know that they're good. Only God knows their identity. But they keep vigil over the rest of us." The pastor paused. "As I said, this is very important in the Jewish faith. If you want to talk to an expert, you should go over to the synagogue on Krystalgade."

Niels glanced at his watch and thought about Kathrine, the tranquilizers, and the plane he needed to catch the next day.

"Is it really so unthinkable?" the pastor went on. "Most of us would acknowledge that evil exists in the world. Evil individuals. Hitler. Stalin. So why not the opposite? Thirty-six people who offer a counterweight on God's balance scale. How many drops of goodness are needed to keep evil in check? Maybe only thirty-six."

Silence settled over them. Rosenberg took the hymnals from Niels and put them back in place on the bookshelf near the exit. Niels shook hands with the pastor. He was the first person on the list whom Niels had even wanted to shake hands with. Maybe the sacred space of the church was having an effect on him after all.

"As I said: I just think you should exercise a little precaution," Niels repeated.

Rosenberg opened the door for him. Outside were bustling crowds, Christmas music, bells ringing, cars, noise—a raging, chaotic world. Niels looked the pastor in the eye, wondering what it was the man had lied about downstairs in the basement.

"In his eulogy for Gerald Ford, Kissinger called the deceased president one of the last good men. Someone also said the same of Oscar Schindler. Or was it Gandhi? Or Churchill?"

"Churchill? Can you send people off to war and still be considered good?"

Rosenberg paused to think about that. "Situations may arise when doing wrong is the right thing to do. But then you're no longer good. That's what Christianity is all about: that we can live with each other only when we've accepted sin as part of the human condition."

Niels looked down at the church floor.

"I can see that I've scared you off now. That's something that we pastors are good at doing." Rosenberg laughed good-naturedly.

"I've got your phone number," said Niels. "So I'll know if you call me on my cell. Promise me that you'll call if anything happens."

Niels walked back to his car. He stopped next to the basement window of the church. Something didn't fit. The basement window. The drug addict. The tattoo. Rosenberg lying to him. A lot of things don't fit, he thought. But things didn't always have to seem logical. That was the bane of a police officer's job. People were liars. It was a matter of finding out which lie covered up not just a sin but a crime.

19

The nun was from the Philippines. Sister Magdalena from the Order of the Sacred Heart. Tommaso liked her. A pretty and smiling face to help those who were terminally ill depart from this world. The newly established hospice was located on the north side of the old Jewish quarter. Tommaso could walk there from the Ghetto in only a few minutes. It was still called the Ghetto, even though the word had acquired a different meaning. It was here that the word had originated—*getto* meant iron-casting in Italian. Several hundred years ago, the Venetian ironworks had been housed in this part of the city, along with the Jews. At one point the gates were slammed shut, cutting off the Jews from the rest of the city. The area then became known as the Ghetto. A place that would later become the model for many urban districts around the world, which all had in common the fact that people were not allowed to leave.

Magdalena said Tommaso's name as he entered the hospice. "Signor di Barbara?" she whispered. A blissful peace reigned over the place. No one ever raised a voice. As if the intent were to prepare the dying for the eternal silence they would soon encounter.

"Your mother was suffering badly last night. I sat with her all night."

She looked at him with her lovely eyes. It was crude of him to have such a thought, but he couldn't help it: Why had she become a nun when she was so beautiful?

"You have a good heart, Sister Magdalena. My mother is lucky to have you at her side."

"And to have a son like you."

She meant what she said—Tommaso had no doubt about that—but like clockwork, his guilty conscience instantly flared up.

"I'll have more time now." He hesitated. Why should he tell her? "I've been suspended from my job."

She took his hand. "Maybe that's a blessing."

He had to suppress a slight chuckle. A blessing?

"Your mother has been asking for you."

"I'm sorry about that, but I was working the night shift at the station."

"It sounded like she was worried about you. She kept saying that there was something you shouldn't pay for."

"Pay for?"

"Something about money that you shouldn't pay. That it was dangerous."

Tommaso gave her a puzzled look. "My mother said that?"

"Yes. Several times. 'Don't pay the money, Tommaso—it's dangerous.'"

Sister Magdalena watched Tommaso di Barbara head down the corridor, carrying a shopping bag in one hand and a big cardboard box under his arm. There was something dejected about him, she thought as he walked past the eight rooms that the only hospice in Venice had at its disposal. Tommaso's mother was in the room at the end, facing the courtyard. Except for one palm tree, the trees were all bare. As if to make up for this, the nurses in the hospice had put up Christmas decorations in the hall: boughs and some shiny garlands around the portrait of Mary and the newborn Savior.

Sister Magdalena always listened carefully to the last wishes of the dying. She knew from experience that those who had one foot on the other side were sometimes allowed a glimpse into the future, into the beyond. Most often what dying people said was sheer gibberish. But not always. Magdalena had taken care of the terminally ill ever since she entered the Order of the Sacred Heart fifteen years ago. She had seen and heard a great deal. She knew that it couldn't always be dismissed as nonsense.

In her former life—that was how she always thought of it—Sister Magdalena had been a prostitute. But God saved her. She had no doubt about that. She even had proof: the receipt for a bicycle that she'd taken in to be repaired.

In Manila she had been the frequent companion of an American who was an ex-pilot. He had settled in the Philippines and spent his pension on girls and alcohol. He'd fought in the Vietnam War and had scars to show for it on his stomach and legs. Probably also on his soul. But now he was dying. It was not a dignified death; he'd never managed to master his desires. Magdalena was supposed to come every day to give him a blow job. He paid her, of course, but as the cancer ate away at his body, it took longer and longer for him to reach orgasm.

This was before she took the name of Magdalena. It was another time, and she was another person. The aging pilot once owned a bar, most likely to give himself an excuse for his alcoholism. It was there that Magdalena had met him. Now he was ill and would die all alone.

But something happened that had changed her life. The last time she went to visit the pilot, he was delirious. He grabbed Magdalena's hand and said, "Don't go there." At first she had tried to comfort him, telling him to "calm down" and "everything will be fine." But he kept insisting. "You mustn't go there." Then he described the building across from the Shaw Boulevard Station, right around the corner from where Magdalena rented a room. There was a bicycle repair shop on the ground floor. Green shutters, peeling blue paint revealing that the facade had once been a different pastel color.

The next day the pilot was dead. The following week the building near the Shaw Boulevard Station collapsed. Magdalena had taken her bicycle to the shop to be repaired, but she hadn't dared to pick it up. Nineteen people had died.

She had taken her vows. Entered the Order of the Sacred Heart. Changed her name to Magdalena—the whore whom Jesus saved from being stoned to death.

Ever since, she had sat at the bedsides of the dying for six days of every week. One week during the nighttime, the next in the daytime. Then one day off, during which she slept and watched *Friends* on TV.

Sister Magdalena had told the doctor in charge of the hospice about her experience, although she'd left out most of the sleazy details. The doctor had smiled and patted her hand. What other proof did anyone need? she asked herself. The old pilot had never seen the building that housed the bicycle repair shop. It was not in a neighborhood frequented by foreigners, and yet he was able to describe it in detail. It's important to listen to the dying, no matter how big a sinner the person might be, she often thought. The pilot had gone to war; he had killed people. Then he had turned to drink, and he'd beaten the girls he hired for sex. Yet God had chosen to speak through him to save her life. It was important to listen to the dying.

Sister Magdalena hoped that Tommaso di Barbara would listen to his dying mother.

Tommaso's mother was asleep, her mouth open. She was snoring very faintly. Tommaso set the bag with his purchases on the small stove and the box containing the murder investigation documents on the floor. The materials from his office wardrobe were all inside the box that Marina had smuggled out of the police station. As if the documents were condemned to shun the light—something that no one wanted to hear about.

Tommaso had brought spicy salami, tomatoes, and garlic for his mother. She had no appetite, but she was fond of the strong smells. That was something Tommaso could understand. He also felt a need to cover up the overwhelming smell of death and cleaning fluids in the hospice. Fortunately, it wasn't hard to do. Even though all the rooms had been newly remodeled, each with a stove and a bed for the patients, no ventilation had been installed over the stoves. The smell of basil and thyme quickly spread through the building. And that was a blessing.

"Mother?"

Tommaso sat down next to her bed and took her hand. Her skin was stretched tight over her knuckles. There was so much they hadn't talked about. So much that he didn't know about her life. Such as the war period, when Tommaso's father had spent several months in prison. He had supported the wrong side, although that was probably not how he viewed it, even later in life. He had remained a faithful fascist for the rest of his days, dying prematurely. "Now we'll finally have peace," Tommaso's mother had said when they buried him in the cemetery. Cremated. The urn was added to an amazing mosaic of urns stacked on top of one another. It was a labyrinth, and Tommaso nearly got lost the first time he paid a visit. The cemetery on the island outside the city couldn't get any bigger. To solve the problem of limited space, it had been built upward. The result was passageways that towered against the sky, one corridor after another stacked with small rectangular boxes. Tommaso doubted his mother would want the space that had been reserved for her next to his father. It was time to ask her.

"Mother?"

She woke up. Looked at him without saying a word and with no sign that she even recognized him.

"It's me."

"I can see that. Do you think I'm blind?"

He smiled. She was a tough cookie. Never reluctant to deliver a good thrashing or a spanking. But also capable of offering comfort. Tommaso took a deep breath. He couldn't put it off any longer. "Mother. You know the place where Father's ashes are kept . . ."

No answer. His mother was staring up at the ceiling.

"When you pass away one day, is that where you'd like to have your ashes?"

"Did you bring the groceries?"

"Mother."

"Cook me some food, my boy. Just so I can enjoy the smell of it."

He shook his head. She patted his hand. "I've told Sister Magdalena everything that you need to know. She'll tell you. Afterward. Be sure to listen to her."

He tried to get up, but she squeezed his hand with astonishing strength. "Do you hear me? I'm going to tell everything to Sister Magdalena. Do as she says."

He hesitated. Remembered the sister telling him some nonsense about money that he wasn't supposed to pay. He smiled, wanting to reassure her. "All right, Mother. I'll do that."

20

A n hour's drive, and a whole new world opened up.
It was as if he saw the city only when he headed out into the countryside. The noise, the crowds, the traffic—he lived in a state of constant upheaval. So the question was whether he would truly see the countryside when he arrived back in the city. The wide-open sky. The flat, expansive landscape dotted with summer houses that he encountered as dusk fell. Fields, paths, and clearings all merged into one. He caught a glimpse of the waters of Øresund beyond a cluster of dark trees.

Niels stomped on the brake. He checked the road sign and backed up a few feet. Gravel crunched under the tires. Then he turned off and drove forward a couple of hundred yards and parked near the only house on the road, at the end. A faint light was visible in a window. The name plate on the mailbox said LUND.

Nobody opened the door when Niels knocked.

He stood there, listening. A mosquito whistled past his ear. He waved it away with surprise. Shouldn't all the mosquitoes be dead now that it was December? He knocked again, this time harder. Still no answer. Niels walked around the side of the house. Not a breath of wind. The air was calm and cold. He stepped onto a small veranda facing the sea. He was about to knock on the terrace door when he heard a faint splashing. He turned around and saw someone standing on the dock below. A woman. Niels could see only the outline of her body. He walked down the slope.

"Excuse me." Niels felt almost guilty at interrupting such a beautiful moment of silence. "I'm looking for Gustav Lund."

The woman turned around and stared at him. She was holding a fishing pole in her hand. "Gustav?"

"I'd like to speak to him."

"He's in Vancouver. Who are you?"

"Niels Bentzon, from the Copenhagen Police."

No reaction at all, which was unusual. Niels was used to prompting all sorts of reactions whenever he announced that he was from the police. Fear, panic, contempt, defiance, relief. The woman merely looked at him and said, "I'm Hannah Lund. Gustav won't be coming back. I live here alone now."

The furniture wasn't really appropriate for a summer house.

It was much too nice. Too expensive. Niels wasn't interested in furniture, but there were periods—or so it seemed to him—when Kathrine talked of nothing else. That was why he recognized a number of designer pieces. Wegener, Mogensen, Klint, Jacobsen. If the furniture in this summer house was genuine, it was worth a fortune.

A pair of gleaming cat eyes regarded Niels with curiosity as he looked around the house. The living room was a huge mess. There were plates and dirty coffee cups on all the tables. Cat toys, shoes, and old newspapers littered the floor. Laundry had been hung up to dry over one of the ceiling crossbeams. A piano took up most of the space at one end of the room. The other end was filled with books. The disarray was in sharp contrast to the expensive furniture, though it somehow lent the pieces a sense of purpose. Maybe because it was nice to see such costly furniture actually being used. Whenever Niels and Kathrine, on rare occasions, visited some of Kathrine's architect colleagues—Niels usually tried to get out of such visits—an uneasy feeling always came over him. A feeling of inadequacy. He didn't like standing in one of those fancy apartments in the Østerbro district, sipping his Corton-Charlemagne white wine, which cost six hundred kroner a bottle, surrounded by Europe's most expensive designer furniture, and hardly daring to sit down on the sofa. Kathrine just laughed at him.

"So Gustav is supposed to be a good person?" Hannah suppressed a smile as she handed Niels a cup of coffee. "Are you sure you've got the right man?"

"That's what they all say. Except for the guy from the Red Cross." Niels stirred his instant coffee, catching sight of a small framed photograph showing Hannah next to a tall, lanky teenage boy. Clearly her son. She had her arm around him. They were standing in front of Foucault's pendulum in Paris.

"Why Gustav?"

"The computer chose him. Because of something he said when he accepted the Fields Medal."

"'In the long run, it will be a mathematician who saves the world.'"

"Exactly."

"And that's why Gustav's name showed up on the screen?"

"Gustav is your ex-husband?"

He studied her as she began explaining her marital status in a long, roundabout way. How old was she? Forty? Forty-five? There was something disorderly about her. Something that matched the house: a bit gloomy and messy, yet interesting and complex. She had dark, serious-looking eyes. Her longish brown hair was tousled, as if she'd just gotten out of bed. Even though the floor was cold, she had kicked off her shoes and walked around barefoot. Jeans, a white shirt, a lovely fair complexion. A slender figure. She wasn't beautiful. If Niels hadn't had other things on his mind, he might have pondered why in the world he was attracted to this woman. It was probably quite simple, he told himself. She wasn't wearing a bra, and Niels could see much more through her shirt than she probably would have liked.

"I started out as his student."

Niels tried to concentrate on what Hannah was saying. She sat down on the sofa, wrapping a gray blanket covered with cat hair around her thin shoulders. "I'm an astrophysicist, and I had lots of discussions with him about mathematics. Gustav is one of Europe's leading mathematicians."

"You're an astrophysicist?"

"Yes. Or rather, I used to be. We started seeing each other socially. At first I was mostly amazed that a genius like Gustav—and I don't hesitate to call him a genius, because he really is—would bother to flirt with me. Later I fell in love with him. And then we had Johannes." She stopped abruptly. Niels saw something else in her expression. Sorrow? Yes, sorrow. He saw it just as he remembered that Gustav Lund had lost his son. Johannes was dead. He had committed suicide.

Silence descended over the room. It wasn't unpleasant. Neither of them tried to salvage the situation with superficial chatter. She knew that he knew.

"Do you live out here all year round?"

"Yes."

"Don't you get lonely?"

"That's not what you're here to talk about."

The abrupt chill in her voice was meant to cover her grief. He could tell by looking at her. It was something she preferred to keep to herself. Dealing with grief was the cornerstone of a negotiator's job; it was what the psychologists had spent the most time teaching Niels and the other police officers. It was when people couldn't handle their grief that things went wrong, leading to guns and hostages and suicide. More than once Niels had been forced to convey the terrible news to parents that their child was gone. He was familiar with the different phases that someone had to move through when overcome by grief. He wondered how long it had been since Hannah's son had committed suicide. She seemed to be in the so-called new orientation phase: that stage when the grief-stricken person attempted to redirect her attention to the world. When she once again—although perhaps only briefly—dared to look toward the future. It was the phase that ultimately involved saying goodbye. Taking leave of the loved one. It was the most difficult phase of all, a long, inward journey, and many were forced to give up along the way. If they lost the battle, the result was a terrifying defeat: a life spent in deep depression. In some cases, the individual would end up as a psychiatric patient, while others found themselves balancing on the edge of a bridge or the top of a building. And then Niels would be summoned to the scene.

"I'm sorry for disturbing you." Niels made a move to leave. "As I said, it's nothing major. No reason to worry."

"I'm not worried. They can go ahead and shoot Gustav, if they like." She fixed her eyes on Niels's face, as if she wanted to underscore that she meant every word she'd said. She was standing a little too close, but Niels was probably the only person who would have noticed that. There was something awkward about her body language. He'd noticed it down at the dock. But maybe that's just how scientists are, he thought. Their expansive intelligence took up more space in their brains, edging out the usual social skills.

Though he could smell the sweetness of her breath, he took a small step back. A phone was ringing somewhere. It took him a moment to pinpoint the sound to his own pocket. He pulled out his cell and looked at the display: a foreign number.

"Excuse me a minute. Hello?" Niels listened. At first there was only noise on the line. "Hello? Who's calling?"

Finally, a voice became audible. It was Tommaso di Barbara, the man Niels had called earlier. He was speaking Italian, although very slowly, as if that might help.

"Do you speak English?" Niels asked.

Tommaso apologetically said no. At least he understood what Niels was asking. "*Scusi.*" And then he suggested French.

"No. Wait a second." Niels turned to look at Hannah. "Do you happen to speak Italian? Or French?"

She nodded hesitantly, then looked as if she instantly regretted admitting to it. "French. A little."

"Just a minute. You can speak to my assistant." Niels held out his cell phone. "The police in Venice. Just listen to what he wants to tell me."

"Assistant?" She refused to take the phone. "What are you talking about?"

"Just tell me what he's saying. That's all."

"No." She sounded quite adamant. Even so, she took the phone from him. "*Oui?*"

Niels studied her as she talked. He couldn't tell how fluent she was in French, but she spoke quickly and seemingly without effort.

"He's asking about the number murders." She held her hand over the cell and looked at Niels.

"The number murders? Are those numbers they have on their backs? Is he sure about that? Ask him to explain."

"Did you say your name was Bentzon? He wants to know your name."

"Bentzon. Yes." Niels nodded. "Niels Bentzon. Ask him if there are any suspects. If there are any particular . . ."

She pressed her hand to her other ear and moved a little farther away.

Niels fixed his gaze on her. Out of the corner of his eye, he saw the cat slowly approaching. He sat down and let the cat sniff at his hand. His attention shifted to the photograph of Hannah and her son. And then to the small bookshelf where a photo album lay open. He went over to look at it. Six pictures told the whole story. Hannah—maybe ten years ago—holding some sort of research award in her hands. Smiling proudly. She was young and beautiful and radiant with life and ambition. The world lay at her feet. And she was well aware of it, savoring the moment. A couple of pictures of Hannah and Gustav. An extraordinarily handsome man of about fifty. Black hair combed back. Dark eyes. Tall and broad-shouldered. Without a doubt a man with plenty of female admirers; open to flirtatious glances, tempting offers. A photo showing a pregnant Hannah. She was standing arm in arm with Gustav on the Brooklyn Bridge. Niels looked at the picture more closely. Maybe he'd become too much of a policeman—sometimes he got sick and tired of the role—but he couldn't help noticing that while Hannah was looking right at the camera, Gustav's eyes were directed slightly off to the side. What was he looking at? A beautiful woman who just happened to be passing by on the bridge?

Then two pictures showing Hannah alone with the boy. Where was Gustav? At some conference? Off somewhere, tending to his career as an international scientist while his wife and son stayed home? The last photograph was from the boy's birthday. There were ten candles on the cake, and *Johannes* had been written in frosting. Hannah and a couple of other adults were sitting around the boy, who was about to blow out the candles. Niels looked at the scene. It was one of those pictures where the person who was absent had the strongest presence. Gustav.

"He was talking about an old myth." Hannah was standing right behind Niels as she handed him the phone. Had she noticed that he was looking at the photographs?

Niels turned around. "Myth? What sort of myth?"

"Something about thirty-six good people. From the Bible, I think. I didn't catch all of it. But don't you think it's fascinating? Most of the murders were committed approximately three thousand kilometers from one another. That's why he contacted your office. Apparently, it's three thousand kilometers between one of the last crime scenes and—"

"Copenhagen," Niels said, interrupting her.

For a moment they simply stared at each other.

———— • ————

Hannah watched as Niels backed his car out of the driveway. She was still holding his business card in her hand. For a second she was blinded by the headlights. Then she caught sight of the license plate on his car:

II 12 041. She took a ballpoint pen out of a drawer. Niels was driving away; maybe she was mistaken. A pair of binoculars lay on the windowsill. She snatched them up and ran to the kitchen window, where she adjusted the focus to see more clearly. There it was. She was right. II 12 041. She wrote down the number on the back of Niels's card and felt the tears well up in her eyes.

21

Bentzon . . ."

Tommaso di Barbara set down his cell phone on the edge of the balcony and looked out across the dark city. He tried pronouncing the whole name: "Niels Bentzon. Who are you?"

While the rest of Venice died when evening arrived, and the restaurant employees rushed to catch the last train back to the mainland, the Ghetto remained lively. Most of the city's population lived in the streets surrounding the old Jewish quarter. Tommaso stood on the balcony. Sirens wailed. In half an hour the water would rise. He was tired. Didn't have the energy to go downstairs and put up the wooden planks over the doors. On the sidewalks below, his neighbors were busy. The small wooden planks were carefully being placed between the rubber strips on either side of every door.

"Tommaso!"

His downstairs neighbor who owned the beauty salon was calling to him. Tommaso waved.

"Didn't you hear the siren?"

"Yes, I'm coming."

The neighbor cast a concerned look in his direction. Tommaso suspected that the man had already heard about his suspension. It was very likely. Tommaso didn't care. In Venice everybody knew everything about everyone else; in that regard, it was like a country village. They also knew that his mother was dying. Especially the neighbors, since his mother owned the entire building. Soon it would belong to Tommaso, and they were worried that he might sell the place to some rich American.

"I'll do it for you," shouted his neighbor. "Where have you stored the planks?"

"Under the stairs."

Tommaso put out his cigarette in a potted plant and went back inside his apartment. Only a single lamp was on. He was headed for bed. His brain needed to rest. But on his way through the living room, he stopped to look at the wall. He had already started pinning up the case material on the south wall. Photographs of the victims. Both men and women. Their eyes, their faces. The world map with the arrows, showing that in some ingenious way, the crime scenes were connected. The dates. All the details about everything having to do with the case. Tommaso stood and stared. Fascinated and mesmerized. Above all, frightened.

He had printed out the last photographs that he'd received from India, showing the back of the dead economist. Raj Bairoliya. The pictures of deceased family members that his mother had hung on the wall had been forced to give up their places for others who had died. Dead people who were more important. Deaths that had a certain significance—Tommaso was sure about that. Because there was no coincidence about these deaths. The victims were linked in some way, he just didn't know how. And he couldn't get anyone else to take up the investigation. They weren't interested. He'd called Interpol a few months ago and was transferred a hundred times until he was finally connected to some bewildered woman. She listened halfheartedly and asked him to send in a report. Three weeks later he had received a reply. The case had been assigned a number. They would look into it as soon as that number came up, but he should count on it taking about eighteen months for that to happen.

Eighteen months. This matter couldn't wait that long. Next to the picture of the dead man from India, Tommaso pinned up the photo of a dead lawyer from the United States. Russell Young. Number 33. Raj Bairoliya was number 34.

22

Night. The best time at police headquarters. Only the cleaning staff quietly moving around, emptying the wastebaskets and dusting the windowsills. They never touched the desks—there was too much paperwork cluttering the desktops.

Niels sent his report to the printer. He had included the list of everyone he'd contacted, stating that they had all been informed and warned. *Timely precaution.* The two most important words for modern police chiefs.

The printer had run out of paper. He found a partial ream and spent twenty minutes figuring out how to insert the paper. He was trying to focus his thoughts on Kathrine, but he kept thinking about Hannah.

The reception area next to Sommersted's office was as neat and tidy as the man himself. Niels decided to place the report on his boss's desk instead of on the secretary's desk, as was customary. He wanted to make sure that Sommersted saw it. And acknowledged that Niels had passed the test to confirm he could still be trusted.

There was only one case file lying on Sommersted's desk. On the cover it said: *Confidential. Top Priority.* Niels had an urge to place his report on top of it, because otherwise Sommersted might never read it. How important could that other file be, anyway? He opened it. Not to snoop but just to find out if it would be all right to put his own report on top. *Suspected terrorist. Landed in Stockholm yesterday. From Yemen. Changed planes in India. Mumbai. Linked to terrorist activities of last year. Possibly on his way to Denmark.* Niels leafed through the pages. There was a blurry photo of the terrorist, taken with a surveillance camera outside the American embassy in Cairo. *The Muslim Brotherhood.*

Niels placed his report next to the file folder. Not on top. Then he turned off the light and murmured: "Goodbye. Have a nice vacation."

23

Southern Sweden

Disturbing sensory impressions. First the stewardess. Now the snow outside the train window. It had been years since Abdul Hadi had last seen snow. Back then he and his brother had gone skiing for the first and only time in Lebanon. They spent half of their monthly allowance on the train trip and rental fees for the ski equipment. On their very first time down the slope, they both fell. His older brother injured himself rather badly. He couldn't move his arm, and for several days Abdul Hadi was forced to assist him with the most intimate activities. Helping him take off his pants. That sort of thing. They couldn't afford to go to a doctor, and they were ashamed. The only money they had came from Yemen, from their family. The funds were meant to pay for their education so they could one day take over the task of supporting their family members.

He felt a hand land solidly on his shoulder.

At the sight of the man's uniform, Abdul Hadi got nervous. Almost panic-stricken. He looked at the other passengers. The woman seated next to him took out her ticket, and finally, he realized what was expected of him.

"Sorry," he mumbled in English.

The conductor punched his ticket and continued through the train car, although he glanced back twice. Both times he fixed his gaze on Abdul Hadi's nervous eyes. Hadi got up, grabbed his bag, and headed for the toilet. It was this type of incident that could ruin everything.

He pulled on the door handle. The toilet was occupied. Maybe it would be better if he stayed in his seat. Maybe it would look suspicious if he moved. The conductor came back, passing Abdul Hadi without a glance. It was only when the man reached the end of the car that he hastily looked over his shoulder as he spoke with a colleague. The colleague turned to look at Abdul Hadi. He'd been noticed. There was no reason to think otherwise. But they had no idea *why* he had caught their attention. Only that he seemed nervous and was behaving suspiciously. Shit! It was all because he'd been taken by surprise. Because the conductor had touched his shoulder. And because he was an Arab. That was why the conductor was calling the police. Abdul Hadi was convinced of it. He would do the same in the man's place.

The train was slowing down, and a voice announced that they were arriving at Linköping. Abdul Hadi remembered that it was the one stop before Malmö. The yellowish light from the train station reminded him of the bazaar in Damascus. But the harsh light was the only thing that reminded him of the old streets lined with vendors in the Middle East. Here, he saw a few people in the station, which was clean and cold, with scores of signs offering information. He tried to spot the conductor. He needed to make a quick decision. Some of the passengers were getting off. If he stayed on the train and the police arrived, he wouldn't have a chance.

He had to get off. He jumped off the train, clutching his bag in his hand. Fuck! The backpack containing the photos of the church. And the explosives. It was lying under his seat in the train compartment. He was about to jump back on board when he caught sight of the conductor talking on a phone as he looked for Abdul Hadi. For a second they stood and stared at each other, separated by a distance of no more than six feet. The mindless henchman of the law, wearing a uniform and cap. The man had no idea what sort of society he was slaving away to uphold. A society built 100 percent on the exploitation of others, on racial prejudices and hatred.

Abdul Hadi turned and ran. The conductor saw him take off and began shouting. Abdul Hadi increased his speed. He ran down the steps that led underneath the tracks and emerged in front of the station building. The train hadn't left the platform. He had to go back. Because of the photos of the church. And the explosives. Otherwise his plan would be discovered.

He started running back. Maybe he could jump on the rear of the last train car. Get hold of his backpack and then pull the emergency brake to make his escape.

It was too late. Abdul Hadi reached the platform just as the train pulled away.

Minutes of stunned disbelief. Seconds that weighed on him. And shame. Everything was ruined. He had failed. Abdul Hadi opened his bag to look for his diary, which held his cousin's phone number. By now he had hurried through the town until he reached the other side because he figured they would be searching for him. Everything was jumbled together inside his bag. He pulled out several pieces of paper and saw that they were actually the photographs of the church. He couldn't recall when he had moved them from his backpack. It took a few moments before he realized that all was not lost. He no longer had the explosives, but he did have the photos. They wouldn't have any idea what his intentions were; they didn't know his plan.

24

Carlsberg silo—Copenhagen

Whenever Niels couldn't sleep, he would get up and read. Preferably some boring book or a day-old newspaper. Wine helped, too, but hard liquor always gave him heart palpitations. He hadn't even opened the bottle of cognac that Anni gave him for his fortieth birthday.

Tonight he just lay in bed. Sleep refused to come. He lay there staring into the dark. His suitcase was packed and ready, his passport and ticket were lying on the table. He had ironed a shirt for himself and hung it on a hanger. He'd made all the preparations. The only thing left for him to do was stare up at the smooth cement ceiling and wait for six o'clock, when he needed to leave. He closed his eyes and tried to envision Kathrine's face. Her eyes. So filled with enthusiasm whenever she talked about her work. The slightly childish dimples that she did her best to hide. She often laughed with her hand held in front of her mouth. Her temperament was always so mercurial. The curve of her cheekbones. Her slender nose. But he couldn't do it. He couldn't put all her features together. He imagined disconnected details that kept bumping into one another, obstructing and preventing any unified picture from emerging.

With relief, he heard his phone ring.

"Hi, sweetheart. I was just lying here thinking about you."

"Did you take the pills?" Kathrine sounded stressed. Tense and nervous. But also filled with anticipation.

"I took a few. I'll take some more in a minute."

"Turn on your computer," she said.

"You want to make sure that I actually take them?"

"Yes."

"Okay, I'll show you." Niels turned on his computer. It took a moment. Neither of them spoke as they waited.

"Hi," he said when he saw her on the screen. She was sitting in her usual place. Niels sometimes felt as if he knew that room—almost eight thousand kilometers away—better than any in their own apartment.

Niels took two pills. He hoped he wasn't approaching an overdose. He'd barely scanned the label on the package. "So. Are you satisfied?" He sounded a bit grumpy even to himself.

"You don't believe they'll work." The words practically shot out of her mouth.

"What do you mean?"

"Fuck! I can tell by looking at you, Niels. You don't believe in them. How hard can it be? Just think of how many people suffer from some sort of phobia. They take a few pills, and then they're back in business!"

"That's what I'm doing. I'm trying."

"Are you trying hard enough, Niels?"

Silence. He hesitated. Was there a latent threat in her voice? A hint of *this is your last chance* in her tone? He couldn't get that notion out of his head. Plenty of emotions were foreign to him, but paranoia was not one of them.

"It was one of the first things I told you when we met. That I have a hard time flying."

"That was a hundred years ago!"

"Do you remember what you said? That it didn't matter, because I was the whole world to you?"

"A thousand years ago!"

"Those were your very words."

"We have no children, Niels. And we've never been farther away than Berlin together."

Niels let that pass. He'd always been bad at arguing. Especially with Kathrine.

"Take a look at this, Niels." She pulled down the neck of her shirt to give him a glimpse of one of her breasts. "This is hard on me, too. I need intimacy. It's biology, you know. I feel like I'm withering away."

"Kathrine." Niels didn't know what to say. Sometimes the right tone of voice was enough. But not at the moment.

"I want you here tomorrow, Niels. You . . ." Her voice broke. "If you're not here tomorrow . . ."

"What?"

"I can't promise anything much longer, Niels."

"What do you mean by that?"

"You know what I mean."

"No, I don't! What the hell are you talking about?"

"You heard me. You have to be here tomorrow or else I can't promise anything. Good night, Niels."

They stared at each other. She was on the verge of tears, but she fought to hide her distress.

Then she cut the connection.

"Shit!" Niels had an urge to fling his wineglass at the computer screen, but he restrained himself. As always.

Loneliness overwhelmed him. All the oxygen seemed to have been sucked out of the room, or at least out of him. The phone rang again. He let it ring several times as he tried to pull himself together. He took a deep breath. He needed to sound positive. "Hi, sweetheart!"

"It's been a long time since anyone called me that."

It took Niels a couple of seconds to identify the voice. Hannah Lund. The astrophysicist.

"Sorry. I thought it was my wife calling."

"I know I shouldn't be calling you this late. It's an old habit from my days as a researcher. Back when I couldn't remember whether it was night or day. Do you know that feeling?"

"I suppose so." Niels could hear how exhausted he sounded.

"Your murders have been keeping me awake."

"My murders?"

"I've been giving them a lot of thought. Could we meet?"

Niels glanced at the clock. Just past two A.M. His alarm clock would go off in less than four hours. "I'm going on vacation. To South Africa. I'm catching a plane early in the morning."

"I've been wondering if there might be some sort of system," said Hannah. "I mean, if there might be numbers and distances that follow a specific pattern."

Niels tried halfheartedly to stop her. "But we're not involved in the investigation."

"Have you thought about it?"

"Thought about what?"

"A system. Maybe we could figure it out."

Niels went over to the window. The streets were dark. "You mean prevent the next murder from happening?"

"Of course, I'll need all the available information and data. But you must have a file on the case."

Niels was thinking. About Kathrine. "As I said—"

"You're not involved in the investigation. I understand. All right, I'm sorry for disturbing you, Niels Bentzon."

"That's okay. Good night."

"Good night, sweetheart."

She hung up the phone.

25

I t's one of the world's oldest civilian airports, built on a grassy meadow outside of Copenhagen. Europe's best-preserved airport in the years immediately following World War II. While most other airports had been heavily bombed, someone had held a protective hand over Kastrup. Higher powers? Coincidence? Or a result of the policy of collaboration with the occupying German forces?

"Did you say the international departures terminal?"

"Yes, please. Terminal three. I'm in a bit of a hurry," said Niels.

The sharp winter sun never rose high enough in the sky to keep it from glaring right in the eyes of the drivers. Niels put on his sunglasses, which were intended for Africa. He looked at the sky: a beautiful, clear deep-blue sky. An Airbus was taking off. Niels tried to suppress a growing feeling of nausea. Every year more than 260,000 planes took off from or landed at Kastrup. Millions of people arrived at the airport or departed from it. Niels had read all the facts. He was familiar with the statistics. He knew that when he got out of the cab in a moment, he ought to breathe a sigh of relief. The most dangerous part of his journey would be over. But the knowledge had no therapeutic effect on him. On the contrary.

"You'll be lucky if there's no delay." The cabdriver stopped the car. "My cousin was supposed to leave for Ankara yesterday. He's still sitting out here waiting."

Niels merely nodded, staring at the wing-shaped building of glass and steel looming in front of him. The climate conference was causing massive flight delays. For the eleven-day duration of the conference, Kastrup was the absolute hub of the world. As far as he'd been able to tell from the Internet, his flight wasn't affected. Most of the heads of state had already arrived. Some had even come and gone.

As soon as Niels entered the departure hall, he began to sweat. He went to the men's room. Swallowed a couple of pills and splashed cold water on his face. He looked at himself in the mirror. His face was sickly pale. The pupils of his eyes were big and shifting nervously, his expression tense.

"Are you okay, mister?"

Niels looked at the man in the mirror. A short, pudgy man from southern Europe with a friendly face.

"I'm fine. Thanks."

For a moment the man didn't move. Just long enough that Niels felt like telling him to quit staring. Finally, he left.

More water. Niels tried to get control of his breathing. He almost managed it, but then he was interrupted by another voice. This one coming from a loudspeaker.

"Last call for passenger Niels Bentzon, traveling on board SAS Flight 565 to Paris, departing at eight forty-five. Boarding at Gate eleven."

The fact that he had to change planes in Paris wasn't making things any easier. He would have to go through the whole hellish process twice.

Niels closed his eyes. Tried to shift tactics. Up until now he had been trying to pretend that nothing was happening. Now he tried the opposite. Tried to ground himself in the present moment. Telling himself to focus and act sensibly. Allow himself to feel the fear, fighting it out with common sense and statistics. Millions of people were always sitting up there in the skies. Good Lord, all he had to do was the same thing they did: sit in an airplane, have a cup of coffee, watch a movie, maybe doze for a while. Accept the fact—maybe even savor the idea—that we're all going to die. That didn't help. It wasn't the plane or death that frightened him. It was the notion of leaving Copenhagen.

Niels dried his face with a paper towel, took a deep breath, and tried to muster his courage. Then he left the restroom and headed for the gate. On his way through the almost deserted departure hall, he had an image in his mind of a condemned man taking his last steps toward the gallows.

He decided that he would have preferred to be executed than go on board a plane.

"Thank you. Have a good trip."

The flight attendant, brimming with confidence, gave him her best professional smile and allowed him to enter the aircraft. No one paid any attention to him. No disapproving glances because he'd arrived so late. Everyone was busy with their own thoughts. Niels found his seat and sat down. Calm and composed, he stared at the seat in front of him. Everything was fine. He was in control. His breathing was almost normal. Maybe the pills were working after all.

Then he caught sight of his hands resting in his lap.

They were twitching as if being jolted by electricity. And the sensation was spreading. He could feel it. Spasms slowly crept up his arms to his shoulders, across his chest, and then down to his diaphragm. All sound around him disappeared. He looked about in panic. A little girl, maybe five years old, turned to stare at him with childish fascination. Her lips were moving. He heard what she was saying.

"What's that man doing, Mommy?"

He saw the young mother hush her daughter. Telling her to stop looking at him, not to pay him any mind.

Niels stood up. He had to get out. Now.

He was about to throw up. And he was sweating again. He staggered down the aisle as if he were drunk but doing his best to hide the fact. He fought to maintain his dignity in an impossible situation.

"You can't leave the aircraft, sir." The stewardess who had greeted him a moment ago was staring at him. Her smile was a bit more strained.

Niels refused to stop. The plane was shaking; the engines had started up.

"You can't—" She looked over her shoulder.

A steward came rushing up. "I'm sorry, sir, but you need to return to your seat."

"I'm a police officer."

Niels continued along the aisle. He was only a couple of yards from the door.

"Did you hear what I said, sir? I need to ask you to go back to your seat."

He took hold of Niels's arm. Quietly and calmly. Displaying an admirable patience. Niels roughly shoved him away and grabbed hold of the door handle.

"Now, look here." The steward again. Still trying to be patient.

Niels took out his police ID. "Copenhagen Police. I need to get off the plane." His voice quavered.

Someone whispered to the stewardess, "Go get the captain."

"I need to get off!" Niels shouted.

Utter silence. The other passengers were all staring at Niels. The steward looked at him. Maybe there was a trace of sympathy in his eyes.

Then he nodded.

———— ◆ ————

The wheel on his suitcase was crooked, and Niels had to fight to keep it rolling in the right direction. He swore under his breath. It had taken forever to locate his suitcase and get it off the plane. The baggage handlers had made it plain that they weren't happy about the extra work he had caused them.

Niels finally gave up. He stopped and picked up his suitcase. Then he found a table and sat down to have a beer.

An uncomfortable seat. The nausea wasn't quite gone. He wasn't in the mood for alcohol; he just wanted to feel better. He wished he were dead. Why couldn't he have stayed on the plane? He wanted to phone Kathrine, but shame was holding him back.

A new chair, this one much more comfortable. A proper seat designed for long periods of waiting. Niels couldn't remember changing places. He was holding his cell phone in his hand. Kathrine. "Beloved Kathrine. I'm not giving up."

She would have to make do with a text message.

He looked out the enormous windows. A Boeing 737 effortlessly took off from the tarmac.

Half an hour went by. Maybe more. Planes landed and departed. People headed off on their travels, people arrived. Businesspeople, tourists, representatives of nongovernmental organizations, government officials, climate negotiators, politicians, journalists, members of various environmental organizations. Niels studied them. Some seemed already tired and discouraged; others were full of hope and anticipation. All of them were in motion. Going from one place to another.

While he was simply sitting.

Niels got up and went over to the line in front of the Alitalia ticket counter. He wasn't consciously thinking; his brain had stopped. Everything had been erased. All the thoughts he'd had about this trip, all the carefully executed preparations, all the statistics. What use were they now? What good had they done him?

"Excuse me, are you Italian?" he asked in English. Niels was as surprised by his words as the young man he had addressed.

"Yes, I am."

"Could you make a phone call for me? It's urgent."

Niels didn't give him time to reply, just punched in the number on his cell and handed it to the man.

"Ask for Tommaso di Barbara. Tell him to fax over everything he has on the case to Niels Bentzon. Here's the number." Niels pointed to the number on his business card.

"But—"

"Everything!"

26

N iels? I thought you were on vacation." Anni glanced up from her computer screen, but she didn't look as surprised as she sounded.

"Maybe later." Niels threw out his arms. "You said it was here."

"What?"

"The fax from Venice."

"Oh, right." She stood up.

"You don't have to get up." Niels tried to stop her. "I can get it myself."

She ignored what he said and moved past him. Niels was annoyed. Anni's curiosity was legendary and usually rather charming. But not at the moment.

The station was practically deserted. The open office plan, the flat screens, the ergonomic office chairs, the new desks that could be raised and lowered, expensive Scandinavian Design models, all seemed better suited to an advertising agency than a police station. But was there that big a difference? Niels had started to doubt it. Marketing terms like "image protection" and "brand identity" were heard more often at their meetings than good old-fashioned police terms. Their superiors had become celebrities. The police chief had become such a media darling that only stand-up comics and pop stars could compete with him. Niels had no idea why. The police force had become one of society's most important political battlegrounds. Countless investigations were testimony to that fact. The police reform of 2007 had provoked more headlines than all of the recent tax reforms put together. Every third-rate politician whose spin doctor had whispered in his ear that it was important to take a stand in the debate could reel off even in his sleep a rock-solid opinion about everything pertaining to the police. Even if the politician's knowledge of police work was based solely on a few episodes of *Miami Vice*.

"Just wait till you see the fax." Anni gave Niels an excited look as she opened the door to the computer room. "I've never seen anything like it."

The computer room didn't have much to do with computers. In fact, it was the only place at headquarters—aside from the restrooms—that didn't contain a single computer. So its name was a common source of amusement. But the space did contain printers, fax machines, and photocopiers, and it was filled with the smell of leftover chemicals, ozone, and toner dust that unquestionably produced nausea and headaches after only a few minutes of exposure.

"There it is." Anni pointed. "As thick as a phone book!"

Niels stared. He didn't know what he'd been expecting, but certainly not a stack of several hundred pages.

"What's it all about?" Anni tried to make her interest sound casual.

"It's just material for a case."

"Well, it can't be an ordinary case." She tried not to smile. "Does it have to do with the climate conference?"

"Yes." Niels gave her a solemn look, thinking that no matter what came out of the climate conference, no matter the results of the efforts made by the world's leaders to save the earth from going under, it would not be in vain. Because without the advent of the climate meeting, Niels wouldn't have been able to keep his secretary from talking about this fax.

"Is there a box I can use?" Niels looked around.

Anni handed him a cardboard box filled with printer paper. He took it without a word but with a growing sense of guilt about the fact that Anni had become like a surrogate mother for him. Niels emptied the box and filled it with the faxed pages. He managed to glance at a couple of the pictures. Forensic photographs from an autopsy. Strange marks on the back of the body. A list of the murder victims. In China and India.

"Look at her dress. Aren't they due to arrive tomorrow?"

Anni was looking at a small TV screen. Barack and Michelle Obama emerging from *Air Force One* someplace on the globe.

"She's got quite a rear end. Is that supposed to be sexy?" Anni asked, turning to Niels.

"I guess. If you're into that sort of thing."

Michelle Obama waved from the stairway, obviously used to this type of scene. Who was she waving to? The huge cadre of security agents?

Barack Obama stepped onto the tarmac and shook hands with a bald man, presumably the American ambassador in whatever country they were in. Niels couldn't take his eyes off Obama. There was something sad in his expression in spite of the big smile. Niels had noticed the same thing the very first time he saw Obama on TV during a debate with Hilary Clinton. A trace of something sorrowful. As if he harbored some doubt about his goals. Not about his will to carry them out, to create a better world. But he seemed to doubt whether the world was actually ready.

A light was on in Sommersted's office, which surprised Niels as he emerged from the computer room. He set the box filled with the faxed pages on the floor, using his foot to shove it under a desk so nobody would see it. India and China. They were the last two murders on the list from Venice. Hadn't that terrorist also been in India?

"Watch yourself," he heard Anni warning him. "He's in a foul mood today."

"Isn't he always?"

Niels knocked on the door and went in. Sommersted was standing next to his desk, still wearing his overcoat. He seemed to be looking for something.

"Yes?" He didn't bother to look at Niels. "I'm on my way out the door."

His tone of voice was hostile. He was clearly a man under pressure. A man who hadn't gotten enough sleep in a long time and whose head was filled with horror scenes of potential security disasters during the conference.

"About that man from Yemen who's wanted—"

"Stop!" Sommersted held up his hand.

Niels chose to ignore it and went on. "I couldn't help seeing the report yesterday. And I happened to notice his most recent destinations."

"What? No."

Sommersted's thoughts were someplace else. That much was obvious. He was out at the Bella Center. Out among all the heads of state he was supposed to keep safe.

"There's a connection with the case from Interpol."

"Bentzon." Sommersted sighed. He was a beast of prey who had decided to give his quarry one last chance. "The Hadi case is top-secret. It's not your concern. We don't need to start a panic right now, for God's sake. Can you imagine it? The combination of highly trained terrorists in Copenhagen with all the world leaders gathered out on Shit Island?"

"I'm not entirely positive," said Niels. "I'll admit that. But I do have my suspicions."

"No!" Sommersted gave up any attempt at self-restraint and raised his voice. "Forget it, Bentzon. Leave it to the others. Do you realize how many presidents and prime ministers will be out at the Bella Center in a couple of hours, expecting me to protect them? Brown and Sarkozy! The whole bunch of them. Even a madman like Mugabe has a right to expect not to be shot through the head while he's visiting Wonderful Copenhagen! Extremists, terrorists, mentally ill lunatics. They're all waiting for me to make a mistake."

"But . . ." Niels had already given up, but he made a last-ditch effort to get through to his boss. He was brutally brushed aside.

"And now the press wants to know why we made a gang of detained anarchists sit on the cold asphalt for a couple of hours. Two of them have apparently developed bladder infections. Do you see the problem here?"

Sommersted didn't wait for an answer but simply slipped past Niels in the doorway and left.

No, goddammit! Niels turned on his heel. This couldn't be right. There had to be a connection. India. Mumbai. Niels debated with himself as he walked back to Sommersted's office. He was a police officer. Hired to prevent and solve crimes. It was not his job to make Sommersted happy. The light was still on in his boss's office. Apparently, the shared responsibility for global warming hadn't penetrated the Copenhagen police force. Niels went in. The documents were still lying on the desk. Niels was surprised at Sommersted's carelessness; no doubt it had to do with stress. He found a profile shot of the man from Yemen. Abdul Hadi. And a slightly blurry photograph taken somewhere in Waziristan, a mountainous area on the border between Pakistan and Afghanistan. Niels was not particularly knowledgeable about international terrorism, but he knew that Waziristan was one of the terrorist hotbeds. The Muslim Brotherhood. It was mentioned several times in the documents. Hadi had been in contact with a leading member of the Muslim Brotherhood. It didn't say how close this contact was, but the fear was that he was a potential terrorist.

Niels looked up. Nobody was watching him. Everyone's eyes were directed at the Bella Center.

He leafed through the file. The Muslim Brotherhood. He ran his eyes over the pages: a political-religious organization founded in Egypt in 1928 by Hasan al-Banna. Their goal was to turn Egypt into an Islamic society, a society based on strict Islamic law, following the same pattern as what had been created on the Arabian peninsula by the Wahhabi brothers. In spite of publicly taking a stand against violence, the organization had been banned many times in Egypt. While in prison during the 1950s, one of its most important members, the now deceased Sayyid Qutb, had written the manifesto *Milestones,* regarded today as a call to arms for Islamic terrorism. Osama bin Laden's right-hand man—and the second in command of Al-Qaeda—Dr. Ayman al-Zawahiri had also started his terrorist career as a member of the Muslim Brotherhood. Ever since its founding, the organization had exerted enormous influence and still did, not only in Egypt but in large parts of the Muslim world. The group had been linked to countless terrorist actions, and it openly supported attacks against Israel, which it regarded as the primary enemy. The Islamic Hamas organization in Gaza originated with the Brotherhood. The Muslim Brotherhood was best known for its part in the assassination of Egypt's president Anwar Sadat on October 6, 1981. He was murdered in retaliation for having reached out in 1978 to the hated Israeli leader Menachem Begin, and for signing the official peace agreement with Israel.

Niels paused. Then he leafed through some more pages until he found what he was looking for. The report of Abdul Hadi's travels until he managed to slip into Sweden. There were obvious gaps, though not many. Niels studied the report carefully. It was thought that Abdul Hadi had been sighted on board a train in Sweden. What was he doing in that country? Was Sweden his final destination, or was he traveling farther? He had arrived by plane from Brussels, and before that—it was assumed—he'd made a side trip to India. Niels was surprised. How was it possible that a man who was the subject of a worldwide manhunt could travel freely, going wherever he pleased? It was a well-known fact that international security procedures left a lot to be desired. The public might not know that, but the police did. In spite of massive improvements in the security measures in most of the world's airports—iris scanners, fingerprints, stricter rules regarding passports and identification documents—the terrorists always seemed to be one step ahead. Or maybe there were so many of them that even though some were caught, others would always manage to slip through.

Niels discovered that he was talking out loud. "What were you doing in India?" he murmured.

No answer. Hadi stared up at him from the photograph. Niels recognized his expression. That was how someone looked right before he pulled the trigger.

"And why are you coming to Denmark?"

27

Christianshavn—Copenhagen

The traffic light on Amagerbrogade wasn't working.

Niels didn't notice that he'd been stopped at the red light for a very long time until the car behind him began honking aggressively. The driver finally drove around him, giving him the finger as he passed. Niels punched in a number on his cell phone and waited. Hannah answered, sounding as if she'd been asleep.

"Niels Bentzon here. Could I drop by?"

"Right now?"

"I've had all the information pertaining to the case faxed over to me. And I might as well warn you, there's a lot of material."

"I thought you were leaving on vacation."

"It's quite comprehensive," he said, ignoring her remark. "Covering all the details. Just like you asked for."

No reply. Niels was about to go on, but before he could speak, she said, "Do I have time to take a bath?"

"I'll be there in an hour."

He ended the conversation, picturing Hannah in the bathtub. Was that why she'd mentioned it? He reached Christmas Møller Square. Part of the area was inaccessible due to a couple of hundred climate activists who were gathering for an unauthorized demonstration. It looked cold to be walking around outside. The demonstrators were moving past the cars, carrying a big banner that said: LAST CHANCE. SAVE THE PLANET. Another one said: NOW OR NEVER. The box with the faxed pages sat on the front seat next to Niels. He opened it and looked at all the typed pages containing information about the murder victims, the crime scenes, and the times of death. Pictures of the victims. Pictures of the strange tattoos on their backs. Niels knew nothing about tattoos, but the images in the photos surprised him. Why would a killer go to the trouble of making such a complicated tattoo on the back of his victims? Tommaso had said they were numbers. Niels couldn't see it. He thought they looked more like a specific pattern. Some sort of abstract design.

A gap appeared in the crowd, which was gradually getting bigger and bigger. Niels continued driving across Christianshavn Torv toward the city. In his mind he kept seeing those strange tattoos. They had taken over his thoughts like an invading army, refusing to go away. On impulse, he made a U-turn, headed back the way he had come, and turned left onto Prinsessegade.

Christiania—Copenhagen

The shop called Tattoo Art was exactly where he remembered it. Niels had never been inside, but he was very familiar with the rest of the Christiania area. Like most other cops in Copenhagen, he had taken part in patrolling Pusher Street and making arrests. He parked the car and got out to look around. A couple of drunken Greenlanders were staggering about in front of the Nemoland bar. Stray dogs eyed Niels with curiosity.

He had a somewhat ambivalent attitude toward Christiania, although it was basically positive. The idea that a group of peace-loving hippies, almost forty years ago, had been able to take over an abandoned military area to create a social experiment was something that appealed to Niels. A free zone inside of a major metropolis. A village in the middle of Copenhagen. A different way of living. It was also in Christiania that he'd had some of his best experiences as a young police officer. He recalled being greeted with the greatest friendliness. Where else in the world would a cop be invited inside for a bottle of Christmas beer and rice pudding at four in the morning during the holiday season?

But the atmosphere had changed during the past ten years. Bikers and immigrant gangs had come down hard, taking over the drug market. The innocence of the hippie era had been replaced by a vicious criminality, with the drug trade now backed by gangster kingpins making big money. Violence and threats had become daily events. It had all come to a head in May 2006, when a nineteen-year-old man was brutally attacked and killed by a group of pushers just outside Christiania. Niels had not been involved in the case, but his colleagues had been deeply shaken by it. Rarely had they encountered such callous cruelty. The perpetrators, with ice-cold deliberation, had used clubs and iron bars to smash in the skull of the young man. It was an execution, pure and simple. A cynical liquidation meant to instill terror and serve as a warning. The case had made Niels change his view of the free zone. The social experiment had been derailed.

"Just give me five minutes."

The tattoo artist nodded in a friendly manner to Niels, who sat down to wait, studying the man. He looked like some sort of monster, with huge, colorful tattoos covering his body and most of his face. The muscles of his torso were about to burst the tight-fitting T-shirt he was wearing. He had rings through his nose and lower lip.

"Would you like a cup of coffee?" The piercing in his lip gave him a slight lisp.

"Sure. Thanks. Black."

The tattoo artist disappeared into a back room, leaving Niels on his own.

The shop was clinically clean. In that sense, it reminded him of a doctor's office. The walls were decorated with pictures of tattooed people. Dragons, snakes, women, and abstract designs. Several of the posters had Japanese characters underneath. Or were they Chinese?

"It's believed that people in Japan were tattooing themselves over ten thousand years ago. Pretty cool, huh?"

The tattoo artist was back. He handed Niels a cup of coffee. "They were called the Ainu. They tattooed their faces."

Niels gave him an inquiring look.

"Mummies with tattoos have been found in China. So it's not exactly a modern phenomenon." The man laughed.

"Have the same techniques always been used?"

"The techniques have developed over time. There are examples of ancient cultures that rubbed ash into open wounds. The Vikings used rose thorns. You have to suffer for beauty." Again that shrill, lisping laugh.

Niels smiled politely. "So what do you use today? From a purely technical standpoint?"

"Take a look." The tattoo artist nodded toward the machine used to make the tattoos. "There's a needle inside that tube. When you turn it on, the needle moves up and down, approximately a thousand times a minute. It's fucking awesome!"

"And what does it spray in?"

"It doesn't spray in anything. It inserts different-colored ink. The tattoo pigments are made up of water, glycerine, and tiny little crystals. Foreign bodies in all the colors of the rainbow."

"That doesn't sound healthy."

"Are you getting cold feet?" He smiled wryly. "Your coffee isn't healthy, either."

"But foreign bodies?"

"A few people develop problems. Sometimes the body tries to get rid of the crystals. That's not much fun. In rare cases the pigments can get into the lymphatic system, make their way into the lymph nodes and then into the bloodstream. But come on, I've never had any problems. And I should know what I'm talking about." He lifted up his T-shirt to display an impressive—and frightening—dragon head. "Do you want one like this? It really turns chicks on."

"No, thanks. But I'd like you to take a look at something."

The man watched with surprise as Niels pulled out a photograph from the pile of faxed pages. "What's that?" The tattoo artist looked with interest at the victim's back. "Is that the kind of design you want?"

"Can you tell me anything about this tattoo?"

"Tell you anything?"

"About the pattern. What is it? How was it made? How much time would it take to make something like that?"

The man didn't speak. Just stared at the photo. Then he said, "Come with me."

The back room was a whole different world. It looked like the home of a junkie. It was strewn with needles and dirty ashtrays. A half-empty bottle of whiskey stood on a filthy table. A puppy was asleep in a basket. The dog woke up and stared at Niels with interest.

"Do you want to buy him? He's an American Staffordshire terrier. He may look sweet right now, but make no mistake, in six months, he'll be able to kill a full-grown horse."

"What about the photo?" Niels said, nudging him back on track.

"Oh, right." The man sat down on the edge of a rickety table and turned on a lamp. "Let me tell you, people show up with the weirdest pictures of what they want tattooed. The other day a guy came in with a picture of his lover's vagina. He wanted to have it tattooed right above his dick so he could look at it while he jerked off."

Niels cleared his throat. The tattoo artist got the hint and fell silent as he studied the picture.

Niels looked at the man. He didn't know what he was expecting, but at least some sort of reaction. Which he didn't get. Nothing happened. The tattoo artist didn't say a word.

"So what do you think?" asked Niels at last.

"Where did you get this?" The man didn't take his eyes off the photo as he broke his silence.

"Can you tell me what it's supposed to be?"

No answer. Niels tried again. "What is it?"

"I have no idea, but . . ."

"But what?" Niels was having a hard time remaining patient. "Say something. How long would it take to make that tattoo?"

At last the tattoo artist raised his head and looked at Niels. "You're mistaken. This isn't a tattoo. At least I don't think it is."

"It's not a tattoo?"

The man shook his head and got up. "The lines are too fine. Besides, there's a lot of white among the other colors. White is almost never used in a tattoo."

"If it's not a tattoo, then what is it?"

The man shrugged. It wasn't his problem.

28

Helsingør—Denmark

The frozen fields were deserted and lonely. The trees lining the horizon looked like skeletons. An explosion of gray. A beautiful sight if melancholy had taken up residence in your heart. Otherwise, it was just dreary, and the only thing to do was to escape—as Kathrine had done.

Niels had the road all to himself. He was driving fast. Then he turned off the highway and onto a gravel track. This time he parked right in front of the house and climbed out of the car, holding the box under his arm.

Before he could knock, he caught sight of her down on the dock. She was standing in the same place as before. He walked down to the water.

Hannah didn't turn around. "I thought you were leaving on vacation."

"It got postponed. Are you catching anything?"

"There are no fish in this lake." She turned around and looked at him. "Although people claim it's filled with fish."

"They're not biting?"

She shook her head. "They can probably smell this." She held up her cigarette. "I'm only out here fishing because it's part of a bigger scheme of things."

"Scheme of things?"

"It involves doing things that I never did while my son was alive."

No hint of tears in her voice. Her composure remained unchanged, and that scared Niels. When people who seemed cold and reserved finally broke down, it happened with terrible ferocity, and they often tried to take other people along with them. That was something he knew from firsthand experience.

"I know it's cold in here." She turned up the thermostat. "That was one of the last things Gustav said before he left for Canada. 'We need to get the furnace fixed,' he told me. And then he was gone." She didn't sound bitter. She was merely making an objective statement. "So you've brought me a whole bunch of murders?"

"Yes."

"Is it too strong?"

"The coffee? No."

"I prefer it as thick as tar."

Niels opened the cardboard box. Carefully, he set the stack of papers on the coffee table.

"And these came from Venice?"

"From Tommaso di Barbara. The police officer you talked to on the phone. He sent the pages by fax this morning." Niels sat down on the sofa in front of the table.

"Have you read all of them?"

"I skimmed through them a bit. It's a detailed account of everything that's known about all the victims. What sort of lives they lived, what jobs they held, and what their accomplishments were. And, of course, everything about their deaths. Time, place, and the circumstances. It's . . ." Niels leafed through the pages until he came to the last one. "A two-hundred-and-twelve page report on life and death. Some of it was translated from Italian to English by using Google. But not all of it."

"Great." She gave him a brief smile.

"First I want you to take a look at this." Niels pulled out a picture showing the back of one of the victims and placed it on the table.

"What's that?"

"Vladimir Zhirkov's back. All the victims have some sort of mark on their back. A tattoo or a symbol of some sort."

"The same symbol?"

"I think so. Tommaso said they're numbers, but I can't see it."

Hannah squinted. Maybe she was skeptical. Or maybe surprised. She pulled out a drawer and found a pair of reading glasses, +1.5 power with a Statoil logo on the frames. The price tag was still on them. She studied the photo. "Are you sure they all have something like this on their back?"

"Yes. Here's another example. The back of Maria Saywa from Peru. Murdered on May twenty-ninth of this year." He placed the picture of Maria Saywa on the table next to the picture of Vladimir Zhirkov. Even though the images were dark, the marks could definitely be seen.

Hannah was holding a magnifying glass. It had come from the same drawer as the glasses, along with an unmistakable smell of marijuana.

Niels studied her. The arch of her nose. The tiny little hairs barely visible on the back of her neck. Niels's eyes kept roaming, and Hannah ran her other hand along her throat, as if she could feel his gaze on her. Several seconds passed. Or maybe it was several minutes. Niels shifted position impatiently. A few swans were making a ruckus out on the lake.

"Can you see anything?" he asked.

"This is really crazy." She didn't look up. Just automatically lit another cigarette.

"What do you mean?"

"Who did this?" She blew a cloud of smoke over the table. "The killer?"

Niels moved closer. "What do you see?"

She ignored his question. Apparently, he was expected to earn an answer. Niels was about to ask his question again when she started murmuring: "Hebrew, Arabic, Indian, Urdu, Devanagari . . ."

Niels stared at her. In a whisper she was intoning: "Mesopotamian, the vigesimal system, Celtic numbers, hieroglyphic numbers, Babylonian numbers . . ."

"Hannah." Niels raised his voice. "What's going on?"

"They're all numbers. Nothing but numbers."

"Where?"

"He's right. The man I talked to."

"Tommaso?"

"Yes. They're numbers. This one is the number thirty-one. Vladimir Zhirkov."

"Thirty-one?"

"It's the number thirty-one in various number systems. In tiny little numbers. It looks like small broken blood vessels under the skin. As if the blood vessels formed the number thirty-one."

"How would that be done?"

She shrugged. "I'm not a dermatologist. But . . ." She changed her mind and fell silent.

"But what?" Niels again sounded impatient.

"I know that the surface of all the blood vessels is formed by a so-called single-layer epithelium. It's called the endothelium."

"Is there anything that you don't know? Sorry. Go on."

"As I was saying, I'm not an expert, but if the endothelium is damaged, the blood comes into contact with other cellular and tissue components—" She stopped abruptly. "No, I can't tell you anything more. I don't really know what I'm talking about. I have no idea how those numbers were made."

"And you're sure that it says thirty-one?"

"I'm positive. I know quite a few different number systems."

"It's the same number repeated over and over? Thirty-one?"

She didn't answer as she looked again at the photo.

"Hannah?"

She nodded. "Yes. Thirty-one. Just thirty-one."

"What about the other one?" asked Niels. "The woman from Peru. Maria."

Hannah studied the pattern on the back of Maria Saywa. "It's a six. The number six written out in hundreds of different number systems. Systems that are used today and systems used in distant places in ancient times. The images aren't clear, so it's hard to see, but this man . . ." She took out another picture from the box and held it up. "He has the number sixteen on his back in hundreds of variations. I recognize the hieratic number."

Niels looked at the photo and searched through the faxed text. "Jonathan Miller. American researcher found at the McMurdo Station in Antarctica on August seventh of this year. But . . ." He put down the picture of Miller, not sure what to say. "How many number systems are there?"

"In every era, every culture has had a need to count. To systematize the world and create an overview. The Greeks, the Romans, the Egyptians, the Indians, the Arabs, the Chinese. All of them have number systems that originated long, long ago. With myriad variations. Bones have been found from the Stone Age, marked with tiny scratches that constitute numbers. The cuneiform from Mesopotamia is from circa 2000 B.C. Initially, numbers were just used for counting, but people soon realized that they were also symbols."

"*Were* symbols? Or do you mean that people made them into symbols?"

"It's that old dilemma of which came first, the chicken or the egg." She shrugged. "Do we create number systems, or do they already exist? And if two plus two equaled four before there were any people around, who then created the system? For the followers of Pythagoras, numbers were the key to the laws of the cosmos. They were symbols in a divine world order."

"That's pretty impressive."

"According to Novalis, God could just as well reveal Himself in mathematics as in any other science. Aristotle said that numbers not only signify a specific quantity, they also possess inherent qualities. He called them the 'qualitative structures' of numbers. Odd numbers were masculine. Even numbers were feminine. Other Greeks talked about spiritual numbers."

The cat jumped up on the table, and Hannah just as quickly removed her without interrupting what she was saying. "Mathematics is filled with mysteries. Mysteries that can solve our problems. That was what Gustav was talking about when he made the statement that brought you here."

"That it will be a mathematician who saves the world?"

"Just think of the work they're doing over there in the Bella Center. Curves, graphs, numbers. Nothing but numbers. The correct interpretation of numbers determines whether we live or die. It's life or death. That's something that every scientist understands. That was why Tycho Brahe got his nose sliced off in a duel."

"Because of numbers?"

"Because he claimed that so-called complex numbers existed. And his adversary claimed that they didn't."

"Who was right?"

"Tycho Brahe. But he lost his nose."

She paused to allow Niels to consider this. "Have you ever heard of Avraham Trakhtman?" She didn't wait for him to answer before going on. "A Russian immigrant to Israel. A professor of mathematics, but he couldn't find a job, so he ended up working as a bouncer in a club. While he stood there trying to calm down hordes of drunken teenagers, he solved one of the greatest mathematical mysteries in recent times: *The Road Coloring Problem*. Does that mean anything to you?" She was breathing so hard that she seemed almost winded.

"Not really."

"The question is extremely simple: A man arrives in a strange city to visit a friend, but he doesn't know where the man lives. The streets have no names, but the friend phones and offers to guide him by saying only, 'Right, left, right, left.' Can the man find his friend's house based on these instructions, regardless of location?"

"If he's lucky."

"The answer is yes. I'll spare you the proof. Are you familiar with Grigori Perelman? He's the Russian who solved the Poincaré conjecture."

"Hannah!" Niels raised his hands in the air like a cowboy surrendering.

She sighed. "Okay. Sorry." She pushed back her chair and looked out at the water, where a couple of motorboats had come into view.

Niels got up. He wanted to ask a lot of questions, but there were so many that they seemed to be colliding in his mind, and he ended up not asking any of them. Hannah was the one who broke the silence.

"But why do the victims have these numbers on their backs?" That was the scientist speaking.

It was the police officer who took over. "And who made those marks?"

Hannah sighed, glancing at her watch and at the stack of papers. Then she smiled. "You've been here almost an hour, and we haven't even started reading yet."

Homicide case: Sarah Johnsson

Niels straightened all the pages into a neat stack on the coffee table. It looked like an oversize brick.

"All these pages are about the murder cases?" Hannah lit a cigarette.

"I think so." Niels cleared his throat. "Sarah Johnsson, forty-two years old. Thunder Bay."

"Does this mean she was the first one to be killed?"

Niels shrugged. "Maybe. For now it just means that she was the first person mentioned in the faxed pages. Here's what she looked like." He placed on the table a photo of a woman with a pageboy haircut and a mournful expression. "She died on July 31, 2009. So she wasn't the first," he said. "The woman from Peru was murdered in May."

"Thunder Bay?" Hannah stared at the big world map that she'd spread out in front of her.

"Canada. On Lake Superior. One of the biggest lakes in the world."

Hannah searched for a moment, then got out a black marker and put an X where Thunder Bay was located.

"Sarah Johnsson was a doctor at a hospital. She lived alone, she was unmarried, and she had no kids."

"Is the text in English?"

"Part of it. The list of basic facts, anyway. I think some of the report is in Italian."

"All right. What's next?" Hannah was ready with her marker.

"There's more about Sarah." Niels scanned the page. "A lot more, in fact. I think this is an obituary from the local newspaper."

"Obtained by the Italian policeman?"

"Apparently. It says that she completed her medical training at the University of Toronto in 1993. There's also an interview in English."

"With Sarah Johnsson?"

"Yes." Niels leafed through more pages.

"She's quite beautiful," said Hannah, staring at the photo. "She looks like Audrey Hepburn."

"Wait. I was wrong. The interview is with someone she studied with. Megan Riley."

"Why was she interviewed?"

"It looks like some sort of transcript. Maybe from a radio interview *about* Sarah Johnsson."

"Why did the Italian send that to you?"

"Good question. Megan Riley describes Sarah as 'antisocial, a bit weird, with a difficult love life. Nice, but she never seemed to be really happy.'"

"Poor girl," said Hannah with sympathy.

Niels nodded. "Look at this. Tommaso even got pictures of Sarah as a child. If this is her, that is."

Hannah looked at the picture of a six-year-old girl perched awkwardly on a swing.

"These pages look like various statements from doctors and psychiatrists," Niels noted.

"Aren't those types of reports confidential? The Italian policeman couldn't have gotten access to those on his own."

"Yes, he could have," said Niels. "If he was persistent enough." He scanned the signatures. Some of them were illegible. "Something must have happened to Sarah in 2005. She began showing signs of psychological instability. Anxiety attacks, insomnia, paranoid tendencies."

"Is there any cause given?"

Niels shook his head and went back to the faxed pages. "Wait a minute. I think I overlooked something in her obituary. Maybe this means something: She was fired from her job in 2005 as the result of an incident that got a lot of attention in the local press."

"What kind of incident?"

"It doesn't say. Give me a minute." Niels fumbled with the pages. "Okay, here's something about it. A newspaper clipping." He considered reading the English out loud, but it was a long article, and he was uncertain of his linguistic abilities.

"What does it say?"

"It says that Sarah Johnsson was fired, effective immediately, when it came out that she had administered an unapproved medication to save the life of a boy who was thought to be incurably ill. The boy recovered, but since the incident had major professional repercussions and prompted considerable criticism, the hospital directors felt they had no option but to fire the doctor."

"An unapproved medication?"

"That's what it says. As far as I know, it can take up to fifteen years to get new medicines approved, and Sarah Johnsson couldn't wait that long. So she broke the rules and saved the boy's life."

"And that had something to do with her subsequent paranoid tendencies?"

"Where are the medical reports?" Niels was looking through the pages. "It doesn't mention anything about that. It just says that her paranoia grew more and more pronounced and that in both 2006 and 2008 she was admitted to the Lakehead Psychiatric Hospital in Thunder Bay. A psychiatrist by the name of Dr. Aspeth Lazarus characterized Sarah as 'periodically almost totally crippled by anxiety. With a growing feeling that someone was out to get her.'"

"Out to get her? Who was out to get her?"

"It doesn't say. But whoever it was, they succeeded, because on July thirty-first, Sarah was found dead in her car in front of the Sobey supermarket. 'The police have refused to rule out . . .'" Niels skimmed over the rest of the article and translated: "They have refused to rule out the possibility of murder, but no arrests have been made in the case. It may have been poison."

"Poison?"

"Yes."

"Does it say anything else?"

"It says that Sarah Johnsson was buried in Riverside Cemetery in Thunder Bay."

"What about the pattern on her back? What does it say about that?"

Niels read some more, then went back to the previous pages. "There's nothing. Wait a minute. Here's an excerpt from an autopsy report. 'Skin eruption or rash on the back.'"

"Could that be why the police suspected poison as the cause of death?"

"Probably. But the case has been closed."

Hannah nodded and put out her cigarette. Niels got up and walked across the room. When he reached the far wall, he turned around and came back. "I don't understand it," he said without looking at her. "Why did Tommaso di Barbara collect so much material?"

Niels sat down again. The wicker chair creaked under his weight. Then there was silence in the room.

"Shall we go on?" asked Niels after a moment. "Do you think there's any point to all this?"

"Let's look at the next case. Open up the Dead Sea Scrolls again, so to speak."

"Okay. Murder number two, based on the order in which the pages were sent. The next one is in the Middle East."

Homicide case: Ludvig Goldberg

This time Niels sat down on the floor and spread out all the material so it looked like pieces of a jigsaw puzzle: twelve pieces covered with text that formed a picture of Goldberg's life and death.

"So what do we have?" asked Hannah.

"Everything, as far as I can tell. Obituaries. Diary excerpts. Interviews. Something that looks like a poem. But a lot of it is in Hebrew. He looks quite nice." Niels handed her a picture of Goldberg. Dark eyes with a worried expression. Intellectual glasses. A narrow face with delicate features.

"What's that?" Hannah pointed at a slightly blurry section on one of the faxed pages.

"IDF. The Israel Defense Forces. His military papers, I think. He was once in prison."

"He doesn't exactly look like a soldier. Where should I put the X?"

"At Ein Kerem."

"Where's that?"

"A suburb of Jerusalem."

Hannah looked at him. Either surprised or impressed. "Have you done a lot of traveling?"

"Quite a bit. In my imagination."

She smiled, but Niels didn't notice. He was reading a police report. "Ludvig Goldberg was found dead on June sixteenth of this year. He was lying in a . . ." He stopped reading and crawled across the floor to another page. "We'll start down here. With the obituary."

"From a newspaper?"

Niels looked at the pages. "From the Shevah Mofet secondary school in Tel Aviv where he worked as a teacher. Written in rather dubious English."

"Maybe the Italian tried to translate it himself," Hannah suggested. "Or used Google."

"Maybe. He was born in 1968 and grew up on the kibbutz Lehavot Haviva near the town of Hadera. His family comes from Ukraine. His mother is from . . ." Niels gave up on trying to read the whole thing aloud. "There's a long section about where all of his ancestors were from."

"Family sagas are very popular in the Middle East," said Hannah, then added drily, "Take the Bible, for example."

Niels was reading a different section now. The page that was blurry and partially illegible. "This *is* a military report. He was suspected of being homosexual." He looked up. "That's what it says. Without comment. Goldberg was apparently in prison after breaching some sort of regulation."

"What did he do?"

"I can't tell. But he was sentenced to a year in a military prison, so it must have been quite serious. There's also an excerpt from an editorial in the *Jerusalem Post* from 1988, in which Ariel Sharon—"

"*The* Ariel Sharon?"

"I assume so, yes. Ariel Sharon calls Goldberg 'everything this country doesn't need.'"

"So the crime he committed must have provoked a lot of attention."

Niels nodded.

"What does it say about his death? Is there an autopsy report?"

Niels looked through the pages. "No, but there's something else," he said. "An excerpt from a speech given by someone named Talal Amar on January 7, 2004, at Birzeit University in Ramallah and printed in *Time* magazine."

"Talal Amar? Who's that?"

Niels shrugged. "He said, 'In the Middle East you never know what the future will bring, but after standing next to Mr. Rabin and Mr. Arafat while they shook hands in front of the White House, I'm quite optimistic. In fact, my hope for the future was already born back in 1988, during the intifada, when a young Israeli soldier disobeyed orders and released me and my brother from an Israeli detention camp and thereby saved us from years in prison. I will never forget the look in the soldier's eyes when he released us. Until that day all Israelis were monsters to me. But from that moment I knew they were humans, just like me.'"

"Rabin and Arafat," said Hannah. "He's talking about the peace accord. What does Goldberg have to do with that?"

"Or rather, what does Talal Amar have to do with it?"

"Presumably a lot. Otherwise he wouldn't be interviewed in *Time* magazine. Or be standing in front of the White House when the accord was signed. He must have been one of the Palestinian peace negotiators."

"Here it says something about how Goldberg died." Niels read through the text to himself before going on. "It says from an 'unknown source.' I'll do my best to translate it. 'In the days leading up to his death, Goldberg was in Ein Kerem, visiting the artist couple Sami and Leah Lehaim. Goldberg seemed to be unwell. He complained of pain in his back and thighs, and according to Leah, he seemed paranoid. As if someone were after him. On the evening of June twenty-sixth, Goldberg stepped outside to smoke a cigarette. When he didn't return, Sami Lehaim went out to look for him. Goldberg was lying on the gravel outside the house. He was dead.'"

"Does it say anything about the mark on his back?"

Niels searched through the pages. "Not from what I can see. No cause of death is given, but it was designated a homicide."

"Why's that?"

Niels shrugged. "Maybe he had enemies."

"It was probably Sharon who killed him." Hannah smiled. "Because of what happened in 1988."

"The incident in 1988." Niels was thinking out loud. "What if the young Israeli soldier who released Talal Amar was . . ."

"Ludvig Goldberg."

Niels nodded. For a moment, maybe for the first time since he had arrived, they looked each other in the eye.

Hannah said, "So that must be why the Italian policeman sent you the excerpt from Amar's speech."

Niels didn't reply.

29

T he veranda railing was covered with a thin layer of frost. Niels's breath formed little clouds in the cold. He looked at Hannah through the windowpane. She was leaning over the map spread out on the coffee table. There was something very attractive about her profile. She was no more than six or seven feet away from him, but she was in another world. She was staring at the twelve X's on the map. Niels thought about what they had just discussed. The fact that every X represented a Sarah Johnsson or a Ludvig Goldberg. A history. A fate. A life. Joys, sorrows, friends, acquaintances, and family. Each X was a story. With a beginning, a middle, and a sudden, brutal end.

A common eider duck dove into the surface of the sea. A moment later, it re-emerged, made a 180-degree turn, and headed south. Away from the wintry chill of Scandinavia. Niels watched it go with envy. He was trapped here, confined to an immense prison. What sort of psychological defect was serving as his prison guard? Fear? Trauma? Again he turned to look at Hannah. Somehow he felt as if he were in the process of discovering the answer to that question. He watched her use her cigarette to light another without taking her eyes off the map.

Niels's fingers were stiff with cold as he took out his cell. A text message from Anni, asking him whether he'd contribute to a gift for Susanne from the archives division. She was turning fifty on Thursday. They wanted to get her a rowing machine or a certificate to a health spa in Hamburg.

"My beloved" was how he'd labeled Kathrine in his list of contacts. He tapped on her number. "You have reached Kathrine at DBB Architects." He'd heard that message in English at least a thousand times, but he still listened to the very end. "I'm unable to take your call right now, but please leave me a message." Then she switched to Danish. "And if it's you, Mother, just be a dear and leave me a message."

"Kathrine. It's me." Niels took a deep breath. "Well, I guess you can see that it's me calling. I can fully understand why you don't want to talk to me. I just want to say that this case I'm working on . . . I have a feeling that . . . I know it probably sounds stupid, but I feel like I'm on to something really important."

Niels ended the call. He was right—it sounded stupid. But he couldn't think of anything else to say.

Homicide case: Vladimir Zhirkov

"Now we move on to Russia." Niels was again sitting on the floor. "Or to be more precise, to Moscow. Vladimir Zhirkov, forty-eight years old."

"Moscow. Okay." Hannah put an X on the map.

"He was a journalist and social critic."

"I didn't think people were allowed to criticize society in Russia." She sat down next to Niels.

"Zhirkov died on November twentieth of this year. According to a report from a Russian human rights organization called Memorial, he was incarcerated in the infamous Butyrka prison in Moscow."

"What was he convicted of?"

Niels hesitated as he leafed through the report. "I don't know, but I'm sure we'll find out. When he was dying, he was discovered by a fellow prisoner named Igor Dasayev, who later recounted that during the afternoon and evening, Zhirkov had complained of being in pain. Dasayev called for help, and, er . . . there's a lengthy text here. Zhirkov reportedly shouted, 'There's a fire in me' and 'It's burning.' Shortly after that he was declared dead. No autopsy. The end." Niels got up from the floor and took a sip of cold coffee.

"What's that?" Hannah pointed to a page on which the text had been reduced so much that the tiny words were practically jammed against each other. "Is that in English?"

Niels nodded. "I can hardly read it. It's a newspaper article from *The Moscow Times*. From October 23, 2003. Listen to this: 'October 23, 2002, is remembered for the attack'—" Niels stopped abruptly.

"What is it?"

"I think I'd better translate it instead."

"I understand English."

"Yes, but I'm feeling embarrassed about reading English to an astrophysicist."

Hannah protested, but Niels insisted on picking his way through a translation. "'On October 23, 2002, forty Chechen terrorists, under the leadership of Movsar Barayev, attacked the Dubrovka Theater, located only a few minutes from Red Square. Approximately nine hundred unsuspecting theatergoers were inside, waiting for the performance to begin, when they found themselves the main actors in a terror drama that sent shock waves throughout Russia. Among the heavily armed terrorists were many women, most of them with explosives strapped to their bodies. The terrorists demanded that all Russian forces be immediately withdrawn from Chechnya. Barayev further underscored his demands by declaring: "I swear by Allah that we are more prepared to die than to live." The enormous amount of explosives and weapons that the terrorists had brought with them proved that they were ready to make good on their threats. Later investigations showed that there were at least a hundred and ten kilos of TNT inside the theater. It was estimated that about twenty kilos of TNT would have been enough to kill everyone in the theater. The Russian authorities had no idea what to do. Putin refused to yield, even as demands mounted from family members of the hostages insisting that something had to be done. One young woman, twenty-six-year-old Olga Romanova, succeeded in entering the theater in an attempt to persuade the captors to release the children. The terrorists replied by shooting her dead on the spot. Over the course of the next forty-eight hours, some of the hostages were released. A number of prominent citizens and organizations tried to initiate negotiations with the captors, including the Red Cross, Doctors Without Borders, and the well-known journalist Anna Politkovskaya. The situation finally became so critical that in the early-morning hours of Saturday, October 26, 2002, Russian Spetsnaz security forces pumped large quantities of fentanyl-based gas into the theater and then stormed the building. The battle didn't last long. Most of the people inside passed out from the gas. The security forces were taking no chances with the unconscious terrorists and shot every one of them, both men and women, through the head. Soon they were all dead. Afterward Russia was in shock. What at first glance looked like a victory turned out to be a tragedy of almost incomprehensible proportions. One hundred and twenty-nine hostages died, including ten children. Sixty-nine children were orphaned by the attack. Some of the hostages had been shot by the terrorists, but most of them had died from the gas or as a consequence of inadequate medical treatment given to the unconscious hostages after they were carried out of the theater. Only a few ambulances were on the scene, and people were not given the medical treatment they needed. Many suffocated in the overcrowded buses that took them away.'"

Niels found himself breathing hard as he set the article aside. He could picture the scene. The terrified children surrounded by terrorists, explosives, and loaded guns. The waiting. The fear. Maybe he'd seen a documentary on TV about the event.

"What does this have to do with Vladimir Zhirkov?" asked Hannah.

"Good question. Maybe he wrote the article. He was a journalist, after all."

"But the Italian police officer could have sent you any number of articles he wrote."

Niels nodded and leafed through the pages of fragmentary information. "Zhirkov grew up in the Moscow suburb of Khimki. His mother was a nurse. His father committed suicide when Vladimir was a boy. Here's a statement from an old team newsletter. I think it's from a hockey coach: 'Twelve-year-old Vladimir Zhirkov has great talent, but we need to work on his psyche if he's to have any hope of a career in ice hockey. He has a tendency to appear resigned and depressed.' I wonder why the Italian translated that? Here's an excerpt from an interview from . . . it doesn't say where it's from. A newspaper or a magazine."

"An interview with Zhirkov?" asked Hannah.

"Unfortunately, no. With a schoolteacher named Aleksey Saenko."

"Who's that?"

"He must have been one of the hostages in the theater. He says, 'The nights inside the theater were the worst. We sat there in the rows of seats as if attending the performance of a nightmare that would never end. There were three dead bodies in the orchestra pit. One of them was a young man who had tried to flee when the terrorists forced their way in. He'd been shot in the stomach. I could see his intestines hanging out. For hours he lay there moaning, and when he died, I thought: Finally. His moans were enough to drive us all mad. The children cried the whole time. Their parents tried to comfort them. The terrorists walked around among us. In the middle of the theater they had placed an enormous pile of explosives. And I mean really enormous. It was a mountain of death. I was sitting only a few yards away from it, and I thought: We're never going to get out of here alive. The leader of the terrorists, Barayev, seemed unbalanced. He had hand grenades strapped all over his body, and he might have been under the influence of some sort of drugs.'"

"'I have come to Moscow to die,'" exclaimed Hannah.

"What?" Niels looked up.

"That's what he said," Hannah explained. "I remember it. 'I have come to Moscow to die.' That statement was repeated in the Danish newspapers."

Niels continued reading: "'At one point an incident occurred between a hostage and one of the terrorists. It was a young mother who had snapped under the pressure. She was holding two little boys on her lap. One of them was only a baby. The other—he may have been five—was shaking with fear. Suddenly, the mother jumped up and began shouting at the terrorists. She called them psychopaths, murderers, and cowards who couldn't think of anything better to do than kill innocent women and children. The terrorists yanked the woman and her children into the aisle. The children screamed. There was no doubt they were about to be shot on the spot. But then a man stood up. He was sitting in the row behind the woman. A very young man. And he said that they could shoot him instead. I remember his exact words: "Let me take her bullet. I don't have as much to lose." A terrible silence settled over the theater. The whole place was holding its breath. The terrorist hesitated. Finally, he nodded and escorted the woman and her children back to their seats. The young man stepped forward. He seemed completely calm. That's the clearest image that I have from those horrific days inside the theater: the calm expression on the man's face as he stepped forward to be shot. Barayev went over to him. At the time I didn't know his name, but it was clear that he was the leader. He started yelling. About the crimes committed against the Chechen people. About the Russians' ruthless actions in Grozny. He was raging. His entire family had been wiped out by the Russians. Hatred flamed from his eyes as he raised his gun and pressed it to the forehead of the young man, and then . . . nothing. Nothing happened. He didn't pull the trigger. The young man looked him in the eye, calmly waiting for the inevitable. But nothing happened. The young man took his seat again as the other terrorists looked at each other in astonishment. Why hadn't Barayev shot the man? What had made him hesitate? Of course, I can't answer that question. But there was something about that young man. Some sort of aura about him. Something in his eyes. I have no doubt that on that day in the Dubrovka Theater, I witnessed a genuine miracle.'"

"This is a picture of the woman and her kids?" Hannah picked up a photograph.

"I assume so." Niels looked at the beautiful mother and her two children. The younger one was no longer an infant. "This must have been taken a couple of years after the tragedy."

"Are you thinking the same thing I am?" Niels couldn't tell whether that was a smile on Hannah's face.

"Yes," he said. "The young man in the theater was Zhirkov. He saved the lives of the mother and her children."

"So why did he end up in prison? He was a hero, after all."

Niels pondered the question. A long pause ensued. Hannah got up and went over to the map where the X's were scattered all over the world, seemingly at random.

"Maybe the experience inside the theater made him criticize the Russian system." Niels was thinking out loud. "And that's why the group called Memorial took an interest in him."

"You mean he was imprisoned because he was critical of the regime?"

"Possibly."

"Then who murdered him?"

Niels was holding another page. "This looks like a printout from an Internet paper. Possibly published by Memorial."

He translated what it said. "Officially, it's still a mystery as to who murdered Vladimir Zhirkov, but in the mind of the well-known social critic and chess genius Garry Kasparov, the matter is quite clear. He has stated, 'Putin killed Zhirkov.' But Zhirkov's fellow prisoner Igor Dasayev, who found his body, has a different explanation. 'On the night before the murder of Vladimir Zhirkov, I saw a man—the shadow of a man—standing right next to the sleeping Zhirkov. I don't know how he got into the cell, and I don't know what he was doing. But I'm pretty sure he had something to do with Zhirkov's death. It was very scary. Like in a horror movie.'"

"I think it sounds good when you speak English."

Niels smiled wryly. "How could anybody get into his cell? The Butyrka prison is heavily guarded. It doesn't sound credible."

"Does it say anything about the mark on his back?"

"Not as far as I can tell."

30

City Center—Copenhagen

The pastor was in his office. Abdul Hadi could see him clearly because the office faced the garden, which was open to the public. Abdul Hadi sat down on a bench a short distance away. A day-care center was right next to the church. There were children and staff inside. Why hadn't his fat cousin mentioned that fact? Not that it would have changed anything; he had decided on his plan, even though he regretted not being able to blow up the church. It would have looked good: the facade of the church facing the famous pedestrian street blasted to smithereens. Photos of smashed shop windows and a destroyed church with a dead pastor inside would have traveled around the world in record time. Copenhagen would have been added to the list on the new map of the world. A world map showing more and more victories. Things were moving in the right direction. The West's own decadence was about to make it implode. A life based on the exploitation of others and the perverse sexual pursuit of children. Children! Abdul Hadi could see it in all of the mannequins posed in the big shop windows. Tiny little breasts, not yet sexually mature; some of the mannequins weren't wearing any clothes at all, but apparently, that didn't bother anyone. People were walking around carrying big packages— their religion was centered around consumerism. On their most important religious holiday, they ate pork, gave a grotesque number of presents to their children, and complained that there was no democracy in the Middle East. Abdul Hadi regretted that his brother had ever come to this place. To Europe. But his death had to be avenged.

Abdul Hadi stuck his hand in his pocket. The knife was still there. His cousin had brought it along to the airport. His fat cousin had been embarrassed that Abdul Hadi had been forced to jump off the train, and he'd almost refused to drive Abdul across the bridge from Sweden to Denmark. *A sleeping army.* Abdul Hadi had chewed his cousin out. Shouted at him in the car when he said that he wasn't happy about driving him.

A Santa Claus walked past with children running after him. Abdul Hadi got up and headed for the church.

The church was empty. A big wooden cross with a Christ figure hung on the wall. This was where he planned to leave the pastor when he was done with him. It was also an image that would end up on the front pages of the Western newspapers. Iconography. That was important. People in the West defined themselves solely through external things. Clothes, appearance, mirrors, pictures, TV, advertisements. Abdul Hadi silently chanted the litany that had been instilled in him as he took note of the church's layout. People in the West had no interior dialogue, no conversations with God.

A woman said something to him but realized at once that he didn't speak Danish. Switching to English, she said, "The church is closing." She smiled and added, "Friday night there's a midnight service, if you're interested."

"Thank you."

He went back outside. The lights were off in the day-care center. The church was closed. Abdul Hadi walked around to the sacristy, where a window had been prepared for him. He would have preferred to say a prayer first, but there wasn't time. He had seen the pastor put on his jacket. It had to be now.

31

H annah poured the coffee, spilling a little on the table. She wiped it up with a dishrag. "Is that all?" she asked.

"Yes. Twenty-one cases."

"From Antarctica to Caracas. With detours to Africa and Asia." Finally, she looked at him. "In theory, there could be more."

"Why do you say that?"

She rummaged through the pages until she found the ones referring to the Russian. "He's number thirty-one."

"And?"

"There's also a number thirty-three and thirty-four. Russell Young in Washington, D.C., and Raj Bairoliya in Mumbai. But maybe it didn't stop there. And there are gaps in the number sequence earlier on." She looked at the map. "We have Chama Kiwete in Olduvai Gorge in Tanzania as number one. Maria Saywa in Peru is number six. Amanda Guerreido in Rio de Janeiro is number seven. Ludvig Goldberg in Tel Aviv is number ten. Nancy Muttendango in Nairobi is number eleven. There are lots of gaps. So where are they?"

"They may turn up later," Niels suggested.

"Did you know that Olduvai Gorge is the site where the first known human beings were found? That was where number one was murdered. Chama Kiwete."

Niels gave her a bewildered look and shook his head. "It's possible that the marks with the numbers weren't always noticed. Or that the cases weren't reported. There are countries so plagued by civil war and famine that they don't have time to pay attention to murders. So we can't rule out that a doctor or aid worker might have dropped dead in Somalia or elsewhere." He couldn't tell if she was listening or not.

"But that Tommaso di Barbara seems like a very thorough man. How on earth did he get hold of all this material?"

Hannah stared at the world map with the twenty-one X's showing all the reported murders. An array of fates. A world of murdered people swathed in the smoke from her cigarette. She was completely absorbed. She was talking to herself out loud, almost intoning the words: "Cusco, Rio, Tel Aviv, Nairobi, Johannesburg, Chicago, Thunder Bay, McMurdo, Beijing—"

"What about the dates of the murders?" Niels interrupted her.

"Seven days between each of them. As far as we can tell." She stared at the map. "Seven days between murders."

"Are there other similarities regarding the chronology? Were the murders committed at the same time of day?"

She hesitated, putting out her cigarette in a saucer. "It's hard to tell. Only a few of the murder reports list a specific time."

"Could they be in alphabetical order?"

"Just a minute."

"What?"

A minute passed. Hannah was sitting so still that Niels thought she looked almost like a wax figure from Madame Tussaud's.

At last she said, "Sundown. I'm almost sure of it." She leafed through the pages. Niels was on the verge of losing patience when she said, "The murders were committed at seven-day intervals, always on a Friday, and in all likelihood at the moment when the sun set in the respective location. That's how it looks to me."

"So what does that mean?"

No reply.

"What about the distances between the crime scenes?" he went on. "Three thousand kilometers. Does that fit?"

Still no answer. Niels sensed that his remarks were disruptive, but that didn't stop him. "Hannah. The three thousand kilometers . . . Or do you see any other connections?"

She raised her head. "I don't understand where the part about good people comes from, now that we've reviewed the material on all the victims— at least those we have reports for. Even though there's a preponderance of doctors and aid workers, not all of them were working to help others, not by a long shot. The Israeli was a schoolteacher and was once a soldier." She shook her head and changed tack. "What was it the Italian said about the Bible?"

"The thirty-six righteous people. It's apparently a Jewish myth."

"This is the first time I regret not paying more attention in religion class. What's the myth about?"

"I don't know." Niels shrugged. "I don't really think it's a viable lead."

"What would you consider a viable lead? Just so I understand your priorities."

"There's no logic in how the victims were chosen. It would be easy to point out people who have accomplished much better things."

"I don't know about that. But look at the map." She threw out her hands. "The locations don't seem to make sense, either, but we think there must be a connection. The question isn't whether it makes sense to *us*."

Niels looked at the map. She was right. The question was whether it made sense to the murderer. Hannah sat down in front of her computer. "*Thirty-six righteous men*—isn't that what it says in the file?" Before Niels could find the page, Hannah was in the process of reading the entry in Wikipedia: "Tzadikim Nistarim. It means the 'The Hidden Righteous Ones.' God's good men on earth. Some people believe that if even one of them is gone, all of humanity will be doomed."

"Which we can hereby confirm." Niels smiled.

Hannah went on, "Others say that all thirty-six have to die before humanity is doomed. Here's the link where you can read about it." With quick, childishly formed letters, she printed out the reference for Niels: http://en.wikipedia.org/wiki/Tzadikim_Nistarim.

"That'll take me an hour. Isn't his name Weizman?"

"Who?"

"The head rabbi at the synagogue on Krystalgade."

"But you can read about it here."

Niels got up. "It may be that most of the world gets its information from Wikipedia, but . . ." He stopped. He felt embarrassed, there was no doubt about it—as if he were a Škoda parked next to a Ferrari. Maybe that was why he sounded so annoyed when he continued. "But to solve a murder, we need to go out into the world."

He gathered up his things and placed them in a small briefcase. His pen, cell phone, appointment book, and notes. His eyes fell on the name Abdul Hadi. Niels took out his notebook and found what he'd written about Abdul Hadi. "The murder in Mumbai. When did that take place?"

Hannah paged through the case material. Niels went over to help her. "You wrote the date on the map."

"Oh, right." She located the X marked in India. "Raj Bairoliya. He was killed on December twelfth. Is something wrong?"

"No, it's probably just a coincidence."

"A coincidence?"

"I'll call you later." Niels was on his way out the door. Hannah said something to him, but he didn't hear what it was. He had only one thought in his head. Abdul Hadi was in Mumbai on December 12.

———◆———

Hannah watched Niels's car as he drove down the road. Again she looked at the license plate: II 12 041.

"That can't be a coincidence," she told herself.

32

Ospedale Fatebenefratelli—Venice

Eighty cents."

Tommaso's mother had not slept well during the past two hours. Each time Sister Magdalena had looked in on her, she was mumbling in her sleep. But now the sister heard for the first time what Tommaso's mother was actually saying. "Eighty cents."

"Why do you say that, Signora di Barbara?"

"He must not pay the eighty cents."

"Who must not pay it?"

"My son."

The old woman tried to free her arm from under the covers. Magdalena helped her, and Tommaso's mother grabbed her hand. There was still some earthly strength left in her body.

"You must tell him."

"All right. What should I tell him?"

"Tell him he must not pay the eighty cents."

"Why not?"

"Because then he will die."

"Where will he die?"

The old woman shook her head.

"What is the eighty cents for?"

Tommaso's mother was on the verge of tears as she replied, "I can't see it."

Sister Magdalena nodded. This was what often happened. People who were dying could see through a crack into the future and the afterlife—but never the big picture, only fragments. Signora di Barbara fell asleep again. Maybe in her dreams, she'd be able to see a more precise picture of what it was her son mustn't buy. Plenty of things cost eighty cents. Pasta. Milk. An espresso. Magdalena went back to her office and called Tommaso's number. He didn't answer.

33

The synagogue—Copenhagen

I t looked like a fortress.

That was Niels's first thought as he climbed out of his car on Krystalgade and looked at the synagogue surrounded by a high fence. Black wrought iron. Two civilian guards stood at either end of the street, stamping their feet on the pavement to keep warm. No doubt hired by the Jewish congregation. The graffiti on the wall explained why: FREE PALESTINE NOW! And underneath: THE WAILING WALL—THE PALESTINIANS ARE WAILING. Niels thought about all the resources that would be freed up if that ancient conflict could be resolved. Recently, there had been a debate on the radio about whether half of the open marketplace in Copenhagen called Israel Square should be renamed Palestine Square. Of all the conflicts on this earth, it was the Israeli-Palestinian dispute that was easiest to export.

Niels pushed the button on the intercom and waited. "Niels Bentzon from the Copenhagen Police," he said.

"Just a moment."

Niels waited some more. He read on the plaque that the building was over 175 years old. The twelve distinctive pillars represented the twelve tribes of Israel. "They've come a long way, those twelve tribes," said Niels to himself. The synagogue was set back a bit from the street, giving it a somewhat reserved appearance in comparison to the other nearby buildings. It had been controversial to build a Jewish house of prayer in the middle of Copenhagen. In that regard, things hadn't changed much since then. But these days the hot topic was whether the Muslims had the right to build a mosque in Copenhagen.

Finally, the gate opened with a faint buzz. Niels stepped inside, and the gate closed behind him. He was unsure which way to go, but then he heard a voice say, "Over here."

A smiling man in his early fifties was coming toward him from the small parking area on one side of the synagogue. Niels immediately recognized the rabbi from the interviews he'd done on TV, with his full beard sprinkled with gray.

"Niels Bentzon."

"Martin Weizman. It's cold today, isn't it?"

Niels nodded.

"Have you been to the synagogue before?"

"No, never."

The rabbi was still gripping Niels's hand. "Well, then, I'd like to welcome you. The word 'synagogue' just means 'meetinghouse' in Greek, so there's nothing really intimidating about it. Please come with me."

They walked around the side of the building. Weizman tapped in a password, and the door opened. "I know it seems like Fort Knox. After the bombing in 1985, we've had to tighten up security."

Niels remembered the incident. A powerful terrorist bomb that miraculously hadn't killed anyone but had caused considerable damage, including shattering all the windows of the nursing home behind the synagogue.

"You just need to put this on." The rabbi turned around. "It's our custom."

Niels looked with surprise at the yarmulke and then put it on.

"And your cell phone, please."

"Should I switch it off?"

"Just turn off the ringer. I do that myself. God didn't say anything about cell phones. He only mentioned sheep and goats."

Niels smiled and put his phone on vibrate. Another door. Then they entered the synagogue.

Niels tried to look impressed because he could feel the rabbi's eyes fixed on him. His first thought was that it looked like an unfamiliar church.

"It's one of Europe's oldest synagogues," the rabbi explained. "Most of them were destroyed in the war. In that regard, the Danish Jews were relatively lucky."

Niels nodded.

"Originally, the task of building a new synagogue in Copenhagen was given to the city architect, Peter Meyn."

"A new synagogue?" Niels said. "Was there one here before this one?"

"Yes." Weizman nodded. "On Læderstræde. But when parts of Copenhagen burned down in 1795, the synagogue was lost. Now, where was I?"

"Peter."

"Oh, yes. Peter Meyn. The city architect. His proposal was considered and found lacking. Instead, the task went to G. F. Hetsch, who was a well-known professor at the Art Academy. His design is what you see here." Weizman gestured with his hand. "He did a good job, don't you think?"

"I thought there would be an altar in a synagogue."

"Since we don't make offerings, we don't have an altar. We call the platform up there the *bimah*. It's there that we pray and read from the Torah. Or rather, sing." He winked, which surprised Niels. "It requires a bit of skill to know when and how to modulate the intonation. You can't tell from the text. And over there," he said, pointing, "is where we keep the Torahs. In the cabinet that faces Jerusalem. It's called *Aron Kodesh* or *Hekhál*. The high point in the service is when the Torah cabinet is opened and the scrolls are unfurled. *Ner tamíd* is the eternal light, reminding us of the menorah, or seven-armed candelabra, in the temple in Jerusalem."

"The Wailing Wall."

"Exactly. The Wailing Wall is the only thing left of the second temple. The Romans destroyed it in the year 70. The Babylonians demolished the first one in 586 B.C. But returning to the service: As you can hear, it's not so different from the Christian church service, except that our weekly service isn't held on Sunday but on our sabbath, which is Saturday morning."

The rabbi took a deep breath and looked at Niels. It was clear that he was used to giving this sort of mini-lecture. Niels knew that he often spoke to school classes visiting the synagogue.

"If I understood correctly, you want to talk about *Tzadikim Nistarim*. The thirty-six righteous men. Often called the *Lamed-Vav Tzadikim*. We can sit here." Niels followed him to the back of the synagogue. The rabbi smelled of tobacco. His index and middle fingers had taken on the color of nicotine. Niels gave him a quick summary of the case.

"To think someone is killing the people who are meant to save us all." Weizman shook his head. "Madness. Sheer madness. I wonder if this is what we deserve." He took a deep breath, drawing fresh oxygen into his lungs, and smiled. "So now you want to know . . ."

"As much as possible. What's the origin of the myth? If that's even the right word for it."

"If that's what you prefer to call it." The rabbi shrugged. "*Tzadikim Nistarim*. The thirty-six righteous men." He paused for a moment, thinking. "It comes from the Talmud."

"You mean Jewish mysticism? The Kabbalah?"

"No, no. We don't need to go there. Fortunately. If we did, we'd be old men before we were done. And above all, mystified." He chuckled. "We'll leave the Kabbalah to Hollywood—it's always good to have that in reserve if they can't come up with the proper ending for a movie." Again he chuckled.

"So, the Talmud?"

"Yes. The Talmud consists of the oral teachings of the Jews. Commentary to the Torah, which was originally written in Aramaic and not in Hebrew, although the two languages are related. Hebrew was given a rebirth when the state of Israel was established, and it became the official language. Before that time, it was used mainly for prayers and services. But we're getting away from the Talmud." The rabbi searched for the proper place to begin. "The Talmud consists of *Mishna* and *Gemara*. *Mishna* refers to the Word of God, exactly as Moses received it from the Lord. *Gemara* refers to the rabbis' comments and discussions regarding *Mishna*. There are two Talmuds: *Yerushalmi* and *Bavli*. Judaism is based on *Bavli*. The Talmud is an extraordinary work in twenty-one volumes, each of which is a thousand pages long. It was compiled after the destruction of the second temple in the year 70. Back then the rabbis were afraid that Judaism would be lost, so they decided to write down the laws and rules for living that formed the basis of Judaism at the time. It's a work that discusses everything under the sun. Political, legal, and ethical issues. You might call it a record of judicial protocols. How should we behave? Who is right in various contested cases?"

"For instance?"

"Quite banal things." The rabbi crossed one leg over the other in a calm, deliberate movement. "Let's say that a man has forgotten his cane at the marketplace and for some reason doesn't go back to get it until three months later. In the meantime, an old woman has been using the cane. Does she have the right to keep it? Or does it still belong to the man? What does it mean to own something? This might also apply to a piece of land."

"The right of ownership?"

"Yes. For instance, a man leaves his house in order to . . . well, it doesn't really matter. There could be any number of reasons. War, famine, whatever. When he returns three years later, the house is occupied by other people. Who has the right to live in that house?"

"It sounds as if there's certainly enough to consider."

"Absolutely. But many of the cases revolve around a basic principle. Once you find a solution to one case, you can draw parallels to a long series of similar cases."

"Rather like a modern legal system."

"You might say that. The Talmud was written down in the form of discussions among rabbis between the years 100 and 500, in accordance with a particular mnemonic technique. A discursive, associative style built around allegories and parables, which makes the work extremely open to interpretation. Remarkably, each volume begins with a type of proof. The conclusion of a specific dilemma. Very much like we find in mathematics. After that, the path to the conclusion is presented. In truth, it's often a long and winding path." Again he smiled. "The Talmud is for people who have a lot of time on their hands. And thick lenses in their glasses."

"I don't. Have a lot of time, that is."

"I realize that. If the Talmud had been written today, it probably would have been very difficult to find a publisher. Nowadays, everything has to go superfast. We're so damned afraid of missing out on something. That's the very reason that we actually miss out on a lot. Do I sound like an old man? That's what my children say, too." He burst out laughing.

Niels smiled, but he wanted to get back on track. "So it's in the Talmud that the thirty-six good men appear?"

"Let's call them the righteous men. That's more correct. *Tzadikim* means righteous. The thirty-six righteous men."

"Why thirty-six? I know that the number eighteen is sacred, but . . ."

"You've done your homework." Again that wolfish smile. "Eighteen is a sacred number, but why it should be thirty-six—twice eighteen—nobody knows. Although I've heard a theory that each of them covers ten days of the year. Thirty-six. Three hundred and sixty. In that case, it probably has more to do with astrology. There's also something about each of them covering ten degrees of the earth's surface." He threw out his arms. "I guess I'll have to get back to you on that. But I do know that in Jewish folklore, the thirty-six are often called the hidden saints. *Lamed-Vovniks,* in Yiddish."

"But do the good—sorry, the righteous—know that they are the righteous ones?"

"Sounds like you know more about all this than I do. No, the righteous don't know that they are righteous. Only God knows that."

"Then how can anyone know who they are?" asked Niels.

"Maybe we're not meant to know."

"Are there always thirty-six?"

"From what we understand, yes."

"What happens if one of them dies?"

"If all of them die, then humanity is doomed. According to the Kabbalah, even God will die if all thirty-six disappear."

"And there are thirty-six in every generation?"

"Exactly. Thirty-six who together carry the sins and burdens of humanity on their shoulders. Something along that line."

"May I ask whether you personally believe in this?"

The rabbi thought about it. "I like the idea of it. Just look at the world around you. Wars, terror, starvation, poverty, disease. Take the Middle East conflict, for example. An area on earth that contains so much hatred, so many frustrations, that a bomber is always lurking around the next corner, and where checkpoints and walls have become a permanent part of daily life. When I look at such a world from here in my little Danish ivory tower, it's a very appealing idea that there might exist at least—*at the very least*—thirty-six righteous people on this earth. Small human pillars to ensure that we maintain a minimum of kindness and righteousness.

"Are you looking for a murderer?" the rabbi asked suddenly.

Niels was caught off guard. He didn't know what to say.

The rabbi went on, "Or a victim?"

34

Helsingør—Denmark

Hannah's attempt to toss the empty cigarette pack into the wastebasket failed. Instead, it landed in the middle of the floor. She didn't get up, just continued to stare at the map and the pages of notes that she'd made. She saw not a hint of a connection between the various crime scenes. Several areas on the map had been largely passed over, while in the Middle East, for instance, murders had been committed in Mecca, Babylon, and Tel Aviv. For a moment she regretted getting involved in this whole thing. Maybe she should call Niels and tell him that she was giving up. This case had nothing to do with her, after all. But something stopped her from doing that. At first she thought it was the system. She knew there had to be some sort of system at work. She just needed to find it. And systems had always attracted her. She enjoyed looking for the key.

If only she had more cigarettes. If only she had—

They're childless. She interrupted her own train of thought. None of the victims had children. Other similarities? She paged through her notes. Religion? No, there were Christians, Jews, Muslims, Buddhists, atheists, even a Baptist minister in Chicago. Skin color? No. Age? She hesitated. That could be something. Hardly anything decisive, but right now even small steps forward were of use. All of the victims were between forty-four and fifty. A coincidence? Maybe. That didn't make it any less interesting. Hannah's years of experience as a scientist had taught her that what at first glance might look like a coincidence could very well turn out to be quite the opposite. Twenty-one murder victims. All between the ages of forty-four and fifty. And childless. That had to be significant.

She began putting all the materials in a box. The faxed pages, her notes, the map. Though her plan to go for a drive had been prompted by a desire to buy more cigarettes, she decided to take everything along with her. She tried to contact Niels to tell him where she was going, but he didn't pick up the phone.

It was cold as she stepped outside the summer house, but the frosty air felt invigorating. Hannah got out far too seldom. Weeks could pass in which she took only a few short walks down to the water or to the Netto supermarket. The rest of the time she just stayed inside and . . . what? She didn't know. That was almost the worst part: realizing that days could go by, so many days, when she would climb into bed at night, unable to describe with even a single word how she'd spent her time that day. Maybe it was acknowledging this fact that made the simple act of starting up her car and driving down the gravel road, headed for the highway, seem like a minor revolution.

35

Niels stood up. An awkward moment followed, as Weizman remained seated. Finally, the rabbi also got to his feet.

"Do the thirty-six have any distinctive characteristics? Anything that would link them to one another?"

"Only righteousness. Or goodness, as you called it. Isn't that enough?"

Niels hesitated. Not entirely. "Can you tell me the names of any people who have been mentioned as one of the thirty-six?"

Weizman shrugged. "It's typical for the topic to come up at funerals. Whenever there's a need to eulogize someone who has had particular significance for many people."

"If you were to name any of them?"

"I don't know. I'm not sure that my guess would be any better than yours. But as Jews, we often look back to the Second World War for examples. Oscar Schindler. The resistance fighters in the occupied countries. The individuals who prevented the total decimation of the Jewish people. But as I said, your guess is as good as mine."

A couple of black-clad men wearing hats came in, greeting Weizman.

"I have a meeting in a few minutes. Have I helped at all?"

"A bit. Thank you for talking to me."

The rabbi accompanied Niels to the door and shook hands with him. "Now you're only two handshakes away from Hitler," said the rabbi, holding on to Niels's hand.

"I don't understand."

"At a conference in Germany, I once interviewed an officer who worked for Hitler. When I shook his hand, I thought, Now I'm just one handshake away from Hitler. So now you're only two handshakes away from evil, Niels Bentzon."

Niels's hand was starting to feel hot in the rabbi's grasp.

"Maybe it's the same thing with goodness. We're never far from what's good. And that's inspiring. Just think about Nelson Mandela. A man who changed an entire country. Like Gandhi. Or your Jesus." The rabbi smiled. "They say that in South Africa, everybody has either met Mandela or knows someone who has. Nobody is more than a handshake away from the former president. It doesn't seem like such a far-fetched idea that it takes only thirty-six people to keep evil at bay. Just remember that all the upheavals in world history, both good and bad, were initiated by individuals."

He released Niels's hand.

———————◆———————

The light was piercing, the cold insistent. At least Niels had a feeling of being back in his own world. He didn't know what to do with his hands. The image of Hitler was still with him. He stuck his hands in his pockets as he tipped his head back and looked up at the synagogue. He felt a faint vibration through the lining of his jacket—his cell phone. When he took it out, he saw that Pastor Rosenberg had tried to call him six times.

"This is Bentzon."

"Rosenberg here!" He seemed to be gasping for breath. "I think there's a man here, trying to break in."

"Are you at the church?"

"Yes. I've locked myself in my office. But the door has a glass pane."

"Are you sure somebody's there?"

"I think I heard someone kick in the front door."

"Have you called emergency 112?"

Noise on the line. Maybe he dropped the phone.

"Rosenberg?"

The pastor was back, whispering. "I can hear him."

"Stay where you are. I can be there in—"

Niels looked down the street. The traffic was at a standstill. He considered calling for backup but changed his mind. Every second counted. He took off running.

"I'll be there in three minutes!"

36

Dark Cosmology Center, Copenhagen University

It was paradoxical that the building housed the offices of international scientists doing research into the dark matter of the universe, since the Dark Cosmology Center was brightly illuminated by exterior lights. Hannah got out of her car. The years since Johannes died, Gustav took off, and her promising academic career waned had not left a single trace on the building. The thought was at once alarming and uplifting. She took the cardboard box from the backseat and went inside the institute. A couple of young scientists or students passed her on the stairs; they barely looked at her. Hannah went up to the third floor, where her old office had been. The floor was deserted. It was the lunch hour. She walked down the hall to her former office, paying no mind to the nameplate on the door. Without knocking, she went in.

Even though only a second passed before she made eye contact with the young male researcher sitting at the desk, she noticed that she felt right at home again. Everything was familiar—the smell, the sounds, the rather stuffy but homelike atmosphere. A couple of posters on the wall were the same. The bookshelves on the walls were where they had always been.

"Excuse me?" said the young researcher. "Do we have an appointment?"

Hannah continued to survey the room. A photo of two little girls. A drawing hung up over the computer. In a child's scrawl, it said: *To Daddy from Ida and Luna.*

"Are you looking for someone?" he asked.

"This is my office." The words flew out of Hannah's mouth.

"There must be some sort of misunderstanding. I've had this office for over two years now." He stood up, and she thought he was angry. But he held out his hand and said, "I'm Thomas Frink. A doctoral student here."

"I'm Hannah. Hannah Lund."

He studied her as if trying to place her name. He seemed about to figure out who she was but then had doubts. "What is it you've written about?"

"Dark matter."

"I'm doing research on cosmic explosions."

"Thomas, have you got a minute?"

Hannah recognized the voice coming from behind her. An elderly man was standing in the doorway, his shoulders hunched, his back stooped, his eyes displaying a childish expression.

"Hannah?" The aging professor looked at her in astonishment. "I thought you were—"

"Holmstrøm!"

He nodded and gave her an awkward hug. He'd gotten thicker around the middle. He looked at her sternly. "Before you tell me what you're doing these days, I'd advise you to think twice. Because it had better be something damned important to make up for the fact that you're no longer here at the institute."

"It's a long story." She held up her hands. "How are things with you?"

"Okay, except for the fact that we've had to deal with cutbacks. The money is going to environmental programs now. All you have to do is call up the minister in charge of funding for research and whisper the word 'climate,' and it doesn't even matter whether it's at three in the morning, you'll have millions." He laughed. It was clearly something he'd said many times. "The money is in climate research. That's just how it is."

"The votes in the next election, too," added Thomas Frink, glancing at his computer screen.

"The climate." Hannah gave Holmstrøm a solemn look. "People worship the wrong gods."

"What gods?"

"Themselves." She smiled.

A momentary silence fell over the room. A silence screaming to be filled.

"You've brought along a box?" Holmstrøm nodded at what Hannah was holding.

"Yes."

He waited. No doubt expecting her to say something about the contents.

Instead, she asked, "Do you know whether the lecture hall over in the old building might be available?"

37

City Center—Copenhagen

Niels turned down the pedestrian street of Købmagergade. The last thing he'd seen was a parking attendant slipping a ticket under his windshield wiper.

"Hey!"

Niels collided with a man, knocking his overflowing shopping bags onto the pavement. Niels didn't have time to stop and apologize. The street was bursting with all the preparations for the holidays: Christmas decorations, crowds shopping for gifts, everyone looking stressed. He turned off at the building housing the university theology department, ran down the narrow passageway, and emerged into a calmer part of town. He glanced at his cell. Rosenberg was calling again.

"What's happening?" asked the pastor.

"Where are you?"

"I'm still in my office." Panic hadn't taken over. But it soon would. Niels could tell by the way the pastor was breathing.

"Where's the man now?"

"I don't know."

"Where did you see him?"

"Inside the church. When will you get here?"

Niels was now running along Skindergade. He heard a loud clattering sound on the line. "Rosenberg?"

More commotion. Questions were flying through Niels's mind. Why the pastor? There were so many others who were more well known.

"Are you still there?"

"He's got a knife in his hand. Oh, God. Is this the punishment?"

Niels could hear somebody pounding on a door. He tried to run faster. "Out of my way!" he shouted to people on the sidewalk. "Police! Let me through!"

He ran down another passageway. A poor choice. He elbowed his way through the crowds. Rosenberg was still on the line. Niels could hear him mumbling something about punishment.

"Are you almost here?" the pastor shouted.

"Yes. In another minute. Find something to defend yourself with." Niels imagined the pastor picking up his Bible. "Are there others with him?" he asked.

"I don't think so. I think he's alone."

"What about inside the church? Are there any other employees in the building?"

The pastor didn't reply. Niels could tell by his irregular breathing that he was listening to something.

"Do you hear something?" asked Niels, gasping for breath. "What's happening now?"

"He's going to break the glass in the door! He's about to get in!"

"Is there any place for you to escape?"

"There's the bathroom. But—"

"Go inside and lock the door and wait for me!"

The pastor stayed on the line.

A huge truck appeared out of nowhere, blocking the way. "Fuck!" Niels slammed his hand against the side of the vehicle.

"Okay, I'm here." Rosenberg was clearly in a state of panic now. "I'm in the bathroom." His voice had dropped any attempt to remain dignified. He sounded like he was on the verge of collapse. "I've locked the door. But it's easy to break open."

"What about the window? Is it closed?"

"Where are you? Where are you?"

"I'll be there in one minute. Tops." Niels was lying, but one of the most important tools for a crisis negotiator was hope. Always give the hostages hope. Even if it was a soldier lying in the middle of the green zone in Helmand province in Afghanistan, his body riddled with bullets and both legs blown off, it was essential that the soldier be told that there was hope. Even if telling a lie was the only way to do it.

The phone went dead. The lifeline had been cut.

"Rosenberg?" Niels raised his voice. As though it would do any good to shout into a phone when there was no connection.

Niels could see Helligåndskirke now. The sight of the beautiful church tower gave him the impetus he needed to run the rest of the way. He crossed the street. A young mother on a bicycle yelled and gave him the finger. Niels didn't blame her. As he jumped over the low wall next to the church, he touched his Heckler & Koch to make sure it was where it should be. The same sentence kept echoing through his head.

I'm going to be too late. I'm going to be too late.

38

Niels Bohr Institute—Copenhagen

Carrying the cardboard box under her arm, Hannah jogged along Blegdamsvej until she reached her destination: the old Niels Bohr Institute. She stuck the key in the lock. It still worked, and she thought that maybe there was something symbolic about the fact that she had never turned in her key. Had she been subconsciously holding open a little door to the world of research? The door closed behind her with an almost inaudible click. As she stood in the vestibule of the old building, she looked around. She saw the famous photo of Niels Bohr and Albert Einstein engrossed in an intense conversation, hurrying along the cobblestone streets on their way to the Solvay Conference in Brussels in 1927.

The idea for the institute had originated with Niels Bohr. He had provided the financing and single-handedly laid out the framework for how the institute would function. It opened in 1921, and in the following decades the institute became the center of the world on research in theoretical physics. It was said that during those years it was impossible to differentiate Niels Bohr the man from the Niels Bohr Institute. That was where he and his family lived. That was where he worked. Teaching, doing research, and holding conferences for the world's leading physicists. Whenever Hannah looked at pictures from those days, they almost took her breath away. She wondered how many Danes even realized what brilliant scientists had walked these halls.

She ran up the stairs, passing Bohr's old office. The door was ajar. She peeked inside. It was like sticking her head through a time warp. The oval table. The bust of Einstein. For a moment she felt overcome with emotion. That surprised her, since she'd been here so many times. She took a deep breath. As if childishly hoping that she might draw into her lungs even a milligram of Bohr's genius. That was something she could really use right now.

Lunchtime. Not a sound in the corridors. She went into the lecture hall. It looked exactly as it had during Bohr's day. With the rock-hard wooden benches and the typical blackboard designed like a clever Chinese box, new boards constantly appearing, one behind the other. The lecture hall had been designated and preserved as one of Denmark's cultural treasures. Photographs taken in the auditorium now hung on the walls, including a famous picture of Bohr sitting with some of the biggest stars in science: Oskar Klein, Lev Davidovich Landau, Wolfgang Pauli, and Werner Heisenberg.

Hannah set her box on a long table and took out the materials, placing everything in front of her. She stared at all the pieces of paper. And at the world map, which seemed to be laughing up at her. *You mean you really can't figure it out?* the map seemed to be saying. *All you have to do is find the system. The rest will follow.*

She could hear the faint sound of traffic outside. She moved all of the case materials aside and focused her attention on the map. She stared at the X's showing the location of the crime scenes, which apparently had been selected at random. Some on the coasts, others inland. She looked at the dates of the murders. Could she find some kind of pattern in the sequence? The same distance apart? The same . . . She went over to the window. It looked like it was going to snow. The sky was covered with pale gray clouds, and frost had settled on the small spikes that were meant to keep the pigeons away from the window ledge. People were walking past on the street below. An elderly woman was approaching. A bus pulled to a stop and passengers got out. The elderly woman fell on the slippery sidewalk. People immediately gathered to help her up. She smiled her gratitude. She was fine. Hannah stood in the window, a spectator staring at . . . *human beings.*

People. The myth had to do with human beings. Thirty-six people who were supposed to take care of everyone else. All the rest of us. People—as opposed to what? earth? water? Hannah strode out of the room and went into the secretary's deserted office to look for a pair of scissors, which she found in a desk drawer. Back in the lecture hall, Hannah was just about to cut into the map when she changed her mind. Instead, she pulled down the big world map at the front of the room, shoved a small bookshelf underneath, and climbed up on top of it. There was no alternative—she needed big continents if there was going to be enough room for all the X's. As she began cutting down the map, she thought, What am I doing? Here I am, cutting Niels Bohr's map into pieces. At the same time, she had a feeling that he would approve. Practical details shouldn't be allowed to stand in the way if you felt that you were on to something.

39

The door of the church was locked. Niels pounded on the tiny little leaded glass panes. "Rosenberg?" he shouted.

Niels gave up any idea of kicking in the door and concentrated on finding another entrance. He couldn't get hold of the pastor. Something Rosenberg had said kept going through Niels's mind: *Is this the punishment?* The punishment for what? he asked himself as he ran around the side of the church. Another door. It might lead down to the basement. Niels grabbed the handle. This door was locked, too. Then he caught sight of a window that stood partway open. A window high up, above a small ledge. But it was December and bitterly cold. No one would keep a window open.

How had the intruder gotten up there? Several abandoned bicycles were leaning against a tree. Niels grabbed two and set them against the wall of the church. He placed one foot on the saddle, steadied himself, then launched himself upward. He managed to reach the ledge of a window four feet below the open window. He was just able to grab the ledge with the tips of his fingers and pull himself up.

He found a foothold on a brick jutting out of the wall and hoisted himself into a better position. From here it might be doable. He had to press his body against the wall to keep his balance. He could feel blood on his knee. He must have scraped it without noticing. He allowed himself two seconds to catch his breath. Come on, now. Then he used both hands to grab the ledge underneath the open window. His feet dangled in the air. If he fell now, he would hit the bicycles or some bishop's headstone in the shape of a marble angel. Panic was about to take over. Niels couldn't pull himself up. He closed his eyes. Tried to muster all his forces for one last attempt. Considered giving up and trying to grab the bars on the other window so he could get down.

"Come on, Niels!" he said out loud.

Using every last ounce of strength, he tried again.

This time he succeeded. He had one arm inside. Strangely enough, it was his free arm that was shaking. If his adversary had really gotten in through this window, it was bad news.

Niels was inside. He assumed he was in the corridors of the old cloister. The ceiling rose in a vault toward the sky. He was aware of the traffic noise outside. And a faint murmuring from the people moving along Strøget. But nothing inside the building.

"Rosenberg!"

He shouted again, adding, "Copenhagen Police!" On the plus side, his shouts would give the pastor hope. Maybe they would enable Rosenberg to hold out longer. But the shouts would also tell the intruder that the police were on the scene.

Niels didn't switch on the lights. The dark could be both his friend and his enemy. He stepped into a small passageway. From here, steps led up to another hall. A loud bang. Then another. And another. Something hard striking something else hard. The bathroom door? The intruder must be trying to bash in a door.

Niels moved faster, taking the last steps at a run. He entered another corridor. Now he could see the outline of a man—a shape—trying to kick in the bathroom door.

"Stop!" Niels already had his gun out.

The man turned around, and for a second he didn't move.

"Drop your weapon!" Niels yelled.

The man took off running. It was at this point that Niels was supposed to fire; that was his duty. Before he'd finished the thought, the intruder was gone. Niels ran down the corridor. The bathroom door frame had been smashed. The hinges were about to fall off. Two more minutes and the man would have been inside.

"You came!"

Rosenberg was down on the tile floor. On his knees. He was preparing himself, ready to face whatever the afterlife had to offer. If the intruder had been able to get in, the pastor would not have put up any resistance. That much Niels could see at once. He helped the pastor to his feet. "Are you okay?" Niels caught sight of the broken cell phone lying on the floor.

"I dropped it. I was scared and . . . Where did he go?"

"Stay here. No. Lock yourself in your office." Niels pointed to the room across the hall.

"Did you see where he went?"

Niels didn't answer. With a rough hand, he shoved Rosenberg inside his office. "Lock the door and call this number." Niels handed him a note. "Say, 'Officer needs backup.' Do you understand what I'm saying?"

Rosenberg didn't reply. Standing there, he seemed almost disappointed. Maybe because he'd been robbed of facing the moment for which he'd spent his whole life preparing. Niels grabbed his arm hard. "'Officer needs backup'—do you hear me? That'll bring the cavalry."

"Yes. All right."

Niels took off.

The man could have gone in only one direction. Niels set off in pursuit. Around a corner. A door was ajar. Niels paused. No sound to give anything away. Niels raised his gun and stepped into the room. Nothing. Hymn books. Ledgers. A dusty old computer.

Back out to the hallway. Keep going. Up some stairs. Narrow corridors, an endless number of doors, more stairs. What the hell was behind all those doors? The sound of a faint bump. Was that Rosenberg? Or . . .

Niels took a deep breath. The man had vanished. Maybe he'd given up and was on his way through the city. At that very instant Niels instinctively put his arm up in front of his face. The knife ripped through his jacket and for a second got caught in the heavy leather. Niels lost his footing. His gun fell out of his hand. Then the man was on him, hitting him hard in the jaw. Niels felt his teeth slam together before he landed on his back with a thud. He tasted blood. He couldn't tell whether he'd been stabbed. Using his knee, the man pinned Niels's arm to the floor. Niels flailed his hands, caught hold of a lock of hair, an ear, and yanked. The man screamed and lost his breath. Niels struck again, this time aiming for the man's head. He hit him in the mouth, splitting his lip and making blood gush out. With a shriek, the man threw himself at Niels. It was the shriek that cost him his momentum. An unnecessary expenditure of energy. Niels grabbed hold of the man's wrist and twisted, intending to break it. The intruder spun around and kicked backward, and Niels had to let go. They stood and faced each other, panting with exertion. Blood was running into Niels's eyes as he grabbed his gun from the floor. He was having a hard time seeing. The man just watched. Waiting.

Niels wanted to shout, but he managed only a whisper: "Put down the knife."

The man shook his head. They stared at each other. Niels recognized him now. Abdul Hadi. The Yemeni terrorist who had slipped into Denmark. He was standing right in front of Niels. With a manic, desperate look in his eyes. Maybe it was because he recognized the intruder that Niels was able to muster the strength to shout, "Put the knife down!"

Nothing happened. Niels knew that it was now he should shoot the man. He raised his gun. Took aim. "Do as I say and drop the knife."

Abdul Hadi screamed again as he threw himself at Niels, who landed on his side. Hadi looked in surprise at Niels. And at the gun. Niels could see the thoughts racing through the man's mind. Why didn't the policeman shoot? Was the gun even loaded? At any rate, it gave Hadi renewed energy as he leaned forward, putting all his weight behind the thrust of his knife. He missed, and at the last second Niels banged his head hard against the Yemeni's face. Blood was dripping down on Niels from the terrorist's broken nose. Desperately, Niels wriggled free and turned. Still lying on his back, he kicked upward and felt both of his feet strike Hadi hard in the abdomen and groin. The man collapsed.

Niels was instantly on his feet, though his gun had slid across the floor. Niels kicked Hadi again. Twice. Once in the face. As Hadi lay on the floor, groaning, Niels tried to get out his handcuffs. At the police academy he'd been trained in karate and jiujitsu, but where the hell was all that training when he needed it? Rosenberg must have put in the call several minutes ago. The message "Officer needs backup" would be given highest priority at police headquarters. They should be here by now. Hadi was trying to crawl over to where the gun lay, but Niels beat him to it. He picked up the weapon, turned around, and . . . Hadi was gone.

Niels took off after him. Down the stairs, taking them two at a time. More stairs. Hadi was standing in front of a door, fumbling with the lock. Niels caught up with him. Then they were outside. A couple of café tables. Where the hell was his backup? That was as much as Niels was able to think before he ran into some sort of advertising sign and just about lost his balance. Out onto Strøget where there were throngs of people. But Hadi was the only one running.

40

Niels Bohr Institute—Copenhagen

Peⱺple, thought Hannah as she carefully cut away the oceans so that only the continents lay on the table side by side. The myth about the thirty-six righteous men is about people. Not water.

She moved away all the seas and stared at the landmasses. It looked like a jigsaw puzzle. The mere thought made it hard for her to breathe. She was reminded of her son, Johannes. And the first time that she and Gustav realized that he was an extraordinarily gifted child. He had put together a jigsaw puzzle meant for adults in under an hour. Seven hundred pieces making up a picture of the Eiffel Tower. He was only four years old. At first they were thrilled, but later on the boy's brilliance began to cause problems. He seemed sad. He was constantly seeking new challenges that never materialized. Hannah had tried to keep up—to do the opposite of what her own parents had done. They had always wanted her to be normal. They told her not to do her homework so quickly and to stay on the same level with her classmates. That had actually had the opposite effect. Hannah had felt more and more alienated from the world for every day that passed. This feeling was strengthened by the fact that her parents were clearly embarrassed by her intelligence. They wanted her to be like all the other children. They wanted her to be *normal*.

When Hannah was admitted to the Niels Bohr Institute at the age of seventeen, it was like finally coming home. She could still recall how she felt on that first day when she stepped inside the door. This was where she belonged. That was why Hannah had done everything possible to make sure that Johannes wouldn't feel abnormal or like an outsider. Everything to ensure that his intellectual gifts wouldn't isolate him from the rest of the world. But Johannes wasn't normal. He was sick. And he got worse every day.

Hannah lit a cigarette. Smoking in here was not allowed anymore. If Niels Bohr came back from Mount Olympus, even he wouldn't be allowed to light his pipe indoors. But that wasn't important. The only thing that mattered was the jigsaw puzzle of continents that she'd cut out of the map and placed on the table.

"Little Johannes," she whispered to herself. "It's about people."

She'd spent her life dealing with numbers, calculations, light from space. But this had to do with people—people who were part of a specific pattern, not just the usual chaos; people who were part of a bigger plan. That was what appealed to her.

She moved one of the continent pieces so that it was lying in a better position. *Human beings.* Life. The origins of life. Back to the time when the continents were formed.

41

Terrorists are well prepared, thought Niels. That was still one of the points where the intelligence services failed time after time. They underestimated who they were up against. They forgot that the terrorists had spent years preparing to carry out their actions. Why wouldn't they have thought through all the various scenarios? Why wouldn't this man fleeing from Niels have considered the possibility that he might be discovered? Of course he had. Of course he'd planned where he would hide.

Niels kept running.

Al-Qaeda sat over there in caves in the border area between Pakistan and Afghanistan, studying Google Earth. They had brought in IT experts who had no trouble outsmarting the experts in the West. That was a known fact. Every time a large-scale terrorist action had been carried out—in Madrid, London, Mumbai, Moscow, New York—the intelligence services had been left asking: How could this happen? It had happened because they were up against someone who was intelligent and well prepared. The events of September 11, 2001, resulted from years of meticulous preparation. Logistically, it was a stroke of genius. The same was true of the bombing of the USS *Cole* in 2000 and the massacre at Hatshepsut Temple in Luxor in 1997, which caught the Egyptian authorities completely off guard. The actions were planned down to the smallest detail.

Niels was all too familiar with the latter case. Kathrine had a friend who had visited the temple two days before the attack. It was a horrific bloodbath. Sixty-two tourists were murdered. Most of them were first shot in the legs so they wouldn't be able to flee, and then, one by one, they were ritually butchered with long knives. The terrorists took their time. The European tourists lay there helplessly, both inside and outside the temple, awaiting their turn. It was thought that the slaughter took at least forty-five minutes. Among the dead was a five-year-old boy. A woman from Switzerland watched as her father was beheaded. *No tourists to Egypt,* said a note found on the stomach of an elderly Japanese man. The terrorists had cut out his intestines.

"Watch where you're going!" a woman shouted angrily at Niels as he brushed past her, making her drop the package she was carrying. "What the hell do you think you're doing?"

People have no clue, thought Niels. They went about in their fairy-tale world beneath the pine boughs and garlands, buying Christmas presents. Nowhere else was it as easy for people to forget all about the dangers in the world than in Copenhagen at Christmastime.

The Round Tower. Niels couldn't believe his eyes when he saw Abdul Hadi turn right and enter the tower. Was the man attempting to hide in the crowds? Niels raced past the ticket booth, ignoring the boy behind the glass who was calling after him. Continued upward. He almost lost his footing on the slippery stone incline. He kept going up the spiral ramp. People protested as Niels barged into them. He was gasping for air. His chest felt like it would burst, and he could feel the lactic acid announcing its presence in his lower calf muscles. Upward. The man in front of him never turned around to look at his pursuer. He just kept on going. Apparently unaffected by the slope. Niels refused to give up. In a moment they would be face-to-face. And the other officers would arrive. They would have been able to follow Niels on their GPS. All the police cell phones could be traced to within a square yard. And then this whole thing would be over.

Shouts and screams. Niels emerged on the viewing platform at the top of the tower. He was holding his gun in his hand. People around him were screaming in panic. Some dropped to the floor.

"Copenhagen Police!" yelled Niels as loud as he could. "Everybody clear the area. Now!"

More panic. Tourists and parents with little children began pushing and shoving to go back down. Niels could hear someone fall on the stairs. Crying and shouting.

Niels moved away from the door, but Hadi was gone. He had let the man out of his sight only a moment, but that was enough. Had he slipped past Niels? Had he managed to hide in the crowd and make his escape down through the tower? Niels cursed his lack of attention. The crowd was thinning out.

Soon only Niels was left. He looked around. He was standing at the top of the world, surrounded by Copenhagen in the grip of winter. He still held his gun. He walked around the platform. There was nowhere to hide. A line of text from his school days kept whirling through his mind: *The doctor with the knife directs the squiggles into the heart of King Christian IV.* Apparently, a popular misreading of the rebus at the top of the tower's facade. Why would he remember something like that now? The doctor with the knife. The assassin with the knife.

Niels caught sight of him at the very last minute. Abdul Hadi launched himself forward, kicking Niels hard in the solar plexus. And again. Making him vomit. Hadi moved around Niels and grabbed him around the throat. He squeezed hard. Niels's eyes filled with tears. He couldn't breathe. Suddenly, Abdul Hadi released his grip. Niels gasped for air. He was just about to straighten up when he was flung to the floor.

Before Niels could figure out what was happening, he felt the muzzle of a gun pressed to his temple, and he heard the reassuring clinking of handcuffs.

"Not him!" cried a voice. "He's one of ours."

The gun disappeared.

"Where'd he go?"

At first Niels could make out only partial sentences, but gradually, he understood. Officers from the intelligence service had arrived. A few policemen, too. One of them helped Niels to his feet and apologized. Another shouted, "What the hell is he doing?"

Niels looked up. Abdul Hadi had climbed over the fence surrounding the platform and was perched on the old outer railing, ready to jump.

Niels made eye contact. Only now did the two men get a good look at each other.

Hadi stared at Niels and then at the abyss below. He had come here to die. There was no trace of fear in his eyes. First he said a few words in his mother tongue. Niels thought it sounded like a prayer. Then he looked at Niels. "Why did you not shoot?"

Niels approached the railing. "I can't," he replied. Abdul Hadi moved closer to the edge.

42

Ospedale Fatebenefratelli—Venice

Sister Magdalena glanced down the hospital corridor before she put on her gloves. Peace and quiet. None of the terminally ill patients was moaning. Yet she always felt guilty when she had to leave; often the other nurses practically had to push her out the door. Today was no different. On the contrary, today was worse. She decided to poke her head in the door of Signora di Barbara's room one last time before she left.

Tommaso's mother looked up just as Magdalena entered the room. "You're leaving, Sister?"

Magdalena gave her a reassuring smile, set down her bag, and took off her gloves. "I'm off duty now. But I'm not in a hurry."

"I'm so afraid."

"Don't be scared. Death just marks the end of our earthly life."

"Not of death. I'm not afraid of dying," she said, annoyed. It was not easy to feel affection for a woman like Signora di Barbara. Over time Magdalena had learned, but a day's respite now and then made it easier.

"What are you afraid of?"

"That he won't get the message. Or that he'll forget about it."

"The message? About the eighty cents?"

"Yes."

"And you still don't know what the eighty cents is for?"

Signora di Barbara didn't hear the question. "Is my purse here?"

"Yes, it's right here."

"Take out my wallet. Put eighty cents in my hand. Then I know that I'll remember to tell him."

Magdalena got out the money. There weren't enough coins to make eighty cents, so she added one of her own. "Here you are."

She put the coins in the old woman's hand. Her knuckles closed firmly around the three coins.

"When my son comes to see me tonight, I will remember. Is he coming tonight?"

"I don't know. He might be on duty."

"The night shift? Well, then he'll come in the morning. At least now I have the coins, so I won't forget."

"I'll remember, too," said Magdalena, stroking the old woman's wispy gray hair. "I promise."

For a moment Signora di Barbara looked content. Magdalena was convinced that the old woman had a few more weeks to live. Most of their patients waited to die until the holidays were over—she didn't know why. Maybe they wanted to have one last Christmas.

Sister Magdalena turned off the light. Signora di Barbara put her hand on her chest, clutching the coins.

43

The Round Tower—Copenhagen

Abdul Hadi stood at the edge of the strange building. How had he ended up here? The Danish policemen were having a discussion on the other side of the fence. One of them was pointing a gun at him.

They were whispering something, but Hadi didn't understand what they said. He gathered his courage. It would have to end here, even though he hadn't achieved the justice that he sought. Why had Allah failed him? The police officer who'd had more than one opportunity to shoot him was now climbing over the fence and coming closer. He looked just as battered as Hadi did. Was the policeman smiling?

"I will jump," said Abdul Hadi.

The Danish officer held up both hands so Hadi could see them. "No gun."

Hadi looked down at the street. He lost all desire to take somebody else with him in death. Normally, he wouldn't have cared, but from up here, all the people below looked so innocent. If he moved a little to the left before he jumped, he wouldn't hit anyone.

"One question!" said the policeman.

Abdul Hadi looked at him.

"Do you have a family?"

"I did this for my family."

The officer stared at him, uncomprehending. "Is there anyone you'd like me to call?" he asked. "Remember: I'm the last person to see you alive."

Abdul Hadi edged away from the policeman. Why is he asking such strange questions? he thought.

"Your last message. What is it?"

A last message? Abdul Hadi paused to think. "I'm sorry" occurred to him. He wanted to apologize to his sister. Because she was never allowed to grow up. Because he had lived all these years. It seemed so unfair. And he wanted to apologize to his eldest brother. Because Abdul Hadi hadn't been able to avenge his death. His brother had wanted nothing more than to seek a better life. He hadn't done anything wrong. Nor had his little sister. She was innocent, too. How clearly he could see her face. His brother and sister were ready to receive him. He was certain of that. He was looking forward to seeing them again.

The policeman moved nearer. He was whispering to Hadi. "I won't close my eyes. Do you hear me?" The policeman reached out toward him. "I'm your last witness."

It was now that Abdul Hadi should jump. Right now. He looked up toward his Creator, toward the deceased members of his family who were standing ready. It looked as if the sky were already sinking down toward him. Then the sky split open, and snow started to fall, first on the Danish officer, then on Hadi, and then it continued on down to the street below. Millions of tiny pieces of white sky, dancing in circles. People on the street looked up and the children cheered. Abdul Hadi heard a loud click from the handcuffs as they closed firmly around his wrists.

44

Niels Bohr Institute—Copenhagen

The old wooden floors creaked and groaned as the institute's largest globe was rolled along the corridor. It was so big that Hannah didn't have to bend down to push the sphere; she could walk along behind it as if maneuvering an unwieldy baby carriage. A splinter of wood flew into the air as the globe struck a door frame. Two young researchers returning from lunch had to jump aside in the narrow passageway so as not to get rolled over.

"Hey! Watch it! Do you have a driver's license for that thing?" one of them inquired with a laugh.

"I just need it to measure something." Hannah didn't slow down. She heard one whisper to the other that she was apparently a bit crazy: "Her name's Hannah Lund. She used to be one of the best, but then . . . something happened to her."

"So what's she doing here now?"

The rest of their words were drowned out by the noise of the rolling globe. Hannah turned the corner and headed for the lecture hall. She worried that the globe might be too big to go through the door, but it just fit. She took out of her pockets the rolls of aluminum foil that she'd found downstairs in the kitchen next to the cafeteria. She began wrapping the globe in foil. She worked purposefully and efficiently. Then she taped the continents that she'd cut from the map onto the globe. But she didn't put them in their familiar positions. Instead, she gathered them around the South Pole and then used a marker to draw on the X's. They were now arranged in an entirely different formation. She looked at the planet. She stood there for a long time, staring, until she broke her own silence. "The world hasn't looked like this since the dawn of creation."

45

Helligåndskirke—Copenhagen

ere, you've earned it." The pastor set a glass on the table in front of Niels and then poured one for himself. "That was a close call."

The golden liquor stung Niels's mouth, and a pink sheen was visible in the glass when he set it down again. His mouth was bleeding. At least he hadn't lost any teeth, and his nose wasn't broken.

"You'd better drop by the ER." Rosenberg was trying to appear calm.

Niels recognized the way he was behaving—a classic response for someone who had been subjected to a life-threatening situation. The victim either fell apart completely and did nothing to hide his feelings, or he reacted in the opposite way: "Good Lord, there was nothing to it. Everything is fine." The latter response was typical of men.

Niels didn't reply. His jaw and cheekbone on the left side of his face ached. His knee was sore. And his pulse refused to slow down.

The church office looked like a combination meeting room and living room, with a touch of day-care center. A box in the corner contained baby rattles and LEGO blocks. The bookshelf behind the pastor was bulging with black leather-bound books.

"So why you?" Niels discovered that he'd said his thoughts out loud.

Rosenberg shrugged.

"How does he choose his victims? Or rather, how *did* he choose them?"

"Might have been a coincidence." The pastor downed his drink and immediately poured himself another.

"I don't believe that."

"More?"

Niels held his hand over his glass, studying the pastor. He could tell the man was lying; he just didn't know why.

"I don't understand this." Niels's tone of voice was affected by his damaged face—it sounded more nasal—but he wanted to put pressure on Rosenberg. "I have no idea why a madman would be going around the world killing good people."

"Stop saying that part about good people," the pastor said. "I'm far from good."

Niels ignored him. "One thing is certain. This was definitely not a coincidence. Just the opposite." He caught the pastor's eye and refused to look away. "You were specifically chosen to die today. You personally. Just like all the others. And I need to find out why."

Niels got up and went over to the window. The office was on the second floor. A redemptive white blanket of snow had settled over the street. On the rooftops, the cars, and the benches. A group of police officers was standing on the street below. Two of them had taken up position near the car where Abdul Hadi was sitting in the backseat with both hands chained to an iron ring on the floor. *This far and no farther.* The intelligence officers had already debriefed Niels and Rosenberg. They would not be allowed to discuss what had happened. Laws pertaining to terrorism. Ongoing investigations, preventing more attacks, and so on. Niels knew full well that not a single word about the incident would ever be mentioned anywhere. It had never happened. Only in Denmark's most secret archives could anyone read about the incident. Archives that not even the Danish prime minister was able to access. Niels was familiar with the new laws regarding terrorism. They had driven a wedge between knowledge and information on the one hand and the Danish population on the other. Censorship. It was nothing short of censorship.

When Niels turned around, he noticed a shadow cross Rosenberg's face. His shoulders were slightly hunched. The reaction, thought Niels. Here it comes. He's going to fall apart now. He's realizing that he was only seconds away from being cut open by a madman. That means he's vulnerable.

"Do you have family that you can stay with tonight?" asked Niels.

The pastor didn't answer.

"I'd be happy to arrange for you to talk with a psychologist. If that would help."

Rosenberg merely nodded. An awkward moment passed. Niels could tell that he wanted desperately to talk. To confess. It was part of his nature. "Of course, don't hesitate to call me if—"

"You've got it all wrong."

Niels stood very still. Waiting for it.

"You've got the wrong man." Rosenberg's voice sounded deep and far away. As if coming from some other place.

"What do you mean?"

Silence.

"What do you mean by the wrong man? That man tried to kill you."

"He's not the one."

"You do know him, right?"

Rosenberg hesitated. Then he nodded, his eyes fixed on the table. Niels sat down.

46

Niels Bohr Institute—Copenhagen

Physical pain was a good sign for a researcher. It was a sign that the person had been sitting too long in the same position, hadn't had enough to eat and nothing at all to drink. Those were the things that a scientist forgot when a breakthrough was imminent. Some of the male researchers called it "discovery labor pains." Hannah ignored the fact that her back was aching and her stomach grumbling as she typed into the search field: http://en.wikipedia.org/wiki/File:Pangea_animation_03.gif.

She stared with fascination at the brief animation showing the movement of the continents. They looked like they were sailing, with North America, South America, and Asia each moving in a different direction. Once again she looked at her own notes. It was so beautiful. So simple, so obvious.

"Hannah? Is that you?" The secretary looked up from her screen in astonishment as Hannah came into the office.

"Could I borrow your phone?"

"How are you? You haven't been here in ages."

"My cell phone is upstairs in my old office." Hannah stopped to take a real look at the woman. "Solvej?"

"How are you, Hannah?"

"I just need to make a call. It's important."

Hannah picked up the receiver as she took out Niels's card. Solvej smiled, shaking her head.

"Hi, Niels. It's me. Call me back when you can. I've discovered something really remarkable. Something . . . I mean . . . it's so beautiful. The system. And I know where the other murders were committed." She put down the phone and stared at the secretary. "It has to do with a series of murders that have been committed all over the world. I've been in touch with a police officer who's looking for—" She came to a standstill.

"For what?" Solvej asked.

"I've been trying to see if I could figure out some sort of system, and I think I have," Hannah went on.

"I don't doubt it."

"Are you all right, Solvej? I remember that your husband was ill."

"Yes, he had cancer. But he's fine now. He still has to go in for regular checkups, but we think he has it beat. What about you?"

"Gustav left me."

"Oh. I'm sorry to hear that. I think it must be ten years ago that I last saw him up here. He was picking up Frodin. They were going to Geneva."

Hannah looked at Solvej. She'd always liked the secretary. She was the institute's mother. Solvej got up and calmly came over to Hannah to give her a hug. "It's good to see you again, Hannah. I've never understood a thing that goes on in that head of yours, but I've always been very fond of you. Don't hesitate to call if there's anything you need."

Hannah nodded and left the office.

47

Helligåndskirke—Copenhagen

This time Niels didn't hold his hand over his glass when the pastor offered to pour him another drink.

"His name was Khaled Hadi. Abdul Hadi's brother." Rosenberg hesitated. It was a different man sitting in front of Niels. Gone were the smiling eyes, the childish demeanor. His voice was deeper. As if it were coming from the depths, from the place where he was going to speak the truth. "Do you remember the photos? The ones you saw in the church basement?"

"Of the refugees you were hiding?"

"Yes. You made a remark about one of the pictures. You said there were more than twelve people in it."

Niels nodded.

"You were right. There were fourteen."

Niels let him set his own tempo. Past experience with interviews and interrogations had taught him to appreciate the pauses. The pauses were the run-up for deciding on a more interesting choice of words once all the standard phrases and rehearsed replies had been used.

The pastor pushed back his chair, took a deep breath, and stood up. "As you know, on several occasions I've used the church to hide people whose application for asylum had been refused. 'Hide' is probably not the right word, since it was no secret what I was doing. I've used the church as a way to publicize the plight of those seeking asylum, as a platform for their causes. On one occasion in particular with great success."

"When a special law was passed."

"Exactly. After lots of articles appeared in the press, a special law was passed allowing the twelve refugees to stay in Denmark. I'm still in touch with some of them. One of them is even my barber." Niels looked at the pastor's sparse hair, and Rosenberg smiled.

"Not all of them have managed equally well. A few of them moved to Sweden. Three of them spent time in prison. One of them—a young man from Sudan—has become a professional soccer player."

"What about the other two?"

"You're right. There were two others." Rosenberg hesitated. Niels sensed that this was the first time the pastor was telling the story. "One of them ran off. A stateless Palestinian. I have no idea what happened to him."

"What about the other one?"

"Khaled."

"The other one was Khaled? Abdul Hadi's brother?"

The pastor nodded.

"What happened to him?"

"He's dead."

"How did he die?"

"Khaled Hadi was a potential terrorist." Rosenberg turned his back to Niels as he went on. "That's what it said in the documents I received from the police. And that's what they told me when they showed up here. A potential terrorist. Something about how he'd been linked to several terrorist actions and had contacts with known terrorists, although it was never confirmed that he actually carried out a terrorist act. But . . ." Rosenberg searched for the right words. He sat down again. "Do you know about Daniel Pearl?"

"The journalist who was murdered?"

"That's right. The American journalist who was lured into a trap by al-Qaeda in Karachi in 2002 and—"

"Beheaded."

Rosenberg nodded. "An appalling case. Publicized around the world."

"Did Khaled have something to do with that case?"

"It was believed that he did. Your colleagues said he had met Pearl shortly before his death. So it was assumed that he most likely participated in luring the American into the trap."

"What was Khaled doing in Denmark?"

"I can't answer that. He may have entered while traveling under an assumed name. Keep in mind that Denmark has housed several international terrorists on the most-wanted lists. The group behind the bombing of the World Trade Center in 1993 had connections to Århus."

The pastor went on. "I was under a lot of pressure from PET, the Danish security and intelligence service. It was not in their interest to have it get out that an alleged top international terrorist was here on Danish soil. At the same time, PET knew that they couldn't just come in and grab him. The other refugees would have defended him. Things would have gotten out of control."

"So they were putting pressure on you. Did they want you to hand him over?"

"Exactly. But the worst part was the other refugees."

"The other refugees?"

The pastor took a deep breath and nodded. "I sensed that I had an opportunity to save the refugees. Several newspapers, a number of prominent politicians, and large segments of the Danish population supported me. Time was on my side and on the side of the refugees. Opinion was beginning to tilt in our favor. But Khaled Hadi was a ticking time bomb underneath the upsurge of sympathy. How would people react if they heard that I had given refuge to an alleged terrorist? The support would instantly vanish. With terrible consequences for the other refugees."

"That's why you gave in?"

The pastor didn't reply. For a moment he sat motionless. Then he got up, went over to the bookshelf, and took an envelope out of a drawer. He held it in his hands as he sat down. "I didn't know what to do. At first I refused. A persecuted man had asked me for refuge. As a Christian, I felt it was my duty to open my door to him."

"The first stone," said Niels.

Rosenberg stared at him. "Yes. The first stone. It was a matter of everything I'd been preaching for years."

"But you were afraid that all sympathy for the refugees would disappear?"

"Slowly, very slowly, images began creeping into my mind, helped along by the information from PET. I began envisioning the scenes: a bomb in a bus at Nørreport Station. Maybe on the metro in rush hour. Or on a domestic flight. Scores of people killed. Blood running in the streets. Finally, I decided that the risk was too great. Just imagine if he was granted a residence permit and went underground. One day I would open the newspaper and read about a terrorist bomb in the heart of Copenhagen. I would read that the terrorist had been given refuge in my church. That I could have prevented it but I did nothing."

"So you turned him in?"

The pastor nodded. "Like some Judas, I lured him up here to my office—right here—where three PET officers were waiting."

Rosenberg paused. He was breathing harder. Finally, he went on. "I'll never forget the look he gave me. A mixture of disappointment, contempt, sorrow, and anger. His eyes said: *I trusted you.*"

"Then what happened?"

"Nothing. Several weeks passed. The other refugees were granted permission to stay. But then . . ."

Tears welled up in Rosenberg's eyes. Niels was starting to like this man.

"One day I got this." He placed the envelope on the desk.

"What is it?"

"Open it."

The envelope contained pictures. Photographs. Niels held his breath. Battered hands bound to a table. A naked man hanging by his arms, a sack over his head. Niels was reminded of Jesus. The last photo showed a bloody corpse hanging head down from something that looked like a meat hook in a slaughterhouse. Niels couldn't utter a word.

"Khaled Hadi. Six weeks after I handed him over. Secret photos taken in a prison in Yemen."

Niels put the pictures back in the envelope.

"Yemen is one of the worst countries in the world when it comes to torture. Most of the torturers in the Middle Ages would have envied their inventiveness. Electrical current to the testicles. Beatings with cables. Submersion in ice-cold water. They force people to eat food laced with crushed glass. I've asked a doctor about . . . all of it."

Niels looked at Rosenberg. He had asked a doctor. Personally suffered every torment on the way to the cross.

"How did Khaled end up back in Yemen?"

The pastor shrugged. "I don't know. The Danish authorities have done a good job of suppressing the case. No journalists have gotten hold of it. PET has discreetly evaded all blame by stating that Khaled ended up in Yemen after being first sent to another country where he was wanted. PET handed him over to the country in question—they won't say which country, but undoubtedly, it was the United States—which officially does not use torture. From a strictly legal standpoint, their hands are clean. Besides, there are plenty of gray areas. But what good is it if they hand him over to a country that doesn't use torture if that country in turn gives him to a country that does? He was simply sent on."

"Who sent you these pictures?"

"Abdul Hadi. He wanted me to know what I had done. He wanted me to know about Khaled's fate."

"So Abdul Hadi was going to kill you out of revenge?"

"Revenge. Yes."

Neither of them spoke. The pastor glanced at the whiskey bottle. Niels could see that he was fighting a battle with himself. He wanted another drink, but he didn't think he should have one. Niels was familiar with that battle.

"I don't think Khaled had anything to do with Daniel Pearl's murder. He was never in Afghanistan. He was a nice young man." Rosenberg looked Niels in the eye. "I threw all sense of judgment out the window."

The pastor lost the battle and refilled his glass. For the first time Niels noticed the tiny burst blood vessels in the skin under his eyes.

Niels could hear voices from the square outside the church. The police officers were talking. He stared at the pastor sitting in front of him. Images merged in his mind: Abdul Hadi. Running after him down Strøget. The disturbing marks on the backs of the murder victims. The various homicide cases. Sarah Johnsson. Vladimir Zhirkov. The good people.

He was grasping at straws. None of it made any sense. He couldn't get it to fit together. The pastor's voice broke into his thoughts. Had he asked a question?

"So I'm not one of the thirty-six righteous people."

Niels gave him an indulgent smile. "That's probably not the theory that's on the top of Interpol's list, anyway."

"Maybe it ought to be."

"Yes, well. You could be right."

Rosenberg got up. He had unburdened his heart. "My job is the opposite of yours."

"How's that?"

"You have to find proof in order to make people believe."

Niels smiled. "And you have to make people believe without proof." He wanted to say something to help the pastor rid himself of guilt. "Maybe PET was right," he said. "Maybe you did the right thing after all."

A heavy sigh escaped Rosenberg. "Who knows what's right? There's a famous Sufi poet named Rumi. He once wrote a story about a little boy who is haunted by dreams of an evil monster. The boy's mother comforts him by saying that he should just think about her and about the evil monster going away. 'But Mommy,' says the boy, 'What if the monster has a mother, too?'" He smiled. "Do you understand what I'm getting at? Evil people have mothers, too, Mr. Bentzon. Mothers who comfort them and tell them that they're doing the right thing. For them, we're the monster."

———————

Soft flakes of snow drifted down from the sky. There was something carefree about their dance through the cold, clear air. The officers were about to drive off. Niels turned to the pastor. "Don't hesitate to call me."

Rosenberg nodded. He seemed about to say something, but one of the policemen came over and handed Niels a package. "What's this?"

"It's from Venice. It came in the embassy mail this morning."

Niels opened the package. A cassette tape labeled with Chinese characters. He wondered what it was all about as he stuck the tape in his pocket.

"There's another possibility," said Rosenberg.

Niels glanced up. The pastor looked like he was freezing.

"Another possibility?"

"Maybe God is deliberately removing the thirty-six righteous people."

"You mean God is a murderer?"

"That's not the way to look at it. If you accept God, you also accept that death is not the end. Look at it as God taking them home."

"God is taking His best people home?"

"Something like that."

The doors of the police car slammed. The engine started up.

"But why would God do that?"

The pastor shrugged. "Maybe to test us."

"Test us?"

"To see how we'll react."

Niels stepped aside so the car could drive off. He made eye contact with Abdul Hadi in the backseat. He looked like a wounded animal. Not a monster.

"Or if we'll react at all."

48

The shop selling radios didn't look like much, squeezed between a pizzeria and a junk shop. Eight televisions stacked on top of each other were broadcasting information from the Bella Center: The world is about to go under. This is the last call. Niels placed the cassette tape labeled with Chinese characters on the counter and tried to make eye contact with the lethargic teenager.

"What's that?" the clerk asked.

"It's a cassette tape. I'm looking for a player so I can listen to it. Do you have such a thing?"

"I have no idea."

Niels looked at him. Waiting. Nothing happened, so he gave up. "Could you check and see?"

"Just a sec." The teenager turned around and yelled, "Dad!" His voice, which was on the verge of changing, hurt Niels's ears and reminded him of the children he didn't have. They would have been about the same age as this boy if Kathrine had gotten pregnant when she and Niels first started trying—a futile process that had gone on for years.

A middle-aged man with remarkably greasy hair emerged from the back room. "Yeah?" he snapped.

"A tape recorder. I'm looking for a tape recorder so I can play this cassette."

The man looked at the tape, snorted, and disappeared into the back room again. Niels moved aside to answer a call on his cell phone. "Yes?"

"I think I've found it, Niels."

"What have you found?"

"The system. It's so beautiful, Niels. So incredibly beautiful. That is, if—"

"Start from the beginning, Hannah. I'm a little tired."

"I'll explain the whole thing later. But just listen to this: I know where the other murders were committed. All of them."

"The other murders?"

"Yes! Based on the theory that it's an unbroken chain of events—the last number we have is thirty-four. A total of twenty-one have been found. So we're missing thirteen murders, but I know where to look for them. One in Santiago, one in Hanoi, one in Belém, one in Cape Town, one in Nuuk—"

Niels interrupted her. "Wait a minute. There's no way I can check up on all these cases. What exactly do you want me to do?"

Neither of them spoke for several seconds.

Then Niels asked, "Did you say Cape Town?"

"What I'm saying is that . . . no, the *system* says that murder number fourteen was committed on Friday, July twenty-fourth, at sundown in Khayelitsha, a suburb of Cape Town. I can text you the precise latitude and longitude."

"Do that." Niels was interrupted as the owner of the radio shop slammed an ancient cassette player down on the counter.

49

I t could have been a painting. The Indian Ocean. The palm trees. As Kathrine sat in her office on the twelfth floor, she often thought about the studio photographs of her and her sister that their parents always commissioned when they were kids.

They would drive into the town of Roskilde from their home out in the country. From far away, they could see the cathedral's twin spires, sharp as awls, pointing toward the sky, toward God, like a declaration of war. *You shall not come any closer.*

Kathrine loved the town. New clothes, a gigantic supermarket where they always lost each other in the endless aisles of jams and spices. And the escalator. She was a little afraid of that. But the escalator carried them up to the floor where they would have their picture taken. She and her sister were never allowed to choose the background themselves, but the photographer always showed them the options. First he would pull down a backdrop showing a forest scene. Her mother loved that scene. Kathrine thought it was creepy. Moss-covered trees deep inside a forest, where the sunlight could shine through only when the trees had shed all their leaves. Her little sister had terrible taste and always wanted something with lots of colors, preferably pink. Then there was the beach scene. That was the one Kathrine had fallen in love with, but her mother had categorically refused to accept it. Even today Kathrine didn't understand why she had never been allowed to choose that one. The photo had been taken from slightly above the beach, as if you were sitting on the dunes and looking down at the sea. They usually had to settle for a compromise: a clearing in the woods, with the trees pushed back into the distance. God only knew what sort of subconscious sexual tendencies were latent in her mother's choice of backdrop. Or what kind of repression motivated it. Kathrine wondered about that. She thought that maybe she was sitting here in this particular office, in this part of the world, because the view resembled the backdrop that had been so forbidden when she was a child. She wanted bright light, but her mother insisted on dim twilight, which better suited the atmosphere in their home. Kathrine's father had suffered from "black holes," as her mother called them. Today he would simply be labeled manic-depressive. Not that he was ever particularly manic. If only he had exhibited a little more manic behavior, like the others Kathrine had read about on the Internet: fathers who were either way down in the dumps or way up in the clouds. When they were up, everything was possible: taking trips, buying new cars, moving abroad. That wasn't how things had been in her childhood home. The old man was either unobtrusive but more or less normal or else he didn't say a word, sitting as motionless as a lizard for weeks on end.

Here she had air-conditioning and soundproof windows. Marc was hovering out there in the open office area where the secretaries and younger architects and engineers all had their desks. He was looking for an excuse to come into her office again. Did she want to sleep with him? They had flirted with each other, there was no doubt about that. The idea of sex with Marc had been more exciting when she thought that Niels was actually coming to visit. Now that he wasn't and having an affair had become a realistic possibility, she wasn't so certain. Marc tried to catch her eye through the glass walls. She turned around to look out the window. Her mother's forbidden view. The sea. The light.

"Hey, Kathrine." Marc was standing in the doorway, his pelvis almost imperceptibly thrust forward.

"Hi, Marc."

"No holiday?" He spoke English with the typical South African Boer accent. Not exactly sexy.

"I'm just sending off the last report," she replied.

"Isn't your husband coming?"

He knew full well that Niels wasn't coming. Right at the moment Marc was being anything but charming. Kathrine could feel tears welling up in her eyes. "Would you mind? I really need to be alone."

Marc looked apologetic. It wasn't his style to be pushy, and she knew it. He was a sweet guy. It wasn't his fault that she'd chosen to marry a man who reminded her so much of her father. Kathrine had spent a lot of time wondering how that could have happened. She hadn't found an answer, but she'd learned to accept that grown people often ended up with a partner who was a copy of their mother or father—usually the parent with whom they still had issues. Just as she did with her father and his gloomy temperament.

Things hadn't always been that way. In the beginning Niels hadn't reminded her at all of her father. He may have had a calm disposition, but he didn't fall into black holes. Back then they had laughed a lot together. All the time. And he seemed ambitious. Or was that something she had imagined? Kathrine asked herself: Do we human beings have some unknown sensory apparatus that's capable of selecting those people who later on in life will start to resemble the mother or father who was difficult? Or do we make our partners turn out that way? Could we make anybody at all assume the role?

Kathrine looked out the window. The crests on the waves looked like champagne bubbles. She got a text from Marc. *Sorry.* She turned around and saw him standing in the middle of the office landscape, looking completely dejected and deflated. He was a handsome man. At that instant her cell phone rang. *Niels calling,* it said on the display.

"I was just sitting here thinking about you," she said.

"What were you thinking?"

"Not anything you'd want to hear."

She smiled at Marc. He was infinitely more sexy when she had Niels on the line. But the thought of Marc as her lover totally turned her off.

"Now, listen here. The reason that I'm not coming to visit you is that—"

She interrupted him. "I think I know why, sweetheart."

"No, you don't. I'm working on a case. A homicide. And it's a really complicated case."

He paused for effect before he told Kathrine all about it. The murders, the crime scene locations, the numbers on the backs of the victims. Kathrine listened without saying a word. Even when he told her the theory about a death, an unreported murder in Khayelitsha. Then Niels fell silent. Waiting. He didn't mention anything about Hannah.

"Have you changed departments?" she asked at last.

"No. Not exactly. It started out as a routine matter. I was just supposed to warn some Danish citizens who might be potential victims. That's how I got involved."

"And that's why you're not coming?"

Niels paused to think. He wanted to say yes. That his ambition demanded he stay home to work on the case. She would like hearing that. She'd often criticized him for a lack of ambition. That and much more.

"I think so."

"You *think* so?"

"I don't know what this is all about, Kathrine. But I have a feeling that it's important, and I need your help."

"You want me to go out to Khayelitsha?"

"Exactly."

"Niels, it's not really safe for a white woman. Khayelitsha is one of the worst slums in South Africa. And that's saying a lot."

Niels didn't reply. The worst thing he could do would be to try and persuade Kathrine to do something. She had to persuade herself. It was not a comfortable silence. He was surprised when she said, without offering any further objections, "Okay."

50

A little piece of China had wedged itself in between two clothes shops on Vesterbrogade.

The restaurant was called the Golden Bamboo. "Restaurant" was a fancy word for a place that had only a few plastic tables, a small open kitchen, and a sullen-looking smiley face in the window, which the owners had attempted to hide behind a plastic palm tree. The health inspector had written with an angry red pen: *Requires improvement in food hygiene.* Niels was trying to shield the cassette player from the snow as he stepped inside, where it was warm. Someone had told him that Asians were very polite. That was something these particular individuals had apparently forgotten, because a war was going on in the kitchen. The manager—the only one wearing a suit—was bawling out his kitchen staff.

Niels cleared his throat to no avail. So he went over to a small counter with a cash register and set down the cassette player. Then he waited. He looked around at the plastic plants in pots lining the windowsills. A map of China on the wall. A big poster advertising the Olympics in Beijing. A menu: noodles, bamboo shoots, spring rolls, Kung Pao beef. A TV was on, showing a report from the climate conference. A tall, hefty man from the island group of Vanuatu in the South Pacific had tears in his eyes as he raged against the industrial nations—especially China—and their exploitation of the environment. His words seemed to be falling on deaf ears, because there was a good deal of chatter going on in the front rows. A couple of Finnish delegates were snickering about something. Most of the conference participants looked as if the island group of Vanuatu and its problems were not going to rob them of any beauty sleep.

"They're out to get us."

Niels turned around and saw the elderly Chinese man, clad in a suit that was a bit too big for him.

"Why is it always us?" the man said. "It's always China. China gets the blame for everything." He gave Niels a bitter smile. "Do you want a table?"

"I'm from the Copenhagen Police." Niels showed him his ID. He was looking for tiny signals in the man's face, but he couldn't read him at all.

"I need to have this translated." Niels didn't allow the man any time to think before he pressed the play button on the tape recorder.

"What's that?"

"Can you tell me what they're saying on the tape?"

They listened. It lasted about a minute. It seemed to be a phone conversation. That much Niels had guessed. A man calling a woman. Apparently asking for help. There was a growing sense of panic in his voice.

The tape stopped.

"Can you understand what they're saying?"

"He's in pain. The man on the tape."

"I can hear that. But what is he saying?"

"He's asking: 'What's happening?' Do you understand?"

"No. I mean, yes, I understand what you're telling me, but not what the significance is."

The man interrupted Niels. "Play it again."

Niels rewound the tape. Then the manager called to one of the kitchen staff. A young man came over to join them, looking submissive. After a conversation in Chinese, the manager pressed the play button.

"Louder," said the manager.

Niels turned up the volume. It was hard to drown out the noise coming from the restaurant kitchen.

"Can you hear what they're saying?" he asked.

The young man translated. And then the manager translated what he'd said into Danish. "The man on the tape is saying: 'What's happening? It's so quiet. Dear God. What's happening to me? It's so quiet. Venus. And the Milky Way.'"

"Venus and the Milky Way?" Niels rewound the tape again to play it one more time. It wasn't quiet on the tape. On the contrary. A bell was clanging in the background; there were loud voices and traffic sounds.

"There's a lot of noise. It's not quiet at all. Are you sure that's what he's saying?"

"Positive. He's from Beijing," said the manager, showing signs of losing interest in this conversation that had nothing to do with him.

"So he's talking about how quiet it is even though there's a lot of noise?"

Niels addressed his question to the younger man, who replied in somewhat broken Danish.

"That is what he says. 'What's happening? It's so quiet. Dear God. What's happening to me? It's so quiet. Venus. And the Milky Way.'"

Niels was asking himself why Tommaso thought it was so important that he hear this tape.

It's so quiet.

51

Between Cape Town and Khayelitsha—South Africa

Most people who had been to Africa talked about the phenomenon afterward, especially those who had traveled deep into the heartland. Away from the tourists, the greed, and the unavoidable European TV teams who wanted to make films of all the misery. *It was a matter of coming to terms with death.* In the heartland—the artery which beat so fiercely for human beings that we were allowed to crawl up out of the mire—it was possible to sense the very origins of the human race. Even though the original color had been washed off, it was here we came from. You could feel it. *The earth.* Home assumed a whole new meaning.

The first time Kathrine stood out in the savanna, she had wept. Wept like a daughter who had returned home to be embraced. She was ready to die here. Marc didn't feel the same way. He had grown up in Africa. He loved the place, but he wasn't ready to die. That was why he hired bodyguards to accompany them. Three Zulus showed up in the afternoon. With big smiles. No matter what Kathrine said to them, they would laugh loudly.

They carried machine guns and rifles. Bobby, Michael, and Andy. All Africans had different names for different situations, just like artists in Europe and America. One name for the whites, and then their real names, which they never revealed. They didn't like to be asked.

"Khayelitsha?"

"Yes."

"Why do you want to go there?" one of them had asked, laughing again. "Nothing there, nothing there," he kept repeating.

"Is that really necessary?" Kathrine asked as Marc placed a pistol in the glove compartment of the dusty pickup.

"Kathy." He turned to her with a smile. She didn't like being called Kathy. "This is not peaceful Scandinavia. This is South Africa. You need a gun." He had quite possibly the whitest teeth in the whole world.

"But . . ." She fell silent. Something in his expression made her hesitate. He didn't even need to say it out loud. She knew what he was thinking: *But what would a pampered woman from a fairy-tale country like Denmark know about it?*

The Zulus followed close behind in their vehicle, and Marc made sure to keep them in his rearview mirror.

"A murder, eh?" he said.

Kathrine smiled and shrugged. "I know. There are lots of murders in South Africa." She lit a cigarette. That was one good thing about Africa. Here you were allowed to smoke yourself to death without encountering a wall of reproachful glances. Here death was part of life. Death was present in an entirely different way than back home, where it almost came as a surprise to people when death one day showed up and knocked on the door. As if it had never occurred to them that one day the party would be over.

Lots of life and lots of death. That was Africa. In Denmark it was just the opposite: People didn't really live. And officially, death didn't exist. All that was left was an existence in which one day followed another, and nobody really noticed.

She coughed. The local cigarettes were strong. It had been a busy day. Meetings. Endless phone calls. She'd found 109 unanswered e-mails in her in-box when she turned on her computer in the morning. It would be the same thing tomorrow.

"Where in Khayelitsha?" Marc's voice was raw and masculine. That was a plus.

She handed him a note with the GPS coordinates and an approximate address. It had required a major effort—and help from the company's IT experts—to convert Niels's GPS coordinates to an actual address.

"Okay." He gave her an indulgent smile. He was everything that Niels was not. Marc had no hidden sides, no inexplicable shifts in mood, no mental chasms to fall into. He was just Marc. Extremely delectable and slightly annoying.

They drove along a twelve-lane highway on shiny black asphalt that had been newly laid. Marc sipped at his takeout coffee and turned on the radio but then changed his mind and switched it off. Kathrine glanced behind them. Andy waved, smiling broadly from the other vehicle. The temperature outside was 85 degrees, and the air was bone-dry, filled with exhaust fumes, dust, and sand, as it blew in from the vast savannas. Construction was going on everywhere. Cranes towered on the horizon, as if pollution had made Africa's giraffes mutate and grow to grotesque heights. Roadwork, sweating laborers shifting earth and cement, the sounds of jackhammers and paving machines as bridges and roads were repaired and upgraded.

"Do you know Bill Shankly?" Marc drove through a red light.

"No."

"A legendary soccer coach from Liverpool. He once said something like this: 'Some people believe that soccer is a matter of life or death. I find that sort of attitude disappointing. I can assure all of you that it's much more important than that.'" Marc looked at Kathrine and laughed. "If you look at what's happening in South Africa right now, with the World Cup only seven months away, you have to admit that Bill Shankly was right. I mean, just because of a little round leather ball, the whole country is preparing to change. At least outwardly," he added.

Kathrine looked out the window.

The modern Western metropolis was now—in an imperceptible transition—in the process of giving way to the big-city Africa so familiar in the media: slums, despair, garbage, heat, and dust. It was impossible to tell where Khayelitsha started. Maybe it was more of a mental border than a geographical one. They had driven across an invisible dividing line, and from that moment there was no longer any hope. All that was left was survival for survival's sake. The daily battle to find something to eat and drink and to avoid falling victim to some random crime. In South Africa, there were fifty thousand murders a year. Every thirty seconds a woman was raped.

Khayelitsha—South Africa

Marc stopped the car and waited several seconds until the vehicle with the bodyguards was once again right behind them. The streets were getting narrower, the houses smaller: huts, sheds made of corrugated tin, primitive mud structures, dusty old jalopies, and dogs everywhere. With drooping tails, they limped along, growling and thirsty. In Khayelitsha children didn't play. That was one of the first things Kathrine noticed. They just stood on the streets, staring and smoking cigarettes. A boy was kicking around a soccer ball. His homemade soccer jersey said MESSI on the back. A woman was yelling at her kids. They paid her no mind. What bothered Kathrine most was all the garbage. It was everywhere. Coke bottles. Tin cans. Plastic bags, car tires, discarded packaging. The stink of dust and heat and piss and hopelessness inevitably seeped inside the car.

Marc followed the GPS, turning first right, then left, and in no time dust covered the windshield like a brown film that lent everything an air of unreality.

Kathrine usually tried to avoid the poor sections of town as much as possible, which made South Africa a pleasant place for her to be. During the first few months, she spent her time largely at the office, in the hotel, and in restaurants and cafés in the financial district. She almost managed to forget where she was. It could have been New York or London during a hot summer.

Marc was talking about one of their colleagues, whom he considered an asshole. Kathrine listened with only half an ear. When Marc changed the subject, it was evident that she hadn't been paying attention.

"Kathy?"

"Yes?"

"How about tonight?" He stopped the car and looked at her. "I know a very nice Indian restaurant."

Kathrine looked at him. He had just asked her out on a date. He'd been on the verge of doing so for weeks. She had known it would come; she'd been expecting such an invitation, but it still took her by surprise. He smiled. Those white teeth. A smile that said there was more to the invitation than dinner in a restaurant. Kathrine had no doubt that if she said yes, she'd end up in bed with him. He was offering her the whole package. Food, drinks, sex. She wanted to say yes. Her body wanted to say yes. She had a warm feeling in the pit of her stomach.

"Why are we stopping?" she said.

She had expected him to demand an answer from her. The idea that she couldn't avoid answering his question was titillating. His shirt was unbuttoned at the neck, revealing a tanned, muscular chest. So maybe she was a little disappointed when he accepted her unwillingness to reply and simply said, "We're here," as he pointed to the GPS.

Kathrine didn't know what she'd expected, but there was nothing special about the house other than that it stood all by itself, apart from the rest of the slum—the only building within a radius of several hundred yards. Piles of garbage formed a border where nature began.

Her next thought was that Marc must have read the GPS wrong. Why would Niels direct her to this particular house—this unremarkable little shack of a house in the midst of the endless slum of millions of other houses? There must be some mistake. On the other hand, the only thing she knew about the house was that back in July a murder supposedly had been committed inside. Niels hadn't told her anything else, but why shouldn't that be plausible?

Marc stayed in the car. The three guards had climbed out of their vehicle, and one of them stayed a few yards behind Kathrine.

She walked across the road, which was little more than a bumpy, scorched stretch of land. The door looked like it had come from an old cabinet and was there mostly for appearance's sake. Several youths were kicking at a bundle of rags outside the house. One of them shouted, "You wanna fuck, white woman?" and laughed with the others. Andy yelled something in Zulu, but that didn't seem to frighten the boys.

Kathrine knocked on the door and waited. Nothing happened. She knocked again. She was afraid she might break the door. At last it was opened by a toothless old woman who stared right through Kathrine as if she were air.

"Hello," said Kathrine, realizing that she had no idea what to say. "Do you live here?" No answer. It occurred to Kathrine that the woman was practically blind. A dull grayish cloud covered her eyes. Many people in Africa were blind. "Do you understand English?"

Kathrine was about to turn around to call for Marc when the woman said in English, "My son is not home."

"Your son?"

"I am taking care of the house."

"Okay." Kathrine was hoping the woman would invite her inside, but that didn't happen. "I've come here to find out if . . . My name is Kathrine. I'm not from South Africa," she added. She'd noticed that usually had a positive effect on the locals. Europeans were popular, or at least more popular than other whites.

Only now did the woman's face betray any sort of reaction. A nervous tic started up under one eye. She raised her voice. "Amnesty?" Before Kathrine could say no, the old woman stuck her head out the door as if to look around. "How many of you are there?"

"My colleague is sitting in the car," Kathrine told her. "There are three bodyguards with us."

"It's about time you got here."

The old woman turned around and vanished inside the house. If she hadn't been blind, she would have seen the big sign painted on the side of the Land Rover: DBB ARCHITECTS. From inside the house, the old woman called: "Come in, Amnesty!"

A couple of rickety wooden chairs, a table, and a rough-hewn bed. Above the bed hung a poster showing the South African soccer team. *Bafana, Bafana. God is on our side,* had been written on the wall above the poster.

The old woman offered Kathrine tea, pouring her a cup without waiting for her to say yes. "Rooibos tea. It's good for you," she said. "It clears your mind." Kathrine looked at the muddy liquid in her cup.

"What are you planning to do to get him out?" asked the old woman. "He didn't kill her. Do you understand? What are you going to do?"

Kathrine swallowed hard. I need to tell her that I'm not from Amnesty International, she thought. Instead, she said, "Maybe it would be best if you tell me a little about what happened."

"He didn't kill her. The woman at the factory. He's innocent, just like Mathijsen said."

"Who?"

"Mathijsen," the old woman repeated. A faint smile crossed her lips, and the furrows on her brow seemed to relax at the thought of this Mathijsen. "He was a good man. He helped us."

The woman spoke quickly, and Kathrine had a hard time understanding what she was saying. "Mat—"

"Mathijsen. My son's lawyer. Joris Mathijsen."

"What about him?" asked Kathrine. "Is he the one your son is accused of killing?"

"No! No!" The old woman shook her head. "Mathijsen died here, in this house. He wanted to help us."

"I don't understand. The lawyer died here? When?"

Before the woman told her the story, Kathrine went to get Marc from the car.

"The old woman thinks that we're from Amnesty International," she whispered to him. "I don't think we should take that hope away from her."

Inside the house, Marc nodded politely to the woman and said hello when he discovered that she couldn't see. Even though the woman had clearly told the story many times, there was a warmth in her voice as she spoke.

Her son, Benny, had been working at a shoe factory in Durbanville. But then he was fired, and in the subsequent tumult, the owner's daughter was stabbed to death. That was how the old woman described the events. Benny was accused of murder. Someone whose name Kathrine didn't catch said later that Benny was standing several yards away and couldn't have done the killing. It was a hopeless situation for Benny. He had no money to hire a proper attorney.

"But then came Joris Mathijsen."

Marc was familiar with the name. Mathijsen was known as one of the brains behind the Truth and Reconciliation Commission, which worked from 1995 until 2000 to expose the violations that had taken place under apartheid. The commission was strikingly different from other tribunals because it wasn't interested in punishing people. It offered amnesty to those criminals willing to present a full accounting of what they had done. If they told the truth, they could go free. How Mathijsen—who had long been out of the public spotlight—had found his way to Benny was a bit of a mystery. The old woman couldn't explain it. All she knew was that Benny and Mathijsen had met several times at the prison, and Benny had been given renewed hope by meeting with the experienced defense lawyer. On July 24 Mathijsen had come to Khayelitsha to pay a visit to Benny's childhood home. He drank tea with the old woman and promised her that he would get Benny out of prison.

"He promised. Do you understand?"

Just as the lawyer was about to leave for home, he saw a shadow pass through the yard behind the house. At first he was going to ignore it, but then he decided to investigate. The old woman stayed inside. Several minutes passed. She didn't dare go outdoors. Finally, she gathered her courage to venture out and found Joris Mathijsen lying on his back with his arms spread out on either side. He was dead. Benny was sentenced to twenty-two years in prison for manslaughter, with no possibility of parole.

Kathrine was on the verge of tears when she saw the hopelessness on the old woman's face: *By the time he gets out of prison, I'll be long dead.* Kathrine promised to help; for a few seconds she even imagined that she was employed by Amnesty International. At any rate, she would contact the group when she got home. She made that promise to herself.

The old woman sat in silence for a moment. Then she got to her feet with an effort and walked the few yards across the room to a door on the far wall. Kathrine hadn't noticed it before. Giving the door a little push, the woman opened it, and they all stepped outside to an enclosed space. They walked over to a spot covered with flowers that had long ago withered under the blazing sun. A small picture of the lawyer hung there. *Born April 26, 1962. Died July 24, 2009.*

52

Niels Bohr Institute—Copenhagen

Niels Bohr night. Everyone who worked at the institute was familiar with that term. Endless nights when the only sound was the faint hum of one of the many machines running experiments in the basement, or the rustling of paper as the research results came in. It was as if the ideas never left the building and the scientists had to be present in order to work with them. Hannah could feel how much she had missed this place as she ransacked the kitchen, looking for some food. Sausage and cheap salami—maybe a bit over the hill. That was par for the course. Physicists weren't exactly gourmets. That was just the way it was. Paper and pencils were always to be found on every table in the cafeteria—that was a house rule. Because what if somebody suddenly had a good idea while he was eating lunch?

Hannah hadn't heard the phone ring. A message. She listened to her voice mail. It was Niels. "Hannah, I just heard from Kathrine. You were right about Khayelitsha. I don't know how you knew. But you were right about both the place and the date. Joris Mathijsen. A well-known defense attorney. Everything fits. I'm really tired. It's been a busy afternoon. Let's talk tomorrow. You're a smart woman."

That was all. Hannah smiled. Of course she was right. And yes, she was a smart woman.

53

Carlsberg silo—Copenhagen

Of all the bad ideas that Niels had come up with over the years, this one took the cake. How could he have sent Kathrine into one of the world's worst slum areas in the middle of the Christmas holidays, which they should have been spending together? He'd talked to her three times; she was very upset, couldn't shake off the experience. At one point in their last conversation, he'd had an urge to shout at her. Goddammit, what did she expect? The world was filled with poverty and death and misery. Kathrine hadn't been aware of it because she spent her days inside buildings with designer furniture and air-conditioning. Hers was a superficial universe. Nothing but surfaces. Marble, steel, copper, aluminum—a gleaming world that ignored the fact that everything all around was in a state of decay. He didn't say that to her. Instead, he said, "I'm sorry. That must have been awful. Get some sleep."

The imaginary argument was raging inside Niels's exhausted mind when he entered his apartment and sensed that somebody had been there.

He looked around the living room. Nothing out of the ordinary caught his eye. The big west-facing room looked exactly as he'd left it. Exactly as it had looked when Kathrine left their shared daily life an eternity ago. Niels had an odd feeling in his body, a feeling that their relationship was over. Maybe he was just sensing Kathrine's shadow, which was always present in the apartment. He was tired and feeling overwhelmed. Also because Hannah had apparently cracked the system and figured out the whole thing. He considered phoning her again but decided to go to bed.

The door to the back stairs stood open.

He never forgot to close and lock the door to the back stairs. He used it so seldom. Carefully, he examined the door. There was no sign that it had been forced. The door, the door frame, the lock, the hinges all looked untouched. He didn't find that reassuring, because it just stirred up another fear. Had someone gotten hold of his key and made a copy? He thought about who might have access to the apartment. He and Kathrine were the only ones. Along with their neighbor, who lived on the floor below. What about the building superintendent? Was there a master key? Niels wasn't sure, but he was inclined to believe there wasn't. If there was any basis to his fear, someone must have borrowed his key or Kathrine's and had a copy made.

The only place where Niels ever left his keys out was at work. The idea was absurd, but could someone at the station have borrowed his apartment key, copied it, and then put it back? But who? And for what reason?

Niels stepped out onto the landing and switched on the light. He heard footsteps on the stairs below.

"Who's there?"

No answer.

"Hello?"

Light footsteps, barely audible, moving away. A door slammed. Niels dashed over to the little window and looked out. Was that a dark figure hurrying away from the building? Something floating? Maybe it was just the light from Carlsberg, which cast long shadows.

The light on the back stairs went out.

54

It was an icy-cold morning. The windchill factor made the temperature a biting five below zero. *Air Force One* landed at precisely nine o'clock. A few seconds later, the door next to the presidential seal opened and President Obama emerged from the plane and walked down the stairs. There was a trace of concern in his otherwise determined expression. A hint of doubt. The most powerful man in the world was not received with any sort of pomp and circumstance. After a quick handshake with the American ambassador, Laurie S. Fulton, he got into a comfortable limousine and headed for the Bella Center. He was a busy man. A man on a very specific mission: He was going to save the world.

Friday, December 18

Niels woke up feeling that his body was filled with an extreme amount of energy. A familiar feeling—and highly preferable to the opposite, which was emptiness. Not depression, as Kathrine claimed. He had either a lot of energy or very little.

Nørrebro district—Copenhagen

Even though Hannah was just sitting there staring into space, there was something different about her.

Niels noticed it at once as he entered the café and caught sight of Hannah sitting at a table in the back, sipping her coffee. It wasn't because she'd made an effort with her appearance—mascara, a trace of lipstick, her hair neatly combed—it was mostly because of the look in her eyes. The way they were surveying the room and the other people in the café. A sense of curiosity had been awakened. A fundamental interest in what was going on around her. She saw him and waved. A childish gesture that made Niels smile. Next to her on the floor stood the cardboard box containing all the case materials.

"Let's celebrate the system." Hannah nodded toward the tray on the table. Pastries, eggs, croissants, slices of melon. "I ordered for both of us."

"The murder in Cape Town. How did you—"

"I figured out the system." She spoke quickly, almost feverishly. "I used the myth and the number thirty-six as my starting point."

"Now wait a minute, Hannah. You're not a religious person."

"Are you sure about that?" She smiled. "To be honest, I don't know whether I am or not. But I do know that everybody is always touting the division between religion and science. Aren't you going to sit down?"

Niels hadn't realized that he was still standing. He sat down.

"That division is based on a false premise. It simply doesn't exist. The first sciences developed from a desire to prove the existence of God. In that sense, science and religion have been hand in hand from the very beginning. Maybe more favorably inclined toward each other during some periods than others, but still."

"Why the number thirty-six?" Niels poured himself some coffee. "Does it have some special meaning?"

"In relationship to the system, yes. And that's exactly what we need. Listen to this: Right now there's a commonly held view among scientists that we know about only four percent of all the matter in the universe. Four percent!"

"So what about the other ninety-six percent?"

"Exactly. What about it? We astrophysicists call it 'dark matter' and 'dark energy.' Maybe we should just call it ignorance. There's so much that we don't know, Niels. It's shocking how little we know. And yet we behave like little gods who think we're in control of everything. Like kids with delusions of grandeur. Isn't that what we've made ourselves into? It's as if we're trying to make ourselves believe that four percent is all there is. That everything else, all that we don't know, doesn't exist. But it does. We know it's there; we just don't understand it."

"There have been reports of only . . . how many murders? Twenty-one? Not thirty-six."

"So far, yes. That's because the others haven't been discovered or reported."

Niels hesitated. He didn't know whether he sounded curious or skeptical when he asked, "What about this murder in Cape Town? How did you know about it?"

"Do you know who Ole Rømer was?"

"Yes, the chief of police in 1700 something."

"And an astrophysicist," she told him. "Like me. He was the first person to measure the speed of light—and he did it with great precision."

"How does he fit into the picture?"

"The king once asked Rømer to find out how big an area Copenhagen covered. So it was just a matter of going out and making meticulous measurements, right? But Rømer figured it out in less than ten minutes. How did he do that?"

A waitress walked past. Hannah caught her attention. "I know this is a strange request, but could I borrow some scissors and a melon?"

The waitress studied Hannah. "Just a sec," she said, and left.

Hannah went on. "Rømer took a balance scale and a cadastral map of Copenhagen and . . . Oh, thanks." The waitress handed her the requested scissors and a melon. "And then he began cutting."

Hannah started cutting up the paper tablecloth. Niels noticed a young couple surreptitiously staring at them. At Hannah.

"Rømer simply cut away all the inhabited areas from the map and placed them in one of the pans of the scale. Then he placed the uninhabited areas in the other pan."

Niels smiled. "And what is it that you've cut out?"

"Doesn't this look like Africa?" She held up a piece of the paper.

"If you say so."

"Okay. I admit that South Africa should probably be a little narrower, but I'll bet you can recognize Australia and South and North America." She held up a few more pieces.

"You removed the continents?"

"No, the water. The oceans. So only the continents were left. The rest I cut away." She started putting together the pieces as if they were a puzzle.

"Hannah?" Niels insisted on making eye contact with her. "I haven't had any physics or math since I finished high school. You're going to have to go slower. So: You cut the continents out of a map. That much I've understood. And you threw away the oceans?"

"Right."

"But why? What would that prove?"

"Didn't I tell you in my phone message? We have to go back in time, Niels. To a very long time ago. To when the continents were first formed. Back when multi-celled organisms appeared."

Niels stared at her.

"It has to do with plate tectonics. Continental plates, plates on the ocean floor, and the specific gravity of granite as opposed to basalt. There's no need to go into all that right now. Let's start at a different place."

"Good idea."

"Because of plate tectonics, the continents move around on the earth. They're virtually always in motion. There's a long and elaborate explanation for why this is true, but I'll spare you the details."

"Thanks."

"What you need to understand is that the continents are made up of granite. Have you ever heard of Minik Rosing?"

Niels shook his head.

"A geologist from Greenland. He proposed a theory that the earth's granite was formed by the oxidation of basalt, and that the oxygen for the oxidation process came from the first photosynthesized bacteria, which appeared approximately three point seven billion years ago."

Niels raised his hands in surrender.

Hannah paused to think. "Okay. We'll skip the explanation and go right to the conclusion. Or at least a partial conclusion. The continents resulted as a consequence of life on earth."

"That's a conclusion?"

"Let's call it a starting point. Look at this."

Niels watched as she moved the continent pieces until they were all connected. The young couple at the next table had given up any attempt to hide their interest as they followed along.

"Once upon a time, all the landmasses were connected, gathered around the South Pole. The continents looked something like this. No, I'll draw you a picture." She took a black marker out of her bag and began drawing the continents on the melon. "This is how they looked, gathered at the South Pole."

Ever since Niels had met Hannah, she'd had a nervous air about her. In the way she walked, in all her movements. But not right now.

"This is approximately how the earth looked about a billion years ago." She held up the melon.

"Back when the continents were all connected?" said Niels.

"Exactly. It's an accepted theory today, but it was less than a century ago that a German astronomer discovered how they all fit together—quite literally. It took years before anyone believed him."

Niels stared at the melon.

"Let's go on to a new world." She looked up at him. "Just for a moment, let's travel to a world called Rodinia."

55

Niels had taken off his jacket. The café was filling up with students hungry for lunch.

"The word 'Rodinia' comes from Russian, meaning 'motherland.' And that's exactly what the supercontinent of Rodinia is: the mother of all the lands."

"Okay." Niels nodded.

"It was when Rodinia split up that life on earth truly began to develop. The subsequent periods are called the Ediacaran and Cambrian periods. There are other periods, but I'm not a geologist."

"Why are we talking about continents and . . ."

"Rodinia."

"Yes. What do they have to do with the murders?"

Hannah poked at her food. "I knew that the system had to do with human beings. With life. According to the myth, the thirty-six are supposed to take care of the rest of humanity. And people live on earth, not on the water. That's why I took away the oceans. And here, in this primitive representation of Rodinia, I discovered something remarkable." She held up the melon.

The young couple at the next table had stopped eating and were paying close attention, as if they were at a lecture in an auditorium.

"I looked at the points from above and saw that they formed a pattern. Then I compared the pattern with the dates of the murders. Meaning the order of the points. I assigned a number to each of them. The seventeenth murder was in Beijing. The fourteenth in Cape Town."

"Khayelitsha. South Africa."

"Precisely. And the ninth was in Mecca. The fifteenth in Thunder Bay."

"Sarah Johnsson."

"Right. Let me draw you a picture."

She cleared all the glasses and plates off the table. The girl at the next table made room so Hannah could move everything over there. Then Hannah drew a big circle on the tablecloth.

"This is the earth. The continents looked something like this." She sketched in the continents so they were gathered around the South Pole. "This will give you a general idea. And the places where the murders occurred—the points—are approximately here."

With impressive speed, she put in thirty-four points. "We'll give each of them a number according to when they occurred. Do you see anything now?"

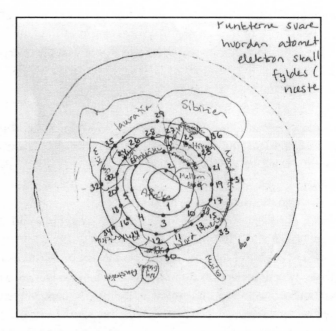

Niels looked at the drawing.

"Do you see that the numbers almost form small circles? Or small concentric shells?"

"Possibly."

"And that they move back and forth from one half of the circle to the other?"

Niels didn't reply. He noticed a cigarette pack in her handbag and had a fierce urge to ask her to step outside with him to have a smoke.

"I figured out that the circles, or shells, are located at the twelfth, twenty-fourth, thirty-sixth, and forty-eighth parallels. But that's not the most important thing at the moment."

"No? What *is* the most important thing?"

"The system you're looking at is an atom. And not just any atom. It's atom number thirty-six."

"Thirty-six. Just like—"

"The myth. It might be a coincidence, but it might not. The Niels Bohr Institute has played a major role in the mapping of the known elements. Maybe I have atoms on the brain, but it's an indisputable fact that this system—down to the smallest detail—is structured exactly like atom number thirty-six. Krypton."

"Kryptonite?" Niels smiled. "Are you telling me this has something to do with Superman?"

"No, unfortunately not. Superman isn't part of the system. Krypton is a noble gas. The word comes from the Greek word *kryptos,* which means 'the hidden.'"

"'The hidden'? Why's that?"

"Presumably because the element krypton is a colorless gas. But it has the special property that it lights up in spectacular green and orange spectral lines when a current passes through it. In other words, it can be activated to emit light. It's also used to define the length of a meter because of something called the krypton-86 isotope."

Niels couldn't help laughing. "Is there anything in this world that you don't know, Hannah?"

"Krypton is a noble gas, as I said, so it's inert. It's one of very few atoms that is perfect. It's in a state of equilibrium. It doesn't go looking for other atoms to combine with. And it's not as if the earth's atmosphere is filled with krypton. Air contains only 0.0001 percent krypton." Hannah fell silent. "The myth of the thirty-six righteous people. Or am I over-interpreting? I just feel like I can sense a connection."

State of equilibrium. The hidden. Perfect. Alone. She was talking so fast that Niels didn't catch everything she said. "Niels, the number thirty-six is a miracle in itself. Three plus six is nine. And if you multiply thirty-six by another number, the digits in the total will always add up to nine. Thirty-six times twelve is four thirty-two. Four plus three plus two is nine. Thirty-six times seven is two fifty-two. Try it yourself. When the numbers get bigger, you just divide them by two."

"Hannah, I'm really sorry, but what exactly are you trying to tell me? Let's just skip the in-between parts."

She stared at him as if weighing what to say. Maybe she was searching for the combination of simple words that would make everything clear to him. Then she said, "Okay, without all the in-between parts: The locations on the earth where the murders took place were established billions of years before any humans even existed. As you know, I figured out where in South Africa that defense lawyer died. And I did it by looking at this system. A precisely determined system based on the continents as they were connected at the beginning of time."

She pointed to the drawing on the table. "I'm telling you that if the system looks the way I think it looks, then we'll know exactly where and when all of the murders took place. Plus where and when the last two murders will occur."

"We will?" Niels discovered that he was whispering. He repeated in a louder voice, "We will?"

"I've written the whole thing down. Look at this." She took out a piece of paper and handed it to Niels. He unfolded it and studied what she'd written.

1. Olduvai Gorge (Tanzania)—Friday, April 24, 2009 (CHAMA KIWETE)
2. Santiago (Chile)—Friday, May 1, 2009 (VICTOR HUELVA)
3. Bangui (Central African Republic)—Friday, May 8, 2009
4. Monrovia (Liberia)—Friday, May 15, 2009
5. Dakar (Senegal)—Friday, May 22, 2009
6. Cusco (Peru)—Friday, May 29, 2009 (MARIA SAYWA)
7. Rio de Janeiro (Brazil)—Friday, June 5, 2009 (AMANDA GUERREIRO)
8. Samarkand (Uzbekistan)—Friday, June 12, 2009
9. Mecca (Saudi Arabia)—Friday, June 19, 2009
10. Tel Aviv (Israel)—Friday, June 26, 2009 (LUDVIG GOLDBERG)
11. Nairobi (Kenya)—Friday, July 3, 2009 (NANCY MUTTEN-DANGO)
12. Johannesburg (South Africa)—Friday, July 10, 2009 (HELEN LUTULI)
13. Chicago (USA)—Friday, July 17, 2009 (ANDREW HITCHENS)
14. Cape Town (South Africa)—Friday, July 24, 2009 (JORIS MATHIJSEN)

15. Thunder Bay (Canada)—Friday, July 31, 2009 (SARAH JOHNSSON)
16. McMurdo Station (Antarctica)—Friday, August 7, 2009 (JONATHAN MILLER)
17. Beijing (China)—Friday, August 14, 2009 (LING ZEDONG)
18. Bangalore (India)—Friday, August 21, 2009
19. Babylon (Iraq)—Friday, August 28, 2009 (SAMIA AL-ASSADI)
20. Chennai (India)—Friday, September 4, 2009
21. Kathmandu (Nepal)—Friday, September 11, 2009
22. Hanoi (Vietnam)—Friday, September 18, 2009 (TRUONG THO)
23. Kaliningrad (Russia)—Friday, September 25, 2009 (MASHA LIONOV)
24. Caracas (Venezuela)—Friday, October 2, 2009
25. Helsinki (Finland)—Friday, October 9, 2009
26. Belém (Brazil)—Friday, October 16, 2009 (JORGE ALMEIDA)
27. Nuuk (Greenland)—Friday, October 23, 2009
28. Athens (Greece)—Friday, October 30, 2009
29. Paris (France)—Friday, November 6, 2009 (MAURICE DELEUZE)
30. Seattle (USA)—Friday, November 13, 2009 (AMY ANISTON)
31. Moscow (Russia)—Friday, November 20, 2009 (VLADIMIR ZHIRKOV)
32. Shanghai (China)—Friday, November 27, 2009
33. Washington, D.C. (USA)—Friday, December 4, 2009 (RUSSELL YOUNG)
34. Mumbai (India)—Friday, December 11, 2009 (RAJ BAIROLIYA)
35.
36.

Niels was staring at the piece of paper. The young man at the next table got up to pay the bill. The girl craned her neck to see what the paper said. Hannah continued her lecture.

"We know that the outermost shell of atom number thirty-six is symmetrical. In other words, once we've located numbers thirty-three and thirty-four, which we have"—she pointed—"we'll know exactly where to find numbers thirty-five and thirty-six."

"And where's that?"

"I think our friend in Venice must have been able to decipher part of the system. Because some of the continents are the same as they've always been.

They've just moved. That's why there's a precise distance between some of the murder locations. And that's why I think he wanted to send a warning—"

Niels interrupted her. "Hannah. Where?"

She turned the paper around and wrote something down. "All right. Now the system is complete."

Niels read what she'd written:

35. Venice OR Copenhagen—Friday, December 18, 2009
36. Venice OR Copenhagen—Friday, December 25, 2009

He stared at the words. Maybe he'd actually known all along. Maybe he'd sensed it from the moment he was assigned the case. Even so, he felt as if all the blood had drained from his head and his heart stood still.

"We know the time and place of the last two murders. We just don't know the order."

"So what you're saying is that . . ."

"That today at sunset a murder will be committed either in Venice or here in Copenhagen."

"Do you really believe that?"

"Believe? This has nothing to do with beliefs, Niels. How else could I have figured out the location in South Africa? The statistical probability of it being a coincidence is . . ."

Niels had stopped listening. He felt his body getting heavier, almost as if it were being pressed downward—as if, without warning, gravity had doubled its intensity. He looked at Hannah. Her thin lips were still moving. Arguing, lecturing. He forced himself to listen to what she was saying.

"I'm telling you, Niels, there's a definite system to this. A system of . . . let's just call it of godlike proportions. It's telling us that the next murder will occur today at sundown in either Venice or Copenhagen."

"But where in Copenhagen?"

Hannah tore off another piece of the paper tablecloth, which was looking quite ragged by now, and wrote down some numbers. The young couple was about to leave. The girl gave Hannah an appreciative look before she exited the café. Hannah didn't notice as she handed the paper with the numbers to Niels.

"What's this?"

"The latitude and longitude here in Copenhagen. Either today or next Friday."

"Are you sure, Hannah?"

"Don't ask me that, Niels. I'm just telling you how the system works. Mathematics never lies. Copenhagen tonight at sundown, or someplace in Venice."

Niels pointed at the numbers she'd written down. "Where exactly is this?"

"I don't understand what you mean. The latitude and longitude are right there on that piece of paper."

"Yes, but Hannah, *where* is this?"

56

Niels came out of the café. The shift from indoor to outdoor lighting was barely noticeable. In a few days' time, it would be the shortest and darkest day of the year. The old streetlights, with their faint yellow glow, were no match for the gathering gloom.

"The sun sets so early," said Hannah. "We have only a few hours, max."

She stood behind him, putting the change from the lunch bill in her wallet. She had set the cardboard box containing the case materials on the sidewalk.

Niels turned around and looked at her. "When does the sun go down?"

"Just before four. Why?"

"Why?" Niels looked at her in astonishment. Was it all just theoretical for her? A parlor game? "Hannah. You said the murder would occur at sunset. Right?"

"Yes, that's right. At the exact moment when the sun goes down."

"Which means that we have five or six hours to find the location. And the person who is about to be murdered."

Hannah gave Niels a look of surprise, as if her theory had taken on new meaning.

"Did you drive here?" he asked.

"Yes."

"Where are you parked?"

"It's that little Audi over there."

"Does it have a GPS?"

"Yes, it came with the car. I've never used it. I don't even know how it works."

Niels was the first to reach the car. Hannah climbed into the passenger seat, holding the cardboard box on her lap. She wasn't used to his practical approach. Niels could see that about her. She had delivered the results, completed her lecture. For her, the world was primarily a theoretical place. A thought occurred to Niels: Had she been flirting with him in the café? Was that how a genius like Hannah flirted? By drawing atoms on the tablecloth and babbling about how the earth looked a billion years ago? Suddenly he understood why her life must be difficult.

"Listen here, Hannah. You were the one who said it first: Maybe we can prevent the next murder. And you called me."

"Yes." She nodded resolutely.

"So I'm ready." Niels took the box from her and tossed it behind them on the backseat. "Let's have a look at the GPS. Can it navigate by latitude and longitude?"

"I don't know. Maybe."

Niels turned the key in the ignition. The little car started up with a low purr. Hannah turned on the GPS and looked to Niels for instructions. It's going to be a long drive, he thought before he pulled out, nearly hitting a truck.

Jagtvej. Another one of the street names that every Copenhagen police officer associated with trouble and adolescent demonstrations. The sort of thing that in the old days could spread, attracting dissatisfied segments of the population to a revolt that might topple kings and governments. But no longer. The time of revolution was past. Back when the citizens decided that the absolute monarchy should be abolished, fewer than ten thousand people marched in a peaceful procession to the royal palace. Nowadays all the climate demonstrators assembled in Copenhagen couldn't expect to get anything but a bad cold from their efforts. On the radio a commentator estimated that there were a hundred thousand people on the streets of Copenhagen at the moment, participating in street theater and protest marches.

Niels shook his head. A million people on the streets of London hadn't been able to influence Tony Blair's decision to send British soldiers to Iraq. So how were a hundred thousand climate activists going to turn down the earth's temperature?

"Is it working?" Niels watched Hannah awkwardly touching the GPS screen. "Is it hard to figure out?"

She gave him an offended look. "Niels! When I was four years old, I was able to solve quadratic equations."

"I was just asking."

Silence. She studied the screen. "Okay, it's ready now. We need to head south a bit."

"South?"

"Southwest, actually."

The traffic wasn't moving at all. It looked like a still photograph. Jagtvej was always like that. Once upon a time the thoroughfare had been reserved for members of the royal family when they left the palace to go out hunting. As soon as it was opened to the general public, the road became instantly popular. In a capital where the urban planning was haphazard and chaotic, to say the least, Jagtvej should have offered some relief: an unbroken line from one end of the city to the other, from the Nordhavn district in the northeast all the way across to Carlsberg in the southwest. Niels endured the traffic on Jagtvej every single day, and he hated it. It was also unhealthy. Modern technology was set up everywhere, measuring the pollution created by the gasoline engines the activists were demonstrating against. The air on this street was about as unhealthy to breathe as the air in Mexico City. If this were Japan, everyone would be walking around wearing masks over their mouths. But it was neither Tokyo nor Osaka. It was Copenhagen, and people here weren't as particular about the air they breathed.

Niels lit a cigarette. "Do you mind if I smoke in your car?"

"It looks like that's what you're already doing."

"I can toss it out the window."

"Go ahead and smoke. I'll have one, too."

Niels pounded on the car horn. "We're not getting anywhere like this," he said.

"No, I can see that."

He swerved the car over into the other lane. An idiot wearing a suit and hiding behind the wheel of a huge BMW instantly pulled out to block the intersection. Niels slapped his police ID against the window. "Jerk!"

"Isn't this street one-way?" asked Hannah as the BMW moved back and Niels sped down the side street.

"Here. Take my cell phone."

"Why?"

"You said there are two places where the next murders will take place, right?"

"Yes, here and in Venice."

"Call Tommaso. The Italian."

"Di Barbara?"

"Tell him that . . . No, give him the coordinates. Tell him what you've figured out."

Reluctantly, Hannah took Niels's cell. He had already punched in the number. Hannah listened. "It's his voice mail."

"Leave a message."

"What should I say?"

Niels gave Hannah an annoyed look. Only a short time ago this woman had been a powerhouse, a fucking explosion of thoughts and ideas, calculations and greatness, yet now she'd been reduced to a blithering amateur. Somebody who was a tourist in real life, who would soon hurry home to the fortress of theory and grief that she'd created inside her summer house.

"Tell Tommaso you've figured out that a murder is going to be committed today, either in Venice or in Copenhagen, when the sun goes down."

Hannah turned back to the Italian's voice mail. "*Bonjour,* Monsieur di Barbara."

Her rusty French proceeded in the same fashion as the car Niels was driving the wrong way up the one-way street: faltering and swerving. Niels clumsily maneuvered around a garbage truck. A man riding a bicycle didn't hesitate to express his anger. He pounded his fist on the roof of the Audi. Hannah gave a start. In Copenhagen it was the bicyclists versus the drivers, and people easily switched from one role to the other.

"Tell him that you'll text him the latitude and longitude. Then he can find the location on a GPS."

Hannah went back to speaking French.

Niels listened. Even though Hannah sometimes came to an abrupt halt in the middle of a sentence, French words had never sounded more beautiful than the ones now issuing from her lips.

57

Venice

The sound of the boat's motor plowing its way through the murky water drowned out the phone. Tommaso's Yamaha outboard had been in the shop for repair since October, but he finally had it back. He was enjoying the sound of its uninterrupted roar without a single discordant note—it ran like a dream. A ray of sun lit up the lagoon, promising better times. Tommaso looked at the dachshund precariously stretched out on top of a pile of rotten ropes. The dog belonged to his mother, and he was on his way to take the animal to the pound.

"Are you seasick?" Tommaso asked the dog as he attempted a smile. The dachshund gave him a woeful look, as if aware of what was in store for him.

Tommaso could see the island now. The sick-bay island, as some people called Santa Maria di Nazareth. When people arrived in the city at the head of the Adriatic four hundred years ago, the plague was ravaging the continent and they had been forced to spend forty days on the island. *Quaranta,* which means "forty" in Italian. That was the origin of the word "quarantine." Forty days for people to prove that their skin wasn't going to break out in blisters. Forty days of not knowing whether the island might be the last place they ever saw on this earth. Maybe it was the thought of the plague, but Tommaso felt as if the flulike symptoms he'd been experiencing for the past few days were getting more insistent. "Swine flu," he murmured as he decreased the speed of the boat. He was having a little trouble breathing. He closed his eyes and savored the warmth of the sun. If he hadn't been suspended, he'd be over at the train station with his fellow officers. The arrival of the politicians and the justice minister was a big event, and Commissario Morante had ordered the entire police force to stand ready. That would happen without Tommaso. And it suited him just fine.

The buildings facing the lagoon were all lopsided. The swampy earth beneath the island had twisted their foundations, and the structures were starting to list. Rust from the iron bars on the windows had run in streaks down the brick walls. After the plague disappeared, the island had been used as a prison for the insane, but these days it was a pound for dogs. Stray dogs from both the mainland and the islands were brought here. Many were euthanized; some waited for a new owner.

Tommaso switched off the motor a few yards from the dock. At that instant he heard his cell phone ringing. Ten missed calls. One from Denmark. From Niels Bentzon. Nine calls from the hospice. That was a bad sign.

58

Copenhagen

Save the planet. Apocalypse if we don't act now. We demand action.

Niels and Hannah sat in the car, staring at the demonstration. Some of the protesters were dancing, while others were about to explode with anger at the injustice in the world.

"How far is it now?" asked Niels.

"That depends on the mode of transportation."

"How many decimals of latitude and longitude?"

"Decimals?" She smiled. "The degrees are divided up into minutes—meaning sixtieths—and seconds. So the number of seconds depends on—"

Niels interrupted her. "Hannah! How far?"

"About a mile and a half."

Niels drove the car up onto the sidewalk, set the hand brake, and yanked the GPS out of the socket.

"What are you doing?" Hannah asked him.

"We're going to walk."

———

From a distance, there was almost something aesthetic about the demonstrators. It was a picture they'd seen a hundred times before—a dense swarm of people following the curve of the streets. But it wasn't the same thing when they joined the throngs and walked among them. Niels held on to Hannah's arm as they forced their way through. Here, in the center of the action, they were surrounded by fierce and chaotic energy. And the stench of liquor. Niels caught the eye of a woman with multiple piercings.

The pupils of her eyes were slightly dilated, and she had a remote expression on her face. Nothing could possibly happen to her; she wouldn't even feel it when the police batons struck her. That was something the people sitting at home in front of their TV sets didn't know. The young people were on drugs, and it often took two or three officers to handle an irate anarchist anesthetized by some bizarre cocktail of potent beer and designer drugs. They didn't react to pain.

Where was Hannah? A few moments ago he was holding on to her arm, but now she was gone. Niels looked around. Everyone was dressed in black, as if for Judgment Day. A big drum was trying to keep the tempo. Suddenly, he saw her. She looked scared. A drunk who was at least ten years too old for this kind of demonstration had put his arm around Hannah and was trying to dance. As if this were Mardi Gras.

"Niels!"

He pushed his way through the crowd, moving against the stream.

"Hey!" A youth had grabbed hold of Niels's jacket. "I know you. You're a cop! A fucking cop!" he cried, and was clearly about to repeat it even louder when Niels shoved him aside. The boy lost his footing and dropped to the ground like summer dew, light and barely noticeable. At least it happened so quickly that Niels was able to get hold of Hannah before anyone discovered the kid. He held on to her hand, which was warm in spite of the cold temperature.

"Are you okay?"

"I want to get out of here."

"Don't worry, I'll get you out of here," said Niels, looking over his shoulder. The boy was on his feet, glancing around. They were barely able to make out his words before they were drowned out by the noise from the big drum: "You fucking pig. You fucking pig."

Copenhagen had become an angry city. People had even scrawled on the yellow stucco walls surrounding Assistens Cemetery, voicing their frustrations. "Fucked" was apparently the word that best described the city's existential crisis. *The earth carries your imprint*, it said above the entrance to the cemetery, friendly-looking letters shaped out of red neon. Maybe yet another climate message. Or it could be the simple truth of a gravedigger: We leave an imprint if we allow ourselves to be buried.

Inside the cemetery, they paused to catch their breath.

"We'll cut through here. Okay?" asked Niels.

Hannah surveyed the cemetery and then looked back at the demonstrators, as if considering turning around.

"As the crow flies. Is something wrong?"

"No. Of course not."

He had an urge to hold her hand again. It had felt so good in his.

"What does the GPS say?"

She took it out of her pocket. "The battery's low."

"Then come on."

Niels touched her elbow. She gave a start. Then her expression changed, and she looked so vulnerable that he wanted to put his arms around her. A thought occurred to Niels, but too late. Was it here that Hannah's son was buried?

Kathrine had dragged him over here on a specially arranged midnight tour a few years ago. The participants had been given burning torches, and they had moved from one grave to another while two pastors, one woman and one man, took turns recounting the history of the cemetery. *The English sweate.* He remembered that term because it sounded so strange. It was a virus that had killed thousands of Copenhagen citizens in the sixteenth century. There were so many bodies that a new cemetery had to be established. Ever since then, the most famous Danes had all been buried here at Assistens Cemetery.

"What does the GPS say now?"

"Straight ahead," replied Hannah, still looking uneasy. The snow had turned the cemetery into a monochrome landscape. The white blanket was broken only by the dark headstones. It looked like a checkerboard in black and white. The smaller headstones belonged to the pawns, the unknown dead. Moss and all manner of weather had long since worn away the names engraved on the stones. High above them towered the kings: Hans Christian Andersen, Søren Kierkegaard, and Niels Bohr. Surrounding them stood the bishops and rooks: the actors and civil servants who had been well known in their day but were now forgotten. Finally, there were those who had achieved immortality because of their unusual exit from life. A young widow, for instance, who had been buried alive a couple of centuries ago. Niels recalled the story that the female pastor had told. In those days a gravedigger also did some moonlighting. He would bury the people in the daytime and then work as a grave robber at night. When he opened the young widow's coffin, her eyes flew open. "Free me from this terrible place!" she screamed. The gravedigger slammed his shovel against her forehead, grabbed her jewelry, and covered the grave back up. Many years later, on his deathbed, the gravedigger confessed to the murder. In modern times the body of the widow was exhumed and found to be lying in disarray and without any jewelry; her body had clearly been disturbed in its coffin. Nowadays her grave received as many visitors as Hans Christian Andersen's.

─────────── ✦ ───────────

Hannah looked relieved as they left the cemetery and once again stood out on the street. They crossed Nørrebrogade and walked along Møllergade, past the Literary Center and the Jewish cemetery. The snow crunched under their feet, and the air was bitterly cold. They walked in silence. Hannah kept her eyes fixed on the GPS. Then she came to an abrupt halt. "Here!"

"Here?" Niels looked around. What had he expected? At any rate, not a drab old co-op apartment building. Two baby strollers were competing with a delivery bicycle to block the sidewalk.

"Are you sure?"

She looked at the GPS doubtfully. "At least I think so," she replied uncertainly. "Although the battery is used up now. It's dead."

"But you think it was here?"

"Yes. Of course, there's room for error. But it has to be within a few yards of here."

Niels walked a few yards back and forth. The co-op building stood all by itself. There had once been adjoining buildings on either side, but they had been torn down. The only other thing in sight was a dreary and deserted playground.

"I don't know," said Hannah, shifting from one foot to the other uneasily.

"What don't you know?"

"There's a small degree of error. Maybe a few hundred yards. If only I had more time."

"This can't be the place."

She looked at him. "What were you expecting to find?"

Niels shook his head. "I don't know. A religious lunatic, maybe. Let's assume that your system is right. Who could have thought up such a thing?"

"Why aren't you looking for the next victim instead?"

Niels shrugged. "It could be anybody. Someone who happens to come walking past." He looked at the nameplates posted next to the door of the building.

"If you think about it, Niels . . . I mean, just think about the mathematical precision." Hannah smiled at the thought.

"What are you getting at?"

"Let's call it a phenomenon," she suggested.

"A phenomenon?" Niels couldn't share Hannah's apparent joy over the theory. Instead, he called Casper back at police headquarters. "Niels Bentzon here. I have a few names that I'd like you to check for me."

Hannah looked at Niels in surprise as he began reading off the names from the building's intercom panel. Carl Petersen, third floor. Lisa O. Jensen, third floor. All of a sudden the door opened. Niels took a step back. An old man gave them a surly look. "What are you doing here?"

Niels didn't even bother to take out his ID. "Copenhagen Police. Keep moving!"

The old man was about to say something else, but Niels interrupted him. "This is none of your concern."

The building tenant headed down the street, although he looked back at least five times. In the meantime, Casper had typed in the names. "I think I have the person you're looking for," he said.

"Who is it?"

"Carl Petersen, third-floor right."

"Really? What about him?"

"He raped and strangled a girl back in 1972. Buried her body near Damhus Lake. He was paroled in 1993. Born in 1951."

59

Ospedale Fatebenefratelli—Venice

Tommaso tied the dachshund's leash to the boat, which he moored behind the ambulance that was quietly rocking from side to side at the covered boat landing. It was possible to bring a boat right into the middle of the hospice, which was what Tommaso had just done. The dog barked and growled, apparently delighted to be at a safe distance from the pound once again. Tommaso jumped up onto the slippery marble floor and took off running. As if that would make any difference. He'd gotten the message that his mother was dead just as he was pulling up at the sick-bay island. He'd been preparing himself for this event for months, but the guilt he felt was stronger than he'd expected. *He should have been here.*

The eldest monk was sitting in the room, but not next to the bed. Instead, he sat next to the window, bending over his rosary. He looked up. Was there a trace of reproach in his eyes? Tommaso didn't care for the man; he wasn't as forgiving and loving as Sister Magdalena.

"It's good that you came," said the monk.

Tommaso walked around the bed and sat down on a chair. His mother didn't look any different. "When did she die?" he asked.

"About an hour ago," said the monk.

"Was she alone?"

"Sister Magdalena had been in to see her before going home. The next time we looked in on her . . ."

He didn't need to say anything more. Signora di Barbara had died alone.

The tears were unexpected. Tommaso had thought that he would feel relieved. But he didn't. For a few moments he sobbed without making a sound, then he gasped for air, letting his lungs take over and give voice to his pain. The monk came to stand behind him, placing his hand on Tommaso's shoulder. At the moment that was all right; it was what he needed.

"I wish I had been here," he managed to stammer.

"She died in her sleep. It's the best kind of death."

The best kind of death. The words tried to find some meaning in Tommaso's mind.

"The best kind of death," the monk repeated.

"Yes."

Tommaso reached for his mother's hand. It was cold. The small knuckles, which had worked so hard all her life, were closed in a fist. A coin fell out of her hand. Ten cents. The little gleaming coin lay on the blanket. Tommaso was surprised, and he turned to look at the monk. He had seen it, too. Tommaso turned his mother's hand over and carefully opened her fingers. There were two more coins. A half euro and a twenty-cent piece. "Why is she holding coins?"

The monk shrugged. "I'll ask Magdalena. We've been trying to call her. I'm sure we'll be able to reach her soon."

Tommaso sat there, holding the three coins, unsure what to do with them. It was as if the unexpected appearance of the coins had put a damper on his grief, adding a slight mystery to the situation. Why was his dead mother holding eighty cents? Tommaso put the coins in his pocket, then turned her hand over and placed it palm down, like the other one.

60

Before Niels knocked on the door, he reached over and pulled up the collar of Hannah's coat.

"Do I look like a cop now?" she asked.

He smiled. "Just let me do the talking."

Niels knocked. There was no nameplate fastened to the door. The tenant had used a marker to write his name directly on the paneling. They could hear noise coming from inside, but no one opened the door. Niels unbuttoned his jacket so he'd have easier access to his gun.

"Copenhagen Police! Open up!"

This time he pounded on the door. Hannah looked alarmed. He shouldn't have brought her along. It was unprofessional of him to bring her here. He was just about to send her back downstairs when an unkempt man with bloodshot eyes opened the door.

"Carl Petersen?"

"What have I done now?"

Niels showed the man his ID. Carl studied it. Niels looked a good deal younger in the photo.

"May we come in for a moment?"

Carl glanced over his shoulder. Maybe making one last survey of his own wretchedness before he allowed strangers inside. He shrugged and opened the door all the way. They were the ones who insisted on coming in. "Hurry up, so the birds don't get out."

The stench inside the apartment was unbearable. Food and piss and animals and decay. Two rooms and a kitchen. For some reason there was a double bed in each of the rooms, which were hardly big enough to hold them.

"Do you live alone?"

"Who the hell would want to live with me? I'm a convicted murderer."

Hannah looked at Carl in astonishment.

"Why are you pretending to be surprised?" he said. "That's why you're here, isn't it? You show up every time some woman in the neighborhood gets raped and you run out of leads. Who is it this time?"

Niels ignored him and went into the kitchen, but Carl wasn't letting him off the hook. "Tell me who I've raped now! Tell me! I've paid my debt, goddammit!"

Newspaper clippings had been taped to the refrigerator door. Random anti-immigrant articles cut out of the newspapers that were distributed for free: *20,000 Polish workmen in Denmark. Bilingual pupils do poorly in school compared to Danes. Fifty percent of Muslim women unemployed.* In the middle was a postcard showing a smiling Pia Kjærsgaard, cofounder of the Danish People's Party: *We need your vote.* Niels turned from the gallery of articles on the fridge to look at Carl. Hate was a commodity. It was possible to sell hatred and receive something in return. Carl got a little extra home help and a cheap meal once a day. In return, he had sold his hatred, which was probably mostly self-hatred, to the arch-conservative woman politician on the fridge. And now she was free to make use of it.

"What do you want from me?" Carl's words were interrupted by a fit of coughing. "Bronchitis," he managed to whisper before the next wave overtook him. He was using a deep royal-blue bowl for the excess phlegm.

I wonder if that used to be a champagne bucket? Hannah managed to ask herself before she glanced inside. She shouldn't have done that. She could feel the nausea rising. With two swift steps, she moved over to the window and was just about to open it when Carl shouted: "No!" He looked at her in fright. "The birds are out." He pointed to an empty cage. A couple of parakeets were watching Carl's every move from a shelf lined with glasses. Only now did Hannah notice the bird shit. Little circular white and gray spots were everywhere, none of them bigger than an old five-øre coin.

"So are you going to tell me what the hell is going on here?" said Carl.

Hannah caught Niels's eye. It couldn't be this man. Impossible.

At that moment they heard the helicopter outside the window. A big Sikorsky was flying low over the rooftops.

"Those fucking choppers. They keep landing day and night," mumbled

Carl as Niels and Hannah moved to look out the kitchen window, which faced southwest. The helicopter was about to land. Carl was grumbling in the background. "I haven't gotten a whole night's sleep since they built that landing pad on top of the hospital."

Niels and Hannah looked at each other. She was the first to say it: "The National Hospital."

61

Ospedale Fatebenefratelli—Venice

Tommaso di Barbara leaned against the wall. The sun had disappeared again. He was the only person on the hospice balcony, but other smokers had been there before him. Two ashtrays with biblical motifs painted on the sides stood on a white plastic table. The ashtrays bore witness to the December rains. Water filled them to the brim, and the cigarette butts swam around, bumping into each other.

He was taking a break. The monk wanted to try again to reach Sister Magdalena on the phone. They had sat in the room together for about half an hour without saying a word. Then Tommaso remembered his mother's dog, left behind in the boat. The monk had promised to go and look after him. He had insisted because he thought Tommaso should have some time alone.

As the monk said, "When a person has looked death in the face, it's important to be alone for a while before going back out into the world."

His family. Should Tommaso call them now? His uncles and aunts. His mother's younger sister, who hadn't visited her even once. He took his cell phone out of his pocket. Someone had left him a message, but he didn't have time to listen to it before he was interrupted.

"I'm sorry about your mother, Signor di Barbara."

Tommaso was startled, even though the voice was so feeble and faint, sounding like it had traveled a thousand miles to reach him. But it hadn't. The man was standing right next to him. Signor Salvatore. Tommaso knew him slightly. He owned a couple of souvenir shops near the Piazza di San Marco. He wasn't nearly as old as Tommaso's mother, but he, too, was ill and would soon die.

"Your mother. I'm so sorry."

The old man's naked legs were visible below the hem of his bathrobe. Covered with varicose veins and gray hair.

"Thank you."

"May I have a cigarette?"

That doesn't sound like such a good idea, thought Tommaso, but what the hell. The party was just about over for Signor Salvatore.

"Thanks."

They smoked in silence. Tommaso remembered that he'd been about to call his mother's sister and dump his guilty conscience on her. He glanced at his phone. He still hadn't listened to the last message. From a number in Denmark. He tapped on his voice mail.

"I used to talk to your mother once in a while, Signor di Barbara."

"Thank you for doing that."

Tommaso listened to the message. *Hannah. Calling you for Niels Bentzon. The Danish policeman. Regarding the case* . . . and then something else in French that he couldn't understand.

"I knew your father, too."

"Excuse me a moment."

Tommaso got up and moved a short distance away. . . . *removed the oceans, all the water. I hope you understand, it's a little difficult to explain on the phone.*

"He wasn't a bad sort, your father."

Tommaso looked in bewilderment at the old man. What the hell was he babbling about? Hannah was struggling with her limited vocabulary in French—or maybe she was having trouble because the subject was so complicated . . . . *I mean, with all the water gone, and all the landmasses pressed together the way the continents used to be at the dawn of time* . . .

Tommaso ignored Salvatore. He was listening to Hannah. *You can look at an atlas and see for yourself. All you have to do is cut the water away. Then you'll see it at once. Just move all the continents around the South Pole.*

"But today we can finally talk about it again. He wasn't all that bad— Benito, I mean."

Tommaso had no idea who the old man was rambling on about. Tommaso's father wasn't named Benito.

Then the old man pronounced the name with a secret glee, as if he were being quite daring. "Il Duce."

Hannah was finishing up her message. . . . *the coordinates here in*

Copenhagen and in Venice. The next murder. I'll send you a text message. Au revoir.

———————————•————————————

Tommaso rushed past the office. Several of the nurses stopped him, wanting to express their condolences. "Thank you. Thank you so much. I appreciate your kindness to my mother," he replied, then hurried on. He knew it was here somewhere. The library. He remembered seeing it the first time he came to visit the hospice. That was three months ago, shortly before his mother was admitted as a patient. He had been given a tour of the whole place, even though everyone knew full well that his mother would probably never leave her bed again.

The smell of chlorine. Tommaso was standing in front of a swimming pool that was used for physical therapy. He wasn't in the right place. "Excuse me. Where is the library?"

The physical therapist looked up at him from the pool. He had his hands under the arms of a patient who was staring blankly up at the ceiling.

"The library? Do you mean the reading room?"

"Yes."

"It's on the second floor. All the way over in the other wing of the building."

Tommaso took off running as he tried in vain to make sense of the strange message that had been left on his phone by the Danish woman. He raced downstairs and through a ward that for once didn't smell of death. Just illness.

The reading room was located in the section of the hospice that had remained unchanged since the days when the building was used as a cloister. An elderly woman was the only person in the room, although she wasn't reading. She sat there looking anxious, both hands clutching her purse. As if Tommaso might try to take it away from her.

"Ciao."

He headed straight for the bookshelves, filled with dusty volumes. Mostly novels. Books intended for the patients, though these days they preferred to watch TV. There had to be an atlas somewhere.

He glanced at the old woman. "Would you mind helping me?"

At first she looked surprised. Then her face lit up and she said, "Yes, of course."

"We need to find an atlas. Why don't you start over there."

It was clearly a welcome break in the monotony of her days. She threw herself into the task, even setting down her purse. Tommaso ran his finger over the spines of the books, looking at the titles. Why were there so many cookbooks? Surely that was the last thing anyone needed in a hospice.

"Here you are." The old woman handed him a children's book. It said *Our World* on the cover, with a picture of cowboys and Indians.

"Thanks. Thanks for your help."

In the center of the book, he found a colored map of the world. Tommaso glanced at the woman. Her smile faded as he swiftly ripped out the pages.

62

The National Hospital—Copenhagen

A direct and immediate connection between theory and proof was something that was completely foreign to Hannah. She was used to spending years discussing theories with her colleagues. When physicists finally came up with a relatively satisfactory theory, they could then begin to look for proof. And it was not at all certain that the proof would emerge during their lifetime. The English physicist Peter Higgs could regard himself as a very lucky man. In 1964 he proposed the theory about the particle that was now being sought, using all available means, in a specially constructed, twenty-seven-kilometer underground tunnel in Switzerland. Higgs was now eighty. Forty years ago he had theorized about the existence of this particle, and if it were found, then he would be one of the few physicists to experience a direct convergence between theory and proof. Along with Hannah Lund.

She looked at the people in the lobby of the National Hospital. Men and women wearing white coats. Last night she had discovered the logic in a pattern of murders. With geographical precision, she had calculated these coordinates without having the faintest idea that they designated the location of Denmark's largest hospital.

Niels came back from his tour of the lobby. "Of course, of course," he murmured.

Hannah didn't know what to say. She was feeling uneasy. She took out the GPS. Maybe she'd read it wrong. She switched it on.

"Is the battery working again?"

"I don't know. Maybe."

The position locator began searching. It instantly picked up the signal from the satellite making its eternal orbit of the earth.

"What do you think?" asked Niels impatiently.

"That's what it says. This is the place." She gave him a resigned look.

Niels shook his head. "Doctors. Midwives."

Hannah took over. "Cancer researchers, lab technicians, surgeons. Almost everybody who works at the hospital is involved with saving lives. All of them would qualify as good people."

"Can't you find a more exact location?" asked Niels.

"We're not going to get any closer. There's no time."

Niels muttered a few swear words and then resumed roaming around the lobby. A thought flitted through his mind: If it hadn't been for his damned travel phobia, he'd be sitting next to a swimming pool right now. He could have sat there, not giving a shit about any of this, and drinking himself silly. Instead, here he stood, looking inside the hospital's employee cafeteria. Hundreds of people wearing white coats. White was a symbol of goodness. Hitler's most trusted soldiers wore black. Doctors always wear white.

Hannah took his hand. She knew what he was thinking. "There are so many of them," she said.

"Yes," he replied. "Too many."

Reception area, the National Hospital—Copenhagen

The receptionist didn't look up from his computer. Maybe he thought Niels was joking when he asked, "How many people work here?"

"General questions about the hospital should be directed to our PR division."

Niels pulled out his police ID. "I asked you how many people work here."

"But—"

"Including all the employees. Doctors, nurses, orderlies, cleaning staff. Everybody."

"Are you here to see a specific patient?"

"Including all the patients and their visitors. Okay, let me ask the question another way: How many people do you think are here in the hospital at this very minute?"

The receptionist gave Niels a helpless look. Hannah tugged at his arm. "Niels."

"And how many of them are between the ages of forty-four and fifty?"

"Niels. This is pointless."

"Why? What do you mean?"

She gave the receptionist an apologetic look. He merely shrugged.

"Niels."

"It has to be possible! These days everything is entered in computers. It should be easy to find out which employees are the right age and are working at the moment."

"And then what?"

"We need to find out which of them most deserves to be called a good, righteous person. And prevent a murder. Wasn't that why you phoned me?"

"I don't know. It seems like such a long shot."

"Why's that? Just look at the list of victims. Pediatricians, pastors, lawyers, teachers—most of them had contact with a lot of people. They were all trying to help others."

Hannah sighed loudly. Like Niels, she'd been thinking about where she could be other than here. At the lake. Sitting in a deck chair. With a pack of cigarettes and a cup of coffee. In her own world.

Nearby was a scale model of the hospital in a glass case. Niels leaned over it, pressing his hands against the glass. He was sweating nervously. When he lifted them away, his palms left marks on the pane. Hannah went over to stand next to him. In silence, they studied the miniature version of the hospital. As if it made everything easier to grasp. They read that the main building was sixteen stories high. The old section of the hospital was spread over an area large enough to contain a small village. Suddenly, Niels turned to Hannah. "Okay, you're right. We need to do this a different way."

63

Amager—Copenhagen

Shit Island. Niels hated that nickname. Nevertheless, two demonstrators stood alongside the highway, holding up a clumsily printed placard: WELCOME TO SHIT ISLAND—MEETING PLACE OF THE WORLD'S SHITTY LEADERS. Hannah saw them, too, but didn't comment. Snow and ice were clinging to the beard of one of the men. He looked like what he undoubtedly was: a madman. The sort of person who was always attracted to events such as the climate conference. COP15 was perfect fodder for the conspiracy theories and paranoid reasoning that is always on the lookout for signs of the apocalypse, such as having all the world leaders gathered in one place. At the site where the citizens of Copenhagen in the old days dumped their human waste. It was almost *too* symbolic. Nowadays a thin layer of asphalt covered the marshland, and on top stood an urban district straight out of the visions of the future depicted in French science fiction films of the 1960s. Elevated tracks for trains that ran without any humans at the controls, and white-painted high-rises that all looked the same. Clinical architecture designed in the days when it was thought that the future would obliterate the individual in favor of the community. That wasn't what happened. Back then, over forty years ago, no one could have foreseen that the world would become a thermostat that could be turned up or down. Mostly up.

A few more activist stragglers were making their way through the snow alongside the highway, heading for the Bella Center.

"Looks like the madhouse has opened its doors," muttered Niels.

Hannah attempted a laugh but failed. "Are you sure I really need to go with you?"

"Yes. You have to explain the whole thing."

Hannah looked out the car window. She was regretting getting involved. She didn't feel up to explaining anything.

The Bella Center. A fancy name for a building made of drab concrete located on Europe's flattest stretch of marshland. Niels parked some distance away. Special permission was required to drive up to the entrance. The Bella Center was not under Danish jurisdiction while the conference was going on. At the moment it belonged to the UN. Otherwise, a handful of despots wouldn't have been able to attend. Heads of state who, according to normal Western standards, ought to be serving thirty-eight consecutive life sentences for crimes against humanity. But they were all here. Mugabe, Ahmadinejad, and the whole gang. For the purposes of turning down the earth's temperature. It was almost touching.

"Have you seen Sommersted?" Niels asked one of the officers.

"Inside somewhere. Everything's in a hell of a mess at the moment. Obama's here." Niels smiled and patted the man on the back. The officer shook his head. "It's hard to say whether the Secret Service is running the show or we are," he told them. Show, thought Niels. Perhaps a better description of things than his colleague knew. The demonstrators were being kept back by a nine-foot-high fence. They stood on the other side, looking like refugees from the Russian Revolution: clad in black, frozen, and harmless. Those considered potentially dangerous had been locked up while Obama was on the scene. All those who had a real chance of breaking through the fence.

Sommersted was standing in front of the TV cameras and reporters, a relaxed smile on his face in spite of the questions being hurled at him. Why were the demonstrators forced to sit on the pavement for so long? Why weren't the police better prepared? *Demonstrators taken to the hospital. Police brutality.* Sommersted's smile seemed to get bigger with every accusation leveled at the Copenhagen Police. Finally, he held up his hands, as if trying to stop a runaway train. "Right now five of my officers are in the ER. Three of them have serious concussions. One of them has a broken nose and jaw. They were struck by iron pipes. But of course, I regret the fact that a few of the demonstrators might have suffered a minor bladder infection from sitting on the cold pavement."

He paused for effect. Suddenly, all the reporters seemed like children, and Sommersted the only adult in the crowd. He put on a sympathetic smile for the cameras. "It's the primary responsibility of the Copenhagen Police to ensure that the world leaders can meet safely and without interference here at the Bella Center. Our secondary responsibility is to make sure that as few demonstrators as possible are injured—even though they're attacking us with bricks and worse. But that is the order of our priorities when it comes to security. Any questions?"

Scattered murmuring. The reporters were feeling repentant. Sommersted was an expert at pacifying members of the media. As the last questions ebbed away, Niels pushed through the crowd. "Sommersted?"

The police chief looked at Niels in surprise. "Bentzon? That was a good job you did, catching Abdul Hadi."

"Thanks."

"Aren't you supposed to be on vacation?"

"I know you're busy," said Niels, ignoring the question, "so I'll make this brief." He pulled Hannah forward. "This is Hannah Lund, a researcher at the Niels Bohr Institute."

Sommersted looked at Hannah in confusion. "Niels Bohr?"

"Actually, a former researcher," Hannah managed to murmur before Niels went on.

"The international homicide cases—good people being killed? Remember that? It turns out that the murders are being committed according to a complex system that's apparently connected to an ancient religious myth." Niels could hear how strange this sounded, and he came to a standstill. A group of Chinese delegates wearing suits began jostling him. What they lacked in height, they made up for in numbers. Niels continued, "Is there someplace else we could talk? This will only take a minute."

Sommersted glanced around, taking fifteen seconds to consider whether to listen to Niels for the minute he had requested. "All right, go ahead."

"Okay. Hannah?"

She cleared her throat and spent a full five seconds looking Sommersted in the eye. "At first we thought the distance between each murder was approximately three thousand kilometers. But it's much bigger and more complicated than that. The system, I mean. You see, at first the numbers didn't make sense. But then I removed all the water, the oceans, and shoved the landmasses together. You have to imagine the surface of the globe consisting only of land—"

"Gathered at the South Pole," Niels interjected.

"The South Pole?" Sommersted asked.

"Exactly. The way the continents looked a billion years ago. The supercontinent of Rodinia. It's a little hard to explain everything in only thirty seconds, but here goes: If we place the thirty-four crime scenes on the twelfth, twenty-fourth, thirty-sixth, and forty-eighth parallels, then"— Hannah glanced at Niels before she continued—"they form small circles or shells and . . ." She came to a halt.

Niels took over. "In short, there are two locations left: Copenhagen and Venice."

Not a word from Sommersted. The seconds ticked past.

"Venice?" Sommersted looked from Hannah to Niels and back. "Venice? I went to Venice on my honeymoon."

His sarcasm was wasted on Hannah. "What does that have to do with this?" she asked.

Niels took over again. He cleared his throat and spoke louder to be heard over a message in English being broadcast over the loudspeakers throughout the entire conference center. "Tonight," he said, "or rather, this afternoon, when the sun goes down just before four—"

"At three thirty-seven P.M.," Hannah interjected.

Niels went on, "At three thirty-seven P.M. a murder will be committed either here or in Venice." People were starting to look at them. Those who understood Danish, that is. Reporters, with their press credentials hanging around their necks on black cords advertising Nokia.

"In Venice the sun will set in less than four hours. Here it will set in three. We don't have much time."

64

Tommaso could remember the location where every single murder had been committed. Even the first ones. Tanzania, Peru, Brazil. He had used a pen to mark them on the map he had ripped out of the children's atlas. With an X-Acto knife, he had removed all the water. Then he had pushed the continents together to form one piece. Even with the naked eye, he could see how it all fit together.

Tommaso had closed the door to the reading room, but he could hear voices out in the corridor. He stared at the childish handiwork lying on the table. A world cut up into pieces and then put back together. Outdoors a siren had started up its lament. It took a moment before it occurred to Tommaso what the siren portended. Only when he stepped over to the small window and saw the Venetians rushing for home did he understand. The city would be flooded in a few minutes. The water in the canals would rise soundlessly. He looked again at the map he had destroyed. It was as if the water in the lagoon were now seeking revenge because Tommaso had removed the seas from the map.

Nonsense.

It was high season for flooding in the lagoon. Several times a week the people of Venice had to pull on waders and rubber boots, barricade their doors, and seal up the cracks. He should be going home, too. Or maybe he could call his downstairs neighbor and ask him to put up the planks. Thinking about using the phone reminded Tommaso of the message he'd received from Denmark. Again he tried to call the Danish woman who had left the voice message. No one answered.

Tommaso's mother was lying in bed just as he'd left her. Alone. Tommaso had a headache, and his back ached. A nurse walked past.

"Excuse me," he said. "Could I trouble you for some painkillers?"

The nurse looked at him and smiled. "I'll get the doctor."

She was gone. The hospice was deserted, with only a few essential staff members present—and the patients, of course. The rest had dashed home, as everyone always did when the waters began to rise. Some of them to reach the mainland, others to protect their homes.

"I can't find him at the moment." The nurse poked her head in the door again. "But I'll let you know as soon as I do."

"Thanks."

She looked at him with a sorrowful expression. "I spoke to Sister Magdalena a little while ago."

"The sister spent a lot of time with my mother, and I'm very grateful for that."

"Sister Magdalena is on her way over here." The nurse smiled. "In spite of the flooding. She said it was important. She said not to leave until she talks with you."

Tommaso had a hard time imagining what could be so important.

"Are there are other family members on their way here?" the nurse asked.

"I don't think so."

"Maybe you'd like to go over to the church and light a candle for your mother."

"I might do that."

"If you do, I'll let Sister Magdalena know that you haven't gone far."

Tommaso smiled, and then his Catholic upbringing made him get to his feet. Of course he would light the candle that his mother would use to navigate her way through purgatory.

He stepped outside the main entrance. The Venetian lion was carved into the stone next to the marble pillars that bore the weight of the old building's roof. The lion looked angry. The square in front of the hospice was already covered with a quarter inch of water. The church wasn't far away. Tommaso's feet would get wet, but there was nothing to be done about that. He needed to light the candle, even though Sister Magdalena had said he shouldn't leave the hospice until she spoke to him. She, if anyone, would understand the importance of lighting a candle for the dead. The fires of purgatory weren't going to wait because of a little flooding.

"Signor di Barbara."

Tommaso saw the old monk.

"Are you leaving?"

"Just to light a candle for my mother. What about you?"

"I won't be gone long. Our cardinal is arriving with the justice minister," replied the monk, his face lighting up at the thought.

"At the train station?"

"Yes. I'll be back soon."

The monk pulled his cowl over his head and set off—well prepared, with big rubber boots just visible under his long robe. For a moment Tommaso felt free. Completely free. Free from standing at attention, wearing his dress uniform, and taking part in one of the police chief's endless welcoming ceremonies; free from visiting this place, this hospice. He was free. With the money from the house . . . if he sold it . . . no. It was too early to think about that. He hadn't even lit a candle for his mother yet. The feeling of freedom was replaced by guilt, and he raced off toward the church.

65

The Bella Center—Copenhagen

A re we under arrest?" asked Hannah after they'd been sitting for a long time inside a shed normally used by workmen.

"Of course not."

Niels caught sight of Sommersted through a window that was sealed shut. The police chief was crossing the square in front of the demonstrators, moving past the line of delegates from NGOs and members of the press who were waiting to pick up their credentials. When the police chief reached the shed, he yanked on the door handle so hard that Hannah jumped. He closed the door behind him, seething with ill temper. "Thanks for waiting," he told them.

"Now, listen," said Niels, "I know it sounds crazy."

Sommersted sat down across from them. He tugged on the bottom of the bulletproof vest he was wearing, revealing a few tendrils of gray hair on his chest, reaching up toward his throat.

Niels went on, "As I was trying to say, the murderer is acting according to an ancient myth about the thirty-six good people who keep the world going. Do you know it? We can even calculate the location of the next murder. We know the precise coordinates, and everything points to the National Hospital."

"The National Hospital?"

"Mathematics never lies. The long and short of it is that we need to evacuate the hospital."

They were interrupted as Leon opened the door. "He's on his way out."

"Are they done?"

"I think they're just taking a break."

"Thanks, Leon."

Leon caught Niels's eye before he shut the door again.

"You gave me an assignment," Niels began. He straightened up and tried a new tactic. "I contacted a number of so-called good Danes and warned them. Because of one of the names on the list, I happened to get in touch with Hannah Lund." Niels glanced at Hannah and then turned back to Sommersted. "You have to realize, Sommersted, that this woman is a genius."

Sommersted shook his head and looked down at the table, his expression sorrowful. "I can't protect you any longer, Niels. First you use your free time to visit criminals in prison, and now this."

"You need to look at the facts," said Niels. "We know when the crime will take place. This afternoon, when the sun sets at three thirty-seven P.M. And we know the location. The National Hospital. We also have a profile of the next victim. A good person who has no children and is between the ages of forty-four and fifty. You just need to look at the facts."

Sommersted slammed his hand down on the table. "Facts?" he shouted. "The fact is that I gave you a chance to handle a simple assignment. It was a matter of regaining my trust." The next second Sommersted obviously regretted his outburst. "No, we're not going to get into this now, Bentzon. There are more important things at the moment. I'll see you next week in my office."

"At least listen to what she has to say."

"Niels. I've just had a background check run on your friend here."

Hannah looked at Sommersted in surprise, then turned to look at Niels.

"Maybe you should have done the same thing before you came trooping in here with this woman. Here, of all places. Today. Passing right through all the security checks to where Obama and all the others are gathered."

"What do you mean?"

Sommersted got up.

"What sort of background check?" said Hannah, standing up, too.

Niels looked at them in confusion. As if the two of them shared some kind of secret. "What's he talking about?" he asked.

Sommersted cast a sympathetic look at Hannah, who exclaimed, "That has nothing to do with this."

Niels interrupted, "What are the two of you talking about?"

Hannah took a deep breath. Sommersted leaned against the door, regarding her expectantly. "Tell him what you found out," she said without looking up.

"I wasn't going to mention it, but since you want me to . . ." Sommersted sounded almost human. "We know that you were a patient in a psychiatric ward. And do you know what that means in my world?"

Hannah was trying not to cry. "But I had lost my child."

"It means that you're unreliable. And unreliable people are a threat to security."

Hannah whispered, "You bastard."

"What I really don't need right now while I'm taking care of him"— Sommersted pointed out the window at Obama, who was walking from the building entrance over to his parked limousine—"is unreliable lunatics. Because they're dangerous."

Obama waved to the demonstrators. He looked smaller in person. HEAL THE WORLD, Niels managed to read on one of the banners before Sommersted opened the door.

"And now I'm going back to my job."

Hannah was crying. Sommersted paused in the doorway. Niels looked at him. He knew that all was lost. That he was no longer employed and most likely wouldn't be hired by any police force in the whole country. He might as well give the last order.

"Get out of here, Sommersted. Goodbye."

———————————

They made the drive back to Copenhagen in silence. Niels was behind the wheel. Hannah looked out the window and was so quiet that Niels began to doubt she was even alive.

"Are you still breathing?" he asked.

"Yes."

"Good."

"But I have no idea why."

Why do we keep breathing? thought Niels. He couldn't answer that question. Not at the moment.

"Drop me wherever you like. It doesn't matter to me. Where did you park your car?" For the first time she looked at him.

"Near the café."

"Oh. Right."

The café. It was strange how things could change over the course of a day. In the morning Hannah had worn mascara. But by now it had all smeared off. In the morning she had been a scientist in her element. Now she was a psychiatric case.

"Niels . . . I should have seen it coming. We went too far. I'm sorry about that."

Niels's cell phone was ringing. "It's the Italian police officer." He handed her the phone.

"What should I say?"

"Tell him that the next murder will be committed in either his city or ours." Niels pulled over. His cell stopped ringing. He turned off the engine and looked at Hannah. "I don't know what happened to you back then. But I know you're not crazy."

She managed a small smile and shrugged. "Not a day passes that I don't compare myself to accepted standards of what's considered normal. I keep a journal. Every time I see a connection, I write it down."

"What do you mean?"

"My brain. It's always looking for systems in everything. It has always done that. It's a supercomputer that never shuts down. From the time I was very young. It's a curse. At one point it stopped. That was when I gave birth to my son. But then I started seeing systems that didn't exist."

"In what way?"

"License plates, for example. I started looking for numerical connections. I still do. I write them down and show them to my psychiatrist. And you know what?"

"No. What?"

"Your license plate. I noticed it when you backed out of my driveway the first time you visited me. It's II 12 041."

"What about it?"

"12 04. That's April twelfth. My son's birthday. Then there's the last digit, which is one, and the double 'I' at the beginning."

"I don't get it."

"The letter 'I' is the ninth letter in the alphabet. So then we have '199.' And if we attach the next number, then we have . . ."

"'1991.' Is that the year your son was born?"

"Exactly. So there you have it, Niels. I'm always seeing systems. All the time. I saw that system on your license plate in less than a second. Do you understand? It's a curse. A calculator that I can't turn off."

Niels paused to think about what she'd said. "Look at the road."

"What do you mean?"

"Just look. Is there a system in the way the cars are driving?"

She smiled. "You're trying to be nice."

"Just answer the question. Pretend that I'm an idiot."

"Okay, yes. There *is* a system."

"Exactly. People drive on the right side of the road. So even though you see systems that aren't important, you also see some that are. I've been called manic-depressive. A victim of stress and depressions and psychoses. All of that. Everybody is always so busy trying to diagnose us. To explain our mood swings by relating them to some disease."

She hesitated. "You're right. But now I'd better get home."

Niels studied her. "I guess that would be best. Because the problem isn't with the fact that you see too many systems." He started up the car.

"What are you talking about?"

"It has to do with people, Hannah. As long as there are systems, theories, something going on inside your brain, everything is fine. But now that it has to do with real people, that's when you shut down. Right?"

She looked at him in surprise. "That's not what I'm saying at all."

"There are systems, black holes, and dark matter. You know all about those sorts of things, Hannah. That's your home turf. But there are also real people. Me . . . the people in your life . . . the next victim . . . your son."

"You . . ."

She was just as taken aback by her loss of control as Niels was. But he was the one who felt the brunt of her anger. First she uttered a half-stifled scream that echoed in the small car. Then she began pummeling Niels with her fist.

"Hannah! Calm down!" shouted Niels, holding up his hands to protect his face. He could have grabbed her arms, but he didn't.

"You, you . . ." she repeated over and over without finishing the sentence. She just kept on hitting him harder.

Then she stopped. He tasted blood. It didn't seem to matter that she could see the results of her rage. The seconds became a minute. Maybe more.

"You're bleeding," she said.

"It's nothing."

She was breathing fast as she reached out to touch his mouth. She wiped away the trickle of blood from his lips, and Niels grabbed her hand. The kiss came as the most natural thing in the world. She turned to face him, got up on one knee, and leaned over him. She was the one doing the kissing. Her tongue slid cautiously over the tiny cut on his lower lip before meeting his. They stayed like that for several moments.

Then Hannah sat back down in the passenger seat and looked out the window. As if nothing had happened. Neither the kiss nor her outburst. She was the first to break the silence.

"You're right," she said.

66

Chiesa dei Santi Geremia e Lucia—Venice

T he call came at the very second the siren stopped wailing. A number with the country code 45. From Denmark. People weren't supposed to take phone calls inside the church, but Tommaso had already lit a candle for his mother, crossed himself, and behaved like a good boy. He'd actually lit two candles, just to be on the safe side. Little Christmas-tree candles that would burn down in no time. He moved into the side aisle so as not to disturb anyone else. In a low voice, he said, "Tommaso di Barbara."

It was the Danish woman. She wanted to know if he'd received her message.

"*Oui.*"

She spoke French with a strong Danish accent. But she pronounced each word with care. "The system works down to the last decimal," she explained.

"That sounds unbelievable."

"If the number is correct—if we're talking about the number thirty-six . . ."

There was a lot of noise on the line. Tommaso looked up at the painting above him: Jesus was standing there with His arms outstretched. Thomas the Doubter was sticking his finger into one of Christ's wounds, at the spot where the Roman spear had pierced the Savior's side.

"Are you still there?"

Hannah replied, "Yes, sorry. There are two more murders. The next one will take place either in your city or in ours."

"Are you sure?"

"Yes." She answered without hesitation, confident in her belief, which suited the place where Tommaso found himself at the moment.

"But . . ." Tommaso struggled to formulate his amazement. Up near the altar, a glass case contained a figure dressed in red. A tourist took a picture of it. Tommaso turned away from the scene. "When?"

"All the murders were apparently committed at sundown."

In his mind, Tommaso quickly ran through the list of victims. Why hadn't he noticed that? Presumably because an exact time of death had been ascertained for only a few of the murders. But still. Every day for the past six months, he had spent hours on the case, and yet this woman had been able to solve the whole thing in no time at all.

"Monsieur di Barbara?"

"*Oui.*"

"I'm sending you a text. It contains the coordinates for the location where the murder will be committed."

"What do you want me to do?"

Hannah was silent for several seconds. Then she said: "What did you want us to do when you sent us all that information about the case?"

Tommaso looked around.

Hannah asked, "When is the sun going to set there in Venice?"

"Very soon, I think."

"Then you could use the time that's left to pinpoint the coordinates that I'm sending you. Find the location where the murder is going to take place. Try to stop it."

"Right. Of course. It's just that my mother . . ."

He considered explaining the situation. That his mother was dead. He had to go back. It would be frowned on if he left so soon after she died. But he didn't say anything.

"There's a certain amount of leeway with the GPS. But it should be accurate to within a few yards. I've got to go now."

Luciano was sitting on the church steps. He was one of the few homeless people left in Venice. They were no longer tolerated because of the tourists. When Tommaso was a child, there had been many more. Now Luciano was practically the only one left. On the other hand, everyone in the neighborhood tried to help him. As if he were the local pet.

"Tommaso. Give me some change."

Tommaso rummaged through his pockets. "I've only got eighty cents."

"Never mind." Luciano dismissed the eighty cents with a wave of his hand and an insulted sigh. Tommaso then found a five-euro bill in his back pocket and handed it to the man.

As Tommaso dashed across the square, he saw that the water had risen another half inch. Except for Luciano on the church steps, the streets were deserted. "Merry Christmas," the old drunk yelled, and then Tommaso turned the corner.

67

The National Hospital—Copenhagen

Hannah was sitting in the lobby of the National Hospital, and Niels was impatiently pacing back and forth, when he caught sight of his colleague through the window. Casper parked his bicycle, removed the bike lights, and came inside.

"I came as fast as I could." Casper sounded out of breath.

"Did you tell anyone where you were going?"

"Nobody asked."

"Good. I want you to meet Hannah. The two of you are going to be working together."

"I've never been out in the field before," he said excitedly. Hannah came over to join them.

Niels introduced her. "Hannah Lund. Professor at the Niels Bohr Institute," he added. She didn't try to correct him. Any other explanation would have been too complicated. Introducing Casper was easier and also closer to the truth: the computer genius from police headquarters.

Personnel office, the National Hospital—Copenhagen

It took forever for the fluorescent lights to turn on. The cold glow lit up the sign on the frosted glass of the door: NATIONAL HOSPITAL PERSONNEL OFFICE.

"I was just leaving for the day," said Thor, the middle-aged man in charge of IT who had let them in.

I wonder if his parents still think Thor is a suitable name for a such a small man, thought Niels. Maybe they knew that he was going to be short before he was born, so they tried to compensate for his size. Thor Jensen. Just over four and a half feet tall.

"Okay. Jurassic Computer Park," said Casper, running his hand over one of the old computer screens.

Thor had no idea what Casper was referring to. "It's Friday. People go home early," he replied.

"Do you know how to turn on the system?"

"Yes."

"Then do it," Niels told him.

With a sigh, Thor set his bag on the desk, went to the back of the room, and turned on the main switch. An electric hum spread through the room.

Casper laughed with delight. "It's like going back in time."

"It actually works great. Better than the old system."

"Which was what? Punch cards?"

Thor apparently didn't feel like discussing the hospital computers with Casper and shrugged. "Is there anything else?"

Casper looked at Niels. Hannah answered him. "Could you print out a complete list of all the hospital employees?"

"Theoretically, yes."

"All the patients too," Niels added.

"I was off duty three minutes ago."

"When am I going to find out exactly what we're doing here?" asked Casper.

Niels looked from Casper to Thor. He knew there was no other option. He would have to explain, as briefly and precisely as possible. "We're trying to find a good person who's at work right now in this hospital."

No one spoke. Thor gaped at Niels.

Casper opened his bag and took out his laptop. The police department's logo was imprinted on the shiny aluminum: two lions rampant, and between them an open hand holding an eye. The eye of the police.

"The same search we did before?" asked Casper.

"No," said Niels. "We need to be more precise this time. We're not interested in people who are well-known public figures."

Casper looked up. "Then how do you want to do this?"

"We're looking for someone between the ages of forty-four and fifty."

Hannah added, "Who doesn't have children."

"That could be me," said Thor. They all turned to stare at him.

Niels went on. "Someone who has contact with lots of people. And who saves lives."

"There must be a few people like that in this place."

"That's why you're here, Casper."

"What do you mean?"

"We need you to sort them out."

Hannah sat down at one of the old computers.

"Hannah, I want you to find possible candidates," Niels said.

Thor cleared his throat. "Excuse me for interrupting, but . . ."

Niels glanced impatiently at Thor. "Yes?"

"What is this all about?"

"We're trying to prevent a murder that is going to be committed in this hospital at three thirty-seven P.M. That's in less than an hour."

Casper stood up, looking anxious. "Maybe you'd better get somebody else."

Niels took him by the arm and said authoritatively, "Take it easy. Sit down, Casper." But Casper remained standing. "We have a chance to prevent it. We need your brainpower. You're the only one who can do this."

"What if I fail?"

"That's not going to happen. We fail only if we don't try. Sit down."

Finally, Casper sat back down. Niels noticed that his hands were shaking slightly. Hannah put her hand on Casper's shoulder to reassure him.

"As I was saying, Hannah and Thor will find the candidates in the hospital's computer."

"I'm sorry, but I'm off the clock."

Niels refused to let him off the hook. "Thor? Have you ever tasted the food in Vestre Prison? Goulash out of a can."

Silence. The little computer guy unbuttoned his jacket and sat down next to the others.

"We're looking for someone between forty-four and fifty."

"That should be possible."

Niels went on. "And Casper, you'll check to see if they qualify or not."

Hannah sighed. "What would disqualify someone? What would knock them off the list?"

Niels paused to think. "Frequent or serious trouble with the law. That sort of person wouldn't be considered good. You'd be surprised how many people have a police record."

"What about the Russian?" said Hannah. "He was in prison."

"Yes, but he was jailed for speaking out against the political system. He hadn't committed a crime against a fellow citizen. On the contrary."

"So what about the man in Israel, the one who released the prisoners?"

"The same thing. He was convicted of doing something good that happened to be against the law."

Casper had logged on. "Where should we start? The doctors? The nurses?"

"What about the orderlies?" asked Hannah. "Could they also be considered good?"

"Sure. But let's start at the top."

Hannah shook her head. "That's not systematic, Niels. It might also be a patient."

"Thor? Can you also tell us who the patients are in the hospital?"

"Of course."

"Okay. But let's start with the employees. Doctors, midwives, researchers. Between forty-four and fifty. With no children."

"I can check that in the civil registry," said Casper.

"We're lucky that it's Friday afternoon. And the Friday before Christmas. Lots of people are already on vacation. Others have left work early. Right, Thor?"

"Yes, that's right."

"Good. I want all of you to feed me the names and departments. Then I'll contact the candidates."

"What are you thinking about saying to them? Are you just going to ask them if they're a good person?" Hannah asked.

For several seconds Niels merely stared at her. "Yes."

"Niels, this is impossible."

Niels thought, then he nodded. "You're right, it's impossible. Almost. Normally, we have to find a murderer. In this case, we know nothing about the killer. The most logical thing would be to evacuate the hospital. But we can't." He paused. "On the other hand, we have quite a few victims. All between forty-four and fifty. All of them childless. And they seem to have had a peculiar ability to find themselves suddenly—almost against their will—in the exact place where their help was needed most. We're looking for someone who has a lot of interaction with many different people. Someone associated with a network."

He was looking only at Hannah. He smiled. "These people are like spiders in a web. They have feelers out everywhere, and they can sense when someone gets caught in the web. Then they're ready to help."

All three were looking at him expectantly. Niels went on, "Why should it be so impossible? I've spent fifteen years searching out evil. And that doesn't surprise anyone. So why should it take an hour or so to find a good person? Is goodness harder to see than evil?"

He pointed out the window at the sinking December sun. It was hovering just above the bare treetops in Amor Park. "We've got an hour before sunset. And yes, it probably does seem impossible. Almost ridiculous. But isn't it worth sacrificing an hour to try? Even though success is statistically improbable?"

A couple of seconds passed as everyone thought about what he'd just said, with the hum of the computers the only sound in the room. Surprisingly enough, it was Thor who answered first. "Yes," he said.

"I agree," said Casper, who had regained his self-confidence.

"Okay. Then let's get started. Check the hospital's records. Take the employees first," Niels said, turning toward the rather bewildered IT expert.

Hannah logged on to her computer.

Niels went on, "Then check the civil registry to see if they have any children. Call me on my cell when you have some names."

Thor looked up from his screen. "I've got one here. Tanja Munck. She's a midwife. She has the night shift, so she's on duty now. I can see that she's already punched in."

"What's her civil registration number?"

Thor read off the number. Casper's fingers danced over the keyboard. "Tanja Munck has three children. Her divorce was finalized in 1993 by the Lyngby district court—"

Niels interrupted impatiently. "Okay. Move on to the next one."

Hannah had found one. "Thomas Jacobsen. Forty-eight years old. How do I find out what sort of work he does?" She turned to Thor.

"What's his CR number?" Niels asked.

"Here he is." Casper found his name in the civil registry. "No children. Registered as living with another man."

Hannah smiled. "Does that mean he's disqualified?"

"Of course not. Find out where he is. Then call me," Niels said.

"Is he at work right now?"

Thor made a call. Niels glanced at his watch as he walked out the door. The last thing he heard was Thor's voice, sounding eager and enthusiastic. "Security? This is the personnel office. Thomas Jacobsen—has he started his shift yet?"

Corridors of the National Hospital—Copenhagen
2:37 P.M.

In an hour someone would die.

People died all the time, especially in a place like this. On average, twenty people each day chose to leave their bodies in this particular hospital. On the other hand, just as many babies were born. Niels's cell rang. It was Hannah. "Thomas Jacobsen is a no-go."

"So who's next?"

"Head for the surgery wing."

A nurse was passing Niels. "Which way to the surgery wing?" he asked her.

"Take the elevator to the sixth floor. Then go left."

"Thanks."

He heard Hannah's voice on the phone. "Can you listen to some statistics while you're on the elevator?"

"Sure, go ahead."

"There are more than seventy-five hundred employees. Half of them are on the job at any one time. But we're looking for those between the ages of forty-four and fifty, and there are eleven hundred people who fit that category."

"How many of them are working right now?"

"About half."

"So we're talking about five hundred and fifty people?" said Niels optimistically.

"Plus we can quickly identify those who have no children. About a third, or a hundred and eighty people."

"And of those, I'm guessing that Casper can find police records for about a third of them."

"So we have a hundred and twenty left. Statistically speaking, at least."

"Who am I looking for now?" asked Niels.

"A senior resident. Dr. Peter Winther."

It was quiet in the corridor. A TV was on, but the sound was off, and nobody was watching it. A nurse looked up from her paperwork. Niels showed her his police ID. "I'm looking for Peter Winther."

"He's doing rounds."

"Where?"

She pointed down the hall. Niels saw a doctor come out of a room with a small group of nurses in tow.

"Peter Winther!" Niels walked toward him, taking out his ID long before reaching the group. The doctor's face went pale.

"Go on ahead and wait for me in the next patient's room," he whispered sharply to the nurses.

"Copenhagen Police." Niels didn't say anything else. He could see that the doctor was about to confess to something. And yet. He turned red as he stared at Niels.

"You know why I'm here," said Niels.

The doctor glanced over his shoulder and took a step closer. "Am I under arrest?"

"No. We just want to hear your side of the story. Before we make a decision."

"My side?" The doctor snorted. "My side of the story is that she's totally and completely insane."

Niels noticed the saliva collecting at the corners of the doctor's mouth.

"And any psychiatrist would agree. She doesn't have a chance in court. Do you understand? Besides, it was self-defense. And I have the scars to prove it."

Peter Winther unfastened the top button of his shirt to show his throat. Long scratches ran from his neck down. "Dammit, I'm the one who should be coming to the police. What would you do if you had a wife who was . . ." He moved closer. He was really working himself up. "Okay, I gave her a slap. But just one! A single slap, and I should have done it three years ago."

Niels looked at his phone. He had a text message: Ida Hansen. The obstetrics clinic. A midwife.

"What the fuck. I can't believe she really went to the police. It's unbelievable. Do I need to think about getting a lawyer?"

Niels shook his head. "No. Thanks for your time."

Niels left Dr. Peter Winther behind to deal with his ruined marriage and his despair.

———

"Talk to me, Hannah." Niels was running.

"She's a midwife, but she's on her lunch break. The cafeteria is on the ground floor."

"Couldn't you organize the list geographically?"

"What do you mean?"

"So I could start at one end of the building and move to the other? We'll never make it if I have to keep running from one part of the hospital to the other every time."

Hannah didn't reply. Niels looked out the window as he waited for the elevator. The sun wasn't red yet, although it was setting fast. He could hear Hannah breathing. A sign pointed toward the maternity ward. A weary mother pushed a little stroller with her newborn son as she absentmindedly devoured a chocolate bar. The baby looked at the sun, just as Niels was doing. I wonder what he's thinking, thought Niels. If I didn't know better, I'd almost think the beech trees in the park were carrying the sun on their shoulders. Like pallbearers in a funeral procession. A dying sun being carried to the west.

With a *ding* that could be heard even by the hearing-impaired, the elevator announced its arrival.

"I'm in the elevator now. On my way down," Niels told Hannah on his cell.

"Okay. Ida Hansen. Forty-eight. Midwife. Hurry."

Hannah ended the call.

68

Cannaregio—Venice

The color of Sister Magdalena's rubber boots could best be described as screaming pink.

Tommaso smiled when he saw her cut across Madonna dell'Orto. The northern section of the city was a bit lower than the rest, which meant that it got flooded faster.

He called to her, "Sister! You were going to tell me something. A message from my mother."

The alarm siren drowned out his words. She vanished inside the hospice without looking back. Unless Tommaso wanted to walk across the bridge at Dell'Orto and get wet to the knees, he would have to go back in order to reach the northern dock, which was seldom flooded. He glanced at his watch. The detour around Fondamenta Nuove would take at least fifteen minutes longer. He had an hour, maybe less, until sundown. The Danish woman had given him the GPS coordinates: 45°26'30" and 12°19'15". His cell phone could display longitude and latitude. Right now his position was at 45°26'45" and 12°19'56". Tommaso had no idea how long it would take him to reach the right location, wherever it was. So he'd better get going. The flooding would keep its grip on the city for at least a couple of hours, and he couldn't imagine that Sister Magdalena would be going anywhere in the meantime. Besides, what could be so important to tell him?

His socks were already soaking wet as he ran south along Fondamenta dei Mori. His shoes splashed through the water. He was the only person on the street. Was this the place? He stopped in front of Tintoretto's house. Tommaso was very fond of the painter. Not so much because of his magnificent painting of the legendary stealing of the body of St. Mark;

rather, because Tintoretto had almost never left Venice. Only once in his lifetime had the painter ventured away from the lagoon, and it was said that he was miserable during the entire journey. Tommaso had never gone far from the lagoon, either.

The GPS signal began frantically jumping around. It was difficult to get a signal in the narrow streets.

He moved on, heading down toward the casino and the Grand Canal, hoping to get a better signal near the wide waterway. His thoughts were still on Tintoretto. No. On St. Mark. Maybe because it was easier to think about the dead evangelist than about his newly deceased mother. He pictured the body of St. Mark, the first painting that every child in Venice sees. The saint was the guardian angel of the city, after all; the central piazza was named for him. Two Venetian merchants had stolen his body in Alexandria—minus the head, if the people of Alexandria were to be believed. The head was supposedly still in Egypt.

The headless corpse, his mother's withered hand, and the colors of death all haunted Tommaso as he reached Strada Nova. The GPS signal jumped again. At the canal he caught sight of the light of the setting sun. He would never find the right place this way; Venice wasn't built for receiving GPS signals or for cars. He had to get hold of a computer.

The entryway was underwater. Ads, dog food, and his mother's black shoes were floating in a lake of canal water; on the surface was a thin film of oil from the boat motors, trying to look like a rainbow. The light went out a second after he turned it on. The main switch had shut off. He reminded himself that his laptop had a battery as he raced up the steps, taking them three at a time. He shook his head. His building had survived four hundred years of monthly floodings. His IBM laptop was only six months old, yet it was already signaling that the battery was almost dead. *Google Earth.* He looked for a spot where he could type in the coordinates, without success. *Low on battery.* Tommaso found the lagoon on the globe, frantically clicked on it, and then zoomed in on Venice. He was getting close. *Low on battery. Save documents now.* He checked the coordinates on his cell and moved the mouse a tad north. There it was.

He sat back, staring at the results. Then his computer shut down.

69

Hannah recognized the methodology from her own experience. Casper's cerebral gears were well oiled, and he had plenty of them. Myriad kinds of information could pass through his head simultaneously, to be handled, assessed, weighed, and categorized. As opposed to Thor, who took one thing at a time.

"I've found one more," exclaimed Casper. "And I think she's at work."

"Think?"

"I'll call security and find out."

Hannah sat down next to Casper. "Listen. The other murder victims—"

"I know. We need to find more common factors, or this is going to take hours. Days. And we don't have that kind of time," said Casper.

"Exactly."

"What do we know aside from their age and the fact that they don't have children?"

"They've all done something remarkable. One was in prison for speaking out against Putin. One was thrown into an Israeli military prison for releasing two Palestinians. A Canadian had used unapproved medicine and was then fired."

"So you're saying that they all ended up in the news for some reason?" said Casper.

"Yes. All of them did something newsworthy."

"If you've been in the news in Denmark, your name can be Googled. Everything is posted on the Internet. Even the smallest article in a local newspaper. If you've worked as a volunteer for only an hour for some charitable organization, your name will be on a list. And that list will be on a website. Even a person's work for a co-op apartment association is posted."

"That's what I mean."

"Let's do a search for . . ." He looked at Hannah.

She finished the sentence for him: "The qualified candidates."

"Right. It'll take two seconds to Google each one. We'll run through all the candidates and then isolate the ones who are the most likely."

Thor put down the phone. "She hasn't punched out yet."

"Quick! Give me a name, Thor!" said Casper.

"Maria Deleuran."

Thor spelled the last name, but even before he was finished, Casper had found her. "She's a nurse," he said.

They studied the picture on her Facebook profile: blond, pretty. Tiny wrinkles that made her even more attractive.

She looks a little like the girl Gustav ran off with, thought Hannah.

"Okay. Here's something." Casper straightened up. "She's a volunteer for IBIS."

A link took Casper to the IBIS website. Aid work in Africa and Latin America. Photographs of Maria Deleuran.

"'Rwanda. HIV. AIDS. Education and prevention,'" he read out loud.

"She's been a project leader down there," said Hannah.

"Twice."

Casper logged off and entered the police database. "Pure as snow. Didn't pass her driving test until the third try. That's the only thing we have on her."

70

The nurse was speaking kindly and patiently to the old man, even though he was badgering her. Niels could hear him complaining from far away. "No, I don't want to go up yet."

"But we promised the doctor. Don't you remember?"

"I don't give a shit about the doctor."

The nurse laughed and patted the old man on the shoulder as she released the brake on his wheelchair and began pushing him back to his room.

Niels stopped her. "Excuse me, where is the employee cafeteria?"

"Back that way. Take a right at the chapel."

The old man snorted. "Chapel."

"Thanks," said Niels. "By the way, I know this sounds like an odd question, but do you have any children?"

"Yes," replied the nurse in surprise. "Why?"

Employee cafeteria—Copenhagen
2:57 P.M.

Niels had a feeling this wasn't going to end well. On the lower floors, it was impossible to see the sun. Instead, he glanced at his watch. Forty minutes left. Tops. Niels didn't feel any better about things when he opened the door to the cafeteria. Men and women wearing white coats. Hundreds of them. It was impossible. No. He had nothing to lose. He climbed up onto a chair.

"I'm from the Copenhagen Police."

Everyone fell silent. The only sound was some machinery clanking in the commercial kitchen. Everyone was staring at Niels. Faces that were used to hearing bad news.

"I'm looking for Ida Hansen."

No one answered. A single hand was timidly raised in the air. Niels jumped down from the chair and walked along the rows of laminated wooden tables. Cafeteria food—the special of the day was chicken, mashed potatoes, and boiled peas. Everyone was looking at him. Especially the doctors. Faces of authority.

"Ida?"

She put her hand down. It couldn't be her. She was too young. "No. I just wanted to say that she has already left. Has something happened?"

"Left? Where did she go?"

He looked at his cell. This was the third time Hannah had called.

"She had to go and help with an emergency birth. She ran out the door."

"How long is it going to take?" Niels could hear how stupid his question sounded. Hannah was still trying to call him. "Just a minute," he said.

He moved away to take the call. "Hannah?"

"Niels. We've come up with a new method. Instead of . . ." She came to a halt. "Well, basically, we have three very qualified candidates. There will probably be more. But start with Maria Deleuran. She works in the Pediatric Department. And she's been an aid worker in Rwanda."

Niels could faintly hear Casper saying something in the background. "And she's written articles about the West's inadequate efforts in fighting AIDS in Africa."

"Okay. I'll find her."

He ended the call and went back to Ida Hansen's younger colleague. "So where did you say she went?"

"To the birthing ward."

Niels hesitated. He had just come from there. It would take five minutes to go back. "What do you think of her?"

The young nurse looked at Niels in astonishment. "What do I think of Ida?" A nervous giggle.

"Do you like her? Is she a nice person?"

"Why are you asking me this? Can't you just wait until—"

Niels interrupted her. "What's your opinion of her?"

"Has she done something wrong?"

"Answer the question! What do you think of her? Is she nice? Is she good? Is she stern? Is she a good person?"

The nurse looked at her other colleagues for a few seconds. "I don't really know. Ida is nice enough, but . . ."

"But what?"

Niels looked at her. No one said a word as she stood up, picked up her tray with the half-eaten chicken thigh and shreds of lettuce, and left.

71

Cannaregio, the Ghetto—Venice

Tommaso had found large quantities of painkillers in his mother's medicine cabinet, and he'd taken some with him. When he got home—without reading the pharmacist's instructions—he had swallowed a cocktail of brightly colored pills, washing them down with a glass of lukewarm water. He thought about his father's test for fever: "Does it hurt when you look up? If yes, you have a fever." Tommaso tried it. Yes, it hurt. He felt dizzy. He racked his brain to remember what had been said during Monday's briefing at police headquarters. Several politicians. He couldn't recall which ones. A judge. A cardinal. It could be anybody. The next victim could be anyone at all, but he or she was on the train that was due to arrive at the station a few minutes from now. Tommaso had no doubt about it. If the coordinates were telling the truth, that is.

Tommaso couldn't see the sun, only its glow behind the building in Santa Croce. There wasn't much time left. If the woman from Denmark was right and the murder was going to be committed when the sun went down, then time was running out. For a moment he lost confidence. He looked at the display on his apartment wall, showing the victims. The case had become the curse of his life. Or was it a blessing? Tommaso didn't know anymore. He happened to think about his mother—he still had her coins in his pocket—and about her dog. He remembered the slightly reproachful look the dog had given him when he left the dachshund to an uncertain fate. Tommaso put the thought out of his mind. He had to get to the train station.

His back hurt as he bent down to pull on his rubber boots. At the bottom of the stairs, he nearly fell on the slippery steps. He sat down. Had to rest for a moment. Maybe he should just call Flavio. Explain the situation to him, say that they had to be on guard. No, it was too late for that. He would have to do it himself.

72

The National Hospital—Copenhagen
3:04 P.M.

A new corridor in the apparently endless universe of sterile corridors, closed doors, and people wearing white coats. "Excuse me, where is the Pediatric Department?" Niels asked a nurse.

"Take a right," she told him.

"Thanks." He set off running.

Pediatric Clinic—Copenhagen
3:07 P.M.

The kids were sitting in a circle in the playroom. Two of them were too sick to get up, so their beds had been rolled into the room. A young man wearing a red-checked shirt was sitting on a chair that was much too small for him, holding a book in his hand. Above him hung a poster that said: MEET THE AUTHOR OF THE HORROR-BOOK SERIES FOR CHILDREN.

"Where do you get all your ideas for the monsters?" asked a child's voice as Niels barged in. The nurse sitting on the floor with a five-year-old girl on her lap looked up at Niels in annoyance.

"Maria Deleuran?" he asked.

"They're all taking a break while the children are here to meet the author."

"It's urgent. I'm from the Copenhagen Police."

Now all the kids turned to look at Niels.

"Why don't you go over to the break room and ask for her there?" The nurse leaned back and pointed down the hall.

THE LAST GOOD MAN   293

Niels glanced at his watch. Less than half an hour until 3:37. He paused to rub his eyes. He couldn't tell if it was because of the children's small faces, but he felt overcome by how unfair things were. Young kids shouldn't have to be sick. There must be some sort of flaw in creation; it was the sort of thing that made a person want to demand an explanation from God. Or maybe it was the task at hand that overwhelmed him. He was going to fail. Hannah was right, it couldn't be done. A new thought: Maybe his reaction was just a manifestation of what others called his manic-depressive personality. Was he in the midst of a manic episode? Niels leaned against the wall for support as he caught his breath. Maybe Hannah was as crazy as Sommersted thought. Or maybe the reverse was true and the murders were all too real. And inexplicable.

The door at the end of the hall opened. He briefly saw a blond woman move off quickly and disappear. He saw her only from the back. Was she the one? "Okay, you need to focus," he whispered to himself. The children were laughing about something, and Niels caught a glimpse of the sun through the window. The children's spontaneous laughter had restored his hope. He found himself running again. He turned the corner and heard the nurses' voices in the break room.

"Maria Deleuran?" No answer. The three nurses continued their conversation. Niels took out his police ID. "I'm looking for Maria Deleuran."

They stopped talking and turned to look at Niels.

"Has something happened?"

"Is she on duty?" he asked.

"She's not here."

Niels looked at the other nurses. The eldest seemed to know her best, or at least she was the one who spoke. "Has something happened?"

"Are you sure she's not here?"

The nurse's gaze wavered. Niels noticed it at once.

"Could you call her?"

"I can try." Without hurrying, she got to her feet. Her rear end had left a big dent in the imitation leather of the sofa.

"Would you mind making it snappy?"

She gave Niels an angry look. An old matron. Domineering. The other nurses were undoubtedly afraid of her.

"We're not supposed to give out cell phone numbers, actually."

"I'm not asking you to give me the number. All you have to do is call her and say that the Copenhagen Police are here and want to talk to her."

"But she's left for the day."

"Then why hasn't she punched out?"

"Sometimes we forget. What's this all about?"

"I need to ask you to make that call. Now!"

I hope you're not married, thought Niels as she tapped in the number. I pity your husband if you are. He looked around. A bulletin board. Postcards, work schedules, photographs, little notes. A beautiful, fair-haired young woman standing in the middle of an African village, surrounded by children.

"Maybe there's something I can help you with instead?" said the old nurse.

Niels ignored her as he removed the photo. "Is this Maria?"

No one answered. The nurses exchanged glances. On the back, it said: *Here are my children. I hope you're all doing well back home in the frozen north. I miss our coffee klatsches.* A smiley face followed by: *Love, Maria.*

"Maria Deleuran?"

"Yes."

"Does she have children?"

"Why?"

"Does Maria Deleuran have any children?"

An inexplicable silence settled over the room.

"No," said the matron after a moment.

"When did she get off work? Are you positive she's not still here? There's somebody's jacket over there." Niels pointed at an empty chair with a jacket draped over the back. "Is that hers?"

One of the nurses got up. She gave him a friendly smile. "Now, look here. Maria was off at two o'clock. She has the morning shift. You can see for yourself on the work schedule." The nurse nodded toward the bulletin board. "She may have been doing a little overtime, but she's not here, at any rate. I'd be happy to take a message for her."

The older matron said, "She's not picking up her phone."

"Does she have any women friends here?" asked Niels. "Does she usually meet up with anybody after work?"

"I'm a friend of hers."

Niels turned. It was the first time this particular nurse had spoken. He looked at her name badge: TOVE FANØ, RN.

"Does she spend time with anyone else at the hospital, Tove? It's a big place."

"I don't think so."

"Friends, lovers, maybe something related to her aid work?"

Tove paused to think and then shook her head. Niels glanced at the matron. She shrugged, her expression surly.

"Do all of you like her?"

"What?"

"Do you have children? All of you?"

Confused looks.

"I asked you a question."

Everyone nodded. Except for Maria's friend. Tove. She could easily be in her midforties. Niels stared at her. Then she moved her hands to reveal a big pregnant belly.

73

N ormally, Hannah preferred the hours just before sundown. For someone who had come to a standstill in the middle of life, the daytime hours could be difficult. People in a hurry, people on their way to or from work, school, the day-care center. In the daytime, other people did all the things that exposed her life for what it was. *Nothing.* No job, no husband, and worst of all, not even her son. Then the sun went down, people disappeared, and things became a bit easier for Hannah. But not today.

She got up, went over to the window, and looked at the sun, which was hiding behind the trees. Just a pale, flat disk that refused to share its warmth with this part of the world. It would be a while yet before the sun went down. At the other end of the office corridor, employees were still at work. A TV was on. Hannah couldn't help getting caught up in the frantic tumult on the screen. Something had happened. Someone was on the ground. People wearing suits had gathered around the poor man; others were rushing to bring water and a blanket. Hannah pictured in her mind the Bella Center— an awful place. Bad air indoors, too many people, and too little time. Who wouldn't faint inside that place?

"Okay!" Casper looked up from his screen with an eager expression. "I've found another angel."

Hannah went back to where Casper and Thor were hunched in front of their computer screens. "All right, tell me," she said.

"At the Center for Medical Parasitology. Professor Samuel Hviid. Forty-nine years old. No children, according to the civil registry. But listen to this." Casper glanced up at Hannah before he went on. "He's one of the world's foremost researchers on malaria. It's thought that his work has already saved the lives of half a million people living near the equator."

"Is he at work right now?"

"He's a researcher at the university, but apparently they have departments connected to the hospital."

"If he's not in the building, he's not in any danger," Hannah told Casper as she looked at the picture of the researcher. *Alexander the Great died of malaria, which is regarded as one of the three greatest challenges to public health, killing three million people every year.* That was as much as she managed to read from the text under the photograph of Samuel Hviid before a thought occurred to her. "Call his department. Find out if he's here in the building."

"Okay." Thor made the call.

Casper continued his search as he muttered, "Gry Libak. Not bad, either—"

Thor interrupted him. "He's in the building. Samuel Hviid. In the administrative wing, Section 5222. He's in a meeting."

3:19 P.M.

Maria Deleuran was still in the hospital. Niels was sure of it. Why were her colleagues lying? He could see that Hannah was trying to call his cell, but he didn't answer it. The nurses were getting up and leaving the break room. Niels waited until the surly matron had left. Then he followed Maria's friend Tove into the women's bathroom.

"What are you doing?" She gave Niels an angry look as he quickly closed the door behind him. "Should I start screaming?"

"You need to tell me where she is."

"What's this all about? Why is it so important? Why can't you just wait until—"

"Her life may be in danger," Niels interrupted her.

Tove paused to consider what he'd said. "But why? Maria is an angel. Nobody would want to hurt her. I just don't believe it."

"Trust me."

Tove weighed whether to tell him something—Niels could see it in her face. Words were on the tip of her tongue. She wore the same expression as a criminal a few minutes before deciding to confess. "She left. I don't know what else to tell you."

Tove resolutely walked out the door. Niels's cell was ringing.

"Hannah?"

"Samuel Hviid. You need to go over to Section 5222. He's a researcher. He matches the profile perfectly. At the moment he's in an administrative meeting."

The secretary looked at Niels's police ID with surprising composure. She was used to having people in authority pass by her desk: the health minister, highly placed government officials, professors, and scientists from all over Europe. It was her job to decide who would be allowed in to see the head of the hospital, and she didn't let anyone slip past easily.

"Professor Hviid is in a meeting with the directors. Can't it wait?"

"No, it can't."

"May I ask what this is about?"

"I need to talk to Samuel Hviid. Now."

She got up, shamelessly taking her time. People in this country make the police feel like we're more of a nuisance than a help, thought Niels. On the other hand, the secretary treated the hospital directors as if they were the oracle of Delphi. She tapped cautiously on the door and then went in, looking apologetic and stooping submissively. On the TV screen behind the secretary, Niels saw the same images that Hannah had seen. The climate conference was in its last stages, and one of the top delegates had suddenly collapsed. Blood was running from his head, and he was gasping for air like a dying codfish that had been pulled out of its natural habitat. The world press was on hand to witness the whole scene.

The secretary was still talking to the directors. The walls of the hospital conference room were glass. Total transparency, as if to underscore that no shady decisions were ever made in the room. Niels stared at the people in the meeting room. They stared back. He couldn't hear what they were saying. Only the faint sounds from the TV broke the silence: *We don't know whether he was just not feeling well . . . or whether his condition is more serious. Possibly a stroke. An ambulance is on its way here right now.*

The secretary came back. "All right. He'll be with you in a minute."

"Good."

Samuel Hviid hitched up his trousers and cleared his throat as he came through the door. The other people in the room tried to hide their curiosity.

"Samuel Hviid?" Niels asked.

"How can I help you?"

"I'm Niels Bentzon. From the Copenhagen Police."

Niels's phone beeped. A text message from Hannah: *We have one more. Gry Libak.*

"What's this about?" The professor looked at Niels with kind, intelligent eyes.

The sun was going to set in a few minutes. Niels could see the pink sky through the big picture windows of the administrative office. "We have reason to believe that your life is in danger."

Samuel Hviid's expression didn't change.

"I need to ask you to leave the hospital. Just for the next half hour."

"Leave the hospital? Why?"

"I can't tell you right now. All I can say is that it's not safe for you to stay here."

Hviid shook his head and than glanced over his shoulder. "I refuse to hide. That case is almost twenty years old." He looked at Niels. Was there a trace of sorrow in his eyes?

"It's just for half an hour. Not even that long."

"And then what?"

"Then we'll have the situation under control."

"No. It's my life, and I have to learn to live with it. I can't do that if I run away with my tail between my legs every time. When did he escape?"

Niels had no idea what to say. "I can't divulge that information."

"Can't divulge? Come on! I'm a doctor. We make mistakes. The man has been threatening me for half my lifetime because of a case that I wasn't even responsible for. I just happened to be the young doctor who was last in contact with his wife before her tragic death. Administering the medication—that was the job of the anesthesiologist. These things happen."

Samuel Hviid glanced back at the directors in the conference room. Niels could see what the man was thinking: He'd come a long way, and no one was going to destroy things for him. The directors sitting behind the thick panes of glass knew nothing about this matter. If he left the meeting now, people would start to wonder.

Yet another text from Hannah. *Forget Hviid. Focus on Gry Libak. Department C. Only a few minutes left.*

74

Cannaregio, the Ghetto—Venice

Sister Magdalena had entered the Order of the Sacred Heart because she believed in God. For the same reason, a little water in the streets wasn't going to hold her back. Signor Tommaso needed to be given the message. Magdalena had made a promise to a dying woman, a woman who had received a last message from the beyond, and it was important to heed messages like that. Magdalena knew this better than anyone. If she hadn't paid attention, she wouldn't be alive today. She would have died at Shaw Station in Manila along with the nineteen other people. But she had been saved by God. In her bag she had the receipt from the bicycle repair shop that she'd kept all these years. For her, it was a form of proof. A tangible proof of God's existence. Mostly as a reminder to herself in case she ever happened to doubt her own memory.

She knocked. The door was ajar, and the entryway was flooded.

"Signor di Barbara? Tommaso? I have a message from your mother."

Not a sound. Magdalena went inside, calling out again. It was against her nature to barge into someone's home, but she had to do it. This was important.

She went upstairs, calling his name, but no one answered. In the living room she saw the display Tommaso had made of the photos of the victims. The worldwide murder case covered the entire wall from floor to ceiling. At first she didn't understand what she was looking at. Then she realized that they were pictures of dead people. Her mouth went dry, and she tasted her own blood. Sister Magdalena didn't understand, but she had a feeling that she was too late.

75

Poul Spreckelsen, the Cardiology Clinic," said Casper, looking up. "His achievements may not be as spectacular as Samuel Hviid's and the fight against malaria. But Spreckelsen has developed . . ."

Hannah wasn't listening. She was looking through the glass pane at the TV screen in the next office. Helicopter cameras showed two ambulances driving up to the Bella Center. Doctors and medics jumping out. The text crawl appeared at the bottom of the screen: *Breaking news. Climate negotiator collapses.*

"Are you listening?"

Hannah wasn't. She left the personnel office and went into the office next door.

"Can I help you?" The woman stared at Hannah.

"Yes. Would you mind turning up the volume?"

The woman didn't move.

"It will only take two minutes. Please."

The woman sighed, fumbled with the remote control, and turned up the sound. *He's being transported through the Bella Center,* said the TV reporter. Casper appeared behind Hannah. "Are you thinking the same thing I am?" he asked.

"Possibly."

The reporter continued to describe in detail what the cameras were showing on the screen: *He's being transported past the press box. Two doctors are walking alongside, and it looks as if an IV has been started.*

"Why don't you tell us his name!" cried Hannah impatiently. At that instant, as if on command, the TV reporter summed up the situation: *What we're watching is a very critical moment. In the midst of the negotiations, the climate negotiator for the NGOs, Yves Devort, has collapsed. He's being taken to the National Hospital.*

Casper and Hannah ran back to their computers.

Google: NGO. Copenhagen and . . . Casper spelled his way through the man's name: "Yves Devort."

"We've only got fifteen minutes left," said Hannah. "Can the ambulance get here in fifteen minutes?"

"Probably not."

Casper had already found Yves Devort. A handsome man. As French as a baguette. "Fifty years old. I can't tell whether he has children. Or what the French police might have on him." They looked at the TV screen. Commotion. Chaos. Delegates, demonstrators, ambulances, security guards, and police officers.

Niels was calling them. Hannah answered. He sounded out of breath. "I'm lost."

"Where are you? Tell me what one of the signs says."

"Orthopedic Department. Section 2162."

Hannah looked at Thor. "What's the fastest way from Section 2162 to the Cardiology Department?"

"Tell him to find the nearest elevator."

"Did you hear that, Niels? It's three twenty-two right now. You have exactly fifteen minutes."

"Hannah?"

"Yes, Niels?"

"It's not going to work. We can't do it."

Hannah hesitated. She looked at the TV screen. The ambulance hadn't left the Bella Center. They were bringing Yves Devort out on a gurney. She wondered whether she should tell Niels about the climate negotiator who had collapsed.

Hannah broke the silence, her voice confident but hoarse. "Niels, what you're doing . . . it's just amazing."

Her voice wavered on the last word. *Amazing.* She sensed that she was on the verge of tears.

"It's too much of a long shot, Hannah. I feel like giving up."

"No, don't do that, Niels. You're trying to find a good person. Just *one* good person."

"All I'm finding are their flaws. That's how it's been from the very beginning. I look for someone good but find only the . . . bad. The flaws."

She could hear Niels breathing as she kept an eye on the TV screen. She had an uneasy feeling in her stomach that reminded her of the time when she and Gustav had a car accident. She was driving. That was what Gustav preferred. To have her behind the wheel while he issued orders. "Slow down, Hannah. Get ready to turn, Hannah." They'd had a fight that day, as was so often the case, and when Hannah was about to exit the highway, she was going too fast. They ended up in the middle of a farmer's field, Gustav's fancy Volvo covered with mud. But just before they veered into the field, at the instant before everything went wrong—in that second when she realized that it wasn't going to end well—she'd had the same feeling she had now.

"Hannah?" said Niels on the phone.

"Yes?"

"Who are they bringing over here in an ambulance?"

"That's what we're trying to find out. Are you okay now?"

"Yes."

"You need to go to Section 2142. The Cardiology Clinic. Find Poul Spreckelsen."

Niels ended the call.

Casper looked up from his computer. "I'm going to start on the patients now."

She nodded. He was indefatigable. She was watching the ambulance on the TV. It had exited the highway and was headed for the National Hospital. A police escort was leading the way.

The phone rang again. "Niels?"

"You're going to have to help me. I don't know if I can make it. And you're closer."

He was out of breath. Was he crying?

"Okay, Niels."

"Gry . . . she's the one. I think it's her. Over in the surgery wing."

"Okay, Niels. I'll go over there."

"Run."

Hannah turned to Casper. "I'm going out to help Niels."

"Shall I call you if I find any candidates among the patients?" he asked.

Hannah looked out the window. Only the very top of the sun was still visible. "No. We don't have time for any more."

76

Santa Croce—Venice

Officially, Venice was a shop that was open 24/7, year-round. Princesses and sheiks and politicians and celebrities, from Italy and abroad, were constantly pouring in. The police used practically all their resources to welcome and escort them from their hotels to the Piazza di San Marco and back again. Tommaso couldn't even remember where the last princess was from. He had accompanied her on a boat along the Grand Canal while tourists stood on the Rialto Bridge, waving. At such moments Venice was nothing more than a Disneyland with better taste and good food. Fortunately, he was supposed to play soccer tonight if he was feeling better. The stadium was all the way out by Arsenale, near the new construction and the shipyard. There was no Disneyland out there. Just an eternally muddy playing field, a rotten stink from the lagoon, harsh light from the floodlights, and a wall of public housing all around.

Tommaso knew that he should be in bed. Instead, he was headed for the train station, this time wearing rubber boots. What a welcome the lagoon had prepared for the justice minister. He couldn't be the next victim— Tommaso was convinced of that. The justice minister, Angelino Alfano, was nothing more than Berlusconi's lackey. Formerly the secretary of the corrupt prime minister, Alfano had been appointed justice minister only to create a network of byzantine laws that would keep Berlusconi out of prison.

Tommaso walked over the Ponte delle Guglie toward the train station. The shopkeepers had long since closed up their businesses because of the rain, and the streets were deserted. The tourists were holed up in their hotel rooms with wet feet, studying their travel insurance policies to find out if flooding was reason enough to demand their money back.

Finally, he caught sight of the station. Santa Lucia. The wide stairs, eagle's wings, and horizontal lines, remnants of the fascist era that Tommaso's father had once supported. A past that was always on the verge of entering into the present. Carabinieri, the military police, stood on the stairs. One of the officers stopped Tommaso. "I'm from the police," he told the man.

"ID?"

Tommaso rummaged in his pockets in vain. He had turned in his police ID. "I can't find it."

"Then you'll have to wait," said the officer. "They'll be out of here in ten minutes."

The fucking military police! The regular police couldn't stand the carabinieri, with their sleek uniforms and gleaming boots. Tommaso went around the back way. The road past the church led up to the freight office, and there was no guard on duty. He paused, then heard the train pull into the station with a roar announcing its arrival. There wasn't much time left. In a moment someone would be murdered here at the train station. Unless he could prevent it.

77

Hannah wasn't running, even though that's what Niels wanted her to do. She still had that feeling—the sense of imminent death.

"Excuse me," she said to an orderly passing by. "Where is the surgery wing?"

"You need to go down one floor. It's all the way over at the other end," replied the man, holding the elevator door open for her.

"Thanks."

She stood in the elevator next to the orderly. She attempted a smile for the sake of the patient in the bed, but it didn't amount to much. There really was no reason to smile. Hannah knew that the system was right—that the likelihood of her calculations being wrong was one in several million. She'd been able to locate thirty-four coordinates with great accuracy. That couldn't be a coincidence.

"You should get off here," said the orderly. "And head back in the other direction."

"Thanks."

Hannah began jogging, but the increase in pulse just provided fodder for her internal calculator. Thirty-four murders. Located with godlike precision. Two were still missing. Hannah was sure of that. She was also convinced that there was nothing they could do about it. It was as if they were at the mercy of the system. It felt like they were fighting to prevent two plus two from equaling four. Or fighting to prevent the car from ending up in the field that time with Gustav—contrary to all the laws of nature.

3:28 P.M.

Niels turned the corner, the sound of Mahler's Third Symphony guiding him. The surgery wing was deserted, but it had an aura of clinical cleanliness. As he raced along, images of people from the past two days whirled through his mind: Amundsen from Amnesty International. The lives he'd saved and the one he was in the process of destroying: his wife's. Niels thought about her innocent expression and her cheerful, clear blue eyes as he said hello to her in the entryway. She wasn't the least suspicious. She loved her husband and had the greatest faith in him. And Pastor Rosenberg. Was it right to sacrifice one person in order to save twelve? Rosenberg knew the answer. He had made the wrong decision. But Niels still liked the man. Thorvaldsen was the only one he didn't care for. He was a little too convinced of his own goodness. And he clearly was a tyrant to his co-workers.

The doors to the operating rooms were all closed. In the past, churches used to engender this feeling of being in contact with the beyond; nowadays operating rooms were the sacred halls. So Niels didn't find it surprising to hear such beautiful music. Operating Room 5. A red light was on above the door. No admittance.

Niels opened the door a crack and saw that some sort of surgery was under way. A team of doctors, nurses, and surgeons all working intently. A woman strode over to Niels. "You're not supposed to be in here!"

"I'm from the police. I'm looking for Gry Libak."

"You'll have to wait until the surgery is over."

"No, I have to talk to her now."

"We're in the middle of an operation! What are you thinking?"

"I'm from the police."

"No unauthorized personnel allowed in here," she interrupted him. "Not even the police. You need to leave!"

"Is she here? Gry Libak? Are you Gry?"

"Gry just left. And now you really have to leave. Or we'll file a complaint tomorrow."

"Left? Is she coming back? Is she off duty?"

"I'm closing the door now."

"One last question." Niels stuck his foot in the door.

"I'm going to have to call security."

"Her life is in danger. That's the only reason I'm here."

The doctors had not looked up from their work. Not even for a second. Only now did one of them glance over at Niels. For a moment the only sound was Mahler and the monotonous beeping that meant the patient was alive. Rhythm meant hope, a constant tone meant death. That's the way it was. A doctor wearing a white mask answered Niels's question. "You might be able to catch her in the locker room. We've been working for twelve hours straight, so she'll probably take a long shower."

"Thanks. Where is the locker room?"

Niels left the operating room as the nurse said, "Section 2141."

Hannah came running toward him. "Niels!"

"Spreckelsen was a dud. But maybe Gry Libak . . ."

"Where?"

"In the locker room. Section 2141."

Niels looked at his watch. Seven minutes.

Section 2141
3:30 P.M.

The women's locker room. Long rows of shiny metal lockers. Narrow benches in between. Not a soul in sight.

Niels shouted, "Gry Libak?"

"The names are in alphabetical order."

Niels paused to think. They should have started down here. People always hid their personal secrets and sins at work, where their loved ones wouldn't find them. "Find her locker. Gry Libak."

"Then what?"

"Break into it."

"Niels?"

"Just do it!"

The padlocks on the doors were mostly for show. Hannah walked down one row. Jakobsen, Signe. Jensen, Puk. Klarlund, Bente. Kristoffersen, Bolette. Lewis, Beth. Libak, Gry. She tugged on the door. Locked.

Niels was working his way backward through the alphabet. Fiola. Finsen. Ejersen. Egilsdottir. Deleuran, Maria.

He tried yanking on the door. That wasn't going to work. He spun around, looking for some kind of tool. Something that could . . . The broom handle! He pulled the broom out of the cleaner's cart, stuck the handle under the padlock, and twisted. The lock yielded easily and dropped to the floor with a metallic clunk. Hannah was standing behind him, looking desperate. "I can't get it open."

"Here. Use this to break off the lock."

Hannah took the broom. It wasn't really her forte.

"She's here!" yelled Niels.

"Who?"

"Maria. The woman we couldn't find. Her clothes are still here."

A coat, scarf, shoes. Maria was in the building.

Taped to the inside of the locker door were several photographs and postcards. A homemade African wallet made of leather was on the shelf. On one of the postcards it said: *You're an angel, Maria. God bless you. Rwinkwavu Hospitals, Rwanda.* Niels studied the picture. A beautiful fair-haired woman seen in profile.

"I saw you," he whispered. "I saw you." He turned to Hannah. "It's her. Everything fits."

"Look at the time. We only have five minutes left."

Niels didn't hear the rest of Hannah's protests. He was already running.

She stayed where she was, watching him go. What had he told her? That people called him manic-depressive? Manic was an appropriate description of his behavior right now, anyway.

78

Santa Lucia train station—Venice

The first people Tommaso caught sight of were the faithful. Men and women clad in religious robes, either all white or all black. Monks and nuns from the cloisters of Venice.

"Who's arriving?" Tommaso asked one of the nuns. His voice sounded hoarse.

The train station was blocked off to regular travelers, and all traffic had been halted to allow the procession to be escorted off the train and out to the Grand Canal. "Excuse me, but who are you waiting for?" he asked again.

The nun gave Tommaso an angry look. He discovered that he was gripping her arm.

"Would you let go of me, please?"

"Sorry."

He released her arm. The nun next to her took pity on him. "It's our cardinal." She mentioned a name, but it was drowned out by all the noise. At that moment the thundering train pulled into the station. Tommaso leaned against the wall. The next victim might be on this train. *Had* to be on the train. If only he could find the police chief. Warn someone. Anyone. The doors opened. The balding justice minister was the first to step into view. He gave an exaggerated wave to those waiting on the platform. Behind him Tommaso could see the cardinal. He recognized the man from TV. Wasn't he the one who had voiced the opinion that the Catholic Church ought to recommend the use of birth control in Africa as something that might save at least ten million lives each year?

Someone was clapping. Or was that just the rain on the roof? The police chief appeared.

79

'm sorry!"

Niels didn't have time to help the woman up. He had collided with her as he came around the corner to the Pediatric Clinic. He glanced into rooms as he passed. At the faces, the nurses. He found her farther down the corridor. Tove Fanø. Maria's friend. He grabbed her by the arm and dragged her inside a supply closet.

"Let go of me!"

He slammed the door behind them. Disposable gloves, bedpans, and sheets. He looked for a deadbolt but didn't find one. "Where is she?"

"I told you—she's not—"

"I know that Maria is here!"

The nurse hesitated. Niels took two steps closer. "Do you know what the penalty is for obstructing the work of the police? Do you want to be blamed for her death?"

She didn't reply. Niels took out his handcuffs. "Tove Fanø. You are hereby arrested for obstruction—"

"Go down to the basement, under Department A," she said. "There are a few rooms down there intended for surgeons who need to get some rest. They're never used."

"What does it say on the door?"

3:34 P.M.

Niels met Hannah on his way downstairs. "She's here. Maria. Down in the basement."

Hannah came to an abrupt halt. Niels looked half crazed. She had an urge to stop him. Make him calm down. Right now she didn't know what to believe.

"How much time?" he asked, out of breath.

Hannah looked at her watch with resignation. "Three minutes."

"Come with me!"

"Niels . . . this is crazy."

He looked at her. Laughed and shook his head. "You, too?"

"What?"

"You think I'm out of my mind, too? Is that what you're saying?" He grabbed her arm and pulled her into the elevator. "You go left. Look for a door marked STAFF ONLY."

The elevator came to a stop in the bowels of the hospital, and the doors slid open.

Basement, the National Hospital—Copenhagen
3:35 P.M.

"What do I do if I find it?"

Niels didn't hear Hannah's question. He was already halfway down the hall. The desperate sound of his footsteps merged with a faint whistling coming from the ventilation shafts.

Hannah took a deep breath. She really missed the theoretical approach. Ideas. Figuring out the universe without ever going farther than to the local newsstand to buy cigarettes.

Most of the doors were unmarked. A few promised supplies. STORAGE ROOM B2. RADIOLOGY DEPT./STORAGE. None that said STAFF ONLY. Hannah thought about Søren Kierkegaard. He had spent his entire life in a space no bigger than a few square yards, pacing the floor, possibly taking a short walk out on the street, but always completely engrossed in his own thoughts. It didn't take a lot of room to figure out the whole world—in fact, it could be accomplished inside of a barrel. STORAGE. SUPPLIES/ANESTHESIOLOGY. She couldn't hear Niels's footsteps as she turned the corner, her thoughts filled with philosophers in barrels. The Greek Diogenes—the inventor of cynicism. Cynicism comes from the Greek word for "dog." Diogenes thought we could learn a lot from dogs. A dog can instinctively differentiate between friend and foe. People don't do that. They can move in and share an apartment with their worst enemy without even knowing it. Why was she thinking about this now? Sometimes she was simply sick and tired of her own associations . . . Oh, now she realized why Diogenes had popped into her mind: because on occasion he would leave his barrel and dash through the streets of Athens in search of a "real person." A good person. Diogenes had come to Hannah's rescue. Like him, she had left her own barrel to find a real human being.

They rounded the corner at the same moment, Hannah and Niels.

"Find anything?" she asked. "It's now. Sundown. It's three thirty-seven."

He whispered, "There it is. It says STAFF ONLY on that door." He took his gun out of the shoulder holster.

I wonder what we'll find. That was all Hannah had time to think before he barged into the room.

Staff only
3:37 P.M.

Niels stepped into darkness. A gloom broken only by the faint glow from a TV and a terrified scream.

"Maria Deleuran?" he shouted.

Was that a girl on the bed? Niels took a step closer as he ran his hand over the wall, trying to find a light switch. "Maria?"

"Yes?"

"Are you alone?"

"Yes," she replied. Niels blinked his eyes. The contours of the room slowly began to take shape. She was lying on the bed. He took another step before he discovered a second person. A shadow—something moving swiftly toward him.

"Stop!"

"What's going on?" shrieked Maria.

Niels took the safety off his gun.

"What the hell is going on?" she screamed again.

Niels didn't hesitate. He reached out into the dark and seized hold of a collar. The other person twisted out of his grasp and punched him in the face. Maria was crying now. Niels accidentally struck her leg with his left arm as he fell. The other person was on him at once, trying to grab hold of his head.

"Turn on the light!" Niels grabbed the man's wrist, wrenched it around, and tried to get up. Again Niels was struck, this time in the back of the head, before he managed to get to his feet.

"Call security!" shouted the man. He had a firm grip on Niels's arm.

"Hannah! Turn on the light!" Niels yanked his arm free and got out his handcuffs. Finally, he managed to grab the man's hand. A quick twist, a cry of pain, and Niels threw the man to the floor with ferocious strength. At that moment Hannah turned on the light. The half-naked man moved a few feet away across the floor before Niels dragged him over to the bed and clamped the handcuff onto an iron bar.

Only now did Niels look at the terrified Maria, who was trying to cover her naked body with a sheet. "What . . . what do you want?"

Niels was gasping for breath. Blood ran out of his nose and down his shirt. His eyes roamed over the room, taking in the scene. He looked at Maria. Then at the almost nude, agile man in his forties who was cuffed to the bed. At the man's coat draped over a chair; the name badge said: MAX ROTHSTEIN, M.D. At an open bottle of white wine standing on a small table. At Maria, who was openly weeping.

"Answer me!" she sobbed. "What's going on?"

"It's not her," muttered Niels. "It's not her."

"What do you want?"

Exhausted, Niels showed her his police ID. Hannah took a step back, moving out into the hall.

"What time is it?" he asked.

"Niels, this is insane."

"Will somebody please tell me what's going on here?" the man shouted.

Niels noticed a little TV in the room. The word "Live" was at the top of the screen, showing helicopter views of an ambulance racing through the city with sirens wailing. "Turn up the sound," he said. The doctor was about to protest when Niels interrupted him. "Turn it up!"

No one reacted. Niels went over to the TV and fumbled with the volume control. *One of the climate negotiators for the NGOs was taken seriously ill during the closing round of negotiations. Sources close to the climate negotiator tell us that this may have been due to the two weeks of inhuman pressure to reach an agreement . . . He is arriving this very minute at the National Hospital.*

"Oh, God," said Hannah.

The TV2 News helicopter captured such a beautiful shot of the sunset over the city. The very last rays.

"The time?"

"It's now, Niels. Or—"

"Where will the ambulance arrive?"

"I demand to know what this is all about," said the doctor.

"*Where?*"

It was Maria who answered. "At the ER. Take the elevator up to the first floor."

3:40 P.M.

Niels was limping. Hannah tried to walk alongside him, but he reached the elevator before she did. He pressed the button repeatedly, but that didn't make the elevator arrive any faster. Hannah caught up with him.

Neither of them said a word in the elevator. She hardly dared look at him. Instead, she registered how other people reacted to him as they stepped out onto the first floor. Surprise, shock. Niels was limping, his gun was drawn, and he made no attempt to hide the blood running out of his nose.

"Police! Where's the ER?" he demanded.

Everyone pointed in the same direction. Niels jogged down the hall with Hannah right behind him. They reached the ER just as the ambulance arrived. A team of doctors stood waiting. The two police motorcycles that had provided an escort through town drove off to make room for the hospital staff. A glass window kept Niels from going any farther.

"How do we get in?"

"Niels!" Hannah tried to grab his arm. He pulled free. The patient on the gurney was lifted out of the ambulance, and the doctors closed ranks around him.

"No!"

They couldn't hear Niels shouting. Panes of glass separated him from the others. He pounded on the window. "Where's the door?"

"Niels." Hannah was tugging at his arm.

"Down here!" someone shouted.

Niels was about to run off, but Hannah stopped him. "Niels! Look at the clock. It's several minutes past the time. The sun has already set."

Niels looked at the climate negotiator on the gurney. The man sat up and smiled to the doctors; he was already feeling better. Niels was all too familiar with the phenomenon. As soon as the ambulance arrived, people often started feeling better. Unfortunately, Sommersted was standing next to the man. His eagle eyes landed on Niels. Of course they did.

80

Santa Lucia train station—Venice

The military police were blocking the way. The official visitors slowly moved past the rows of government officials and police officers.

"Commissario!"

Tommaso tried to shout, but his words were drowned out. "The cardinal is in danger!"

He caught sight of Flavio and called to him. Finally, someone who could hear him. But Flavio didn't react. He stood at attention as the justice minister shook hands with the police chief, wiped his sweaty brow, and introduced the others accompanying him. More nervous handshakes, kisses on the cheek, and an exchange of well-rehearsed phrases. The cardinal stood in the middle of the group. Tommaso looked around. No one suspicious except a man hiding behind a pair of sunglasses. There was no sun at the train station, so why was he wearing shades?

"Flavio!"

At last Flavio responded. He stepped away from the ranks of police officers and came over to Tommaso. "What are you doing here?" he asked.

"Somebody's life is in danger," Tommaso told him.

"What are you talking about?"

"You have to believe me—"

Flavio interrupted him. "You look like shit. You're ill. You shouldn't be here. You should be with your mother."

Tommaso pushed him away. The man with the sunglasses had disappeared in the crowd. No, there he was, standing not far from the cardinal. His hand was resting on a bag.

"That man over there, Flavio!" shouted Tommaso, pointing.

The commissario noticed Tommaso. Flavio took his arm. "You need to leave. You're ruining everything for yourself. Do you hear me?"

The procession of dignitaries began moving away from the train station. The man with the sunglasses followed.

81

A lone drop of blood landed on the floor. It had dripped from Niels's nose. Dr. Max Rothstein studied Niels as he unlocked the handcuffs.

"Police officers make mistakes, just like you do," muttered Niels in an attempt to cut off all the questions and angry accusations issuing from Maria Deleuran and her secret lover, Max Rothstein.

"You certainly do."

"I'm sorry."

Maria had long since put on her clothes. The doctor cast an uncertain glance at her. "Is there going to be a report filed about this incident?"

Niels gave him a puzzled look, wondering what answer the man most wanted to hear. "Report?"

The doctor cleared his throat. "Listen here. I have a family. You made a mistake. And I don't think I should be made to suffer because you need to write up a report about what happened here."

"No, of course not. Not a word."

Rothstein tried to catch Maria's eye, but his protective attitude toward his "family" had left her cold. Hannah was wondering if Maria had just failed the test, or if she could be considered a "good person" even though she was having an affair with another woman's husband. Rothstein turned to Hannah. "And you are?"

"Hannah Lund."

"Gustav's wife."

"Yes." She was surprised he knew who she was.

"We both lived in the Regensen dormitory when we were students."

"I see."

Rothstein rubbed his wrists. They were red and swollen. "Shall I take a look at your nose?"

Rothstein went over to Niels and studied his nose. Cautiously, he tipped Niels's head back so he could peer into his nostrils. The balance of power between the two men had shifted. Maybe that was exactly what Rothstein had in mind: to regain some of his lost dignity.

Maria rolled some cotton into a ball and handed it to Rothstein. He stuck it into one of Niels's nostrils and said, "Okay. I think that makes us even."

Rothstein left the room, giving Hannah a nod as he passed her. Perhaps it was his way of acknowledging her as an equal, one academic to another. While leaving the nurse and policeman to fend for themselves.

Lobby, the National Hospital—Copenhagen

Niels insisted on sitting down to wait for a while. Maybe someone had died unexpectedly somewhere in the hospital just as the sun set. They waited for half an hour without saying a word. Finally, Hannah got up.

82

Santa Lucia train station—Venice

The sun was about to set in Venice. Tommaso stood outside the train station, watching the cream of the Italian justice system disappear into the police boat. No one had died. The man with the sunglasses had taken them off and disappeared in the direction of the Ghetto.

Tommaso was not feeling well at all. He could feel snot running out of his nose. When he wiped it off, he saw that it was blood.

He was also having problems keeping his balance. He needed to find something to drink and just sit down by himself without anyone seeing him. Flavio was on his way back. He waved to Tommaso, who hurried away. He bumped into a young couple wrapped in an embrace, kissing. "Sorry," he muttered.

There was a line outside the women's bathroom. He went into the men's room, but a metal bar blocked the entrance. "You have to pay," someone behind him said. Tommaso felt dizzy as he searched his pockets for a couple of coins. The man behind him was getting impatient. Tommaso finally found the three coins. He put the fifty-cent piece into the slot. The metal bar still wouldn't budge. The man behind him snarled, "It costs eighty cents!"

Tommaso tossed in the last two coins. EIGHTY CENTS, it said on the display. The metal bar slid aside.

83

Kongens Nytorv—Copenhagen

A Christmas tree on a sled. A father and son pulling the sled across the thin layer of snow. Niels watched them through the car's windshield, which was starting to fog up. He should be in Africa right now. Celebrating Christmas Eve in a swimming pool, going out to look at lions on Christmas Day, and feeling the Indian Ocean caress his bare feet. Instead, he felt the cold whistling up from the floor of Hannah's car.

"Do you want me to drive?" she asked.

"No, that's okay."

The stoplight turned red, yellow, green. First gear, he released the clutch, and the front tires skidded across the snow. For a couple of seconds he lost control of the vehicle, but then he got it pointed in the right direction, and they headed out. Control? At the moment he felt that anything could happen and he wouldn't be able to do a thing about it. His hands would start shaking if he let go of the steering wheel, and he would collapse, sobbing, if Hannah so much as touched him. She didn't, and Niels kept a firm grip on the wheel. That was how they drove. Across the bridge between the lakes. Past Kongens Have. By the time they reached Kongens Nytorv, neither of them had said a word, but they both stared at Santa Claus walking past with a flock of little kids in tow.

In the middle of the square, five-foot-tall posters had been set up, showing hundreds of places on earth that were in danger of disappearing because of climate change. From inside the car, they could faintly hear the man holding the microphone, speaking to a modest crowd: "More than seven hundred thousand workers make their living from tea production in Sri Lanka. Drought will destroy all production."

Traffic was at a standstill. People were lugging their Christmas purchases across the square. Past the posters of the Solomon Islands, where the local population lived on coconuts and fish, only seven feet above sea level. Heading for the antiques shops on Bredgade, where they passed the illuminated photos of Lake Chad, which was in the process of evaporating, transforming yet another corner of Africa into a wasteland of dust and sand. The traffic began moving again. Hesitantly, uncertainly, as if all the drivers at the square were considering whether to take the lead in the battle: shut off their engines, throw away the car keys, and try to save the Solomon Islands. At the last minute, the drivers changed their minds and the cars rolled on as usual. If they were very quiet, they might hear the last coconut pull loose from its branch and float down toward the sea that intended to swallow up everything.

Hannah was the first to break the silence. "Where are we headed?" She looked out the window as she spoke. As if her question were directed not at Niels but at all of humanity.

"I don't know."

She looked at him and smiled.

"This whole day . . . I'm sorry, Hannah."

"You don't need to apologize."

"There's just one last thing I'd like to ask you."

"What's that?"

He hesitated. "I don't think I can be alone tonight." He cleared his throat. That sounded all wrong. Like an invitation. "I mean," he muttered, "not anything—"

"That's all right. I understand."

He looked at her. She did understand.

"Would that be okay with you? I have a good pull-out sofa. We could have a glass of wine."

She smiled. "You know what? I just realized this. There were three things that Gustav never said to me. 'I don't know,' 'I'm sorry,' and 'Would that be okay with you?'"

84

Carlsberg silo—Copenhagen

My wife is an architect," said Niels as the elevator doors slid open to reveal his apartment.

Hannah didn't say a word about the size of the place. She merely sank onto the sofa as if she lived there. Everyone else was always spellbound by the 360-degree view. Not Hannah. I suppose she's seen much more impressive things, thought Niels as he uncorked a bottle of red wine. As an astronomer, she had probably lain under the open skies in the Andes Mountains, watched suns explode in Orion's Belt, and all sorts of things like that. By comparison, looking out at the view of Carlsberg probably didn't rate. He handed her a glass of wine. "It's okay to smoke in here."

He felt a sudden pang of guilt. As if he'd been unfaithful. Hannah now stood next to the window.

"It has always struck me . . ."

"What?" He moved closer.

"When I look at cities from above. Like here. Or when I look down at Europe at night. With all the lights. Do you know the feeling?"

"No. I'm not very good at flying."

She looked taken aback. "You're not?" She stared at him. As if she'd just realized something.

"You were saying?" Niels prompted her.

"That the lights around the cities look exactly the way light looks in space. When we gaze out into the galaxies, Niels. That's the way it looks." She pointed at a distant light on the horizon. "Amazing areas of nothingness. And then all of a sudden a cluster of lights. Life. Almost like a city."

Niels didn't know what to say. He refilled their glasses. "Maybe we should call Tommaso. To hear if he found out anything."

"Found out anything? I don't know if I can stand any more of this tonight."

"Then I'll call him. I just want to see if he answers. Could you translate if he does?" Niels punched in the number. No answer. He tried again. "Hello? English? Is this Tommaso di Barbara's phone?"

———————————

Hannah poured herself some more red wine. She could hear Niels talking on the phone in the bedroom. What was it he'd just told her? Hannah couldn't get the words out of her head. *I'm not good at flying. Traveling.* He was shouting in the bedroom: "What? Can I talk to him? I don't understand."

After a few minutes, he came out of the bedroom and went toward the bathroom. She caught a glimpse of his confused expression. "I think they're trying to find him. I can't really tell what's happening."

Hannah followed him. At a distance. In the bathroom he took off his shirt and tossed it on the floor. She looked at him. There was blood on his shirt. He turned his back to her. Hannah knew what she was going to see, but it still came as a shock.

"What? No? Tommaso?" said Niels on his cell.

Niels was trying to make sense of the phone conversation, but the person on the other end had already gone. He put down his cell. He was standing in front of the sink, leaning on both hands. Hannah didn't take her eyes off him. Finally, he turned around.

"It . . . he . . ." Niels stammered.

"He's dead," she said.

"How did you know that?"

"The question is, why didn't I realize it earlier?"

"What do you mean?"

"Niels. He was number thirty-five."

She had lost him. She could clearly see that. She stepped inside the bathroom and carefully took Niels by the hand.

"What it is?"

"Turn around."

Cautiously, she turned him around in front of the mirror. She picked up a small mirror from the sink and handed it to him. "Use this."

At first he couldn't see it. Then he did. A mark had appeared on his back. Not yet very clear. It looked almost like eczema. But the shape was unmistakable. He dropped the mirror, and it shattered on the tile floor. Seven years of bad luck. He dashed out of the bathroom.

"Niels?"

He was gone. He slammed the door to the bedroom behind him. She called after him, "The two of you found yourselves. It's obvious. You're the only ones who would listen."

She could hear him rummaging around in the bedroom. "You're the only ones who would listen," she repeated to herself. Niels tore open the door. Wearing a new shirt with a suitcase in his hand. The suitcase that he'd packed long ago—the one that hadn't wanted to leave. But it did now.

85

Ospedale dell'Angelo—Venice

Commissario Morante was holding Tommaso's cell phone in his hand.

Heavy. That was exactly how the responsibility felt. *Heavy.* A responsibility that he had neglected. It felt like a lump in his lungs, something that was reducing his ability to inhale oxygen. Responsibility can be weighed like an actual physical weight, the commissario managed to think before Flavio interrupted him by saying, "I should have listened to him."

Morante looked at Flavio, who was sitting on one of the pink plastic seats in the hospital. They were waiting for the doctor to come and get them so they could ask him a few questions. A Swedish tourist had found Tommaso dead in the men's bathroom. From what they'd been told, the tourist's screams could be heard through the whole train station.

"He said we were in danger. That someone was in danger," Flavio explained.

"When?"

"At the train station. I thought he was ill. You said he'd been suspended after all."

"I did? So it's my fault? Is that what you're saying?"

Flavio gave the commissario a surprised look. He'd never heard his boss shout before.

Morante tried to stand up straight and look composed in spite of his outburst. There would have to be an investigation, he knew that. He would be interviewed. Why had he suspended Tommaso? Should he have paid more attention to what the man was saying? The medics had tried to revive Tommaso in the men's room. That was when they saw his back. When they had cut off his jacket in order to use the defibrillator on his heart, they saw the bizarre mark, stretching from one shoulder to the other. His skin was swollen with patterns. One of the medics had said, "His back was hot, like it was on fire."

The doctor stuck his head out the door and yelled, "Come with me!"

Nobody ever spoke to the Venice police chief in that tone of voice. Maybe this was a foretaste of what was in store for him. Demotion. Humiliation. Perhaps derisive articles printed in the newspapers.

Even in a situation with a dead colleague, the foremost thing on Commissario Morante's mind was his own status.

The morgue—Venice

A single garland adorned the entrance. It was Christmas here, too, in the medical examiner's domain.

The body of Tommaso di Barbara lay with the head slanting down on the ice-cold steel table. But it wasn't just a body on the table. It was a decorated body.

The commissario took a step closer to examine Tommaso's back. "What's that?"

"I was hoping you could tell me." The doctor remained next to the window with an accusatory look on his face. As if this whole situation were Morante's fault.

"How would I know?"

The doctor shrugged.

"This is what Tommaso was talking about." Flavio's voice was barely audible. He looked down at the floor and went on. "He talked about people who had died with marks on their backs. That case he kept babbling about. The package from China. All his newspaper clippings. We just didn't believe him."

Silence settled over the autopsy suite.

"What was the cause of death?" asked the commissario.

The doctor shrugged. "Until somebody tells me what that is, I would say murder."

"Murder?"

"Murder by poison. I don't know what else could have caused that."

A deep breath. Flavio had retreated to the far side of the room. "Flavio," called Commissario Morante.

"Yes, sir?"

"Get hold of Tommaso's secretary. She knows a lot about the case. Tommaso used to ask her to translate things for him."

"Okay."

"And let's get in touch with Interpol." Morante looked at the doctor and then at Flavio. "It's important to act promptly. And that means now."

Part II

THE BOOK OF THE RIGHTEOUS

And Abraham drew near and said, Wilt thou also destroy the righteous with the wicked?

Peradventure there be fifty righteous within the city: wilt thou also destroy and not spare the place for the fifty righteous that are therein?

And the Lord said, If I find in Sodom fifty righteous within the city, then I will spare all the place for their sakes.

—Genesis 18:23–24, 26

1

Vesterbro—Copenhagen

The snow crunched under Niels's shoes as he trotted over to the parking lot. He couldn't hear Hannah, but he knew she was there.

"Niels!"

He gave up trying to pull the suitcase through the fallen snow and picked it up to carry it. There was something protective about the heavy suitcase. Almost like an oversize bulletproof vest.

"You've known all along, Niels."

She was right behind him now.

"I don't know what you're talking about."

"It's you, Niels."

"Can't you hear how ridiculous that sounds?"

"Ridiculous?"

He slowed down.

"Is it because it now has to do with real people? Is that what makes it ridiculous?" She caught up with him and grabbed hold of his arm. "Wasn't that what you said to me?"

Niels didn't reply. They had reached the car.

"When was the last time you traveled anywhere?"

Niels avoided looking at her. He refused to answer the question. Hannah raised her voice. "Answer me! If it's so ridiculous, you might as well answer."

Niels was searching his pockets.

"Is this what you're looking for?" She held up the car key.

"Dammit. It's your car."

"Exactly. Shall we go?"

She unlocked the doors. Niels tossed the suitcase into the backseat next to the small cardboard box containing all the documents regarding the murder cases. Then he got into the driver's seat and slammed the door. Hannah climbed in beside him. "Okay, Niels Bentzon," she said. "Where are we going?"

She looked at him, waiting for him to say something. Finally, he did. "I'm not a doctor," he said tensely. "But I've heard of psychosomatic reactions. Bewildering sensory perceptions. Abnormal states of consciousness. Take the phenomenon of stigmata, for instance."

Niels's brain was working feverishly. The memory of a TV program came to his rescue. "St. Francis of Assisi."

"What about him?"

"During the last years of his life, he walked around with constantly bleeding hands and feet. It came from inside of him. Or what about that other man—what's his name?" Niels buried his face in his hands as he replayed the TV program in his mind. "A short, fat monk. Was he Italian? They've even put a statue of him underwater off the Tremiti Islands. Padre Pio! Have you heard of him? He's from the twentieth century. For over fifty years he suffered from stigmata. The human body can produce the most inexplicable phenomena. That's what we're dealing with here. It can't have any other meaning."

"Why are you talking about meaning?"

Niels didn't reply.

She persisted, "Who says there has to be a meaning? Is there a meaning behind the fact that the planets move in an ellipse around the sun? Or that—"

"I'm not a religious person, Hannah. For me, there has to be a natural explanation."

"Yes. And we've found the natural explanation. We just don't understand it. That's how all discoveries start out."

He shook his head.

"Think of it as the phenomenon behaving like a law of nature."

"A law of nature?"

"The definition is something like this: a well-founded connection between physical entities. Essentially, a law of nature cannot be altered. You can scream and cry, Niels, but you can't do anything about it. Look at me."

He complied. Without saying a word.

"Why is it so unthinkable that the phenomenon follows a specific pattern?"

"How is that possible?"

"It's like in mathematics. At first chaos seems to rule. You can't make heads or tails of it. But suddenly—when you're able to get some distance, when you crack the code—the system becomes apparent. The system emerges from the chaos. Coincidences dissolve right before your eyes. Things, numbers, converge and can be inserted into formulas. That's something that every mathematician knows."

"Hannah."

She refused to let him speak. "The whole thing may look random, Niels. The way you were brought into the case. Tommaso. Your meeting with me. But it all fits. It's all part of the system. The law of nature."

"That's too far out there for me," Niels said, but he was really talking to himself. Shaking his head.

"None of you can travel," she went on. "You're all like cell-phone towers waiting for a signal. And then suddenly, you do something. *You take action.* A deed that is part of something larger."

"Something larger?"

"Like the soldier who released the prisoners and in that way made them have faith in—"

"That's just one example," Niels interrupted her. "What about the Russian?"

"He saved the mother and her children in the theater. Who knows what will result from that? Or from the boy who was given unapproved medicine and then survived? All of you are like little islands, Niels. You're bound to specific geographic locations. That's where you act as protectors."

"Protectors!" Niels gave her a scornful look. "I can't even protect myself."

"That's not true. You told me yourself that you're the one they call whenever people have had enough and try to commit suicide. You're just like the other thirty-five. Doctors, human rights defenders. Just think about that Russian in the theater who volunteered to be shot instead of the young mother and her children. That's exactly what you do. From the very beginning, you've taken the threat seriously. You're the only one who has."

He noticed that she was holding his hand tightly. She loosened her grip but didn't let go. "There's an old proverb that goes like this: 'The devil's greatest stroke of genius was'—"

Niels finished the sentence: "—'convincing people that he existed.'"

"The biggest mistake we can make is to think that we've figured the whole thing out. The people I know who are the greatest skeptics, who are least certain about how the world and the universe work, are also the most intelligent. The most brilliant.

"God does not exist. It started with the Big Bang. We can turn the temperature up or down, like a thermostat." She shook her head and smiled at him. "Absolute certainty is only for stupid people. It requires a certain intelligence to realize how little we actually know."

"That's why we don't know what's happening to me? Is that what you mean?"

"Yes. But we can see a system. It's the same way with gravity. We have no idea why it works the way it does. But we do know that the ball will come back down when we throw it up in the air. No matter what you do, Niels, no matter what, you're going to end up at the National Hospital six days from now. On Friday."

Niels didn't reply. He turned the key in the ignition. There was something liberating about putting an end to the silence.

"Where are we going?" Hannah asked.

He looked at her and said, "On vacation. I need a break."

Heading west

Snow began sweeping over the road as they drove out of Copenhagen. At first they headed north. The high-rise apartment buildings gave way to single-family homes. The houses got bigger and bigger, eventually becoming mansions before nature took over.

"No." Niels changed his mind. "Let's drive west."

He took the exit for Odense. He wanted to get as far away as possible. On the radio, agitated voices were discussing the climate conference fiasco. Obama had left by now. Some callers claimed the world was doomed. "And maybe we don't really deserve to be here. Human beings. The destroyers." The words on the radio flew through the air like the snow outside the car windows.

"Look at that," said Hannah quietly, almost as if speaking to herself.

She was staring with enchantment at the billions of snowflakes they were driving through. "I wonder if this is what it's like to float through space."

The car's headlights lit up the snow-covered fields on either side. "We need to listen to some music." Niels rummaged through the stack of CDs. Milli Vanilli and Nina Hagen in a broken case.

"Keep your eyes on the road."

"Don't you have any Beatles? Or Dylan?" he asked Hannah. "Something from before 1975?"

"I only have music that I never listened to while Johannes was alive."

He looked at her. "Part of your so-called project?"

"Exactly. But watch out!"

They started to skid. For just a few seconds, Niels lost control of the car.

"I told you to keep your eyes on the road."

Niels smiled. Hannah lit two cigarettes and handed one to him. She rolled down the window.

"Thanks." He turned on the music. A monotone pop tune that somehow suited the moment. "But it doesn't really matter, does it?"

"What do you mean?"

"If the car skids off the road. Or if I have an accident. You said yourself that it's a law of nature that I'm going to end up at the National Hospital on Friday. No matter what I do."

"I'm not the one deciding that. It's the system. It's mathematics. But it doesn't apply to me. And I'm not sure that I'm ready to—"

Niels looked at her. "I'm not, either."

They drove through little hamlets that all looked alike. The same view from the car windows: streetlamps, a train station, a grocery store, a pizzeria, a newsstand, designed by the same architect who had designed all Danish provincial towns. He must have been a busy man.

They stopped for a red light. Not a soul in sight. No lights on in any of the windows. Not in the veterinarian's office or the community health clinic. Nor in the pharmacy or pub.

"The light's green."

Niels didn't move.

"Niels?"

He pulled over to the side of the road.

"What's going on? Where are we?"

"Somewhere or other."

"Somewhere or other?"

"That's a good enough name for this place, don't you think?"

"Niels. Why are we stopping?"

He looked at her. "To defeat your mathematics."

2

Kathrine usually said that there were two types of people. The ones who felt reassured when they went to see a doctor, and the ones who were terrified. Niels belonged to the second category. Doctors in any medical setting: health centers, hospitals, and clinics. He did everything possible to avoid them. He always tried to postpone any sort of contact until it was absolutely necessary. Six years earlier, he had pushed his luck too far. A harmless respiratory infection that could have been cured in a matter of a few days with a dose of penicillin had almost cost him his life. Because he'd refused to do anything about it, the infection had spread to his pleurae, lung tissues, and alveoli. When Niels agreed to be admitted to the hospital, he was in such a weakened condition that the doctors at first guessed he might be suffering from aggressive lung cancer. Kathrine was furious with him. Why hadn't he gone to see a doctor earlier? "I belong to the second category" was the only thing he could say.

At first nothing happened when Niels slammed his elbow through the glass pane. Then the alarm started up. An ugly sound. A loud, shrill shrieking. His hand was bleeding, and he hesitated. Then he began rummaging through drawers and cabinets, trying to read the labels in the dark. Prednisolone, albuterol, aspirin, Terbasmin. What was morphine called? He scanned the labels: *Sedative. Sleeping pills. Laxative. Antihistamine.* Most ended up on the floor, but anything that might have a tranquilizing effect got stuffed into his pockets. How much time had passed? It could take ten minutes for the police to arrive on the scene. At least. This type of break-in wasn't given high priority. In his mind, Niels could hear the officers down at the station when they received the call. "Fucking drug addicts!" They might just have a little more coffee. Because what use would it be? What officer wanted to go out in the dark, in the middle of a snowstorm, to deal with a desperate junkie probably infected with HIV? There would always be more poor souls ready to swallow a handful of pills—it didn't matter what kind—in the hope of suppressing the cravings. Cortisone, baclofen, bromhexine. Some Niels tossed on the floor, others went into his pockets, before he found some of the good stuff: two different brands of morphine.

"What the hell are you doing in here?"

The lights went on. Sharp and relentless, blinding Niels.

The man was younger than Niels. Tall and broad-shouldered and furious.

Niels couldn't think of a single word to say. That was what often happened when someone was arrested. Silence. As if the person under arrest was in a state of shock. But that wasn't always the case. Sometimes the person simply had nothing to say.

"Don't move. I'm calling the police."

Niels glanced around. There was no other exit. He had to get past the man. Now. Niels took a step closer.

"Stay where you are!"

Niels was standing right in front of him. The man reached out to grab Niels. Instinctively, Niels knocked his hands away. The man tried to punch Niels but landed only a glancing blow. Niels didn't want to hit the man. He just wanted to get past. He tried to squeeze through the door. The man grabbed him, and for a few awful seconds, they staggered around like a couple of amateur wrestlers. The man was stronger than Niels, but he didn't have desperation on his side. With a roar, Niels threw off his opponent. The man then dragged Niels into some freestanding shelves. For an instant—or was it Niels's imagination?—the alarm stopped shrieking and yielded to the sound of the toppling cabinet. Then it started up again.

Niels was the first to get up. He pushed the man away, noticing that a shard of glass was sticking out of his cheek just under his eye. He had blood on his face. Blood on his hair.

Then Niels was out of there.

He ran for the car. He almost lost his footing on the slippery, snow-covered sidewalk. Hannah already had the door open. They could hear police sirens in the distance.

"Niels! What the hell!"

He started the car.

"What happened back there, Niels?"

They took off.

------ ✦ ------

They were parked at the side of the road. The snow had retreated, presumably to gather its troops and return with renewed force. Not a sound could be heard in the whole world.

Niels was staring out the windshield. Out into the dark. The dashboard clock showed that it was just past three A.M.

"I've never done anything like that before," he said.

"If you keep on this way, maybe you'll get out of showing up on Friday."

"What do you mean?" Niels turned to look at Hannah.

"Maybe this is what you should be doing. Bad things. So you'll no longer be considered a good person."

Niels didn't answer. He emptied his pockets and read the labels on the stolen medicines. "I think I got everything."

"What are you planning to do with that stuff?"

"Syringes, alcohol, and enough morphine to knock out an elephant."

He could tell that his words rolled right off her. She wasn't listening. That didn't stop him.

"We've got a week left. A little less than a week. So—" He stopped abruptly.

"What about it, Niels?"

"So I'll take the morphine, hide on some boat, and sail away."

"Sail away?"

"Yes."

"Where?"

He shrugged.

"Where would you like to sail to?"

"Argentina, I think."

"Argentina?" Was she smiling? "That's quite a voyage."

"Buenos Aires. I have a friend there. She's told me all about the green lakes in Patagonia. Green like emeralds."

"Who's your friend?"

He hesitated. "I don't know. I've never actually met her." He turned to look at Hannah. She was beautiful. Happy, scared, sad. Was that a tear sliding down her cheek? "No, it has to be with you, Hannah."

"I thought you couldn't travel."

"Maybe I can. If I'm sound asleep."

"You don't understand, Niels. You really don't understand." Yes, it was a tear. He could see it now. Hannah hurried to wipe it away. "The laws of nature don't care whether you're asleep or not."

3

The Great Belt Bridge

Niels could remember when the bridge across the waters of the Great Belt was opened in 1998, linking the Danish islands of Sjælland and Fyn. Kathrine had been glued to the TV screen, watching the ceremony with envy, fascinated by the eleven-mile-long monstrosity of a bridge that stretched as far as the eye could see. She knew the numbers: 230 feet to the surface of the water. More than 4,900 feet between the two pylons, which each rose up 820 feet into the sky. Nineteen bridge supports, each weighing 6,000 tons. Niels didn't share her enthusiasm. He thought the bridge was a waste of money. And what was worse, it meant the loss of the ferryboats. The loss of an opportunity to meet people, to fall into a conversation with truck drivers and politicians and all sorts of people from every part of the country. Kathrine wanted to design a bridge one day. She sometimes spent whole evenings surfing the Internet, looking at the Golden Gate, Ponte Vecchio, Karlsbroen, Akashi Kaikyō, and the South Congress Bridge in Austin, from which a million and a half bats flew out at dusk every evening in search of food. She told Niels that he was wrong about the Great Belt Bridge. She said it would connect people. Get them talking to each other.

Niels looked out at the traffic gathering around the toll machines at the foot of the bridge. Nobody was talking to one another. People rushed past faster than ever as the sun came up over the sea.

The Great Belt Bridge
Saturday, December 19

The early-morning rays colored the water orange. The line of cars at the tollbooths hadn't moved in at least ten minutes. Hannah was asleep. Niels looked at her. A peaceful expression, unmarred by worry. A barely perceptible trembling under her delicate eyelids. She was dreaming.

At last he was able to move forward to the tollbooth.

"Good morning." Niels handed the man his credit card.

"Be careful. It can get slippery."

"Thanks."

Niels headed the car for the island of Fyn.

"Niels?" Hannah was only half awake. She sounded groggy.

"Go back to sleep."

He turned on the radio. Christmas music. Then the news, which dealt mostly with the climate conference. The government was purporting it was a huge success, while the opposition parties thundered that it had been a disaster. The Chinese were scoundrels. Everyone agreed about that. One politician declared, "It was as if the Chinese thought they were on a different planet from everyone else. Otherwise why would they be so indifferent to the climate?" New topics: a politician demanding tax reform; another complaining about fraud with foodstuffs; fighting on the border of Gaza; an oil spill off the coast of Canada. Niels was looking for something else. Everything else. When he heard the news bulletin, it took a moment before he realized who the radio announcer was talking about. "Danish in appearance, approximately six foot one inch tall, wearing jeans and a dark coat. Considered dangerous." It was the last word in particular that made an impression on Niels. He'd been called many things in his life—naive, cowardly, diplomatic, vague, aloof, smart, stupid, manic-depressive—but he had never been called dangerous.

"Dangerous." The word haunted him for several kilometers as he drove along the highway. He drove faster as he found himself casting paranoid glances in the rearview mirror. Had anyone seen their car as he ran from the community health clinic? Niels replayed the scene in his mind. At first he was convinced that there had been no witnesses except the man who discovered him inside the building. And he couldn't have seen the car.

Then Niels began to have doubts. Had the man gotten up and run over to the window? Had he reacted so quickly that he was able to see the car's license plate? Niels wasn't sure. He wasn't sure of anything but that he felt physically sick about the whole situation. Just as he turned off the highway and headed along a smaller road, he was almost certain he remembered the man standing at the window. Niels had caught a glimpse of his silhouette. If he'd managed to get their license number, it wouldn't take the police long to catch them. A few hours at most. Especially since Niels had been labeled dangerous. He felt a prickling sensation in his legs; he needed to get out and stretch. He decided to hell with it—he would find someplace to stop. He decided not to tell Hannah that the police were looking for them.

They ended up down by the water at a small harbor area. Possibly Kerteminde Harbor.

Hannah woke up as he stopped the car. "Where are we?"

"Good morning. We're going to get some coffee. And take some time to think."

Hannah stretched with a pleased expression. Niels couldn't tell whether it was the thought of coffee that made her happy or because they were going to stop and think.

They found a small harbor building with a kiosk. Hannah waited outside while Niels bought the coffee. The kiosk girl stared at him suspiciously. Or maybe he was imagining that. It was normal for the police to notify gas stations about people they were looking for. But what about this kiosk? Had the girl already received a description of him, and was it lying under the counter? Or had she seen it on the small laptop over by the window? Niels caught her eye. Was she looking at him and trying to determine his height? His weight? Niels tried to relax, attempting to make his shoulders and face less tense. The result, he was sure, was that he looked like a neurotic robot. As he left the kiosk, he imagined the girl rushing to call the nearest police station. He pushed the thought out of his mind and went over to Hannah.

"I can't believe how far we've driven," she said, sounding tired.

"Did you get some sleep?" He handed her the coffee cup.

"A little." She moved her head from side to side to ease the stiffness in her neck.

"Is it too cold to stand out here?"

"No, it's fine."

They looked out at the water. Soon the clouds of water vapor on the surface would turn into tiny ice crystals and the bay would freeze over. Niels switched on his cell phone. No messages.

"I once had a colleague at the institute," Hannah said as she watched a couple of fishermen getting ready to head out in their boat. One of them waved. She waved back. "He found it impossible to say no. It was as if 'no' wasn't part of his vocabulary. Whenever anyone asked him to do something, he always said yes." She paused. "That became a real problem for him because he just couldn't keep up. He couldn't do everything he'd agreed to do. Committees, meetings, conferences, reports. So in the end . . ." She turned to look Niels in the eye. "In the end, opinion turned against him."

"What's your point?"

"Goodness is a problem, Niels. That's my point. His goodness became a problem for the whole institute. Pretty soon we started holding meetings without him. Just to spare him, so that he wouldn't disappoint either us or himself. Do you understand?"

"I don't think so."

"What does it mean to be good, Niels?"

He shook his head as he studied the gravel underfoot.

She went on, "The philosopher Hannah Arendt talks about the banality of evil. In her view, most people possess evil lying dormant inside of them. All that's required are the right—or rather the wrong—conditions for that evil to be released. But what about goodness? The banality of goodness. When I think about my colleague and about you, I'd almost say that you have no free will. You have no choice. You *are* good. So does that mean that goodness is still good?"

"Hannah."

"No, wait a minute. This is important. You haven't chosen to be good. In our understanding of goodness and the good deed, we think from an existential point of view that we have a choice. But you don't. Just think of the story about Job! You're a piece in a bigger puzzle, and someone else—or rather, *something* else—has made up the rules of the game. What's paradoxical in the Job story is that there's nobody else God thinks more about than Job, even though He takes everything away from him. It's the same thing with all of you. With you personally, Niels. You've also been stripped of your free will, the possibility of moving freely."

"Stop right there!"

"They say that most people in prison today suffer from ADHD. Varying degrees of autism. Neuropsychological disorders that we're only just beginning to understand. What if we're much less in control of our own lives than we imagine? What if most of our actions are biologically determined?"

"Hannah! It's very hard to forget about everything if you keep on talking about it. We're on vacation. Okay?"

"Okay." She was smiling.

"Let's get going."

They walked back to the car and got in. They sat there, enjoying being out of the icy wind. Niels was about to start up the engine when Hannah said, "Who's that?" She was looking past him.

"Where?"

"Behind us. They're coming this way."

He turned around. Two police officers. One of them leaned forward and rapped hard on the window.

4

Nyborg

The place really did have potential. At first Niels hadn't seen it, but now he did.

The cell looked almost like a dorm room, although the space was slightly bigger. There wasn't much similarity with Alcatraz. No slamming iron gates, no sound of clattering key rings or the military stomp of boots belonging to sadistic prison guards. No psychopathic prisoners with tattoos on their faces, locked up for quadruple murders as a result of robberies gone wrong, just waiting to assault him while he slept. No anxious muttering from the corridor where prisoners on death row trudged the long way to the electric chair. Just a perfectly ordinary dorm room that stank of vomit. The cell was like a hotel. People arrived, checked in, stayed a brief time, and then moved on. Today's guest was Niels Bentzon.

Niels surveyed his surroundings: a bunk, a chair, a table, a cupboard, four bare walls. Somebody had used a marker to write *The polees suck* on the wall, spelling error and all. But the place had potential. He was *locked up*. All they had to do was give him a carton of canned food and throw away the key for a week.

Where was Hannah? In a different jail? Being interviewed? Maybe they had let her go. Niels kept thinking about how the arrest had taken place. He wondered how they'd found him so quickly. Maybe it was because of the girl in the kiosk. As far as he knew, there were normally no surveillance cameras on the bridges. He gave up trying to figure it out. It had been years since he'd participated in any manhunts, and so much new technology had appeared in the past few years. Maybe a satellite had tracked them down.

It was cold in the cell. The local police station must be trying to save on the heating bill. Or else it was part of a larger strategy. Since they couldn't make life miserable for the prisoners by starving them or beating them, the police could always turn down the heat in the winter months. Niels was familiar with that tactic.

He heard the sound of a door being unlocked. A woman came in. Lisa Larsson. That would be a good name for a porn actress, thought Niels when she introduced herself. Or a Swedish detective novelist. She smiled briefly, but there was nothing pleasant about her tone of voice when she asked him to come with her.

"You're a police officer?" Lisa Larsson—young, attractive, her expression chilly—sounded genuinely surprised. Niels's eyes roamed over the Christmas elf figures on the windowsill.

"Yes. I'm a police negotiator for hostage situations. And if people are threatening to commit suicide."

"Why didn't you say so before?" The other officer, Hans Rishøj, was an older man who reminded Niels of a schoolteacher he'd had in another life. The man glanced down at some papers, looking confused as he scratched his short, well-trimmed beard, which was clearly meant to lend him the authority that he didn't naturally possess.

Niels shrugged. "How the hell did you find me so fast?"

They ignored his question.

"You work in Copenhagen?"

"Yes."

They exchanged glances. Several painful seconds of silence went by. Niels wouldn't have been surprised if they decided to release him on the spot. A mistake must have been made—that thought was palpable. They obviously suffered from the widespread notion that police officers never got into trouble with the law. They were uncomfortable sitting across from a fellow officer under these circumstances. Niels could tell from the looks they kept giving each other. He fully understood how they felt. As if they were being uncollegial. Like traitors. Since everyone else hated the police, what would happen if they started arresting one another?

"In Copenhagen?" Hans pushed up his glasses. "Under Sommersted?"

"Yes. Do you know Sommersted?"

"A little. We're not exactly best friends, but we've run into each other on various occasions."

"Sommersted doesn't have any friends." Niels attempted a smile.

"What happened at the community health clinic?" Lisa was less impressed by Niels's status.

Niels looked at her. Newly trained, eager to play by the book, and she could still remember what the rules were. He decided that he would look only at her during this conversation. He would like to follow the rules, and he didn't feel like carrying on any small talk with Hans.

"What did he tell you? The guy I punched?"

"Allan . . ." She scanned the report. She was efficient and intelligent. Obviously, she had ambitions to rise through the ranks. It was not her intention to give up on the island of Fyn and risk being here twenty years from now, standing outside the pub and asking the locals to blow into a Breathalyzer as they staggered out the door after Christmas lunch. "He said that at approximately two-thirty A.M. you broke into the clinic, knocked him down, and then took off. With this." She pointed at the morphine lying on the table along with some plastic syringes and the other pills Niels had collected. Clear evidence that he was a drug addict. Niels wasn't planning to contradict that idea. The truth was too complicated—it almost always is.

Silence. Hans stood up. "I'm just going to give Sommersted a call." He went into the office next door but returned shortly. "Your boss wants to talk to you."

Niels could tell as soon as he picked up the phone: Sommersted was trying to act calm and sympathetic, but he wasn't having much luck with either. He was breathing fast, in a halting manner, and that gave him away.

"What's going on?"

"I know, I know." Niels was annoyed that his voice sounded so weak.

"What do you know?"

"I know that I've been arrested for breaking into a health clinic."

"What's going on, Niels?" his boss asked again, casting aside any attempt to seem sympathetic. What remained was a thoroughly furious Sommersted. "And what the hell are you doing on Fyn?"

Niels didn't reply. He found silence preferable to trying to offer impossible explanations. What was he supposed to say?

"I'm waiting, Bentzon." Sommersted had toned down his rage.

"It has to do with the case of the good people who are being murdered."

"That again?" A resigned, melodramatic sigh. Followed by silence.

Sommersted was working up to something. Niels could sense it. And sure enough: "So it's true, what they've been saying."

"They?"

"That was why you needed the pills. For yourself. You're not well, Niels."

"No."

"I don't think you're at all well."

Niels could practically hear Sommersted thinking over the phone.

"All right. I want you to come back to Copenhagen. I'll get Rishøj to drive you across the bridge. Leon will pick you up there."

"Rishøj?" Niels made eye contact with Hans, who smiled.

"Exactly. Leave now, and then I'll see you at headquarters around . . . Give me a call when you're getting close. We won't be able to avoid an internal investigation."

Niels wasn't listening. He heard only one sentence: *I want you to come back to Copenhagen.* "I'm not going back to Copenhagen."

"What do you mean?" Sommersted sounded hostile.

"I'm not going back to Copenhagen."

Niels hung up. He stood there, looking around at the local station. The police force's answer to *Little House on the Prairie*. A couple of computers. The walls decorated with photos of children and grandchildren. An article clipped from the local paper. *Police Doing Battle with Obesity.* Niels wondered what that was about but didn't bother to read the article. What exactly were they doing? Had they started handing out tickets to people for not keeping up with their weekly jogging?

"We've got to go now." Rishøj sounded almost apologetic.

Niels didn't move.

"Niels? Your wife is waiting out in the car."

"She's not my wife."

Rishøj put on his coat.

"Rishøj? I know this probably sounds crazy. But what if I ask you to lock me up until Saturday morning?"

5

Fyn

The snow's encounter with northern Fyn was not a pretty sight. All around the station, the clumps of white crystals were mixed with swirling dirt. Instead of white, this part of the world had turned light brown.

The police car was also covered with dirty snow and slush. Hannah was sitting in the front passenger seat, which surprised Niels. It was a clear breach of regulations, but maybe it was because Rishøj regarded them more as friends than as enemies. Hannah didn't say a word as Niels and Hans got in. Niels sat in back. The doors couldn't be opened from the inside.

Rishøj turned the key in the ignition. Lisa was still inside the office, which was also against the rules. One officer for two prisoners. *Prisoners.* The word seemed all wrong.

The aging police officer turned so he could see both Hannah and Niels. As if he were a schoolteacher about to take the kids out for a field trip and he wanted to issue a few admonitions. Niels was almost expecting him to say: "We'll be at Hans Christian Andersen's house in an hour. Did you remember to bring your bag lunches and milk?" Instead, he said, "I've got to be honest. I've never seen the likes of this before."

Both Niels and Hannah hoped that the other person would say something. But their continued silence didn't seem to bother Rishøj.

"Not much happens out here. Young toughs getting into trouble. Brawls down at the bodega. That sort of thing. Occasionally, we've gone over to Vollsmose to help out when the young Arabs get out of hand. And you know what?"

"No, what?" Hannah hurried to ask.

"Most of them are okay. Sure, some of them are off the deep end, but most of them are just bored. So why not just give them a youth center or a soccer field? Oh well, that wasn't what I meant to talk about."

Niels stared at him. Rishøj smiled, looking like a man who had long ago lost all connection with the world around him. A bewildered, slightly absentminded man who ought to get rid of the police uniform and realize that his future battles would be waged out at his summer house where the enemies weren't "young Arabs" but knotgrass, saltbush, and other garden weeds.

Whenever Hans Rishøj paused in his monologue, they rode in silence. It was snowing harder. Drifts swept across the road from the fields, and the traffic moved slowly. Hans talked a lot. Mostly about his daughter who was a hairdresser. Hannah nodded now and then, but Niels wasn't listening. He was thinking about what would happen when they reached Copenhagen. He could just picture it: Sommersted's anger. Leon's scorn. Worst of all: the psychological evaluation he'd have to undergo in the National Hospital's psychiatric unit. He felt like screaming: *I don't want to die!* But it was as if something—*something*—were tugging at him.

"One of your colleagues is waiting for us on the other side of the bridge," Rishøj explained. "He'll drive you the rest of the way back to the city."

Hannah turned to look at Niels. "You see, Niels? No matter what you do. Now we're on our way back."

"Just like you said."

"But look at the other side of it: This is something bigger than us. Something we don't know anything about. And now you can sense it."

"Are you trying to console me?"

"Yes."

"Okay."

Rishøj gave her a puzzled look.

Niels felt an urge to curl up in a fetal position. In less than two hours, he would be back in Copenhagen. Up ahead they could see the line starting to form for the Great Belt Bridge. I'm not going back across that bridge, he promised himself. If I reach the other side, it's all over.

A long line of cars was waiting in front of the bridge.

"What's going on?" Rishøj muttered to himself.

"Closed because of the weather, maybe?" Hannah suggested.

The officer nodded. He sat there, impatiently drumming his fingers on the steering wheel. "My pipe is calling to me," he murmured, and opened the door. "Anyone else?" he asked.

Niels nodded.

Hannah was right. The bridge had been temporarily closed because of poor visibility. Niels caught her eye as she climbed out of the car, too.

"I'm going to call your colleagues on the other side. Just so they don't think we've forgotten them." Rishøj moved a few yards away to make the call.

"Are you ready?" Niels whispered to Hannah.

"What do you mean?"

"I'm not going across that bridge."

"Niels, it doesn't matter what—" Hannah didn't manage to say anything else before Rishøj was back.

"They say the wind is starting to die down." He got out his pipe and tried to light it, but his lighter refused to work.

Niels thought fast. "I have a lighter in my suitcase in the trunk."

Rishøj nodded and fished out his keys. The trunk opened with a faint clack. Niels reached inside his suitcase.

"There's more snow on the way. Look over there," Hannah said, and the aging policeman looked toward the north with concern. When he turned, he was in the direct line of fire from Niels's Heckler & Koch. But he didn't notice. He had long ago tossed all instinctive reflexes overboard. It was lucky that the national police force had any use for him at all. "It's always this stretch of water that gets hit the hardest," he muttered. "I've got a boat in Kerteminde that—"

Niels had to raise his gun and tap him on the shoulder before the officer noticed the pistol. He wasn't afraid. Not even surprised. He simply couldn't comprehend what was happening.

"Get in the car," Niels said to Rishøj. He picked up his suitcase and handed it to Hannah.

"What?"

"I want you to get in the backseat of the car."

"But why?" Rishøj's voice was barely audible.

Niels didn't answer, just opened the door. "Give me the keys."

"All right, but—"

"Now!" Niels raised his voice.

The clicking sound when Niels opened the door to the backseat made

Rishøj's expression change. Niels saw it at once. Everything came into focus. Niels realized that he had actually done Rishøj a service. The moment was of crucial importance for the officer. His image of the world as an oversize Duckburg, where everyone was basically good at heart—an image that he had cultivated for decades—collapsed as Niels and Hannah looked on. Nothing remained but disappointment. *I thought we were on the same team,* his expression said.

"Get in the car," Niels calmly insisted.

"But why?"

"Because I'm not going back to Copenhagen. I need to get away." Niels leaned inside and pounded the butt of his gun against the police radio until it was smashed, leaving a couple of wires sticking out. "Give me your cell phone."

The blow to his head caught Niels completely off guard. Pain spread through his skull, and he heard a screaming sound in his left ear.

"What the hell do you think you're doing?" roared Rishøj. "Do you think you can lock me up in here?"

Another blow. This one harder. Niels staggered and dropped his gun. Rishøj was fumbling to take out his weapon. Niels spun around and punched him.

"Niels!" Hannah's shout seemed to come from another world, even though she was standing right next to him. Niels took a second to gather his thoughts. *The morphine. The syringes.* They were in the glove compartment. He was aware that Rishøj was wailing in pain and desperation. Niels found the morphine packet inside one of the clinically clean plastic bags used by the police to collect evidence.

"The suitcase!" Niels said. He snatched up the suitcase and then grabbed Hannah by the hand, and they set off running.

They climbed over the traffic divider, leaped over a frozen puddle, and raced across the frost-covered fields. Taking a quick glance over his shoulder, Niels saw the old policeman aiming his pistol at them. "Hannah, I think he's—"

The sound of a faint bang resounded across the frozen ground. Another bang. They sounded like firecrackers.

"He's shooting at us!" shouted Niels, gasping for breath as they ran, finally disappearing into the swirling snow.

Their shoes sank deep into the powdery snow between the trees.

"Is he coming after us?" Hannah turned around.

"I can see a road up ahead."

She was crying. "Where?"

In Denmark there was always a road up ahead. "Just keep going."

They left the trees behind and clambered across the honest efforts of a landscape architect to unite farm fields with a picnic area.

"What now? Which way?" She started walking along the road. "Maybe a car will give us a lift or—" She was interrupted by the sound of a bus coming toward them.

"Here comes the cavalry," muttered Niels, sticking out his hand, knowing that was the way to flag down a bus out in the country.

The bus stopped.

"Your car couldn't take the cold, is that it?" yelled the driver in his lilting Fyn accent. "I'm only going as far as the station, but from there you can catch a train to Odense."

"Thanks." Niels boarded the bus first, trying to avoid the driver's eye.

They sat down in the last seat in the back and looked out the window. The icy road forced the driver to proceed slowly, which was not at all in keeping with Niels's racing pulse. But the driver set the pace, which was fine. It was a matter of staying calm. Acting like everybody else.

Niels knew of professional criminals who had committed the most meticulously planned robberies—stealing from banks, armored cars, jewelry stores—only to be overwhelmed by panic afterward, when the job was done. It was a behavior that was deeply embedded in the human psyche. After committing a crime, the impulse was to get away fast. Far away.

The bus pulled into a small station, and the driver got off along with the passengers.

Hannah and Niels went inside a minuscule waiting room. The coffee vending machine wasn't working. The whole place smelled of urine.

"The train station is over there." Niels pointed. "We'll go and buy tickets. Where should we go?"

She touched his lower lip. "You're bleeding."

Niels nodded. He felt dizzy. Rishøj had hit him hard. "You don't really need to . . ." He stopped.

"What? Flee with you?"

"Yes. It's not you that someone's after."

"*Something's* after," she said, smiling. "Not someone. If it was a person,

I wouldn't be here. But since it's something, that makes it much more interesting."

"Worth going to prison for? If things go that far?"

"I'll just tell them that you kidnapped me."

The train stopped every time two houses stood close enough together to be called a village. But it didn't matter. They sat across from each other, and it felt good. Niels kept trying to steal glances at Hannah, but she caught him at it. Niels turned to look out the window, trying to fix his eyes on what they were passing. When they headed into a tunnel, he saw Hannah's reflection in the windowpane. She was studying him. In a way that pleased him.

"Look at me," she said.

He complied. He thought the tunnel suddenly seemed very long. Just before they emerged into the light again, he happened to think about Kathrine—his guilty conscience calling to him. He tried to imagine it was Kathrine sitting across from him, but he saw only Hannah.

An experience from his childhood rescued him from the awkward situation. Niels began talking and talking, as if Hannah might attack him and strip off his clothes if he stopped. "I was six years old," he said. "On the way to Costa Brava on a bus with my mother. By the time we reached Flensburg, things started to go wrong. It was late at night, and most of the other passengers were asleep. I woke up feeling sick, almost as if I were suffocating. My mother was worried, and she asked the driver to stop the bus. The other passengers got mad. They were headed off on vacation and didn't want to have to stop because of a boy suffering from motion sickness. But when they saw the boy—when they saw me—lying in the center aisle and gasping for breath, my whole body racked by convulsions, they didn't say another word.

"An ambulance was called. It was all very confusing because at first the ambulance wasn't allowed to enter Germany. Finally, the bus drove me back to the Danish border, and the medics carried me across. I don't think I was conscious; at least I don't remember what happened. I woke up a few hours later in the Aabenraa hospital, and I felt fine."

"You can't leave your territory. That's fantastic."

He looked down at the floor.

"Sorry. I meant fascinating. As a phenomenon."

"Maybe." Niels didn't know what to think about being called a fascinating phenomenon.

"So what happened with your vacation?" Hannah asked when she realized there was a human aspect to the story.

Niels shrugged. "We spent a week in a summer house on the fjord, catching a lot of crabs. So many that it bordered on mass murder." He chuckled at the memory. "Since then things have gotten a little better," he went on. "Maybe it's my age, but nowadays I can drag myself all the way to Berlin. Although I end up feeling sick then, too."

They changed trains in Odense and continued west toward Esbjerg. Niels was now sitting next to Hannah. Not across from her. They had taken backward-facing seats.

"Just imagine a very long train without separate cars," she said suddenly. "Meaning one long space, so it's possible to stand in the middle of it and look from one end to the other."

"You mean I'm on the train?"

"No, you're standing on the platform. I'm standing inside the train." She got up. The other passengers stared at her, but she didn't care. "Imagine that I'm holding a flashlight in each hand." Hannah was standing in the center aisle, holding two imaginary flashlights. "Can you picture it? The flashlights are shining in opposite directions. One is aimed at the front of the train, the other at the rear. It's a very long train."

The three other passengers had stopped pretending they weren't listening. They put down their newspapers and closed their laptops and were looking at Hannah. She was looking at them. "All of you are on the platform. The train is moving fast. It's very long. Are you following me?"

"Yes." They all nodded.

"The train rushes past, and you're all standing on the platform. The second that I'm right in front of you, I turn on the flashlights simultaneously." She allowed the image to sink in. "Which beam of light strikes first?"

They pondered the problem. Niels was just about to answer when a young man near the door beat him to it. "The beam pointed at the rear."

"Exactly. Why?"

"Because the train catches up with it. While the front of the train is traveling away from the other one," he replied.

"That's right!"

Hannah was in her natural habitat: the lecture hall. Immersed in theories and ideas and the conveying of knowledge.

"Now imagine that all of you are standing here, inside the train. And you're holding the flashlights. The train rushes along. Then you turn them on simultaneously. Which beam strikes first? The one pointing toward the rear or the one pointing toward the front of the train?"

A few seconds of silence followed. Niels was the one to speak first. "They strike simultaneously."

"Precisely. They strike at the same time."

"An optical illusion?" suggested a voice behind Niels.

"No. It's not an illusion. Both results are equally correct. It just depends on the position where you're standing. It's . . . *relative.*" She smiled.

The theory of relativity became their bridge from Fyn to Jutland. Hannah wanted to remind Niels of how little humans actually knew. Einstein developed the theory a hundred years ago, and it turned the view of the world upside down, even though very few people truly understood it. Niels could tell that she had no intention of stopping. Apparently, she saw it as her mission to convince him.

They forgot all about the time, and when they next looked out the window, the fences were tall and white, in the best style of horse country. They had arrived in Jutland.

It was impossible to tell when they'd be captured, but Niels was hoping that several days would pass, maybe even a few weeks. He was hardly a top priority, and time was on their side. New cases would appear, more pressing manhunts, and slowly but surely, they would be moved down on the list of priorities. Of course they would be caught. It was just a matter of time.

6

Jutland

Middle-aged mothers and fathers were waiting at the station to welcome home their grown children returning to celebrate Christmas. Were people looking at them? Niels could feel his paranoia grow as they stepped out onto the platform. They could have been spotted a hundred times between Odense and Esbjerg.

Niels saw the man before he spotted them. The cold expression, a piece of paper in his hand, his eyes roaming over the arriving passengers. Niels pulled Hannah into the train station men's room.

"What's going on?" she asked.

He didn't reply. He was trying to collect his thoughts. How could they have found him so quickly? Just like when they were discovered down by the harbor. It was too fast. Someone must have made a call to the police. Was it Hannah? Niels stared at her, thinking back. At the harbor he had gone into the kiosk, so she could have used her cell. And on the train she had left at one point to use the bathroom.

"Why are you looking at me like that?" she asked.

Niels shifted his glance to the floor. "There was a man out there. A plainclothes policeman. He's looking for us."

"How do you know that?"

"That sort of thing is easy to spot."

Niels pondered the situation. Hannah was the only one who could have given him away. Or else it was . . . He pulled his cell out of his pocket. It was turned on. "Shit!"

"What's wrong?"

"Nothing."

"They're tracking you through your cell?"

"Yes."

Niels waited a couple of minutes before he looked out the bathroom window. Passengers were still getting on and off the train. There were heaps of baggage, and everyone was lugging heavy suitcases as they pushed their way through the crowd. The world must weigh significantly more at Christmastime, he thought. At that instant he caught sight of the man again. At the end of the platform.

"Is he still there?"

Niels shut the door. The police officer gave himself away not so much by the way he was staring; but every time a middle-aged man passed, he looked down at the piece of paper he was holding.

Niels pulled Hannah into one of the toilet stalls. Someone went into the next stall to pee. Hannah smiled and held her breath. The walls were covered with desperate invitations. *Guy seeks guy. Young man seeks mature male partner.*

"I guess this isn't an easy place for anyone who doesn't fit into the sexual norms," said Niels once they were alone again.

"No. But it's never easy." She sounded as if she spoke from experience.

"You go out first. Keep an eye on the exit. A middle-aged man, about five-eleven, wearing a light suede jacket. He's looking for us. If he's still there, cough."

"Then what?"

"Turn around and calmly go into the toilet next door. As if you just went into the wrong one."

She left. A moment later he heard a surprisingly natural-sounding cough, then the door to the ladies' room as it banged closed. He waited for five long minutes. Then he looked out. The man was on his way down the stairs. He had given up.

Outside the train station, before they jumped on a bus, Niels cursed himself. It had been years since he'd been part of a manhunt. He was a negotiator— he wasn't used to thinking about things like tracking devices, satellites, GPS signals, and cell towers. First he ripped out the SIM card, then he stomped on his cell phone. It gave him a satisfying feeling.

"Can I have your cell, too?" he asked.

Hannah handed it to him without protest. An elderly couple watched from across the street as Niels threw Hannah's cell to the ground and then crushed it underfoot. They shook their heads.

The bus started out along the highway but then turned off and continued on small country roads.

"I think I know where we are," said Hannah, looking out at the landscape. "I haven't been here in thirty years. And back then it was in the summertime."

"There's a hotel?"

"There must be. Don't you think?"

They drove into the town. Like most other Danish towns, it looked rather boring at first: a supermarket and redbrick one-story buildings. It ended up looking quite lovely down by the area that used to be the old fishing village. The bus pulled over and stopped.

Hannah got up. "This is it."

Outside, they saw two locals, elderly men standing next to their bicycles.

"Hi." Niels went over to them. "Do you know if there's a hotel that's open?"

Suspicious glances and the sort of silent treatment practiced only in small towns. Niels was about to ask again when the man who still had teeth spat out his wad of snuff and answered, "It's closed to tourists. Come back in the summer."

"*Closed,* or just closed to tourists?"

The men didn't reply. Hannah intervened. "Are you sure there's no place where we could spend the night in this town?"

The toothless man said, "Go down to the shore and head north. But watch out for the freight trains. The gate at the crossing isn't working properly."

"Thanks."

They followed the traces of sand that got bigger as they approached the sea. The sound also served as a guide. The waves bombarding the coastline. Niels had never understood why anyone would want to live on the coast. It was never quiet.

"Watch out!" Niels grabbed Hannah's arm and yanked her back. The train raced past them, and only then did the train driver sound the horn, more as a greeting than a warning.

"Idiot," said Niels.

"They did warn us that the gate wasn't working."

"Sure, but what about people who weren't warned?"

The tracks were nearly covered with sand and snow, and the roar from the sea drowned out the sound of the diesel engine. The gate was trying hard to come down, but it refused to budge. For a moment neither of them spoke. Like all policemen, Niels felt an ingrained aversion to unsafe traffic conditions. Someday one of his colleagues would be standing here, comforting the survivors, coordinating ambulances and fire engines, and trying to figure out who was responsible for the accident.

The North Sea shoreline was wide and hard-packed; tiny rivulets and lagoons had wedged their way into the sand. They had to keep stepping over them, while the wind tried to knock them over. Hannah laughed.

"What are you laughing about?"

She couldn't stop.

"What is it? Why are you laughing?"

She held her hand over her mouth while she laughed. They kept on walking as she chuckled to herself.

Maybe it was just because he looked so foolish.

7

The North Sea

The hotel smelled of school field trips, of sack lunches and damp clothes. The floors and walls were made of wood, and the only pictures on display were of the sea, even though it was right outside the door. The lobby was deserted, and Niels looked for a bell on the front desk that he might pound with his frozen fist. The hotel clerk finally appeared behind them. "Good evening," she said.

"Good evening." Niels's face felt stiff with cold. "Is the hotel open?"

"Yes. We're open all year round. How many nights?" She took her place behind the counter.

"Er . . ." Hannah looked at Niels.

"Five, for the time being," he said. "Maybe more."

The clerk stared at a computer screen. "A double room?"

"No." Niels caught Hannah's eye. "Two single rooms."

The window faced the sea. A chair, a rickety table, a wardrobe, and a thick red carpet. Niels stretched out on the bed just for a moment. It creaked, and the mattress sagged. It was almost like lying in a hammock. But he didn't care. He closed his eyes, turned onto his side, tucked up his legs, and used his hands as a pillow. He imagined someone looking at him from above. Maybe he was doing that himself. Or a bird. He ought to go into the bathroom to take a look at the mark on his back. He pushed the thought away as quickly as it appeared. He sank another quarter inch into the mattress. Other disturbing thoughts passed through his mind: about his mother, about the climate conference and Abdul Hadi. The pastor's words: *But Mommy, what if the monster has a mother, too?*

"Niels?"

A voice from far away. Had he fallen asleep?

"Niels."

Hannah. Out in the hallway. "We need to eat. How about meeting in the restaurant in ten minutes? It's on the third floor."

"Okay." He propped himself up on his elbows. "See you in ten minutes."

———————————

The restaurant decor was white-painted wood, with dried North Sea flowers adorning the walls. Christmas decorations stood on the windowsills. There were no other guests. Hannah appeared from the far end of the restaurant.

Niels had a feeling that she'd been there a while but had waited in the wings in order to make a grand entrance. She looked different.

"Have you ordered yet?" she asked him.

"No. The girl from the front desk is the waitress. She's probably the cook, too."

"And the hotel manager."

They laughed. The desk clerk came over to their table. "Have you decided?"

"We'll start with something to drink."

"White wine," said Hannah at once.

"Any particular kind?"

"The best you have." Niels smiled at the clerk. "If the world is going to end this weekend anyway, we might as well have the best."

"I don't understand." The young woman gave him a puzzled look.

"Me, neither."

An uncertain smile and a slight laugh. Then the clerk disappeared.

"There's no reason to make her nervous," Hannah said.

"She might as well know what's going to happen. Maybe there's something she needs to do."

"We often talk about that up at the institute."

"The end of the world?"

"Of course. We sit there staring out into space, looking at dying suns and colliding galaxies."

"And meteors?"

"They're a little harder to see. But my work is a constant reminder of the end. Fortunately, it's also a reminder of the birth of new worlds."

The hotel clerk was back. She uncorked the wine and filled their glasses. After she left, a comfortable silence settled over them.

Niels ruined the moment. "Your son."

"Yes. My son. My beloved son."

He may have regretted broaching the subject, but it was too late now. She grew distant, but still she said, "He killed himself."

Niels looked down at the table.

"Johannes was a child prodigy. An extraordinarily gifted boy." She sipped her wine.

"How old was he when he died?"

She ignored the question. "He started showing signs that he was psychologically disturbed. He was schizophrenic. Do you understand what I'm saying?"

"Yes."

"The day we got the diagnosis out at Bispebjerg Hospital, it felt like the whole world came crashing down around me and Johannes."

"What about your husband?"

"Gustav was somewhere else. He was always away giving guest lectures whenever things got complicated from an emotional point of view. When I told him about the diagnosis on the phone, he said, 'Well, at least we now have an explanation, Hannah. I've got to run. I have a meeting.'"

"I'm sorry."

"Maybe it was a good thing he said that. His way of dealing with the situation was to continue on with his life as if nothing had happened. So there was at least one thing that was the same as before. Gustav."

"Was Johannes committed to an institution?"

She nodded. She didn't speak for so long that Niels thought she was done with the topic.

"I left him at the hospital and visited only on Sundays. And there he sat."

Another pause, even longer than the previous one. The silence was starting to feel uncomfortable.

"Do you know what day he chose to hang himself?" she asked at last.

Niels kept his eyes on the table.

"The day that Gustav received the Fields Medal. It was the clearest message a son ever sent to his parents: 'Congratulations. You abandoned me.' You won't find that part of the story in Wikipedia if you look us up."

"You shouldn't look at it like that." Niels could hear how feeble his protest sounded.

"The first few months, my only thought was to leave this place."

"You mean . . . commit suicide?"

"I didn't deserve to live. I even got hold of the necessary pills. Planned the whole thing."

"What made you change your mind?"

"I don't know. I just decided not to do it. Maybe because I needed to . . ." She stopped.

"What, Hannah?"

"Because I needed to meet you, Niels." She looked at him. "And do something right."

Niels wanted to say something—he had to say something—but Hannah put her hands on top of his, and that made all words superfluous.

8

The wind from the North Sea was tearing at the old hotel. As Niels and Hannah walked down the corridor toward their rooms, he imagined that the wind might shove the hotel so fiercely during the night that the building would end up in Copenhagen. He seemed to have voiced this thought aloud, because Hannah giggled and said, "We better not make so much noise. I think it's really late."

"Why do you say that?" Only now did Niels realize how much he'd had to drink. "We're the only guests here."

Hannah stopped and took out her key. "Thank you for a lovely evening."

"I'm the one who should be thanking you."

There was something very deliberate about the way she turned her back to him. Without looking at him, she asked, "Would you like to come in?"

"The condemned prisoner's last wish?"

She turned around. "I just thought it might be comforting. Or wonderful. You know what I mean."

Niels stroked her cheek. That was stupid of him. If he'd taken a few seconds to think things through, he could have come up with at least ten things he would have rather done.

"I don't think it would be a good idea," said Niels. "Sleep well."

He didn't move. Everything in his body was telling him to go to his own room—except his feet.

"You should do something wrong once in a while." Her voice caught him off guard.

"What do you mean?"

"You should do something evil."

"Maybe. But there's nothing evil about going to your room with you."

Niels closed his door behind him. He could hear Hannah talking to herself out in the hall. *Do something evil,* she said twice before she opened the door to her own room and went inside.

The mark was getting clearer. Niels studied his back in the bathroom mirror. He turned his head as far as his body would allow, examining the swollen, reddish skin. Just some sort of rash. A rash with a will of its own. He couldn't see any numbers yet. Yet?

Niels went over to the table and sat down. He couldn't sleep. Half drunk and half exhausted didn't equal the calm necessary to fall asleep. He ignored the NO SMOKING sign on the door and lit a cigarette, then counted how many were left in the pack. He looked around the room. Thought about Hannah. About her grief. About Kathrine and how much he longed for her when she was thousands of kilometers away. More than when she was standing right in front of him. He tried to push that thought out of his mind, but it wouldn't budge. Two cigarettes later, he saw the scene from their latest fight play out word for word in the middle of the room. He pictured the two of them so clearly: Like amateur actors, they stood before him, yelling at each other. He was just about to step in like a referee at a boxing match and shout "Break it up" and then send each of them back to their separate corners—him to the North Sea and her to Cape Town.

Something made him open the drawer in the table. He found a local phone book, a postcard that had never been sent to someone's grandmother in Gudhjem. And a Bible. He picked up the book with the dark cover and leafed through the pages. Abraham. Isaac. Rebecca. It was an eternity since he'd held a Bible in his hands. He hung his shoulder holster and pistol on the back of the chair. It seemed wrong to have those two things so close together—a gun and a Bible. The Beatles came to his rescue, as only pop music can when contradictory emotions need to be resolved. He was still half drunk—actually more than half—or he would have started singing "Rocky Raccoon."

Niels went over to the bed and lay down on his back. He closed his eyes and hoarsely hummed a verse before he floated off to dreamland.

9

Niels opened the medicine cabinet in the bathroom. Someone had left behind some mosquito spray and a bottle of sunblock, SPF 25. Niels spread some of the lotion on his hand and sniffed at the mosquito spray. The scent of summer. Don't be silly, he thought. It was probably manufactured in some factory in Poland five winters ago. And yet the memories came flooding over him. Sunshine and mosquitoes, water and ice cream and elder flowers.

He sat down on the edge of the bathtub. He felt a powerful sensation in his chest. He wanted to live. He didn't want to die. There was so much he still hadn't done.

Sunday, December 20

Of course he could do it, thought Niels as he turned on the shower. He had a plan. The morphine pills were in his bag, and there were plenty of them. He would board a boat, take enough to knock himself out, and stay far away for a very long time.

"Niels?"

Hannah. She was in his room.

"Niels?"

"Just a minute." He turned off the shower, wrapped a towel around his waist, and then stuck his head out the bathroom door.

"Do you want to have breakfast? They stop serving at nine."

Only now did he notice that she was holding his gun in her hand. "Hannah! It's loaded!"

"Sorry. It was on the chair, and . . . here." She handed him the pistol.

He took out the magazine and handed the gun back to her. "Okay. Now it can't hurt anyone."

"Are you sure?"

"Yes. It's safe at the moment. But if you do this. . ." He handed her the magazine and showed her how to shove it into the gun. "Then you can fire it."

"I like it better the other way. Have you ever shot anyone?"

He shook his head and smiled. "Have you forgotten that I'm supposed to be good?"

"Is that why you've been reading that?" She pointed at the Bible, which lay on his unmade bed.

"Maybe."

She smiled. "I'll see you downstairs."

After she left, Niels got dressed and meticulously made the bed. Then he put the Bible back in the drawer. He went into the bathroom and looked at himself in the mirror, lifting up his shirt. The mark stretched from one shoulder to the other and ran almost halfway down his back. Fine lines that were pushing up under his skin. He leaned closer to the mirror. Could he see any numbers? Maybe it would go away if he stopped thinking about it.

Later, they took a walk along the beach. The wind never let up out here, but at least the storm clouds were taking a break.

"I remember going inside a German bunker on the coast somewhere," said Hannah.

"When you were a kid?"

"Do you think we can find one?"

Niels looked ahead at the shoreline. Sea fog. Cars driving across the sand. He turned to look at Hannah. The way her hair was fluttering in the wind, blowing into her face, blocking her vision.

"What's wrong?"

"Nothing," he said. "What do you mean?"

"You're giving me a weird look." She poked him in the side. "Come on, old man. I'll race you up to the dunes."

Hannah set off running. Niels followed. Sand got into his shoes, his hair, his eyes. He stumbled on the way up the slope and heard Hannah laugh. "Are you laughing at me?"

"You're so clumsy."

He put more effort into climbing the dunes, struggling to be the first to the top, but they reached it at the same time. Out of breath and practically covered in sand, they dropped onto the heather and frozen grass. Here they were protected from the wind.

For a moment they lay still without speaking.

"You said you were reading the Bible," she said.

"A little."

"What were you reading?"

"The story about Abraham. And Isaac."

"God tells Abraham to take his only son, Isaac, up on the mountain to sacrifice him there," she summed up the story.

"I once heard a pastor talk about it on the radio. He said the story should be banned from the Danish Lutheran Church."

"But it has something important to tell us," she said. "Something we've forgotten."

"And you're going to tell me what that is, right?"

She laughed. "It's the teacher in me. Sorry." She sat up. "I think the story about Abraham is telling us that we need to listen. At least once in a while."

Niels didn't reply.

"But you're right. It's a troubling story. Wasn't there any other way God could have said the same thing?"

"Do you believe in it?" Niels asked.

"In what?"

"You know."

"You can't even say the word."

"In God."

Hannah lay back on the sand, staring up at the sky. "I believe in what we don't yet know. And that's so much—much more than we realize."

"You're talking about the four percent you mentioned?" said Niels.

"Exactly. Four percent. We know what makes up four percent of the universe. But try telling that to a politician when you're asking for money for research. It's much better to shout that you're absolutely positive that the oceans are going to rise eight feet over the next—" She stopped abruptly. She sat up and gave Niels a solemn look. "Polycrates. Do you remember the story about him?"

"I don't think I know it."

"A Greek king. Whatever he tried his hand at turned out to be a success.

He was rolling in success: He had women, wealth, military victories. Polycrates had a friend—I think he was an Egyptian ruler—who wrote to say that Polycrates needed to sacrifice something. And it had to be the most precious thing he owned. Otherwise the gods would be jealous. Polycrates thought about this long and hard. Finally, he rowed out to sea and threw his most beloved and valuable ring into the water. A couple of days later, a fisherman brought a fish he had caught, wanting to give it to his king. When they cut the fish open to eat it, what do you think they found?"

"The ring."

"Exactly. The ring. Polycrates wrote at once to his friend in Egypt, who replied that he was putting an end to their friendship. He didn't dare be anywhere near Polycrates when the gods one day decided to unleash their wrath on him."

Hannah knelt in the sand, and the wind began playing with her hair. "It's the same theme as the Abraham and Isaac story. The theme of sacrificing something."

"What exactly should we sacrifice, Hannah?"

She thought about that. "Our reckless self-belief. Is that a real word?" She smiled. "I mean, it's one thing to believe in yourself. It's a whole different thing to worship ourselves as if we're little gods."

A deprecating smile. As if she'd said something silly. She looked at him. Then she leaned over him as quickly as she'd done before and gave him a kiss.

They were very much aware of that kiss a little while later as they walked back along the beach, which they had all to themselves. Niels savored the cold wind against his face, the fresh air that tasted of salt. Later in the day he would go down to the harbor and find a fisherman who was planning to go to sea before Christmas. That shouldn't be so hard, he told himself. Thousands of codfish had to be caught before New Year's Eve. He'd offer the fisherman a few thousand kroner for a berth on his boat and then take enough pills to make himself black out.

"What are you thinking about?" asked Hannah.

"Nothing."

"Let's have a drink," she exclaimed. "We're on vacation, after all. I keep forgetting what that's like."

"Gin and tonic?"

"And then an afternoon nap. Or is it the other way around?"

"I don't think there are any formulas for that sort of thing."

"Don't say that." She smiled. "Let's go into town."

Niels stopped next to an old-fashioned phone booth. There was a convenience store right across from it. "I'll just make a quick call."

"Have you got any coins?"

He nodded. She went inside the store while he stepped into the phone booth, inserted coins in the slot, and began punching in the mile-long number in South Africa. He stopped before he reached the last digit. He could see Hannah inside the store. She waved to him. He waved back and then turned away. Winter light was bathing the sea in a cautious white. The earth under his feet shook slightly. Or was that just something he imagined? The tremor continued, making its way up through his body. A weak electrical shock or a tiny earthquake. He shook his head, ascribing it to stress. He tapped in the number again. To Kathrine. Or so he thought. But it was Rosenberg who answered. Niels was surprised. Had he memorized the pastor's phone number?

"Who's calling?" The pastor's voice was deeper than Niels remembered.

Niels hesitated. He wanted to say something, but he couldn't find the words.

"Is anyone there?"

Hannah waved again. She was standing at the counter, about to pay for her cigarettes. His eye was caught by something else. A car was driving along, farther up the road. Niels looked at the gate at the railroad crossing. It was trying to come down, like last time. Or was it the wind that was making it move?

"I don't know who this is, but I think you're calling me because you're ready to listen," said the pastor.

Niels could see the train. Had the driver seen it?

The pastor again, his voice almost intoning: "Perhaps you've experienced something that has made you doubt. Something that has made you ready to listen."

Silence. The pastor wanted to give him a chance to say something, but Niels didn't speak.

"You don't have to say anything."

Two little girls came out of the store. Laughing, each carried a bag of candy. Their cheeks were red with cold, and they were wearing knitted caps. They walked over to their bicycles.

Rosenberg cleared his throat and said, "It's enough that you're ready to listen. It's enough that you show that you're listening."

Niels could hear the pastor breathing. He sounded a bit short of breath. "Are you still there?"

Niels hung up the phone and stepped out of the booth. The car was getting closer. He could see it was a Volvo, one of the old boxy models. It hadn't slowed down. The girls were standing next to their bicycles in front of the store. One of them was fumbling with her scarf. Niels took a few steps forward and waved at the car.

"Hey!" He put his hand up to signal to the driver. But the car kept on coming. "Stop!" The sea and the icy wind drowned out all other sounds. The driver couldn't hear him, but Niels yelled again: "Stop!"

One of the girls was startled by Niels's shouts and turned around. At that instant, she slipped on the snow and lost her grip on the bike, which fell against the door of the convenience store. Niels looked at Hannah. She hadn't noticed anything. He looked back: the train, the Volvo, the gate that wasn't working, the little girls, the bicycles, Hannah inside the store, the blocked door. Niels began running toward the car, waving to make it stop.

"Stop!" Niels thought the driver had heard his shouts. The car slowed down. Niels stopped. He was standing midway between the store and the train tracks. For a second he had the same feeling as when he was sitting in the backseat of the patrol car on his way back to Copenhagen. As if something were tugging at him.

By the time the driver caught sight of the train and stomped on the brakes, it was too late. The brakes locked and the car slid with a screech over the tracks. The snow acted as a lubricant, causing the vehicle to accelerate even more. The train struck the rear of the Volvo with an awful thud unlike any sound Niels had ever heard. He glanced back at the store. Hannah was pushing on the door to get out. The girls. The Volvo was going to hit the girls. "Get out of there! Run!" The girls did just the opposite. They froze where they were, staring dumbfounded at Niels, who came running toward them. Somewhere behind him he could hear the car, out of control.

"Run! Get out of here!"

One of the girls realized what was about to happen. If only he could reach them in time. He yelled at the girls, flailing his arms. "Get out of here! Run!" Niels glanced over his shoulder to see where the car was now. He managed to see the horrified expression of the driver before disaster . . . Before the car rammed into Hannah, the store, and himself.

10

Darkness

The sound of something dripping far away. Or very close. It didn't mean anything. A magnificent calm. The darkness protected him. Like a blanket he could remove if he wanted to. But he didn't want to. He was lying so comfortably in the dark.

Voices. Someone shouting. Crying. Screaming. Something struck his nose. The smell of gasoline. The smell of alcohol, gin. The taste of blood in his mouth. He wanted to shut it all out. Wished that everything would disappear again. Someone was pulling the blanket off him. The eyes of a stranger were peering down.

"Are you okay?" The voice shook. Niels could hardly hear it.

"The gate didn't come down, and . . . I've called for an ambulance."

Niels moved his lips. Or did he?

"I don't know," said the man. He was crying. "What? The girls? Is that what you're asking me?"

Darkness.

This time it lasted an eternity. Or was it only a few seconds? Niels was underwater. Going away. Diving down into the darkness. Wanting to disappear. Allowing himself to be swallowed up. Vanish. No. He had to leave. Find a boat. He was thinking about eating cod at New Year's.

Voices again. This time a deeper voice. Why couldn't they leave him in peace?

"Lie still. Don't try to say anything."

Was the voice talking to him?

"Just think about breathing calmly. Nice and calm. We'll take care of the rest."

Another voice. This one loud and clear. "Are they sending a chopper?"

A reply that he didn't hear.

He did hear his own voice. "No . . . I don't want to. I don't want to . . ."

"Lie still now. We're going to help you."

No pain yet. Niels couldn't feel his body. What happened? He pictured Hannah in his mind. And the sea. And the wide, frozen shore. And two little girls with bags of candy and knitted caps. Two little . . .

"The girls?" That was his own voice again. It had a life of its own.

"Yes?"

The sound of rotating blades. Was that something he was dreaming?

"There were two little girls."

The second man's voice intervened. "We need to get him out."

"The girls."

Someone lifted him up. Like in a dream from his earliest childhood. His mother lifting him up, holding him close. Kathrine. Now he pictured her. She stepped out of the darkness and leaned over him, whispering, "Niels. Aren't you supposed to be out at the airport?"

"One, two, three."

Was he the one screaming?

"Morphine. Now," said a voice from far away. Yes, morphine. And then out to the boat. A berth, sailing far away from Copenhagen. The Dogger Bank, he thought. Or even farther.

"We're going to put an oxygen mask on you." The voice went right through him. It was almost unbearably loud. "Your lungs . . ."

He heard someone say, "His lungs have collapsed." A feeling of heat. He turned his head.

"We need to cut his shirt off."

The sound of fabric being torn.

"Hannah?" She was lying next to him. Her eyes closed, an IV, an oxygen mask. She looked almost comical. He was about to laugh. He wanted to ask, "Why are you lying there like that?" Instead, he heard a sound inside his head that could only mean the world around him had come crashing in, followed by an ominous silence.

"Can you hear me?"

A new voice.

"I'm a doctor."

"Hannah . . ."

"Your wife is unconscious. We're flying you to Skejby. There you'll be given the best of care, and—"

He was interrupted. Someone was talking to the man. A brief discussion. *Burns on his back.* The doctor was speaking to him again. "We're taking you to the National Hospital instead. It will just take a few minutes longer. They have the only burn unit in Denmark."

"The National Hospital . . ."

"In Copenhagen. Do you understand what I'm saying? Can you hear me? It looks as though you have a bad burn on your back."

"The National Hospital . . ."

The doctor was carrying on a whispered conversation with someone else. The voices came and went. "Was the car on fire?"

"I don't think so."

"I don't understand."

A face came close to him. A pair of eyes, gray, serious-looking.

"He's completely out of it."

Another voice. "Are we losing him?"

"He's back."

"Not the National . . . Hospi . . . not . . ."

It occurred to Niels that he was incapable of moving his lips. He was talking, but no sound came out.

Someone put the blanket over him again.

Part III

BOOK OF ABRAHAM

And Isaac spake unto Abraham his father and said, My father: and he said, Here am I, my son. And he said, Behold the fire and the wood: but where is the lamb for a burnt offering?

And Abraham said, My son, God will provide himself a lamb for a burnt offering, so they went both of them together.

—Genesis 22:7–8

1

The National Hospital—Copenhagen

Niels was out. If he had been conscious, he would have seen the helicopter land on the roof of the National Hospital, seen the doctors and orderlies waiting to receive him, felt himself being lifted onto a gurney and transported along a narrow passageway that led to an elevator.

———————◆———————

He was riding alongside Hannah. Maybe he woke up. In any case, he heard scattered voices, partial sentences, words that floated past: *Hit by a train . . . No, hit by a car at a train crossing . . . Why not Skejby? . . . Poor weather conditions . . . burn unit . . . trauma center. . .*

One sentence he heard very clearly. *I can't get a pulse on her.*

Someone answered. It sounded like a discussion, but Niels wasn't sure. He saw his hand reach out toward her. He heard himself whisper: "Hannah."

"We're almost there."

"Hannah."

"We're losing her. We need to start—"

They stopped. At least that's what Niels thought. Until he realized, in a haze of morphine, that it was only Hannah who had stopped. He kept going, and that was the worst moment of all. Worse than the accident itself. Worse than the instant when the car crashed into him. Niels had a feeling that he'd been torn in half, and out of the corner of his eye, he saw—or maybe just sensed—that doctors were leaning over her and . . .

He was out again.

It didn't matter. It was over now. It was good. It lasted only a moment. Because a moment later . . .

Wednesday, December 23

. . . the light came toward him. He thought: So that's that. He felt no fear, could manage only a resigned shrug for the light that was approaching at the end of the darkness, his life that was slowly ebbing away, a face that leaned over him, a beautiful woman, maybe an angel who . . .

"Is he awake?"

The angel was talking to him.

"Yes. He's coming around now."

Two nurses were looking at him. The younger one—the angel—seemed genuinely curious. The other's expression was merely matter-of-fact, observant.

"Hannah," he whispered.

"I'll get the doctor."

Niels couldn't tell which nurse had spoken. He was having a hard time separating their words from his thoughts. He looked out a window: snowflakes lit up by the hospital's lights, eternally burning. He tried to remember, tried to gather all the fragments into a memory of what had happened.

"Niels Bentzon?"

Niels suppressed an inappropriate smile that was presumably due to something as banal as the joy he felt at being able to remember his own name.

"You're awake. I'm glad to see that. My name is Asger Gammeltoft. I'm the head surgeon here. I was part of the team that operated on you. We worked on you for almost eight hours."

"Hannah?" Niels couldn't hear his own voice. "And the children?"

"Can you speak a little louder?" The doctor bent down closer.

"Were they hurt?"

"Are you asking about the children?" The doctor straightened up and conferred briefly with the nurses, whispering, conspiratorial. "The girls weren't hurt. They escaped unscathed. You saved their lives." He pushed up his glasses. He wore a kind but slightly arrogant expression. He was a man who was making an honest effort to be attentive, though he had other things on his mind. "I'm going to be frank and tell you that you have a number of serious injuries. Many of them are typical for people who have been involved in a car accident. Injuries to your hips and back, lesions in your abdominal cavity, broken ribs and bruised cervical vertebrae, blood accumulations in your lungs. I won't burden you with all the details at the moment. The important thing is that you've pulled through."

He wiped the sweat from his brow with a handkerchief and then put it back where he'd found it. "During the first hours of the operation, we weren't sure you'd survive." He sighed. "Are you thirsty?"

Before Niels could answer, a nurse was pressing a straw into his mouth. "Drink some of that. It's juice. You need lots of fluids."

Strawberry and raspberry. Sickly sweet. The straw in his mouth stirred up some lost memories from his childhood. The wild rhubarb plants behind the soccer field. The tomato plants, with furry stalks, like the legs of a spider.

"Good. Tomorrow you may be able to have some solid food."

Maybe it was the thought of solid food that made Niels look down at his body. His arms were sticking out from under the covers. He saw an IV and bandages. "What happened to me?"

"Maybe we should talk more at some later time."

"No! I want to know now."

The nurse whispered something in the doctor's ear. Dr. Gammeltoft nodded.

"Niels. You've lost a lot of blood, but we've got you stabilized, so we're optimistic." He corrected himself: "I mean we're *very* optimistic. We also discovered some extremely atypical accumulations of blood on your back. The medics at the accident scene thought they were burns. That was why you were brought here. But those aren't burns on your back."

He cleared his throat. "At first we thought it was an old tattoo that had developed a rash, but it's more likely that the tiny blood vessels in the skin, or rather *under* the skin, expanded or . . . We'll have a dermatologist take a look at it. But it's quite common to develop a fungal infection after an operation. It's a sign that your immune system is fighting.

"Right now you need to rest. We'll probably have to operate again, but for the time being, the most important thing is for you to have peace and quiet. As we usually say here: The best doctor is your own body." The doctor nodded, which apparently indicated that the conversation was over.

Niels tried to stop him. He whispered: "Hannah."

"I can't hear what you're saying."

Niels tried to summon the last of his energy in order to speak. "Hannah . . ."

Dr. Gammeltoft still couldn't hear. Her name was made up of too many indistinct sounds that were almost nothing but air. "Han . . ." Niels tried again.

"You need to rest." The doctor was about to leave but changed his mind and again came closer.

". . . nah . . ."

"You've been unconscious for almost seventy-two hours. You've suffered serious injuries. You need to rest."

Seventy-two hours? Niels looked out the window. It was as if the date woke up his slumbering brain. Seventy-two hours.

"Wednesday?"

"Yes, it's Wednesday. December twenty-third. You've been out for three days."

"Friday."

"What?"

"It's going to happen on Friday."

The doctor looked at the nurse. Their eyes carried on a conversation that Niels didn't understand, but it didn't matter. He had to get out of here. As far away as possible. He looked out the window and thought about how to do that. He couldn't walk. Or could he? He looked around. The doctor had left the room.

The young nurse came over to Niels. "You need to understand that it's very common to have lapses in memory after a serious accident. But your memory will slowly come back. It's not a sign of significant brain injury. I'm sure you're going to make a full recovery."

"Hannah?"

The older nurse offered some sort of explanation. Niels heard a somewhat distorted version of what she said. "He's talking about his girlfriend."

"Hannah!"

"Take it easy. You need to relax."

"Tell me."

The young nurse looked down at his stomach. With a great effort he turned his head and looked down too. He saw that he was gripping her wrist hard. His fingernails were digging into her skin.

"Let's take one thing at a time. Okay? The most important thing right now is for you to regain your strength."

"Tell me!"

"We'll get a doctor, Niels. Just a minute."

The older nurse disappeared. Niels struggled not to fall asleep. He wanted to wait until the new white-coat arrived to offer some reassuring words and a sedative. He wanted to feel the nurse take his hand and squeeze it with genuine sympathy as the doctor told Niels the news that he already knew. The news that he had long since read in the eyes of the young nurse as she tried to avoid looking at him. The news that Hannah was dead.

2

She felt better than she ever had. An explosive feeling of freedom. Able to think so clearly, without any limits. Here she had room for her thoughts.

Thursday, December 24

A fissure of darkness in an overwhelming light. Hannah turned away. She didn't care. Until she happened to think of Niels. Then the darkness opened, and there was nothing she could do except allow it to swallow her up.

I've just experienced something incredible.

Hazy, dreamlike shapes in a white room. One of the shapes came closer. Leaned over her. Shined something in her eyes . . .

"She's back!"

"What?"

"Come and look."

A murmuring all around her. *Amazing.* Someone laughed with relief. *What a tough woman.*

The voices were coming through louder. Especially a woman's voice. The other shapes came closer. They attached things to her body, fiddled with various machines, talked quietly as they focused on their work.

"Unbelievable," someone said.

Another person said that she needed to be stabilized. Who did they mean by "she"?

They shined lights in her eyes. Stuck needles in her hands. She sensed a faint beeping somewhere in the room.

"Where . . . ?"

Could that be Hannah whispering? There was no reaction. She tried to clear her throat. Only now she did feel her body. And that was an unpleasant encounter. A searing pain in her chest and throat. A prickling sensation in her legs. The voice was talking louder. "Where is—" She was interrupted by the sound of a helicopter. She glanced out the window and saw it fly off. The National Hospital. Of course.

"She's trying to say something."

Faces stared at her. She lay still, gathering her strength to swing her legs off the bed. She had to find Niels and warn him. But it was impossible. She couldn't move. She was not in terrible pain. Her body was numb.

"Can you hear me?"

They were talking to her. A frantic male voice trying to sound gentle.

"Hannah Lund? Can you hear what I'm saying?"

"Yes."

"You've been unconscious for several days. You've been more than unconscious. Do you know where you are?"

The National Hospital. The words refused to go from thought to speech. They refused to leave her mouth.

"Do you know that you're in the National Hospital in Copenhagen? You were involved in a serious accident in Jutland, and you were brought here by helicopter."

Hannah didn't try to reply. The doctor was speaking to her as if she were a child.

"Can you hear everything that I'm saying?"

"Yes."

"Good. Because it's important that you—"

"What day is it?"

"Thursday. December twenty-fourth. Merry Christmas." The face was becoming clearer, and Hannah noticed a little smile. A young man wearing black-framed glasses.

"Tomorrow . . ."

"What?"

"Where is Niels?"

"She's talking about her friend. The man who was also involved in the accident," said a voice.

"Where is Niels?"

Only when the stand with the IV toppled did Hannah realize that she'd succeeded in swinging her legs over the side of the bed. Pain in her head. She seemed to have hit it on something. Presumably the floor or the IV stand. The door opened. White coats came rushing in. More anonymous, well-intentioned faces. A voice said, "She's in shock. She needs . . ."

Hannah didn't hear the name of the sedative they wanted to give her, but it occurred to her that the voice was right. She was in shock. Her brain was a jumble of scattered thoughts. Briefly, she could feel every single artery and vein in her body, as well as the blood surging through her brain. She heard herself saying, "I'm not in shock."

She was put back in bed. She was incapable of resisting. A soothing, almost drawling voice said, "You've been in a serious car accident. You were hit by a car moving at high speed."

"Tomorrow . . ."

"You need to rest, Hannah."

"When the sun goes down . . . Niels."

"Listen to me, Hannah. Your husband, or your friend, is still alive. You both need to rest."

"What day is it?"

The whispering voice again: "Can we hurry it up a bit?"

"Don't . . ."

A warm sensation in her hand.

"What day is it?"

"We've already talked about that. It's Thursday morning. Christmas Eve. But you shouldn't be thinking about anything except getting some rest. You were both very, very lucky. We've given you something that will help you relax."

The voice grew muddy. Hannah could still hear it, though the words made no sense. The medicine was taking over her body. She fought against it, but she wasn't equal to the battle, and the darkness came back. Releasing her.

3

Every awakening felt like an endless climb out of death toward life. The light hurt his eyes. It was as if his body were subject to the gravitational force of the realm of death, which was much stronger than the earth's. This must be how Lazarus felt when Jesus brought him back to life, thought Niels, squinting his eyes and noticing how his body was being pressed against the mattress, down toward the floor, down toward the ground.

He was breathing heavily. He looked around. The hospital. Always the hospital. He closed his eyes. Let himself fall.

Thursday, December 24

"Niels?"

He recognized the voice.

"Niels."

The bald head. The kind eyes that reminded him of his father's.

"Can you hear me? It's Willy. Your uncle."

"Willy?"

"I've been here a couple of times. You've been completely out of it, my boy. Good thing your father and mother don't have to see you like this. They wouldn't have survived it."

Niels smiled. Willy was just about the only family he had left. At least the only one he cared about of those who were left.

"Can you tell me where Kathrine is working? Is it somewhere abroad? I want to give her a call."

Niels shook his head. "No. I'll call her when I'm feeling better."

"Okay. Okay, my boy. You'll be fine. That's what the doctors say, too. You're strong. You've always been a strong boy. Your father's boy."

Niels wanted to go back to the darkness and the heaviness. Away. He heard Willy rambling on as he let himself fall. Something about flowers. And chocolate. And all the family members who had died. It was a pleasant voice to accompany him down into the darkness.

"Merry Christmas," someone said. Or sang. Maybe he was already dreaming.

———————

"Niels Bentzon?"

A man wearing a white coat. A new man. This place seemed to have an endless number of them. Where was Uncle Willy? Had he been here or not? The hopeless bouquet of flowers on the table was proof of the visit. Only Willy would show up at a hospital with a bouquet better suited for a funeral.

"Can you hear me?" asked the man in the white coat.

"Yes."

"I have good news."

Niels tried to focus. A veil seemed to have settled over his eyes, making him feel as if he had his eyes open underwater. "Good news?"

"About your girlfriend."

"Hannah?" said Niels.

"She's not dead."

"Not dead?"

"She's going to pull through, Niels." The man smiled. "It's highly unusual to be brought back to life twice. I'm a doctor, so I very seldom use the word 'miracle.' But if I've ever personally witnessed a miracle, it has to be when your girlfriend opened her eyes a couple of hours ago. She may not even suffer any permanent injury."

"Girlfriend." The word annoyed Niels. The doctor was saying something else, but Niels wasn't listening.

"I want to see her." He spoke the words loudly and clearly.

"We'll have to arrange that. As soon as possible."

"I need to see her."

"You'll need to stay here a little while longer first." The doctor looked around and made eye contact with a nurse. He didn't say anything out loud, but Niels had no doubt what he meant: I can't keep standing here talking to this patient. I have other things to do. You'll have to explain to him that he needs to stay here.

The nurse came closer. "I'm afraid that's not possible at the moment, Niels. You're in separate wards of the hospital. Your girlfriend has been taken to the cardiology department. All the way over there."

She pointed out the window. The hospital was built in the shape of an incomplete H, which meant that two patients could be quite a distance from each other even though they were in the same building. So far away that it was impossible to see the people behind the windows on the other side.

"Every time we move a patient, we increase the risk of stress and complications. The two of you will have to wait for a while. It's for your own good. We've contacted family members for both of you."

"But it's important."

"Maybe we can arrange something on the phone. How does that sound?" She smiled and touched the bandage on his head.

"Good."

She left. Niels stared at the opposite wing of the building. He let his memory take over: the North Sea. The freight train. The convenience store. The accident. *No matter what you do, Niels, you're going to end up at the National Hospital in a week.* That's what Hannah had said. Because of the *system.*

"Niels Bentzon?"

Niels was jolted out of his thoughts. How much time had passed? The man introduced himself. "My name is Jørgen Wass. I'm a dermatologist. This young man is a student making rounds with me."

A younger man wearing glasses stood at the doctor's side.

"I've been asked to take a look at your back."

"Now?"

"That's why I'm here." He smiled. "I'm not on staff here, you see. The National Hospital no longer has a dermatology department. But it's been decided that you shouldn't be moved back and forth to various doctors' offices. I won't be able to make a thorough examination right now; I'm just going to have a look to determine whether any sort of treatment is required, and if so, what we should do for you. Could you turn over onto your stomach?"

Without waiting for a reply, and using a tone of voice that made Niels feel like a baby who hasn't yet learned to talk, the dermatologist looked at the nurse and said, "Okay? Shall we turn him over?"

Dr. Wass pulled on a pair of latex gloves. Niels had decided not to make a peep when they took hold of him. The nurse pulled up his shirt. The dermatologist sat down. He took his time. Niels found the waiting time humiliating.

"Do you need anything?" The student came closer to the doctor.

"No, thanks. This will only take a minute. I hope this isn't too uncomfortable." The last remark was directed at Niels.

Niels didn't say a word as the doctor touched his back.

"Is there any tenderness? Itching?"

"Not really."

"When did you have this done?"

"What do you mean?"

"The tattoo. Or . . ." The dermatologist fell silent. "Is this a tattoo?"

"I don't have any tattoos." Niels could tell that the doctor didn't believe him.

"Are you sure? What about a henna tattoo? Have you been traveling abroad?"

"I want to see it."

"That must be what it is." The student had decided to voice his opinion. He spoke in a low voice to the doctor. "Or could it be Mongolian spot?"

"I don't have any tattoos on my back." Niels tried to speak louder, but it was difficult while lying in such an awkward position, with his face pressed against the pillow.

"You haven't had one removed?" asked the dermatologist. "Have you ever had problems with fungal infections?"

"No."

Niels couldn't tell whether the doctor was talking to the student, the nurses, or him when he murmured, "A slight swelling of the epidermis. Signs of pigment variation and inflammation."

"I want to see it." Niels tried to turn over.

"If you wouldn't mind waiting a moment." Dr. Wass scratched Niels's back with something sharp. "I need to take a sample. Does that hurt?"

"Yes."

"There's not much to see. Shall we turn him over again?"

"No! I want to see it."

Silence. The doctor didn't want to comply. Niels could sense his opposition. "All right, but we'll need a couple of mirrors."

Niels lay still while the nurses brought two full-length mirrors into the room. It took a few minutes to set them up.

"It looks worse than it is," the dermatologist warned him. "Don't be shocked. With the proper treatment, maybe some cortisone cream, you should be fine in no time."

Niels looked at his back. The mark had taken on a shape similar to the other ones, stretching from one shoulder to the other. The pattern was starting to emerge. He couldn't see the numbers, but he knew they were there. Three and six. Thirty-six.

The doctor straightened up and glanced at his student. "I've seen this before," he said.

"Where?" asked the student.

"What do you mean?" asked Niels, insisting on making eye contact with the doctor. "You've seen it before? Where?"

"A long time ago. But . . ."

"But what?"

The doctor stood up. "I'm going to have to do some research, and then I'll get back to you."

He nodded to the student. Without another word to Niels, they both left the room.

4

Hannah's parents thanked the nurse when she brought them some food. Hannah had been inhaling the smell for several hours. Roast pork and gravy. Her father ate his own portion, and then he ate his wife's as she continued to weep, not saying a word. *We shouldn't let it go to waste.* That was the motto of his life. A glance at his enormous belly might make anyone question whether the words were as sensible as they sounded.

Hannah had always found it embarrassing to have her father around. She remembered with horror the time her parents showed up for her Ph.D. defense, sitting in the last row of the auditorium. Her father kept making a chuffing sound; he was so huge that he took up one and a half seats. Her mother didn't say a word. Just like now.

It was a lengthy visit, although little was said. Hannah had long had the impression that her parents had given up on her. After Johannes's illness and death. And after Gustav had left her. It was all too much for them. Too foreign. Even as a child, Hannah had seemed like a stranger to them.

Finally they left. One last question at the door: Did she want them to stay longer?

"No, you should go. It's best if I get some rest."

Hannah's parents were planning to stay overnight with her half brother, but her father had back problems, and he could sleep well only in his own bed. He would sleep sitting up in a chair. Just for a few hours. Tomorrow they would go home.

"My sweet little girl," her mother whispered before she left. But Hannah was no longer anyone's girl. Not Gustav's and not her parents'.

"Are you sure you don't want anything?" asked the nurse as she cleared away the dishes from her parents' visit.

"I want to talk to Niels."

The nurse looked at her, uncomprehending.

"Niels Bentzon! The man who was involved in the accident."

"Is he here in the hospital?"

Hannah shook her head in amazement. It must be because of Christmas, she thought. A lot of substitute nurses, who were less experienced, had been brought in for the holidays. Finally, a familiar nurse showed up. Pudgy cheeks, smiling eyes. Was her name Randi? Yes, that was it. "Randi?" said Hannah.

"Are you awake?"

"I want to talk to Niels."

"Yes, I know. But he keeps slipping off to sleep, just like you do. They've given him some pain meds that make him drowsy. He's awake for ten minutes, and then he falls asleep for three or four hours."

"Could we talk to each other on the phone? It's really important."

Randi smiled. "The most important thing is for both of you to regain your strength. Am I right?" She took Hannah's hand. "But I'll try to arrange it. Shall I go and see him? Try to set up a time when you can call each other?"

"Yes, please."

Randi left. Hannah looked out the window. It was dark now. Christmas Eve at the National Hospital. Hannah closed her eyes until she again heard cautious footsteps approaching. At first she thought the elderly woman must have gotten lost. She wasn't wearing a white coat, and there was something rather confused and remote about the look in her eyes.

"Hannah Lund?" said the woman, coming closer. "Is that you?"

Hannah didn't answer. She felt sluggish and weak.

"My name is Agnes Davidsen." The woman held out a frail-looking hand. Then she changed her mind and merely gave Hannah's hand a quick squeeze. "Could I talk to you for a moment?"

She had to be well over seventy. Her skin was like parchment, and her hair was reminiscent of a potted plant that had withered, but she had lively, intelligent eyes.

"You were in a car accident, is that right?"

"Yes."

"You were in a car that was hit by another car?"

"I wasn't in a car. I was hit by a car."

"And this happened five days ago?"

"What's this all about?"

"I'm here to ask you about your near-death experience."

Hannah smiled and shook her head. "Doesn't a person's heart have to stop for that to happen?"

Agnes looked at her in surprise. "Didn't anyone tell you anything about what happened?"

"Yes. They said that it was . . . serious."

"Hannah." Agnes moved closer. "You died. Twice."

"You must be mistaken."

"I can't understand why they haven't told you. I guess that's typical for the National Hospital. During the holidays, communication with the patients seems to break down entirely. Trust me: I know. I've worked here all my life."

"I don't understand."

The nurse came in as Hannah was trying to climb out of bed, knocking over the IV stand. Someone started protesting. She wanted to shout, "What's happened to me?" But all she managed was a hoarse cry: "I want answers! Now!"

"Spontaneous pneumothorax."

The doctor had decided that Hannah was "one of our own," as he put it. Not just an academic but a respected scientist. For that reason, he didn't hold back from giving her a complex explanation.

"The small pleurae on the surface of the lungs rupture, causing the air in the pleural cavity and lung to compress. This rupture will often close spontaneously, and then the lung expands again." He looked at her. "Do you need to rest?"

"I want to hear all of it."

"In your case, because of the crash, a leak was created, which acts as a valve so that air entered the pleural cavity but not the lungs. At that point, pressure-induced pneumothorax occurred, with more and more air trapped inside the pleural cavity. That's a serious and potentially fatal condition. But . . ." He smiled. "Now we've got your lungs under control again. As well as the contusion on your heart."

"The old woman said that I died."

"I've been trying to figure out what went wrong with conveying this information to you. It looks like we need to do a better job of doctor-patient communication during the holidays."

"Is it true?" Hannah insisted. "Was I dead?"

He took a deep breath, as if it were his fault that her heart had stopped beating. "Yes. You should have been told about it long ago. I apologize. Your heart stopped. Twice. The first time we got your heart going again after a few minutes. But when I got you on the table—"

"The table?"

"The operating table. Your heart stopped again. Actually . . ." He smiled and shook his head. "We thought you were dead."

"For how long?"

"Almost nine minutes. It's extremely rare."

Silence. "I was dead for nine minutes?"

He cleared his throat. Looked at his watch. "You can trust Agnes. If you want to talk to her, that is. If not, just tell her to leave. She's been sitting out in the hall, waiting for you to wake up."

"What day is it?"

"It's still Christmas Eve." He gave her a sympathetic smile. "I guess it's not going to be much of a Christmas for you this year. But they always try to make something special for the holidays in the hospital kitchen."

"How long will I be here?"

"Let's just see how things go."

He stood up with a strange expression that seemed to be his attempt to smile again.

5

"Niels."

Niels woke up with a jolt and looked around in bewilderment. He hadn't seen this particular nurse before.

"How are you doing?" she asked.

"Who are you? What day is it?"

"My name is Randi. I work in the cardiology ward, where your girlfriend is a patient. Hannah."

"How is she?"

"She'll be okay. She's been asking about you. Would you like to talk to her on the phone?"

"What day is it?"

Randi ventured a kindly smile. "You both keep asking the same question. Is there something you need to do on a certain day?"

Niels attempted to sit up, but it hurt so much in his hip and chest that he quit trying.

"Just stay there, and I'll go get a phone. Be back in two seconds." She left the room.

Niels tried again to sit up. He needed to get control of his body, find out how to move his limbs enough so that he could get away. Away from the hospital. He thought about the participants in the Special Olympics. Some of them had no arms or legs, but they were able to accomplish the most remarkable things. Surely he could drag his carcass downstairs to a taxi.

Randi came back with a phone. "All right. Here we are." She punched in the number. "This is Randi. I'm over here with Hannah's friend. Is she awake? Gone? Who was it?" She listened, looking concerned. "Okay." She put down the phone and looked at Niels. "Someone has taken her out of her room."

"I don't understand."

"Me, neither. Unless she was feeling worse."

"What do you mean by 'worse'?"

Randi left the room after promising to return soon. Outside, Niels heard a voice that was all too familiar. Self-confident, brusque, capable of being charming if he felt like it. Niels closed his eyes and pretended to be asleep. It wasn't hard to do. He heard footsteps approaching. Hugo Boss aftershave. The slight trace of a woman's perfume clinging to his jacket.

"Bentzon?" Sommersted whispered. "Bentzon? Can you hear me? No. You're not looking too good, are you?"

Sommersted didn't speak for several minutes. He just sat there. Niels pretended to be far away.

"Well. I'll come back tomorrow, Niels. I hope you're going to be all right. I—" Sommersted stopped abruptly. Then he leaned forward and whispered, "You were right, dammit. About Venice. I don't know how you knew. But you were right."

Sommersted stood up. Muttered something about what Niels had told him, that the National Hospital would be next. Followed by total silence. Niels was convinced that his boss had left. Or else he had fallen asleep.

6

Doesn't she have anywhere else to be on Christmas Eve? Hannah couldn't help thinking as Agnes pushed her hospital bed into the elevator.

"So far, so good. Be sure and tell me if you're in pain." The old woman smiled. From her chapped lips came a hoarse, almost soundless laugh that revealed a long life as a smoker. "I'm a retired midwife, and I worked here in the maternity ward until ten years ago, when I was diagnosed with cancer. The doctors gave me two years, tops. So I've devoted my time to something that has always interested me. And that's why I've come to see you."

"You're interested in car accidents?"

"Not exactly. Near-death experiences. Maybe it's because I've spent so much time thinking about death that I'm still here. You might even say that death scared my cancer away." She smiled. "At any rate, it hasn't got me yet. Do I sound morbid? Feel free to say whatever you're thinking. You think I'm a crazy woman, right?"

"No."

"It's okay. For me, there's a certain logic in following up my work as a midwife with a study of near-death experiences. I spent the first part of my life helping people into the world; I'm using the second part to try and understand what happens after we leave it."

Hannah looked at the woman, who cleared her throat. Maybe she was expecting Hannah to say something.

"But I didn't have a near-death experience."

"I want to show you what happened. Where you died. Maybe it will jog your memory."

The elevator arrived at the ground floor, and Agnes rolled the bed out into the corridor. She was clearly on familiar turf. Holding on to the headboard with both hands, she pushed the bed along the hall. Hannah stared up at her chin until Agnes noticed and said, "Let's start with the phenomenon of the near-death experience. What is it, exactly?" She took a deep breath. "The phenomenon has been known for a very long time. People who died but then came back to life and recounted what they'd experienced."

"The last convulsions of the brain?"

"Perhaps. Few people take the stories seriously. Most people merely laugh. But medical techniques have gradually gotten better, and we've been able to revive more and more people, so we know a lot more. Doctors and scientists are beginning to take the phenomenon seriously. Have you heard of Elisabeth Kübler-Ross and Raymond Moody?"

"I'm not sure."

"Two doctors who carried out groundbreaking research into the phenomenon in the seventies. According to them, there are nine basic elements often seen in connection with near-death experiences. Am I talking too fast?"

"I'm an astrophysicist."

Agnes laughed. "The nine elements are: a humming or ringing sound; pains that subside; an out-of-body experience in which the dying person floats, so to speak, out of his body; the feeling of being pulled through a dark tunnel at a furious speed; the feeling of hovering above the earth and looking down on it as if from the vantage point of another planet; encounters with people who seem pervaded by an inner light, often friends and relatives who have died; an encounter with a spiritual force . . ."

"God?"

"Perhaps. This encounter is followed by a brief summing up of the dying person's life. His life passes before his eyes, as we say. Finally—and this may be the strangest thing of all—an offer either to return to life or to remain where he is."

"You mean the person is asked whether he wants to live or die?"

"That's one way to put it."

"And at that point most people choose the new place?"

"Apparently."

"Holy shit! Life after death."

"Yes, at least according to Kübler-Ross and Moody. For them, there was no doubt. They considered it proof that a significant number of patients were able to describe these experiences. Of course, there were tons of skeptics.

One of them was the well-known cardiologist Michael Sabom. Dr. Sabom carried out his own research. To his great surprise, his studies showed that up to sixty percent of the patients who were revived at the heart clinic where he worked were able to describe near-death experiences. And in these cases, with great detail."

Agnes glanced at Hannah before she continued. "There is also a biological explanation. The pupils of the eyes noticeably expand when the body is about to die. So we're talking about a very real visual perception. You might call it a form of sophisticated visual illusion. Another physical explanation is that the body experiences a type of carbon dioxide poisoning at the moment of death. Carbon dioxide poisoning is known to give people a feeling of being pulled through a tunnel. Others say that it's simply a matter of hallucinations. A type of mental defense."

Agnes Davidsen shrugged. "Maybe it has to do with the subconscious trying to hide the almost unbearable fact from the person that he's about to die. So the mind creates an experience to show that it's not so bad. The person is heading toward light and warmth and love. But this doesn't explain everything."

"I thought you'd say that."

"There are examples of people who died, and when they come back to life, they're able to describe meeting others in death, even though at that time they couldn't have known those other people were dead. Isn't that fascinating? Now even the UN has entered the picture."

"What do you mean?"

Agnes pushed Hannah's bed through a door, turned it around, and set the brake. "In 2008, under the auspices of the UN, a major conference on near-death experiences was held. Researchers were able to publicly voice their doubts about our perception of consciousness and all the experiences that we can't explain without being mocked."

"Science is merciless."

"Yes. For the same reason, during the following year a group of doctors decided to initiate an investigation into near-death experiences."

"I wouldn't think it'd be easy to establish verifiable facts."

"No. And yet a British doctor came up with a very simple, almost silly method."

"What's that?"

"In emergency rooms and trauma centers in many different countries, small shelves have been set up near the ceiling. High up, where no one can see what's lying on the shelves. Various pictures have been placed up there."

Hannah was beginning to guess where Agnes was headed with all this. She looked up. At first she didn't see it, but then she looked over at the other side of the room. Yes, there it was. High up, four inches below the ceiling, was a small black shelf.

Agnes was looking at her. "No one knows what sort of picture is up there. Not even me. It arrived in a sealed envelope from headquarters in London."

Hannah felt her mouth go dry, and she could feel her heart pounding. She wanted out of here.

7

Intensive Care, the National Hospital—Copenhagen

A nurse came into the room.

"This is for you, Niels." She was holding a book in her hand. "From the dermatologist. What was his name?"

"Jørgen Wass."

She smiled. "You're good with names."

"I'm a police officer."

She handed him the book. "Dr. Wass found this for you. He even marked the place. He said that he'd stop by to examine you again after Christmas."

Niels looked at the book. There was no writing on the black leather cover.

"I think it has to do with skin diseases."

A small yellow slip of paper was sticking out of the book.

The nurse said something else, but Niels wasn't listening. He was staring at an old black-and-white photo of somebody's back.

"What's that?" She couldn't hide her curiosity. "Is it a tattoo?"

Niels didn't answer. He was having a hard time breathing. The person's back was practically identical to Niels's. Thirty-six. The number thirty-six in scores of variations, shaped with a virtuosity that made his stomach turn over.

"Is something wrong?"

He kept staring at the photo.

"Niels?"

"Who is the man in this picture?" Niels pulled himself together enough to look at the caption. "A patient. The National Hospital. Nineteen forty-three. *Worning syndrome.*"

"Is he Danish?" asked the nurse.

Niels paged through the thick book. Worning. Was that someone's name? Was there any other information? He had to give up. "That's all it says." He looked up at the nurse. "Where did the book come from?"

"The dermatologist. I have no idea where he got it."

"I need to know where this book came from. I need to know who the patient is. I need to know everything. Call the dermatologist and ask him."

"But it's Christmas Eve."

"Now!"

"Just a minute." She took the book away from Niels. He was about to protest but restrained himself.

She left the room. Before the door closed behind her, she automatically switched off the light. In the dark, Niels thought about Hannah.

Light.

The nurse was standing in the doorway. "Did I turn off the light? Sorry about that." She came closer.

Niels tried to calm his breathing.

"Are you in pain? Would you like some water?"

"Did you get hold of him?" Niels looked at the book she was holding.

"Yes. He said not to worry. It's not something people die from." She smiled. Niels doubted that she'd talked to the doctor at all. "He'll be in to see you after Christmas." She handed the book back to Niels. "Do you want to read more of it?"

Again Niels studied the photograph, hoping to see something more. A thin body. The arms stretched out on either side. The man was standing up when the picture was taken. Black and white. *Worning syndrome.* Maybe Worning was the name of the patient.

Niels could feel how tired he was. "Are there any sort of archives here at the hospital?"

"Yes, there are. Quite extensive archives."

"Have you ever seen them?"

"Twice in fifteen years. But we're not going down there now. Right now we're going to sleep. And enjoy Christmas. Right, Niels?"

She took the book away. Niels said, "The man in the picture was a dermatological patient here. A patient in the National Hospital. That's what it says."

"We don't even know his name."

"Worning. *Worning syndrome.*"

"Worning could also be the doctor who discovered the disease."

She pulled the covers up to his shoulders. Like a solicitous mother.

8

A gnes took out a small notebook and began reading aloud. It contained reports of the near-death experiences of other people.

"Take this one, for example. It's an edited version of a well-documented near-death experience by an American woman. I translated it into Danish myself. If the language seems a little clumsy, it's not necessarily the fault of Kimberly Clark Sharp. So don't blame her."

"Kimberly . . ."

"Kimberly Clark Sharp. We have to go back to the fifties, when she collapsed on the sidewalk after suffering a severe heart attack. She stopped breathing. Had no pulse. Listen to this: 'The first thing I remember was a woman shouting in panic: "There's no pulse! No pulse!" But I felt fine. Really fine. In fact, I thought that I'd never felt better in my life. I had a feeling of great calm and connection like I'd never had before. I couldn't see anything, but I could hear everything. The voices of people bending over me. Then I had a feeling of being in another place—a place where I knew I wasn't alone, but I still couldn't see clearly because of the dark fog that surrounded me.'"

Agnes looked up. "Should I keep reading?" She went on before Hannah could reply. Hannah suspected the old woman of subjecting her to a simple psychological ploy: By telling Hannah about the near-death experiences of other people, Agnes would make her feel that it wasn't so strange to go through something like that. And that, in turn, might make Hannah willing to talk about her own experience. The ploy was working.

"'Suddenly, I heard a huge explosion underneath me. An explosion of light that filled my vision. I was at the center of the light, and all trace of fog was gone. I could see the whole universe, reflected in endless layers. It was eternity showing itself to me. The light was stronger than a hundred suns, but it didn't burn me. I had never seen God before, but I recognized this light as God's light.

"'I understood the light even though I didn't have words for it. We didn't communicate in English or any other language. Communication was on an entirely different level than what you can do with something as banal as a language. It was more like music or mathematics.'"

With an effort, Hannah lifted her head from the pillow. "Does it really say that?"

"Yes."

Agnes looked at her. Hesitating. Then she continued reading. "'A nonverbal language. And I knew the answers to all the big questions, the questions that border on cliché: Why are we here? To learn. What's the meaning of life? To love. It was as if I was reminded of something that I already knew but had forgotten. Then I realized that it was time for me to go back.'"

Agnes paused to catch her breath. "This is how Kimberly Clark Sharp concludes her report: 'I could hardly bear the thought. After seeing all of this, after having met God, did I really need to go back to the old world? But there was nothing to be done about it. I had to go back. Then, for the first time, I saw my body and understood that I was no longer part of that body. I had no connection to it. What I now understood was that my "self" was not a part of my body. My consciousness, my personality, my memories were someplace else, not in the prison of flesh that my body represented.'"

Agnes looked up.

"Is there more?" asked Hannah.

"That's her story. Here's a picture of her." She handed the notebook to Hannah, who looked at the picture of a typical American housewife, as if taken straight from Oprah Winfrey's show.

"The body as a prison." Hannah was thinking out loud.

"It's a very common feeling in connection with near-death experiences. The separation of body and soul. Shall we go to India?"

"Excuse me?"

"Near-death experiences can be found in all religions and all cultures. This is one that I haven't yet written down, but I remember what happened. An Indian named Vasudev Pandey. When he was ten years old, he developed a mysterious illness that killed him."

"I've always been suspicious of stories that start out with a mysterious illness."

"He describes it as a paratyphoid disease. At any rate, he died. After he was pronounced dead, his body was transported to the crematorium. All of a sudden he showed signs of life. Pandey was quickly taken to the hospital, where he was examined by several doctors. They tried various means to revive him, including injections. Finally, the doctors managed to restart his heart, but he didn't regain consciousness. Only after three days in a deep coma did he wake up."

"So what did he experience?" asked Hannah.

"There, you see." The old woman smiled. "You're curious. When I give speeches on the subject, I usually say that near-death experiences get under your skin. That might sound ridiculous, but it's true. Vasudev Pandey later described the experience, or rather, the *feeling,* of two people lifting him up and taking him away with them. Pandey quickly grew tired, so the two people had to drag him along. Soon they met a creepy man."

Hannah laughed. "A creepy man?"

"I know it sounds funny. But that's how he described him. The creepy man was furious and started yelling at the two men who had brought Pandey. 'I asked you for the gardener named Pandey,' he told them. 'Take a look around. I need a gardener. But here you come with a boy named Pandey.'"

"It sounds like some sort of comedy."

"Maybe. Pandey explained that when he regained consciousness, a large group of family members and friends stood around what they thought was a child's bier. Among them was the gardener named Pandey. The boy told the man what he'd heard, but the gardener and everyone else just laughed. Pandey the gardener was a strong, young man. But the next day . . ." Agnes paused for effect.

"He died," Hannah whispered.

"Yes."

Silence settled like a soundproof bubble over the room.

"A very well-documented story. Later, Pandey—the boy—said that the creepy man was Yama, the Hindu god of death. The boy also said that the same two men brought him back when it became clear that they had taken the wrong Pandey."

The old woman took a deep breath. It was clearly taking a lot out of her to talk so much. "Vasudev Pandey's story will undoubtedly end up in the book too."

"The book?"

Agnes smiled. "Just think how much death means to all of us. It's the only thing we know with certainty: We're all going to die. The only thing that genuinely connects us as human beings. The only thing we have in common that transcends all national borders, cultural differences, and religious differences. All such things. Some psychologists would say that everything we do is somehow related to the fact that death awaits us. That's why we love. That's why we have children. That's why we express ourselves. In other words, death is present at all times. So why not try to find out as much as possible about it? I've thought about the fact—and this may sound absurd, so feel free to laugh; I'm used to it—that many people read guidebooks before they take a trip. They want to know something about Paris or London or wherever they're going. So they'll be prepared. Death is the ultimate destination, and I want to write the guidebook. Does that sound crazy?"

Hannah shook her head. "Not when you explain it like that."

Agnes Davidsen leaned forward and looked Hannah in the eye. "Will you tell me what happened to you when you were dead?"

Hannah hesitated. Somewhere a radio was playing Christmas music. *I am driving home for Christmas.*

"Hannah . . . We talk about the *moment* of death, but it's more like a process. The breathing stops, the heart stops beating, and the brain ceases all activity. Even when this process comes to an end, there's a period—for some individuals, it may last up to an hour—when it might be possible to revive the person. So the question is: What does the deceased experience during that time? That's what we're researching." She placed her hand on Hannah's arm. "How long were you dead?"

"I don't know." With an effort, Hannah shrugged.

"For approximately nine minutes," Agnes told her. "At least that's what I've been told."

Hannah didn't reply.

"You can speak freely to me. I won't use your experience for anything that you don't want me to. My primary interest is simply to hear what you have to say. Keep in mind that there are many common elements in near-death experiences, yet no two are completely alike. There are always slight differences. Would you be willing to tell me about it?"

Hannah looked up at the shelf. "Maybe not."

"Why not?"

She hesitated. "Maybe I don't want to be the proof . . ."

Agnes's hoarse laughter. "The proof of life after death? That's not what we're looking for. We call this a study of consciousness. That way, it doesn't sound so scary."

Silence. Finally, Agnes asked, "Hannah, do you know what's up there on the shelf? Have you seen it?"

Agnes tried a different approach. "Do you believe in God?"

"I don't know."

"I'm asking because many people interpret their near-death experience—the glimpse they're given of what might be an afterlife—as a definitive proof of God's existence. In my opinion, the two things should be kept separate. On this point, I disagree with my colleagues. In my world, it's possible to imagine an afterlife that doesn't involve God."

"What do you mean?"

"The most important thing for me is to prove the existence of a consciousness that is separate from the body. These days we seem to believe more and more that everything can be explained and analyzed and categorized."

Hannah closed her eyes. She thought about Johannes. How he was. How he looked. Several times over the past few months she'd had a hard time recalling his face. The details were missing, and she'd resorted to looking at photographs. The first time this happened—late in the summer last year—she had been completely devastated. She'd felt like a murderer. She had often thought about the fact that even though Johannes was dead, he somehow lived on. In her memory. All she had to do was close her eyes and she would see him right in front of her, as large as life. Now that it was no longer possible, she had pushed him definitively out into the darkness.

"Hannah?"

The voice was far away. With a slight echo. "Just keep your eyes closed if that's better for you."

Hannah didn't say anything. She kept her eyes closed and tried to get used to the darkness that had closed in around her. "I found myself inside an impenetrable darkness."

Hannah could hear Agnes open her bag and take out something. Maybe a tape recorder. Or a pen.

"There was air all around me, on all sides. But then—out of the darkness—a sliver of light started to grow. At first it was only a white stripe. Like a single line of chalk on a huge soccer field. A black field. Something flat. Do you understand?"

"Yes."

"Slowly, it opened up and turned into a sort of entrance. The light was all-pervasive, soft, and pleasant."

Agnes was breathing quietly. Hannah didn't open her eyes. Now it would have to come out.

"I wasn't moving on my own. I was lifted up and pulled along. As if I had strings attached to me—I just couldn't see them. There was a stillness that I've never experienced anywhere else. A calm so . . . no . . . I was fully conscious. I was thinking so clearly!"

Hannah smiled at the memory, and Agnes gave her arm a maternal pat. "And then what happened?"

"I thought about Niels."

"Your husband?"

Hannah paused to think. Is Niels my husband?

"You started coming back."

"Yes. But not the same way. It was darker."

"Then what?"

Hannah sounded on the verge of tears. "Then I was hovering above myself. And watching the doctors working and working on my body. It looked so foreign. So unpleasant. White and wrecked. Ugly."

"You were hovering above yourself?"

"Yes."

"In this room?"

"Yes."

"Did you see anything that surprised you?"

Hannah was silent.

"Hannah?"

"Yes."

"What?"

"A picture. A picture of a naked baby. An illustration. A striped baby."

"Striped?"

"Yes. You know: flower power—red, yellow, green, blue, all the colors of the rainbow. The brightest colors."

"And then you woke up?"

"No. Then everything went black. And I disappeared."

Hannah opened her eyes and wiped away the tears. Agnes was smiling at her.

"Okay, so hurry up," said Hannah. "I'm an astrophysicist. I know what it's like to wait for the proof."

Agnes went out, and Hannah was left alone for a minute. Then Agnes was back, carrying a ladder. She climbed up. The ladder slipped an inch or two on the linoleum floor, and Agnes glanced down, frightened.

"Maybe you should get someone to hold the ladder," said Hannah.

"No, it's all right."

Agnes Davidsen climbed up the last rungs and picked up the paper lying on the shelf. Without looking at it, she came back down and stood in front of Hannah. "Are you ready?"

9

A t first Niels had begged the night nurse to lend him a computer. She protested that it was Christmas Eve. He had to threaten her, telling her to open the cupboard and get out his gun and handcuffs. She laughed, shaking her head, but she did come back with an old laptop. His fingers could hardly strike the small keys. Worning syndrome. *Enter.* Lots of hits on the word "syndrome," but only a few for Worning syndrome. Niels clicked on one of the links. The same picture as in the book. The gaunt man with short, dark hair and skinny legs. There he stood in the nude, with his back to the photographer. Niels read what it said:

> Rare skin disease usually connected to religious hysteria. Worning
> syndrome begins as depressed lines or thin bands of reddened skin,
> which later become white, smooth, shiny, and further depressed,
> occurring in response to changes in weight or muscle mass and skin
> tension.

Niels wished he had his reading glasses. He turned up the brightness on the screen and kept reading. The first known case was in South America in 1942. After that a couple of cases in the United States, and then the case at the National Hospital in Denmark. Thorkild Worning. A telegraphist. How strange. Usually, a syndrome was named after the first known patient. Or after the doctor who discovered the disease. Niels's heart skipped a beat. He went back to reading: In most cases, considered fatal—*affecting the body's organs*. But not when it came to Thorkild Worning. He was discharged from the hospital. He survived.

11:15 P.M., Thursday, December 24

The nurse in charge of the ward straightened her white coat and gave Niels an unsympathetic look.

"But why not?" said Niels. "I have a name. Thorkild Worning. And he must have died long ago."

"We have to comply with privacy laws."

Niels gave her his most insistent look. The nurse seemed to waver.

"What if you come with me? Or maybe we can get a doctor to go down there with us." Then Niels changed tactics and raised his voice a bit. "Now look here. I need to go downstairs to the archives. This is of the utmost importance."

"I'm not the one who makes the rules," she told him. "A nurse is only allowed to enter the archives if a doctor requests a specific medical record. And that hardly ever happens. Besides, it's nighttime. And Christmas Eve. The place is locked!"

Niels sighed. He wasn't going to have any luck pressuring her. Of course not. And he was only pretending to be clueless. Naturally, the archives housing patient records in the basement of the National Hospital wouldn't be accessible to just anybody. Illnesses, medical treatments, and the cause of death were undeniably the most sensitive personal information imaginable. He thought about what Casper over at police headquarters would say if some chance passerby demanded access to the police case files.

"And you can't get a key?"

"Mr. Bentzon. You don't understand. Among all the thousands of hospital employees, only two or three have access to the archives. That's Bjarne's territory."

"Bjarne?"

"The archivist. All patients who have been admitted to the hospital for the past seventy years are on file. Every single blood test has been recorded; every little pill a patient has taken has been entered into a complicated system that very few people would even understand."

"But Bjarne's one of them?"

"He could find things in his sleep."

"Is a password required? We're talking about a computerized database, right?"

"Only since the year 2000."

"What do you mean since the year 2000?" Niels could hear how impatient he sounded.

"The medical records have only been entered electronically since 2000. The rest are part of a good old-fashioned archive. On paper, in folders."

"That must take up a lot of space."

"Fifteen kilometers. More than fifteen kilometers of shelving. Apparently, it's too expensive to enter all the data in a computer. Some people say that it would take up to ten years to complete the transfer. So the archives consist of metal file cabinets, bookshelves, drawers, logbooks, card catalog files, and patient records. It's a whole world unto itself. Secrets about everybody and everything. Astrid Lindgren, the author of *Pippi Longstocking,* gave birth in all secrecy here at this hospital. I'm sure there's a record of that, too."

Niels looked at the nurse and saw the excitement in her eyes, which had come to life. "So I'm sorry." She shrugged. "Is there anything else I can do for you?"

"No. Thanks anyway. Can I keep the book for a while?"

"Of course."

She went out the door, leaving him in the whiteness of the room. He opened the book and looked at the photo of Thorkild Worning's back. Again he felt his stomach turn over. Thirty-six. There was nothing about Thorkild Worning in the accompanying text. Niels leafed through the book, scanning the pages in the hope of stumbling on something he might be able to use. There was a lot about burns. Horrible pictures: the children at the French School on Frederiksberg Allé in Copenhagen. In the spring of 1945, the school was mistakenly bombed by the RAF. One hundred and four people perished in the flames. Eighty-six were children. Many suffered terrible burns.

There were articles about all sorts of skin diseases. It was under "rare skin diseases" that he found Worning syndrome.

Niels couldn't manage anything more. His body simply refused. The last thing he did was slip the book under his pillow. "Worning," he muttered. "Worning was discharged. He survived."

Survived.

10

Maybe she had dreamed it. Hannah opened her eyes. She knew she'd been asleep, at least. She looked down at herself, at the hand that was so stubbornly clutching a piece of paper. Names, websites—places that Agnes wanted Hannah to see when she was feeling better. YouTube: Dr. Bruce Greyson, speaking at the United Nations. Also on YouTube: Dr. Sam Parnia on MSNBC.

It was real. The study of near-death experiences was going on all over the world. Hannah had seen the proof. Proof that consciousness could exist separate from the body. Hannah *was* the proof.

She wanted to go back. That was the only thing she knew for certain. Back to the place where her consciousness existed outside of her body. The place where she would be able to find Johannes. Thoughts ricocheted inside her thick skull, which for all these years had managed to hold together a deeply problematic intelligence. An intelligence that had made her a stranger to her own family, to her friends, to life itself, and that first found a home at the Niels Bohr Institute. Those were good years. Especially in the beginning, before she met Gustav. They shouldn't have had a child together. It was too much of a handicap for one person to bear. And "handicap" was the right word for it. Possessing such an overload of intelligence was a handicap, she had no doubt about that. It wouldn't bother her at all to leave the physical world behind.

Then everything fell into place. Like an equation. Values that were seemingly irreconcilable coalesced right before her eyes. Hannah was lying in bed, clutching the piece of paper with the names of American and British scientists as she pictured all the elements: Johannes. His suicide.

Consciousness. Niels. The system. The thirty-six. She knew that she had to go on, she had to leave her body.

And she knew how Niels could be saved.

"How bad is it?" she whispered to herself as she lifted off the covers to study her injured body. She couldn't tell. Bandages covered almost everything. Maybe it was because of the Christmas decorations that some determined nurse had hung up in the room, or maybe it was the chemicals that had been pumped into her, but when she looked down at herself, she had a childish image of a Christmas present. All she needed was some ribbon and she'd be ready to be put under the tree.

Hannah tried to swing her legs over the side of the bed, but they resisted. "Come on!"

She tried again. This time she put all her strength into the effort. The cold sweat that broke out on her skin followed the pain: from the back of her neck to her spine to her thighs. She persisted and got her legs out of bed. She stood still. Then, with a swift motion, she yanked the IV out of her hand. She felt warm blood run down between her fingers, and she pressed her other hand over the wound to stanch the flow. Then she headed for the door.

Even the National Hospital was saving on energy. The light didn't switch on until Hannah hobbled past a sensor. A nurse rushed past her at the end of the corridor. Otherwise, the ward was deserted. Hannah was having a hard time walking. She felt a tugging sensation in one calf, as if the floor were trying to hold on to her leg. She had no idea where she was in the hospital. Two doctors were coming toward her. Hannah opened the door to a room and went in, closing the door behind her. Waiting.

"That was fast." The voice gave Hannah a shock.

A girl who looked about twenty was lying in a hospital bed. She had a cast around her neck and spoke with difficulty. "I'm in a lot of pain. That's why I rang for you."

Hannah took a step closer. The girl must have broken her neck, because she couldn't hold up her head on her own. "I'm not a nurse. I'm a patient here, like you."

"Are you lost?"

"Yes."

They looked at each other, searching for words that might make sense of the situation.

"Get well. I hope you feel better," said Hannah, then left. She could feel the girl's disappointment prickling at the back of her neck as she closed the door. But there was no time. She had to find Niels.

"What are you doing here?"

Hannah had run right into a nurse. "You're supposed to be in bed." The woman was trying to sound kind, but anger and fatigue were right below the surface.

"I need to find . . ." Hannah realized that she was gripping the nurse's hand. She was leaning on her and might fall over if she let go.

"No, you need to stay in bed. You've been in a serious car accident, and you need to rest."

"I have to find Niels. You have to help me."

Hannah tore herself away. She didn't know how she found the strength, but she managed to set off at a trot down the corridor. She heard the nurse shouting behind her: "I need some help here!"

Hannah fell. When the nurse reached her, Hannah lashed out. It wasn't a hard blow, but her hand struck the nurse on the cheek. People in white coats appeared from all directions. Hannah had no idea where they'd come from or where they'd been only a moment ago.

"She hit me." The nurse was on the verge of tears.

Strong arms lifted Hannah up. She reached for the nurse's hand and whispered, "I'm sorry." She didn't know whether the woman heard her or not.

They put her back in bed. With a new IV. Hannah tried to fight them off. "Let go of me!"

Soothing voices intoned: *Rest, everything will be fine, take it easy.*

"Let go!" she screamed. "Niels! Niels!"

She heard an echo in her voice, and she couldn't tell whether she had merely dreamed the whole thing.

11

Maybe it was still Christmas Eve. Niels stared outside at the snow. He didn't know how long he'd been awake. The door opened.

"Niels? There's a phone call for you. It's Hannah." Randi was standing in the doorway with the phone in her hand. "Are you up to it? I think she really wants to talk to you. She even tried to run away from her room to find you."

He tried to say yes, but the word got stuck in his throat. The nurse handed him the phone. "Hannah?" he said.

"Niels?"

"You're alive."

He could tell that she was smiling. "Yes. I'm alive. Niels, something really incredible happened."

"Did you see it, too?"

"The striped baby?"

"Baby? What are you talking about?"

"Niels. I died. Twice. I was gone for nine minutes."

Niels looked out the window as Hannah told him how she had died and then come back to life. How she saw what was lying on the little shelf near the ceiling. For several long moments they savored the silence, listening to each other breathing.

"I wish I could see you."

He could hear the yearning in her voice. Then she had an idea. "Try to aim your lamp at the window. Can you do that? Can you move your arms?"

"Yes."

"Okay. I'll do the same."

Niels pushed the desk lamp against the window and aimed the light out toward the snow. At that instant he saw a light in the opposite wing of the building, from a window at almost the same level, shining at him. "Can you see my light?"

"Yes."

Silence.

"Niels, I'm so glad I met you. Even though we've ended up here in the hospital."

Niels interrupted her. "There's a precedent, Hannah."

"A precedent for what?"

"Here at the hospital. In 1943. I've seen a picture of the man. His name was Thorkild Worning. And he had exactly the same mark on his back. Number thirty-six. The dermatologist showed it to me."

The door to his room opened. It was Randi. "That's about enough for now."

"Hannah. Can you hear me? He survived. It's not certain that everything has to end tomorrow."

The nurse was standing in front of Niels. "Two more minutes." She shook her head and left.

"Can you walk, Hannah?"

There was a clattering sound on the phone. Maybe she'd dropped it. He waited for her to call him back. Nothing happened except the nurse came in, took away the phone, and left again.

He reached for the lamp. Switched it off and turned it on twice. A moment later, with precisely the same timing, the lamp in the opposite wing did the same. Niels and Hannah. Separate but connected.

12

Friday, December 25, 2009

Niels tried to move his legs. It hurt, but after a short time, he managed to regain control of his feet. He couldn't feel his thigh muscles. He struggled to get some life into them. At first without success, but slowly, very slowly, he was able to lift his legs.

The question was whether that would be enough for him to make it all the way down to the archives.

12:01 A.M.—15 hours and 40 minutes until sundown

Niels stopped abruptly at the sound of a scream. Could that be Hannah? Impossible. She was too far away.

Niels was moving like an old man. The pain in his ankles allowed him only to shuffle forward. His head felt heavy, like a weight that he was forced to drag along with him; he wished he could take it off and carry it under his arm. A couple of broken ribs kept trying to poke through his skin, or at least that was how it felt. Like a body that should be split into pieces and put into storage to await better times.

He waited an eternity for the elevator, and when it finally arrived, he was met by the sleepy gaze of an orderly coming out. The man didn't look at all surprised to see an injured patient out of bed.

The elevator landed on the basement level with a jolt, and Niels almost lost his balance. He stepped out and looked around. A sign said ADMITTANCE FOR AUTHORIZED PERSONNEL ONLY. Stacked up in one corner were dozens of plastic-wrapped mattresses. A row of worn metal lockers lining the wall reminded Niels of an American high school. And then there were all the doors—what seemed like an endless number of them along the hallways, like a series of secrets. Niels tugged on a few handles, but all were locked. The only room he was able to enter—presumably due to an oversight—was some sort of workshop. In spite of the dim lighting, he could see the toolboxes, workbenches, saws, hammers, and screwdrivers. Niels went back out to the corridor. Was he even anywhere near the archives? He tried to think back; it was only a week ago that he'd been running around inside the hospital. Had he seen the archives back then?

Voices.

From his hiding place behind a mattress standing on end against the wall, Niels heard two men walk past. One of them—the man with the high voice—was saying that his wife had a sex phobia. The other man laughed. Then they disappeared into the elevator. Niels waited a moment before he headed in the opposite direction. It still hurt to walk, and he made only slow progress, but he was getting used to the pain. His ribs hurt the most, while his ankles had simply gone numb. He leaned against the wall as he crept along.

CENTRAL ARCHIVES.

The sign and the arrow gave him a little boost of energy. He continued down the hall, rounded the corner, and found himself in front of a door. It didn't say ARCHIVES, but it was the only door that the arrow could be pointing to. The door was locked. Of course. What now? Could he kick it open? That might have been possible if he were in top physical condition. But not at the moment. Besides, it would make too much noise. What about the workshop?

Niels's legs responded before his brain did; he was already on his way back down the hall. The door was still open. He took his chances and switched on the light. Posters of nude girls hung on the walls. An FCK soccer scarf was draped over a chair. Niels opened a drawer and took out a big screwdriver. A hammer hung from two nails on the wall. Someone had even drawn the outline in ink around it, which reminded Niels of a murder scene and the neat lines that the crime techs often drew on the ground around the victim.

Niels managed to wedge the tip of the screwdriver into the small crack between the door and the frame, just above the lock. Then he gave it a hard whack with the hammer. Even after the first try, he could tell it wouldn't take long to get the door open. The screwdriver was now lodged a bit deeper in the crack. After ten more tries, the metal lock released. Niels had to stop and collect himself. He took a deep breath, trying to focus.

Then he stepped inside the Central Archives of the National Hospital.

Fifteen kilometers of patient records. Niels remembered the nurse telling him that.

How many files would there be? Hundreds of thousands? Millions? For men, women, and children of all ages. Everyone who had ever been treated at the National Hospital over the past seventy years would be listed in these files.

There was a faint scent of ammonia. Niels stood still and listened. A low, constant hum came from electrical installations and various pipes, the type of sound that was noticed only when it stopped. He switched on the light. He held his breath as he looked with dismay at the seemingly endless rows of file cabinets, catalog systems, and shelves that stretched farther than the eye could see. The nurse had said the archives were a complicated system that very few people would understand. Niels believed her. When the archivist—wasn't Bjarne his name?—decided to retire, it would probably be wise to hire his successor well in advance so there would be plenty of time for training.

Niels heard a sound that made him turn off the light.

Voices. Maybe someone had noticed that the door was open. Maybe they'd seen the light on and wondered why anyone would be in the archives in the middle of the night. Or had he merely imagined the sounds? Voices produced by the growing paranoia that was starting to take over his mind. Niels decided to take his chances and continue on. Fumbling his way forward, he walked down the aisles of shelves and file cabinets. He wasn't positive, but he had the feeling he'd entered through the back door. Maybe it would be easier to get an overview of the place if he started at the other end. When he reached the door on the opposite side, he found a table. A worn-out old metal table with rusty legs and cluttered with coffee cups, half-empty water glasses, a box of throat lozenges. Niels looked around. It had to be possible to form some sort of overview.

His gaze fell on a number of leather-bound books standing side by side on the bottom shelf of a bookcase. They continued on to other shelves. Niels pulled one out: *Admittance Records.* He was holding the one for October to November 1971. That wasn't what he needed. 1966. 1965. He went over to the other side of the aisle. 1952. 1951. The 1940s. Niels felt his heart beating faster. 1946. 1945. 1944. Finally: 1943. There were several books for that year. He leafed through one of them. The pages were as thin as rice paper and kept sticking together; it must have been years since the books had been opened. He looked under "W" for "Worning" but found nothing. Why? Weren't the patients listed in alphabetical order? Then he saw it: The names were alphabetical, but the list started over each month. This book contained patient names only for the months of January, February, and March 1943. He put the book back and took out the next one. April, May, June 1943. There were two patients named Worning. Julia and Frank but no Thorkild. He tried another book. A couple of pages had come loose. July, August, September. None in July or August. But in the admittance records for December 1943, at the very bottom of the page, it said Thorkild Worning. Niels found a ballpoint pen in a drawer. On top of the bandage on his hand covering the incision from the IV, he wrote what he saw in the book: *Section H, file no. 6,458.* Then he went back to the aisles of shelves.

What next? Only now did he notice the tiny handwritten labels on the bookcases. Letters of the alphabet: A, B, C, D, E, F, G, H. Niels looked at the bookshelf in front of him. It stood so close to the others that it would be impossible for him to squeeze between them. Then Niels caught sight of a handle sticking out from the shelves. He grabbed it and pulled. The bookcase slid to the side, and Niels stepped in between. He saw boxes holding small index cards, again labeled by year. There were several boxes for each year. 1940, 1941, 1942, 1943. Niels pulled out one of the boxes for 1943. January, February, March. The next box. September, October, November. And finally: December. Niels ran his fingers over the tops of the index cards. Yellow pieces of paper. Rosenhøj, Roslund, Sørensen, Taft, Torning, Ulriksen. There it was! Thorkild Worning. Niels took out the card and stared at it. *Thorkild Worning, admitted on December 17, 1943.*

Dermatological patient. Medical record number 49,452. Niels stared at the number. 49,452. He stuck the card in his pocket and stepped back out into the aisle. The shelves on the other side contained the patients' records: 26,000 to 32,000. He walked down the long row: 35,000 to 39,000. He was so stressed he was thinking about cigarettes. 48,000 to 51,000. He stopped. This was it. He pulled on the handle, and the bookshelves slid away from each other. He paused and took a deep breath, sensing that his body was wound up tight. He had a bad chemical taste in his mouth. He cast a quick glance at the card he was holding, even though that wasn't really necessary. He had memorized the number: 49,452. The medical record belonging to Thorkild Worning.

Niels quickly found the right place. Descriptions of the patients' medical conditions and types of treatment. Some took up half a page, while others were practically a novella. 49,452. "Thorkild Worning," it said at the top of the page. Admitted on December 17, 1943. There were two photographs, both black and white. One of them was the same picture that he'd seen in the book. The photo of Thorkild Worning's back. With the same mark as on all the others who had died. Just showing a different number. Thirty-six. Like on Niels's back. The other picture showed the patient's face. At first glance, there was something remarkably ordinary about Thorkild Worning. He looked like a man who might be found behind a bank teller's window in 1943. Dark hair, slicked back and with an impeccable part; not a strand out of place. A narrow, well-proportioned face. Round steel-rimmed glasses. But there was something about his eyes. Something manic, almost demonic about the man's expression. The text under the photographs was disappointingly brief, written in a cold, clinical style:

Admitted 12-17-1943

Clinical findings:

The patient has today been given a preliminary examination. Complained of bad pain in his back. He was offered relief in the form of cool compresses, but without effect. The patient has significant swelling on his back. He seems hostile and detached. The patient says the mark appeared of its own accord, and the pain is increasing. The patient described the pain as a "searing, corrosive sensation." And later as "the feeling that my skin is burning from the inside." He stated that the pain is active not only in his skin but inside his back as well. "In my blood," as the patient said. The patient was treated with aspirin without the desired effect. The patient appears to be extremely unbalanced and takes a mocking tone with the doctors. An examination of the patient's back indicated a form of severe eczema, erosion, or possibly an unknown state of inflammation. Testing for metal allergy at Finsen's dermatology clinic is recommended. No pus was found seeping from his back, though the skin is red and swollen. His skin has taken on a distinct pattern. The patient's aggressive behavior is increasing. He is delirious and producing bloody vomit.

Patient's occupation and marital status:
Telegraphist. Married his present wife in 1933. Resides in a one-bedroom apartment on Rahbæks Allé.

Tobacco and alcohol consumption:
Moderate.

Other organs:
No specific complaints except for some arthritis in one shoulder. Not thought to be related.

Psychological evaluation:
12-23-43: Condition presumed to be a result of mental imbalance. The patient was moved to the psychiatric department of the National Hospital on the morning of December 23.

Dr. W. F. Pitzelberger

Niels reread the medical report several times before he stuck it in his pocket. He didn't know what he'd expected, but he'd been hoping for more. He stepped back out into the aisle, trying to shake off his disappointment and convince himself that this was a necessary intermediate step. It was in the psychiatric department that he would find the answer to . . . what? Wasn't this exactly what Hannah had tried to tell him? That science had established long ago that human ignorance was monumental? And that every time an advance was made, it merely revealed more and larger layers of ignorance? Finally, Niels asked himself: How did Worning survive?

Like every police officer in Copenhagen, Niels was familiar with the National Hospital's psychiatric department, which was located kitty-corner from the hospital. It was there that the police delivered the crazies—those people who couldn't handle prison. There were plenty of repeat offenders. Too many. It was a frequent topic of discussion at police headquarters: The number of beds in the psychiatric wards was constantly being cut. If the politicians only knew how often psychiatric patients whose treatment wasn't adequately financed became part of the crime statistics, they might have second thoughts about the budget cuts.

Niels left the archives, but he had to leave the door standing open.

Voices were approaching. From the elevator. It was bound to happen sooner or later; of course they would be looking for him.

"There he is!" someone shouted behind him.

Niels turned the corner into another corridor, then another corner, and entered a narrower hallway that was almost completely dark. Were they still after him? He paused to listen.

He heard a lot of well-intentioned words spoken in a harsh voice. "Hey, you! Hey, pal. Patients aren't allowed down here."

Niels didn't stop. Another hallway. His foot struck something, and he almost fell. But he stayed on his feet and kept going. More than two people were after him; that much he could hear. He didn't turn around; that would be a waste of precious energy. But it wouldn't be long before they caught up with him.

Niels found himself inside the elevator. He must have been going in a circle.

An orderly reached out and grabbed him. Niels couldn't see his face, but the man was wearing a lab coat, and he seemed determined to keep a firm grip on Niels's arm. Niels thought the man might break his wrist. Other people were standing behind him. What are they waiting for? thought Niels.

"Time to go back to bed, pal."

The orderly attempted to pull him out of the elevator. Niels used his anger to call up his last vestiges of strength. He spun around and slammed his knee into the man's groin. The orderly swore as he loosened his grip. Only for a moment, but enough for Niels to shove him out of the elevator. The last thing he saw before the doors slid shut was the orderly toppling over and hitting the cement floor.

13

The cold was malicious and personal. It followed Niels wherever he went. He was running in his socks through the snow. Across the parking lot, heading toward the psychiatric department. He pulled off the socks and tossed them away. They weren't helping. A taxi driver gave him a startled look as he climbed out of a cab. Niels knew what he was thinking: Good thing that lunatic is running toward the loony bin and not away from it. Niels wondered if he should get into the cab. Go home, pick up some cash from his apartment to pay the driver. Find his passport and . . .

The psych ward's ER was open around the clock. Sudden attacks of anxiety, disturbed behavior, depression, paranoia, or thoughts of suicide weren't restricted to regular office hours. A pair of uncomprehending parents were trying to calm their anorexic teenage daughter as the girl screamed that she didn't fucking want to live anymore. The mother was crying. The father looked as if he felt like giving the girl a good slap. Just inside the door, a man was lying on the floor, asleep. Or was he—Niels dismissed the idea. Of course he wasn't dead.

Niels took a number and sat down with the other patients, not wanting to attract attention, even though quite a few eyes were directed at him. Niels looked down at his bare feet. They were red and steaming slightly now that he was inside the warmth of the waiting room. He couldn't feel his toes. The woman behind the counter sent most people home after a brief conversation. That was her job. She was the system's first line of defense. A human bulwark. She made a lot of people cry. It was heartbreaking, but Niels knew that there was good reason for her actions. More than any other place, the twenty-four-hour psych ER drew lonely souls who eagerly made all sorts of claims just to win a moment's attention from another human being. *Remember that Danes are the happiest people in the world* had been written on the wall by someone trying to be funny.

The anorexic teenager was allowed through the eye of the needle and would soon disappear into the system. The woman behind the counter got up to accompany the girl and her parents. It was the moment that Niels had been waiting for. He slipped behind the counter and into a long corridor, then stopped to look around. The pastel-colored walls were decorated to a degree that verged on fanatical: scores of Christmas hearts, elves, and garlands. A door opened behind him.

"Do you want to play?" A beautiful woman in her forties with a shifting, manic look in her eyes was standing behind Niels, giggling like a schoolgirl. She had smeared lipstick over the lower half of her face and didn't seem to be quite sober. She moved close to Niels. "Come on, Carsten. The kids are asleep. And it's been so long since we—"

"Carsten will be here any minute," said Niels, and hurried down the hall.

The archives wouldn't be located in the psych ward, he decided. Archives were always in the basement. That's just the way it was.

———————

Brick walls. An old, worn-out basement that had been admitting the damp for years. These corridors were considerably shorter than the ones he'd traversed in the other hospital building. Niels found a couple of empty offices and a room filled with folding chairs and patio tables. But no archives. He kept on going. They had to be here. More offices. And then the door at the end of the corridor. There was no sign on the door, but stacked up outside were boxes containing medical records. Niels glanced around for something he could use to break in. He found an empty yellow oxygen tank. Just before he slammed it against the heavy door, he changed his mind and grabbed the door handle. He was in luck. It wasn't locked.

These archives were minuscule compared to the ones he'd just visited. This time he knew the drill: Find the admittance logbook with the file number, then the file card with the record number, then the actual patient's file. It took him only a few minutes to locate the bookcase containing files for patients from 1943. After that, it was easy to find patient number 40.12, Thorkild Worning. The psychiatric report was much more extensive and detailed than the dermatological report.

December 23, 1943

The patient was processed by admissions. The patient complains of severe pain in his back.

Clinical findings:

The patient has a skin disease on his back, which at the present time cannot be definitively diagnosed, but it is thought to be due to some form of bacterial infection. A dermatologist from Finsen's clinic was summoned. The patient suffers from mood swings and in seconds can switch from utter silence to shouting and disturbing behavior. He is being treated with an anti-anxiety medicine, but without effect. The patient clearly demonstrates his disapproval of both being examined and the questions I ask him. Signs of schizophrenia. At times he is lucid and understands why he has been hospitalized.

On the first day the patient was apathetic as he lay in bed. He refused to speak to anyone. He asked for his wife and demanded that she bring him his radio equipment so he could talk to his contacts. Refused to eat anything. In the afternoon he was asked if he'd like to get out of bed, which provoked an outburst of rage, ending with the patient throwing himself to his knees and praying to God to forgive him. Yet later in the evening, he declared that he is not a religious person. He was relatively calm during the night.

Medications:

No previous treatment with medication.

December 23, 1943

Talked about voices that kept him from sleeping.

The patient said he was unable to sleep in the night because of an internal voice that kept him awake. The patient didn't want to explain who the voice belonged to or what it said. He was calm during the daytime. He was seen kneeling in his room as he murmured Bible verses. Asked what verse he was reciting, he refused to answer and seemed on the verge of taking a hostile attitude but calmed down after having a conversation with a psychiatrist. The conversation ended with the patient again stating that he doesn't believe in God but that he finds it "expedient to pray once in a while." In the evening he complained of insomnia and pain.

Medication:
Otherwise recommended: morphine—scopolamine 0.75 ml.

Remarks:
Conversation with Levin requested.
Dr. G. O. Berthelsen called in.

December 24, 1943

The patient had a restless night. He didn't sleep, he threatened an attendant, and he repeatedly shouted that he "promises to listen." This morning the patient suffered an attack of rage. "I'm going berserk," he yelled. It's worth noting that during this attack, as well as during previous aggressive spells, the patient directed all his anger at himself. At no time was he a danger to those around him. On the other hand, he hit, bit, and scratched himself to a degree that must be labeled extensive. He repeatedly said, "I'm going to rip you out of my body." It is unknown who this "you" is. The patient's self-destructive tendencies are so pronounced that it is feared he might commit suicide.

The patient's family brought to the ward a couple of notebooks, which the patient, during the days just before he was hospitalized, had filled with his "automatic writing" correspondence with God. Appearing in the patient's customary handwriting is a series of questions, which God then answers in a large, childishly formed script that is actually the patient's own handwriting but larger. In places God's writing is so faint that it's illegible, apparently even to the patient himself, since in the next line he asks for the answer to be written more clearly. At times God's answer is nothing but gibberish. The contents of these notebooks is very stereotypical, naive, and lacking in imagination, characterized by an inferiority complex and references to the patient's so-called mission. Furthermore, the patient had prepared a couple of pompous documents addressed to the people of the world. In a Norwegian newspaper, he had entered check marks next to a number of articles.

Treatment:
It is recommended that the patient be treated with the new electroshock therapy.

Remarks:
In spite of aggressive treatment with electroshock therapy, it has not been possible to induce the patient to give up his self-destructive behavior. Hence it was decided to put him in restraints.

December 24, 1943

For the first time since he was admitted, the patient was willing to see his wife, Amalie Hjort Worning. Mrs. Worning, who seems extremely upset by the situation, tried to calm her husband. They spent the morning together in his room. When she left around lunchtime, she told a nurse that her husband seemed calm, although what he was saying didn't make any sense. He wanted her to bring him his radio equipment.

Radiology:
An appointment has been ordered.

Supervised conversation with a stenographer present. Doctor of psychiatry P. W. Levin.

14

Niels leafed through the remaining pages of transcripts from conversations with the patient. A stamp in the upper-left-hand corner stated: *Approved for training purposes.* Niels read:

Levin: Mr. Worning. The stenographer here is going to write down our conversation. It saves a lot of time if I don't have to write my own summaries of my conversations with patients. But it's only for my own use. Do you understand?

Worning: You can do whatever you like with it.

Levin: For my report, I first need to get some general information from you. Where were you born?

Worning: I was born in Århus.

Levin: In 1897? Mr. Worning, it would be best if you answer the questions in words, otherwise the stenographer can't—

Worning: YES!

Levin: Can you tell me a little about your family background? Your mother and father?

Worning: My father worked down at the harbor as a longshoreman. My mother was a housewife.

Levin: Would you say that you had a good childhood?

Worning: I was never beaten or abused.

Levin: Did you have any sisters or brothers?

Worning: They both died of typhoid. But two years apart. My mother never recovered from their deaths.

Levin: What about your father?

Worning: He just drank a little more. A lot more.

Levin: You went to school, didn't you? Would you describe your school years as normal?

Worning: Yes.

Levin: And you didn't notice anything . . . unusual about yourself?

Worning: Unusual?

Levin: Were you like all the other children? Did you have friends?

Worning: Yes.

Levin: Did you ever feel particularly depressed or . . .

Worning: I think I was pretty much like everybody else.

Levin: What did you do after finishing your schooling?

Worning: I went to work at the harbor with my father. That was a good period until . . .

Levin: Until what?

Worning: The accident.

Levin: What accident?

Worning: He fell in the water. He thought the ice would hold. We couldn't even pull him out. He just slipped under. Two weeks later, my mother died.

Levin: How did she die?

Worning: She never went to the doctor. She just kept coughing until her lungs gave out. And then one morning—exactly two weeks after my father died—she started coughing up blood. A lot of blood. I remember it quite clearly. It was horrible. A few hours later, she was dead.

Levin: I'm very sorry to hear that.

Worning: It was the best thing that could have happened to her. After Thea's and Anna's deaths, she was . . .

Levin: Were they your sisters?

Worning: Am I going to get my radio today?

Levin: What?

Worning: My shortwave radio. I've been asking for it for two days now.

Levin: I wasn't aware of that. I'll look into it after we're done here. Shall we talk a bit about your wife?

Worning: Why? What does she have to do with anything?

Levin: How about your work, then? You are a . . .

Worning: I'm a radiotelegraphist. I never had any sort of proper training, but I had a friend who . . . Do we really need to go into all the details?

Levin: Only if they're important.

Worning: Good. I worked for the military. Hitler's power was increasing. I think that I was . . . meant to work as a radiotelegraphist.

Levin: You were meant to? You mean there was some sort of higher meaning?

Worning: Is that a question?

Levin: Yes.

Worning: I've stumbled onto the track of something. Yes, that's it precisely. I'm on the track of something.

Levin: And what do you mean by that?

Worning: Some people have died. In different parts of the world.

Levin: In the war?

Worning: This has nothing to do with the war. At least I don't think so. They just died.

Levin: Where did you hear about this?

Worning: You wouldn't believe what I can pick up on my radio. Shortwave. Longwave. It's like tentacles that are sent out into the world. Messages in bottles. And some of them come back.

By the time Niels realized that the door had opened, it was too late. He'd been engrossed in a conversation that had taken place over half a century ago. But now there was someone else in the room.

15

It was an effort for Hannah simply to open her eyes. Her body felt weighted down, and the room was spinning in a slow elliptical movement like some sort of cheap amusement-park ride. She wasn't sure, but she had the feeling that the doctors had increased her pain meds. They were making her sluggish. She struggled to wake up properly, telling herself that it was Friday. She tried to see the sun, but the curtains were drawn. Was it still night? She needed to get up. Tonight when the sun went down . . . She closed her eyes for a few seconds. Just for a moment.

"Hannah?"

An unfamiliar voice.

"Are you awake?"

"What?"

"You just need to take this." A nurse—Hannah wasn't sure if she had seen her before—stuck a pill in her mouth, raised her head a bit, and helped her drink some water.

"Please. No. Don't give me any more sedatives."

"It's just something to help you sleep."

"You don't understand."

Hannah managed to spit out the pill. It landed on the nurse's arm, partially dissolved in pink saliva.

"Now look what you've done."

"I need to see Niels."

"Your husband?"

"No, my . . ." She gave up trying to explain. "I need to see him."

The nurse headed for the door.

"Wait," said Hannah.

"What?"

"What time is it?"

"It's still nighttime, Hannah."

The nurse left. They didn't have much time. "You have to think of something," Hannah told herself. "Get control of your body." She pushed the sheet aside so she could examine her injuries. Her legs would pass. It was her upper body that was the biggest problem. Her shoulder and her chest.

"What's the problem here?" The doctor spoke loudly, sounding annoyed, as he came into the room. The nurse was behind him, preparing a syringe.

"There's no problem."

"You need to rest. You've had heart failure."

"No. I'm begging you. Please don't put me out again."

"I can understand that it's not exactly pleasant."

"You don't understand a fucking thing! You're not going to stick that in me. I need to have a clear head."

The doctor and nurse exchanged glances. The nurse left the room. The doctor patted Hannah on the arm. "You need to stay calm so your body can recover. Otherwise you may go into cardiac arrest again. I hear that you've been out of bed and running around. That just won't do."

Two nurses came in.

"Please. I'm begging you. Please don't."

"If you'll just hold on to her," the doctor said to the nurses.

They each grabbed one of Hannah's arms.

"No! Do you hear me? You can't do this! This is an assault."

The doctor searched for a vein and then stuck the needle in Hannah's arm. "It's for your own good."

16

Niels leaned against the boxes stacked in front of him. He needed to stretch out his leg, but he was afraid of giving himself away. He closed his eyes and prayed that the woman would hurry up and finish her phone conversation.

". . . I just want to come home to you, Carsten. And talk everything over."

She'd already said that five times. She had wept and accused the man of lying. Now she'd entered the final phase: pleading.

"Just for ten minutes, Carsten. Don't you have time to see me for just ten minutes?"

Niels wasn't sure how it ended, but the woman stopped talking. He heard a couple of grunts. Maybe that was her way of sobbing. Then the light went off and the door slammed shut. He heard her footsteps fading down the hall. Then he got up and went back to reading.

———————————

Levin: How did they die? Who died?

Worning: They each had a mark on their back. Will Amalie be here soon? She has my shortwave radio.

Levin: A mark?

Worning: When is Amalie coming?

Levin: What kind of mark?

Worning: Like mine.

Levin: You're talking about the mark on your back? Who made that mark?

Worning: May I ask whether you believe in God?

Levin: No.

Worning: No, I can't ask you? Or no, you don't believe in God?

Levin: No, I don't believe in God. But that's not what we're talking about here.

Worning: I need my shortwave radio.

Levin: Who do you want to talk to?

Worning: The others.

Levin: What do you mean by "the others"? Please be a little more specific.

Worning: The ones who have been marked. The other righteous men.

Levin: Righteous men? Are they the ones who have a mark on their back?

Worning: I want to see Amalie. I'm tired now.

Levin: All right. We'll leave you in peace. But would you be willing to answer one last question?

Worning: Yes.

Levin: Can you tell me who you think made the mark on your back?

Worning: The one that you don't believe in.

Levin: God? You're saying that God made the mark on your—

Worning: Not just on mine. On the others, too.

Levin: God made the mark on your back?

Worning: Yes. God did it. It can't be anyone else. But it might be possible to get it removed.

Levin: The mark can be removed?

Worning: Maybe. Before I get killed.

Levin: Who is going to kill you?

Worning: But first I have to do something evil.

Levin: What do you mean?

Worning: I don't want to say any more.

Levin: What do you mean you have to do something evil?

Worning: I don't want to say any more.

December 25, 1943

Clinical findings:

Classic example of paranoid schizophrenia. The patient believes that he is the center of the universe at the same time that he feels persecuted. Multiple traumatic experiences in his childhood may have caused this condition.

He has been given electroshock therapy but without the desired effect. His wife came to visit him this morning, which seemed to calm him down at least temporarily. Around lunchtime, he was again extremely depressed and was seen pounding his head against the floor as he shouted, "I can't be the one. I can't be the one." And later: "I'm listening. I promise to listen." Anti-anxiety medication did not have the desired effect. In the afternoon the patient was so upset that his wife was summoned. This turned out to be a mistake, because shortly after two P.M. it was discovered that both the patient and his wife had disappeared. The patient had managed to break open a secured window and then fled along with his wife. Half an hour later, the patient was found wandering around in front of the hospital, holding a knife. No one knows where he got the knife. He tried to kill his wife before the attendants managed to grab him. His wife was admitted with deep stab wounds in the throat, but she is expected to survive.

The patient was sedated and restrained.

December 28, 1943

The patient is calm and has been asleep for most of the day. For the first time since being admitted, he has slept soundly for several hours in a row. When he woke up, he wanted to speak to his wife. This request was denied. In the evening a discovery was made by the dermatologists who had been sent for. They described what they found as "highly unusual": The severe psychosomatic eczema on the patient's back has dramatically improved. The swelling has disappeared, and only a faint red mark remains.

January 26, 1944

The patient was discharged around noon.

Niels was sitting with his back against the wall. He couldn't remember actually sitting down in that position. The medical file was lying open on his lap. He could hear footsteps outside. Voices. Had he fallen asleep? Someone must have noticed that the light was on in the room. He didn't have the strength to make another attempt to flee. Two men entered the archives.

"There he is!" said one of them, aiming the beam of his flashlight at Niels even though he was bathed in light.

"What the hell are you doing down here?" asked the other man.

They may have said more, but Niels didn't hear them.

When they placed Niels on the bed and began rolling it back to his room, he glanced at his watch. It was just past ten o'clock in the morning. Outside, the day was still gray, and the air was heavy with snow. He couldn't see the sun. Maybe it hadn't bothered to come up. If it stayed away . . . "Stay away! Stay away!" Niels muttered before his system reacted to the injection and he was out.

17

Yet another resurfacing to consciousness. It happened in small waves that made her open her eyes for a moment and then retreat once again.

"I . . ." said Hannah, then came to a halt. This time she wouldn't speak to anyone. She wouldn't ask for help. Or plead with the staff to let her stay awake. This was a hospital; they would do everything possible to save her life. But they misunderstood. Hannah knew that now. She was supposed to die. Today. By sundown, Hannah would be dead.

She needed to move calmly—to keep pace with her thoughts, which were still under the influence of the drugs. First she pulled out the IV and pressed the tape over the wound. Then she swung her legs over the side of the bed and stood up, wavering like a toddler taking her first steps. One leg was almost useless. She needed a crutch. Or a wheelchair.

She leaned on the wall and worked her way over to the cupboard. The only thing inside was her jacket. Still muddy from the accident, it reeked of juniper and alcohol. She remembered the smashed bottle of gin. The light blue shards of glass. She put on her jacket. At first she didn't recognize the woman standing in front of her, looking angry. Then came the painful realization that she was looking at her own reflection in a mirror. One side of her face was swollen. But it didn't matter. Very soon she would be leaving her earthly husk for good.

2:24 P.M.—1 hour, 17 minutes before sundown

"Two more. They'll take the edge off the pain."

The nurse was leaning over Niels as he swallowed the two big pills with difficulty. She looked at him.

"Is today Friday?" he heard himself ask.

"Yes, it's Friday. Christmas Day. You've been asleep for a long time, Niels."

"This afternoon . . ."

"What about this afternoon, Niels?"

"When the sun goes down . . ."

"I hear that you've been running around the hospital in the middle of the night." She smiled. Maybe because of the word "running," which made him sound like a dog in heat. "It was lucky they found you so quickly. I think you're just feeling a little confused about the whole situation."

Niels didn't reply.

"Do you know what, Niels?" she went on. "It's actually quite common for patients to wake up and feel completely bewildered. It's perfectly normal."

She took his hand. He looked out the window, trying to catch sight of the sun. For a moment he thought it was the bright light that dazzled his eyes so much that he couldn't see the trees. But it was just the reflection from the lamp. He tried to whisper something, but the nurse didn't hear him.

"You need to stay here, Niels. So we can take care of you." Her hand rested on top of his. "Did you say something?"

"Turn off the light."

"Sure. Of course."

She turned off the lamp next to his bed, and the reflection in the window disappeared. The sun was hovering above the treetops in the park. Crimson and impatient. There wasn't much time left. He gave up. He thought: Go ahead and take me to the realm of the dead. Just let the whole world go to hell.

The nurse interrupted his thoughts. "There are a couple of men outside who want to talk to you. They've been here every day since you were admitted." She stood up and went to get them.

Sommersted and Leon came into the room. Leon stayed next to the door. Like a bodyguard for a Mob boss. Sommersted came closer.

"Just for a moment," said the nurse, and left the room.

Niels couldn't read Sommersted's expression. It wasn't recognition or compassion, coldness or contempt. If it weren't for that scrap of humanity that manifested itself as jealousy when it came to his wife, Sommersted easily could have fooled Niels into believing that he was a robot consisting of nothing more than wires and intricate mechanisms.

"To be honest, Niels, I don't understand any of this." Sommersted spoke in measured tones. Like a man who had all the time in the world and knew that he wouldn't be interrupted. "But you were right. Last Saturday a police officer was found murdered in Venice. And it was just like you said—he had a mark on his back. We're still waiting for the final report from the Italian ME, but it looks like we're talking about the number thirty-five possibly tattooed onto the victim's skin. Interpol is actively working on the case."

Sommersted took a deep breath, which Niels interpreted as a form of apology. *I'm sorry for not listening to you.* Niels made eye contact with Leon. It was like looking into the eyes of a dead fish.

"What about you, Niels?" asked Sommersted. All of a sudden there was an undertone of empathy in his voice.

"What about me?"

"How are you doing? The doctor says you had a narrow escape. Was it a train?"

"A car at a railroad crossing."

"Ah, so that was it." Sommersted nodded. "Great thing you did for those girls. I heard they would have been killed if you hadn't been there. First that family in the Nordvest district, now those two girls. You've saved quite a few lives." He shook his head and looked down at the floor before he continued. "As I said, we can't really make sense of the whole thing. But we're going to increase the police presence here at the hospital for the next few days and see what happens."

"Just until this afternoon. At sundown," said Niels. He looked out the window. The sun had begun to caress the tops of the trees.

"Okay. We can certainly manage that. Right, Leon?"

Leon jumped into the conversation. "Of course, we're not talking about the same level of security that we had for the climate conference. But we've informed the hospital's own security officers and asked them to be extra-vigilant. We'll be watching the four main entrances and keeping an eye on the parking garage." He kept his gaze fixed on Sommersted. Like a boy pleading for recognition from his father. And he got what he wanted.

Sommersted nodded. "That's good, Leon." The police chief turned to leave, but then he changed his mind and came back. He said, "I can never figure you out, Niels. Do you know what I'm getting at?"

"Not really." Niels sensed that Sommersted was about to get tangled up in his own words.

"Maybe I should have listened to you. But I just never know with you. You seem so . . . maybe the word is 'naive'?"

He came to an abrupt halt. Niels could tell that his boss was on the verge of offering a major concession.

"I'm glad that you're going to be okay. I really am. I can't evacuate the hospital—I'm sure you realize that. But Leon and a couple of the other boys are going to keep an eye on things here."

Niels nodded, surprised at his use of the word "boys." That was not a term that Sommersted had ever used. It made him sound like a Little League coach. And it suited him. Maybe it was that very word that made Leon clench his fist and exclaim, "Goddammit, Bentzon, we're all thinking about you. So you'd better see about getting back on your feet."

Niels looked at him but couldn't think of anything to say. Sommersted clearly noticed the awkward silence and hurried to intervene. "By the way, everything went fine here—with Hopenhagen, as they called the city. We took good care of all the heads of state." He shrugged. "It looks like the world has been saved this time around."

Leon smiled. He'd always known how to play by the rules. Even the unwritten ones. One of the rules was that you should always smile when the boss attempted to make a joke.

Niels nodded. He didn't know why.

Someone knocked on the door a bit too loudly. The nurse stuck her head in. "Are you done in here?"

"I think so." Sommersted gave Niels a clumsy collegial pat on the shoulder and left the room.

"Bentzon," said Leon, and gave a little wave. Then he followed his boss. The nurse closed the door after them.

Niels didn't notice when it opened again. But he did hear someone quietly whisper his name. "Niels."

He turned over in bed.

Hannah was sitting in a wheelchair. It pained Niels to see her like that, but one glance at her face gave him hope. There was something different about her.

"Niels."

"Hannah."

She rolled the chair over to his bed and put her hand on his arm. "I'm glad to see you. I've been looking for you." Her voice was weak but determined. "I tried to find you, but they sent me back to my room."

"We need to get out of here, Hannah. There's not much time left."

"Niels. We have time. I just need to explain the whole thing. And you need to listen."

"The sun is on its way down."

"When I died, it wasn't all darkness." She squeezed his hand. "There's more than this life. And now there's proof."

"Proof?"

"Like I told you on the phone. But maybe you were a little out of it." She smiled. "They're carrying out a major research experiment, Niels. They've put pictures on shelves up near the ceiling in hospital emergency rooms all over the world. Pictures that you can see only if you're hovering near the ceiling. It's not some hocus-pocus; it's a scientific study. Carried out by doctors and scientists under the auspices of the UN—people like me who have been trained with strict adherence to scientific integrity. I've been told that you can read about the whole thing on the Internet. Wait. Just listen to the rest of it before you interrupt. I saw what they put on that shelf near the ceiling. I was able to describe the picture, which I couldn't possibly have seen any other way except if my consciousness had left my body."

"Consciousness." Niels sighed. Hannah had a fanatical glint in her eye that he didn't care for.

"Call it whatever you like. The soul? I don't know. All I know is that because of this proof, we need to rethink everything."

"What we need to do is get out of here before the sun goes down, Hannah."

"Do you remember the story I told you? About my colleague at the Niels Bohr Institute who could never say no? The guy whose goodness became a problem?"

"We need to leave, Hannah. Will you help me?"

"Look at yourself, Niels. You tried to save those girls. You wanted to stop that car with your bare hands."

"I just did what anyone else would have done."

"Go running around the National Hospital looking for a good person? Is that something everyone else would do, Niels?"

"It's because I'm manic. Manic-depressive. I'm not well."

"Yes, you are! You're a good person who does good things."

"We need to get out of here."

"We can't. And you know it. You know full well what I'm getting at."

Niels didn't reply. A sentence was echoing in his mind: *But first I have to do something evil.*

"Remember the story about Abraham? God commanded Abraham to take Isaac up on the mountain. You told me about it when we were lying on the sand dunes by the North Sea."

"I don't want to hear about it."

"You're going to have to," said Hannah.

Niels shoved aside the covers and tried to swing his legs down.

"You need to stop being good, Niels. It's your only chance."

"Hannah." Niels stopped. He remembered Worning's words: *But first I have to do something evil.* He sat forward and looked out the window at the sun.

"You need to sacrifice something. Something you love. Something to show that you're listening. Do you understand what I'm saying, Niels? I was dead, and then I was brought back to life. I saw with my own eyes an opening into . . . *something else.*"

Niels let her talk.

"We—*you, Niels*—have to accept it. There's something bigger than us. And you need to show that you understand."

"What do I need to show? What exactly do I need to show?"

"You have to show that we're capable of believing in something other than ourselves."

Niels felt like throwing up. Or hitting her. Giving her a good slap. Like they used to do to hysterical women in the old days. He looked with sympathy at her swollen face. Those intelligent eyes of hers. She could be reached only through rational arguments. "And then what, Hannah?" he heard himself say. "What happens then?"

"I don't know. Maybe . . . maybe we just go on. And then a new generation is born. The new thirty-six."

He shook his head. "We need to get out of here," he whispered without any conviction. "How much time do we have?"

"It's no good, Niels. Think about the Italian. He was also part of the system. You need to stop being good. You—"

He interrupted her, shouting, "How much time do we have?"

"About ten minutes. Then the sun will set."

Niels yanked the IV out of his arm. A spurt of dark red blood shot up. Outside in the corridor, they heard people yelling and running. Hannah got up from her wheelchair to hand Niels a tissue. For a moment she wavered. Then she regained her balance. While Niels got himself out of bed, Hannah rummaged through the cupboard in the room.

Niels was as pale as a corpse when he grabbed her hand and said, "Help me, Hannah. Help me so I can at least try to escape."

She turned around. She was holding his gun in her hand. "Okay."

18

L eon had heard it on the police radio several minutes ago: *Dark green van drove through a red light at Town Hall Square. At high speed. A police cruiser giving chase a few hundred yards behind.* It had nothing to do with him, but he stood up and went over to look out the window.

"Are you a doctor?" a voice asked behind him. "I need some help."

Leon was about to correct the patient's mistake when he heard the radio again: *Dark green van being pursued along Østersøgade. We're blocking off Fredensbro.* A faint alarm bell sounded inside Leon's head. Christmas Day. Not an entirely normal day; in fact, it tended to be sleepier—aside from those family patriarchs who insisted on driving after having downed four Christmas beers and five shots of aquavit. It was highly unusual to see a car speeding through the city streets, slippery with snow, on Christmas Day. Leon grabbed the radio. "Albrectsen? Have you got a view of Fælledvej?"

His question was answered at once: "Great view. All calm."

Leon stared out the window. At first he wasn't sure. But when he saw other cars veering out of the way, he caught sight of the vehicle through the blowing snow. Tinted windows. An old van. *Dark green Citroën van on its way across the bridge and heading for the National Hospital.*

"Fuck!" Leon raised his voice as he spoke into his walkie-talkie. "Albrectsen! Have you been listening to the chase in progress?"

"Yes! I'll cover the main entrance."

"Team two! Have you got the driveway to the basement parking garage covered?" He waited for their answer. "Team two? Jensen?" No answer. "Albrectsen? Can you see team two?"

"No. They were here a minute ago."

Leon could hear the sirens from two patrol cars in pursuit of the van. "Shit!" He set off running as he shouted: "Albrectsen! Take up position farther down the street so you can cover both the entrance and the driveway."

He stopped abruptly. He couldn't believe his eyes when he saw Niels come limping down the hallway. "Bentzon? What are you doing here? Shouldn't you be in bed?"

Niels was leaning on Hannah, and she was leaning on a crutch. They made quite a pair. "What's happening, Leon?"

"Nothing that you need to worry about. We've got it under control."

They both heard Albrectsen's desperate shouting on the radio: *"It drove past me! Heading for the parking garage!"*

Leon took off running. He sounded like a general in a war. "No one gets out of that van! Understand?"

"We need to go, Hannah." Niels's voice was weak. Just getting out of bed had drained most of his strength. And his back was burning.

"We can't, Niels. What about the roof? We'll have a good view from up there."

"Okay. Where's the elevator?" Niels staggered toward the nearest elevator. As he passed a window, he looked outside. A strong wind was making the trees nearly bend in half. A few cars had hydroplaned on the slick streets and were stranded like beached whales in the big snowdrifts—no doubt because they had tried to avoid colliding with the speeding van. And through the whole scene, the last rays of the sun were fighting a losing battle, trying to penetrate the snow and the gathering dusk. The reddish-yellow rays made it look as if all of Copenhagen—the rooftops, the streets, the air—were on fire. "Judgment Day," whispered Niels. "So this is how it looks: quiet and calm and red."

He saw a dark van speeding along the street, turning with a screech, and heading down the ramp to the parking garage under the hospital. The van crashed into several parked bicycles that were thrown into the air.

"Come on, Niels!" Hannah was standing next to the elevators.

Niels went over to join her. He couldn't get the image of the dark van out of his mind. "Not the roof," he said as he practically fell into the elevator.

"It's our only chance, Niels. The exits are all blocked. It's impossible. And the basement . . . you heard it yourself—it's full of police."

"The main entrance. We'll have to risk it. We just have to get past them." Niels pressed the button for the ground floor and then collapsed.

"Niels!" Hannah sat down next to him. "What's happening to you?"

"My back. It's burning. . . . How much time left?" Niels could taste blood. "My mouth." He gave up.

"Come on, Niels." She tried to haul him to his feet.

He heard her words, but they didn't make sense. He was sitting on the floor of the elevator, hunched over. The pain in his back was unbearable. It felt like he was leaning against burning coals.

"Your nose is bleeding."

As if in a trance, Niels lifted his hand to his nose. Hannah was right.

"We need to go up on the roof, Niels."

"Why?" he managed to stammer.

"We only have a few minutes left."

"I'm going to die, Hannah. And so will—"

"No, Niels."

She took something out of her bag. "We're going to use this."

With an effort, he raised his head. "No, Hannah."

She was holding his gun in her hand.

3:37 P.M.—4 minutes until sundown

The dark van came roaring down the ramp, going much too fast. For a moment it seemed about to skid. The brakes locked, and only sheer luck saved it from torpedoing into one of the cement pillars.

Leon and the other officers surrounded the vehicle, their guns raised.

Albrectsen moved into position behind the van as Leon approached the side door. "Copenhagen Police! Open the door! Do it slowly. Very slowly."

Then they heard it. A voice. At first plaintive. Followed by a scream. Terrible and loud, sending shivers down their backs.

A man stepped out of the van. He couldn't be more than twenty. His hair was sticking out all over, and he looked scared.

"Down on the ground!" shouted Leon.

"I—"

"Shut up and get down before I shoot you!"

At that moment Albrectsen opened the back door of the van. Inside, he saw a woman lying on a mattress. She was screaming.

"What the hell is going on, Albrectsen?" yelled Leon as he cuffed the young man.

"Boss?" Albrectsen sounded almost like he was laughing.

"What?"

"It's my girlfriend. She . . ." the young man started to explain.

Leon stood up. He went around to the back of the van and looked inside. The woman was lying there with her legs spread apart. Leon was positive that he could see a small head on its way out.

For two seconds the police officers stood frozen in place. Then the woman yelled at them, "Are you just going to stand there staring?"

19

From up here they had a view of all of Copenhagen.

The sun, partially obscured by clouds and snow, was hovering on the horizon. Niels looked back as Hannah continued toward the middle of the helicopter pad. The blowing snow struck their skin like tiny needles. "This is a good place," she whispered, but her words were instantly whirled away by the wind. "Take it!" Hannah had to shout to make herself heard. "Take the gun."

"No, Hannah."

"Look at me." She came back, grabbed hold of Niels, and tried to force him to look her in the eye.

"I can't do it."

"You have to, Niels."

"Leave me alone." He tried to push her away, but he was too weak, and she refused to release her grip.

"It ends here, Niels. Do you understand?" She pressed the gun into his hand. Even though he could have thrown it away—tossed it in a gentle arc into the dusk—he didn't. "It ends here," Hannah repeated.

He released the safety and glanced toward the door. A tiny movement that nonetheless required all his strength. He raised the gun and pointed it at the only entrance to the roof. The elevator door.

"No one's going to come up here, Niels."

"Get away from me!"

She didn't move.

He shouted, "I said, 'Get away from me!'"

She moved a few feet away.

"Farther." He staggered but kept a tight grip on the gun. As if that small object, created for the sole purpose of taking lives, was now, paradoxically enough, his only remaining lifeline.

"Niels!"

She was shouting in vain. He didn't hear her.

"Niels!" She came very close. Grabbed hold of him again and refused to let him push her away.

"Get away from me."

"Listen to me, Niels. Nobody's going to come up here. There's no murderer. It's just us."

He didn't reply.

"You need to stop being good. You need to sacrifice me."

"Stop it, Hannah." He tried again to push her away.

"It's the only option. Can't you see that? You have to act."

He didn't say a word. Blood was running out of his nose and down his lips. His knees were buckling. Hannah thought he was going to fall. She thought it might be too late. A quick glance toward the west told her that the sun was still hesitating on the horizon.

"No murderer is going to make an appearance up here, Niels. Can't you understand that? There's no terrorist. No stupid serial killer. This is about us."

"Stop it right now."

"Shoot me, Niels."

"No."

"You have to act. You have to show that you're listening. That's what this is all about. You have to sacrifice what you love." Hannah took hold of the cold barrel of the gun and pointed it at her own heart. "It doesn't make any difference to me, Niels. That's what I've been trying to tell you. I was dead when you found me. I died when Johannes died."

"Hannah . . ."

She leaned in close; her lips touched his ear as she whispered, "We have to show that we're listening. That we know there's something more." She placed his finger on the trigger. "You need to fire the gun, Niels. Just do it. I want to go back. I've seen what awaits us. It's the only thing I want. To go back. To Johannes."

"No."

"No one will suspect you. Everyone will think it was suicide. I'm an emotional wreck. Your boss was right." An unexpected smile appeared on her lips. "I have nothing to lose, Niels. Nothing."

"No, I can't do it."

Suddenly, all sound disappeared. Niels could see her lips moving, but no words came out. The noise of the wind and the storm and the city far below them had vanished. All that remained was a silence that he didn't know was possible. A silence so moving that it made him close his eyes, just to savor it.

"It's so quiet," he whispered. "So quiet."

A warmth streamed through his body. A wondrous warmth that made the pain in his back disappear and brought him peace—respite at last. Maybe Hannah was right; maybe this was a promise of what awaited him. Warmth, calm, peace. It felt as if the storm had stopped altogether. The snow was gone, and the clouds parted to let him glimpse the stars overhead, close enough to touch. Again he looked at Hannah, who was screaming, pleading with him, though he heard nothing. She pressed the muzzle of the gun to her heart and mouthed the words "Do it now, Niels," but he still couldn't hear her. Niels closed his eyes. He knew she was right. He didn't want to listen to her. He couldn't do it.

But he pulled the trigger.

The firing pin sent a powerful jolt through his hand.

Hannah jerked away. Seemed to stagger. Niels looked at her, saw her take a step back. There was no blood.

At that instant, sound returned to his ears, striking his eardrums with a bang.

"But . . ."

Hannah turned around. Looked toward the west. The sun was gone. Twilight had descended. "You did it, Niels."

Niels could feel his legs shaking. He was looking for the entrance wound in Hannah's chest. He couldn't understand why blood wasn't pouring out of her. Tiny spasms passed through his body, and he sank to the ground.

She held out her fist to him and slowly opened it. There, in the palm of her hand, was the gun magazine.

She sat down and put her arms around him. He shut his eyes.

He could hear footsteps and voices. Leon was calling him. "Bentzon? Are you up here?"

Niels opened his eyes.

"Bentzon?" Leon shouted again.

But Niels saw only Hannah—and the soft snowflakes dancing in the air between them.

20

Niels could clearly feel the change in his body as he packed his suitcase in the hospital. Not only was the pain in his back gone, but he was also having an easier time walking. Something inside him had changed. Normally, the mere act of packing a suitcase would have reminded him so much of traveling that anxiety would have settled over his body, getting ready, like some invincible adversary, to defeat him.

This time it was different. He was totally calm as he carefully placed his clothes inside the suitcase. With his police ID and gun on top. He felt no apprehension as he zipped up the bag.

"You're going home today?" The nurse was changing the sheets on the bed.

"Yes. It's about time. I'm putting on weight, eating all this good food." He patted his stomach.

"I'm glad that you're feeling so much better."

"Thanks for all your help." He held out his hand, but to his surprise, the nurse gave him a hug instead.

"Good luck with everything, Niels." She sounded almost sad, as if she was going to miss him. But she was smiling.

Hannah wouldn't be discharged for a few days. When Niels went to her room to say goodbye, he brought a bouquet of flowers with him. He couldn't find a vase.

"Just put them here," Hannah said, patting the bedcovers. "They're lovely. What kind are they?"

Niels shrugged. "I don't know anything about flowers."

"I once dreamed of making a real garden out at the summer house. Putting in all sorts of plants and, well . . . you know."

He kissed her on the mouth. Just briefly. Her warm, soft lips. He may have been a bit clumsy, but it worked—he could feel the effect deep down inside him.

He handed her a present, wrapped in newspaper.

"What's this?" Hannah said, flushed from the kiss.

"Open it."

She tore off the wrapping paper with childish glee. But her expression changed when she saw what was inside. The gun magazine.

"Don't worry. I took out the bullets."

She picked it up, sighing as she turned it this way and that. "I was positive that I had to die," she said. "That I was meant to die."

"When did you change your mind?"

She looked up at him. "You know what? I didn't. I'm not sure that I even took out the magazine. Or whether . . ."

She didn't finish what she was thinking. "I'll walk you to the door," she said.

They'd talked about it several times over the past few days. About what had actually happened up there on the roof. Every time Niels had asked who had done it, Hannah had corrected him. "Not who but *what*, Niels. What did it?"

Niels had no answer.

A long white corridor. A swarm of doctors, nurses, patients, and family members. One sound pierced all the other sounds: a baby crying. Niels stopped and looked around. A young mother, looking tired but happy, was carrying her baby in her arms. Coming toward Niels and Hannah. He turned his head to look at the new little creature as the woman passed. Maybe that was why he bumped into a nurse.

"Sorry."

She was about to move on, but he stopped her. "Could I ask you a question?"

She turned to look at him.

"How can I find out if a baby was born here last Friday at sundown?"

The nurse considered his question. "You need to go over to the maternity ward."

"Thanks."

Hannah tugged at his sleeve.

"What?" he asked.

"Niels. Isn't that a bit far-fetched?"

"Why? Don't you believe that the baton has been passed?"

Niels knocked politely, and when no one answered, he simply went into the room. Hannah remained outside.

Flowers, boxes of chocolate, teddy bears, and infant clothes. The mother was lying in bed, dozing with her newborn in her arms. The young father was sitting in a chair, snoring. They perfectly matched Leon's description of the couple who had arrived in the dark-colored van. The mother looked up.

"Congratulations," said Niels. It was the first word that came to him.

"Thanks." She gave him a puzzled look, trying to place him. "Do we know each other?"

Niels shrugged and looked at the baby, who was stirring. "A boy?"

"Yes." She smiled. "An impatient little guy. He arrived a month early."

"Will you promise me something?"

She looked at him in surprise.

"When he gets older, if he has trouble traveling, will you promise not to get mad at him?"

"I don't think I understand what you mean."

"Just promise me that."

And Niels left the room.

21

S etting out on a trip for the very first time. Most people can remember that experience—the childish sense of adventure when the plane takes off. How everything is new: the flight attendants, the food, the little cups and plastic utensils and accessories that look like they belong in a dollhouse. The way you leave all worries behind and allow someone else to determine the destination and route.

Venice

The smell of the lagoon was like no other Niels had ever experienced. Welcoming, even though it was also musty. The brackish water was blue-black, and yet it was so inviting that Lord Byron had jumped into the canal. That was something Niels had read about in his guidebook.

For most of the flight, he had simply stared out the window of the plane. As they flew over the Alps, he wept without making a sound, without moving. It was a good thing that Hannah wasn't with him. She would have told him that the Alps were nothing more than the result of two continental plates ramming into each other. And that in a few hundred million years, the Mediterranean would be gone when the African continent caught up with Europe. Kathrine probably couldn't wait that long, so Niels had bought himself a ticket from Venice to South Africa. He had to change planes three times along the way, and it would take a whole day to get there.

One of the young men at the water taxis called out: "Venice, mister?"

Niels got out his guidebook and pointed to the island with the cemetery.

"San Michele? The cemetery?"

Niels ventured a faint *si*. Which prompted the young man to name a price: ninety euros. What the hell. Even though Hannah had told him to haggle over all the prices in Venice, especially at this time of year when everyone was desperate to make money.

Niels started laughing as the taxi driver floored the throttle and the boat leaped over the water like a skipping stone. The young man looked at Niels and couldn't help sharing his passenger's genuine joy at the speed.

At San Michele they had to wait for a coffin to be unloaded from a small black-varnished boat before they could dock. As Niels hopped up onto the wharf, the driver held on to his arm and then waved enthusiastically as he headed off in the water taxi. Only then did Niels realize he had no idea how he would get back from the island.

If the cemetery was a preview of the beauty of the rest of the city, then it boded well. Chapels, colonnades, palm trees and willows, ornamentation, angel faces and wings—a cornucopia of sacred art to help people depart this life in style. Niels spent almost an hour walking around, feeling both amazed and bewildered. Slowly, he began to see the system: where the newest urns had been placed and where the Protestants were interred.

Niels walked down the endless rows of urns placed on top of urns. Faces and names. Flowers and lit candles placed in little red glasses that protected the flames from the rain.

He found Tommaso's earthly remains squeezed in between those of Negrim Emilio and Zanovello Edvigne. TOMMASO DI BARBARA. There was also a small photograph: a face and enough of his shoulders to show that he was in uniform. A pleasant-looking man. A friend.

Niels sat down on the bench under the weeping willow, right next to Tommaso. He hadn't brought anything with him. No flowers or candles. He'd brought only himself. No longer good. Just himself.

Acknowledgments

A. J. Kazinski would like to thank:

For ideas, systems, theories, patience, and for making us realize the full extent of our glaring ignorance: astrophysicist Anja C. Andersen from the Dark Cosmology Center, the Niels Bohr Institute, Copenhagen.

In Venice: For invaluable details about work shifts, tourists, and island eccentrics: Luca Cosson of the Venice Police.

For giving us a tour and guiding us around the flooding: Sister Mary Grace and Father Elisio of the Order of St. John of God Hospital at the hospice Ospedale Fatebenefratelli.

In Copenhagen: For conversations and e-mails about the Talmud, the Torah, and the thirty-six: Head Rabbi Bent Lexner.

For a glimpse into eternity: Anja Lysholm.

For showing us the world below: Bjarne Rødtjer, Bent Jensen, and Susanne Hansen of the National Hospital's Central Archives.

For a tour of Copenhagen's most beautiful villa, and for helping us take the first step on the Diamond Way: Jørn Jensen and Mikkel Uth of the Buddhist Center.

For willingly sharing his experiences about police work: Jørn Moos.

For at least a handful of religious legends: Sara Møldrup Thejls, professor of religious history, Copenhagen University.

For a dizzying tour of the mysterious world of mathematics: Professor Christian Berg of the Institute of Mathematics Studies, Copenhagen University.

For his indefatigable reading of the manuscript and his impeccable notes: David Drachman.

For a conversation about skin: Professor Jørgen Serup of the Dermatological Department, Bispebjerg Hospital.

Special thanks to our supporters: Lars Ringhof, Lene Juul, Charlotte Weiss, Anne-Marie Christensen, and Peter Aalbæk Jensen.